Praise for *Mary Clay's DAFFODILS* Mysteries*

(*Divorced And Finally Free Of Deceitful, Insensitive, Licentious Scum)

"Witty and hilarious..."
Midwest Book Review

" ... a crisp pace with plenty of humor ..."
Romantic Times BookClub

"*The Ya Ya Sisterhood* meets *The First Wives Club*. A cleverly done light mystery that's a rare find ..."
The Examiner (Beaumont, Texas)

"The Turtle Mound Murder is light and accentuated with the familiar mannerisms of Southern women. ... A fun book."
Southern Halifax Magazine

"Bike Week Blues is one of the funniest capers this reviewer has had the privilege of reading."
Harriet Klausner, #1 Reviewer, Amazon.com

"Sometimes we just need something fun to read. The DAFFODILS Mysteries fit the bill."
The DeLand-Deltona Beacon

DAFFODILS Mysteries
by
Mary Clay

The Turtle Mound Murder

Bike Week Blues

Murder is the Pits

A DAFFODILS* MYSTERY

**Divorced And Finally Free Of Deceitful, Insensitive, Licentious Scum*

Murder is the Pits

Wishing you calm seas & gentle breezes —

Mary Clay

A DAFFODILS* MYSTERY
**Divorced And Finally Free Of Deceitful, Insensitive, Licentious Scum*

Murder is the Pits

Mary Clay

An if Mystery
An Imprint of Inspirational Fiction
New Smyrna Beach, Florida

Published by Inspirational Fiction

P. O. Box 2509

New Smyrna Beach, FL 32170-2509

www.inspirationalfiction.com

Cover Design: Peri Poloni, www.knockoutbooks.com

This is a work of fiction. All places, names, characters and incidents are either invented or used fictitiously. The events described are purely imaginary.

ISBN: 0-9710429-3-4
EAN: 978-0-9710429-3-3

Library of Congress Control Number: 2005934347

Printed in the United States of America

For

Elizabeth, Shelby, Grace, Kate,
Annabelle Lee, and darling
grandchildren yet to come ...

Like most authors, I benefited from the suggestions, corrections, and good humor of generous friends and colleagues: Cathy Edwards, Mimi Hall, Beverly Poitier-Henderson, Chris Jenkins, Tom Kingston, Deborah Mallard, Chris Miller, and Elizabeth Owens—thank you!

Thanks, also, to Adele Hodson, a creative genius with frozen food; Dick Grantham, inventor of the fishing machine; Patrick McDaniels, weapons expert; Becky Wood, realtor extraordinaire; and Patti Hill, mini-car racing champ.

Hats off to the entire staff of New Smyrna Speedway for their assistance and patience, particularly Andrew, Jane, and Robert Hart.

Finally, a deep bow to Emily Ellis, a Tennessee belle, who knows more Southern sayings than anyone on the planet!

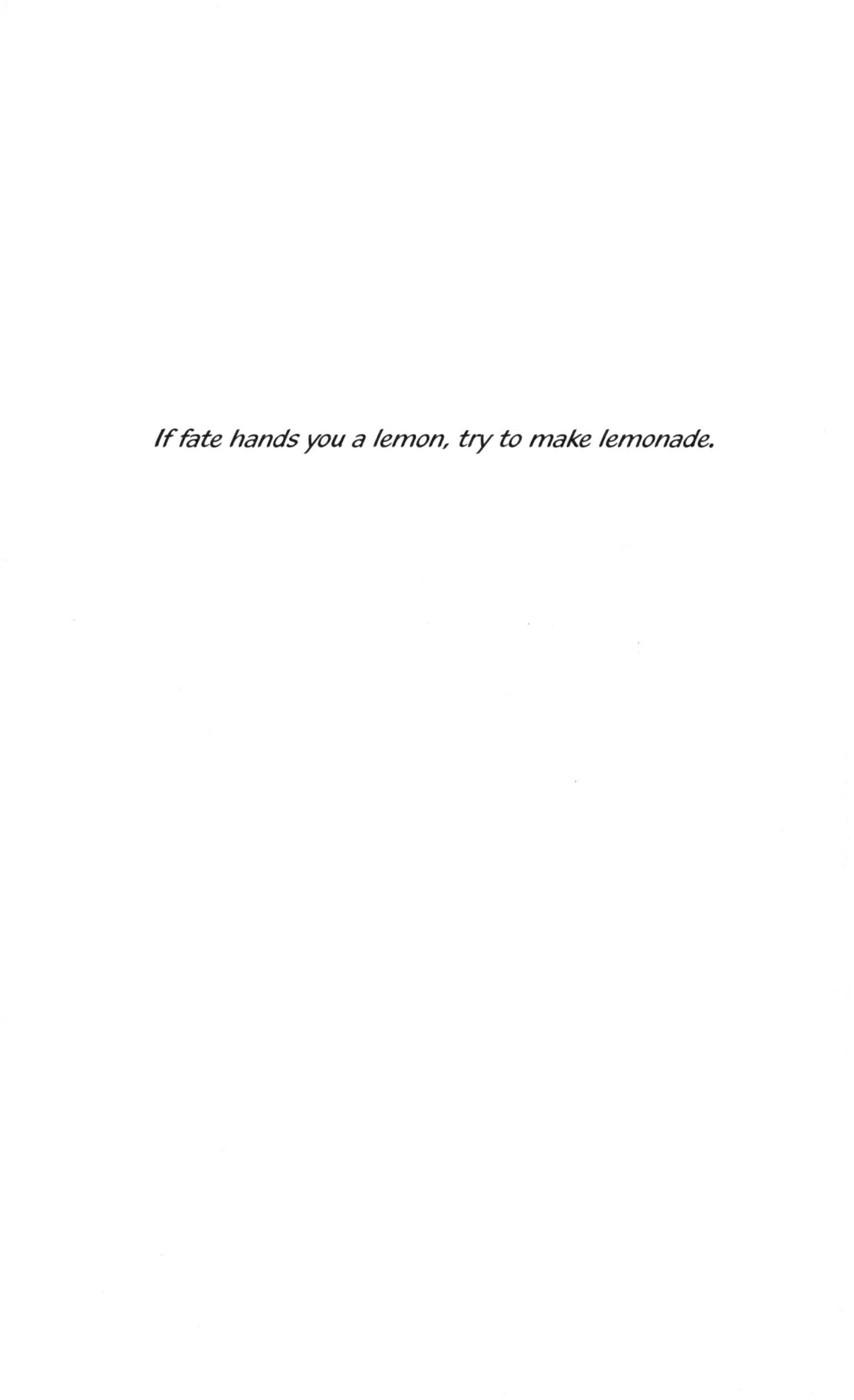

If fate hands you a lemon, try to make lemonade.

Chapter 1

August 12

Our car crested the hill, and the headlights caught the outline of a man directly ahead.

"Who the hell is that?" Penny Sue screeched. She slammed on brakes and the Mercedes slid sideways, narrowly missing a hunched man pulling a wheeled cart. Lucky for him, she was driving slowly over the rutted sand driveway. Illuminated by the headlights, he nodded slightly and kept walking toward the path that ran under the elevated beach access.

I tensed, fearing Penny Sue might lose her cool and respond with a rude hand gesture or profanity. "I think he lives in the next complex. I've seen him a lot lately on the beach in front of our place. I asked him once if he was catching anything. He laughed and said the spot was a mother lode. Apparently, there's a trough out there where fish like to hang out."

"Fishing in the middle of the night?" Penny Sue asked skeptically. "And, what's that thing he's pulling?"

"He calls it his fishing machine," I answered. "It holds his poles and other gear."

"Well, he scared the fool out of me and almost became fish food himself."

I bit my lip. I doubted anything could scare the fool out of Penny Sue. She wasn't a complete dingbat, just—how to say it?—impetuous. And, that was putting it kindly.

She parked in the front of our condo, snatched the CD from its player, and got out in a huff. "We were having such a good time, too."

"No harm done. Put it out of your mind," Ruthie, our peacemaker, advised.

"You're right. I'm not going to let a crazy, old coot ruin my birthday." Penny Sue jammed the key into the weathered lock and bumped her hip against the door. The warped wood gave with a loud pop. She stomped down the hallway, security alarm screeching its armed-state, as a robotic voice demanded, "Halt! Who goes there?" Penny Sue keyed in the code to the alarm with one hand and elbowed a button on top of Lu Nee 2's head—our robotic security guard and maid (massive exaggeration). "Boy, that was a good show. Y'all couldn't have given me a better birthday present." She flipped on lights and headed for the kitchen. "I laughed until my face hurt. The person who wrote that play had to be a woman."

The play in question was *Midlife Crisis*, a fitting birthday gift because Penny Sue had just turned forty-seven and experienced much of the play's subject matter—whether she admitted it or not. The *y'alls* who couldn't have given Penny Sue Parker a better gift were Ruthie Jo Nichols, and me, Rebecca Leigh Stratton, her old-time college sorority sisters and new-time cohorts in the DAFFODILS (Divorced And Finally Free Of Deceitful, Insensitive, Licentious Scum).

Virtually The Three Musketeers at the University of Georgia, we'd grown apart over the years, what with all our marriages, kids, and whatnot. It was my divorce that brought us back together and to New Smyrna Beach. I'd been living in Penny Sue's daddy's condo since my house in Roswell, Georgia sold last year. The condo was intended to be a stopgap move to tide me over until my property settlement was finalized. But, I'd grown attached to the place and made little effort to move, even though my share of the settlement had finally come through.

The complex was a rare find that I couldn't duplicate elsewhere, because it was built on an incline and arranged so each condo had an ocean view. Our unit was in the single story oceanfront building. Up the hill a short distance, two-story duplexes flanked our building—their back balconies overlooking our parking lot and the Atlantic Ocean. Finally, a three-story duplex rounded out the cluster. Centered behind the two-story buildings, the tall duplex's balconies had a great view over our roof.

I cruised the sand driveways of each cluster daily, searching for sale signs, desperately hoping to get a jump on the competition. And, there was a lot of competition for property on this quarter-mile stretch of wide, car-free beach. Yep, that's car-free, not carefree, though it's that, too.

New Smyrna and Daytona Beaches are two of the last ocean resorts that allow beach driving. The famous Daytona Beach races were originally run on the hard-packed sand, establishing a tradition that most old-timers considered an inalienable right, in the same class with free speech and the right to bear arms. Yet, times change, and sea turtles—facing extinction—were no match for the cars and campers that cruised the ocean's edge. So, a deal was struck between the county and Federal environmentalists, where half of the beach permitted driving and half didn't. That way, sea turtles had a place to nest where they wouldn't have to dodge cars, and locals had a place to park, picnic, and swim for the day.

A side benefit of the compromise was a massive increase in real estate values for beachfront property in the non-driving section. Predictably, tourists with young children clamored to buy or rent apartments in the "safe" zone, sending real estate values through the roof. It's the "through the roof" part that worried me. I wanted to buy a beachfront unit like Judge Parker's. At current prices, I could just afford it on my divorce settlement. The way the market was moving, beachfront would be out of range within a few months. To call it a seller's market was an understatement. A couple of B-units—the two story duplexes in the middle of each cluster—came on the market and were sold before I could get the owner on the telephone. And I was calling from their driveway on my cell phone! In each case, I'd waited until eight-thirty AM to phone, judging that a respectable hour. Both times I was told the owner had just accepted an offer. The buyers, whoever they were, could not have been Southerners, or least not mannerly ones. Calling before nine was pushing the envelope of civility, calling before eight-thirty was downright barbaric. After that, I decided I'd better cruise the development twice a day.

"Which will it be?" Penny Sue asked, holding up a bottle of Bailey's Irish Cream in one hand and a coffee pot in the other. "A cordial or decaf?"

Ruthie was oblivious to the question, preoccupied with tuning the television to the Weather Channel. An insatiable news junkie who read newspapers and watched cable news every chance she got—"One must be informed"—Ruthie had been fretting about two tropical storms, Bonnie and Charley, which had formed in the Caribbean. Thankfully, Bonnie had moved into the Gulf of Mexico and out of our range, while the jury was still out on Charley.

Penny Sue curled her lip peevishly. "Well, what will it be?" she snapped.

"Both," I said quickly. "How about decaf with a little Bailey's in it?"

"That would be great," Ruthie said distractedly, eyes glued to Dr. Steve, the Weather Channel's hurricane expert.

I took the coffee pot from Penny Sue. "Sit down, birthday girl. This is your day." I looked at the clock. Eleven PM. "Only one more hour to enjoy."

Penny Sue hopped—hefted might be more accurate—onto the stool at the end of the L-shaped bar separating the kitchen from the great room and dining area. The focal point of the condominium, the spacious area had a vaulted ceiling and two walls with sliding glass doors that overlooked the Atlantic Ocean to the east and natural vegetation on the south.

With the moon overhead a mere sliver and the No Outside Light Ordinance in effect for turtle nesting season, the natural beauty was invisible. Still, you knew it was there and could feel the energy of the ocean, plants, and wildlife all around, which is what I loved about the place. Although New Smyrna had the foresight to pass a high-rise ordinance that limited complexes to nine stories, the new condos, for all their glitz and glamour, could not match the majestic—almost spiritual—atmosphere of this low rise, natural community. Geez, I hoped I'd get to buy one. After living in the Judge's place, I didn't think anything else would be the same.

I dumped water into Mr. Coffee and flipped the switch. The water started to drip, sending a pleasant hazelnut scent though the room.

Penny Sue swiveled her stool to face Ruthie, perched on the edge of the sofa and listening intently to Dr. Steve.

"Another hurricane, wouldn't you know it?" Penny Sue moaned.

On our first visit—the Let's-Cheer-Up-Leigh-After-Her-Rotten-Divorce trip—there'd been a hurricane. That storm turned out to be the least of our worries. I tripped over a body on the second day, which unleashed absolute hell. None of it was our doing, mind you. Pure and simply a matter of being in the wrong place, at the wrong time. Still, for all the torment, the trip was a success since it *did* take my mind off my divorce and my two-timing, asset-hiding ex-husband, Zack. It also convinced me to leave Atlanta and move to New Smyrna Beach.

"What does Dr. Steve have to say?" Penny Sue called to Ruthie.

"Bonnie's safely into the Gulf and about to make landfall in the Panhandle," Ruthie replied without shifting her eyes from the television. "Charley's south of Cuba, headed for the Gulf, but may take a northerly turn." She looked up grimly as I handed her a cup of Bailey's coffee. "I sure hope it follows Bonnie's path. After our first trip, I don't relish the thought of going back into that owner's closet."

The owner's closet is a large storage room found in most resort condos. Designed to keep personal items away from renters' prying eyes and sticky fingers, the closet turned into a prison on our first stay, thanks to some mobsters who thought we had something we didn't. Which brought me to the other reason for our reunion in Florida, besides Penny Sue's birthday. We'd been notified that we might be called next week to give depositions for the trial of the head honcho of a drug smuggling ring.

Judge Parker, Penny Sue's daddy, said we probably wouldn't have to appear—the government had a mountain of evidence from undercover operations—still, we had to be available, and it was a good excuse to get together.

Penny Sue hopped down from her stool and strode our way. "Have you put up a hurricane box?" she asked me.

I stared into my mug, as if looking for bugs or other foreign matter. "No." I squirmed under her scrutiny. "I've been busy with the property settlement, Ann (my daughter—a long story

I'll explain later), and I do have a job, you know. Besides, New Smyrna Beach has never taken a direct hit from a hurricane."

Penny Sue sipped her coffee thoughtfully. I marveled that smoke didn't billow from her ears, the wheels in her head were whirling so fast.

"Better safe than sorry. That's our first priority tomorrow. You have the day off, don't you, Leigh?"

"I took the whole week off in case we have to go to Orlando for the depositions."

"Good," she said emphatically. "A box of supplies won't take much effort, and we really should do it before a storm heads this way. If we wait, grocery shelves will be bare. It may already be too late. Stores sell out of water, bread, and toilet paper first thing."

Water and bread I could understand. Toilet paper? The stress of the storms gave everyone the runs? Possible, I suppose. In any event, I wasn't going to argue with Penny Sue. She'd morphed into her take-charge, schoolteacher persona. There was no reasoning with that one.

Understand, Penny Sue is not a multiple personality. She's simply a Leo, who has to be on top and in charge. God forbid something should happen that she wasn't prepared for. Yet, a kinder person you'd never find. "You've never been loved until you've been loved by a Leo," Ruthie had said repeatedly. "They're generous to a fault." But, like the lion in the *Wizard of Oz*, you'd better acknowledge a Leo's generosity and importance or that big ego was shattered. She didn't cry like Dorothy's hairy friend in Oz—a pout was more Penny Sue's style. You could tell her feelings were hurt when her lower lip protruded.

Of course, with the silicon lip injections Hollywood stars got nowadays, it was hard to tell when they were sulking. To me, most movie stars looked like they were pouting or, worse, had recently been backhanded in the mouth.

"I don't want to stay in that closet again. If Charley heads this way, we should evacuate, don't you think?" Ruthie said nervously.

Penny Sue ran her fingers through her meticulously streaked hair—four colors, she'd informed us, a three hundred dollar job. "There's no need to run if it's only a Category 1 storm that's moving fast. Heck, those things only last a few hours. A little champagne and caviar and you won't even notice it."

Ruthie looked doubtful. "Don't you remember how hot the room got the last time?"

I snatched a coaster and put my mug on the coffee table. "Guess what? There's a vent at the back of the closet. I found it when I packed away my linens and discovered it was closed."

"All that sweating for nothing?" Penny Sue went to the closet and peeked in. She reeled backward, bumping Lu Nee 2, which unleashed a torrent of "Whoops!, Watch outs!, Take me to your leader."

"Lord," she grumbled, smacking the button on Lu Nee's head. "Where did all this stuff come from?"

I cleared my throat. "Well," I started sheepishly, "I had to move out of my house fast and didn't have time to sort through everything. So I brought it with me."

Penny Sue stared, pointing at the closet. "Don't tell me these are the linens Zack took half of? Like these are all bottom sheets, no tops?"

Yep, the rat took all the tops, no bottoms. One of each pair of pillowcases. I smiled weakly, hating to admit my foolishness.

"Well, it's got to go. We need room for a cooler and some chairs." Penny Sue screwed her nose up. "Why do you want that stuff? It's no good—you don't have a complete set of anything. Bad memories, it's nothing but bad memories. Put the past behind you. Throw them away."

She was right; I didn't have a whole set of anything, thanks to my sleazy ex-husband. The worm took half of everything in our house. Half the pictures on the wall, half the furniture, and half of each set of china and crystal, and we had a lot—several generations of china from both our families. As the old joke goes, if Jesus came back to feed the ten thousand, a Southern woman would have a place setting for everyone.

The sneaky beast had waited until I went to visit my parents then swooped in like a vulture. The hatefulness stunned me, considering he was responsible for the divorce. Mr. Big Shot Attorney found himself a young stripper while he entertained clients. And the sleazebag had the gall to rent a house for his mistress in our neighborhood. Every night I went to bed thinking he was sanding wood in his garage workshop. Hell, he was stroking silicon breasts!

His scam worked for over a year, until our daughter, Ann, was picked up for DUI late one night. I went to the garage to tell Zack. His car was gone.

"Why are you glaring at me?" Penny Sue asked, her bottom lip inching forward. "Keep the linens, if you want. It was only a suggestion."

"Sorry," I said, shaking off the rotten memories. "I was thinking of Zack."

Penny Sue nodded sympathetically. A person who'd been around the altar three times, she had her own regrets—the worst being Sydney, her second husband, who turned out to be bisexual. It's one thing to be dumped for a woman, and quite another to be dumped for a man. That was a real slap in the face for her, as well as for Judge Parker. Yep, her daddy took Sydney's shenanigans very personally. Penny Sue is quite wealthy as a result of that parting.

"Sorry, Leigh, I didn't mean to drag up dirty linen." She smirked, pleased with her witticism.

I rolled my eyes.

"What if it's a Category 2 storm?" Ruthie asked anxiously, having missed the whole conversation about Zack. "We won't stay then, will we? There would probably be storm surge; we could be flooded."

Penny Sue huffed. "There are two big dunes between us and the beach, for crissakes. If it makes you feel better, we'll evacuate for a Category 2. Of course, that means we'll have to go to a school and sit in a hallway with a bunch of screaming kids."

"School?" Ruthie repeated, biting her fingernail. "I figured we'd go to one of the hotels in Orlando or St. Augustine."

"*If* we can get a room. This is tourist season—everything's already booked."

"I hadn't thought of that," Ruthie replied.

Our sensitive friend was working herself into a tizzy. Ruthie had run her hands through her hair so many times her bangs were standing straight up. I patted her knee reassuringly. "Don't worry—the storm won't hit us. It's south of Cuba and headed for the Gulf. We'll lay in supplies as a precaution. New Smyrna has never taken a direct hit."

"Everyone keeps saying that. Did you ever think that we might be overdue? Besides, a glancing blow from a Category 2 storm is nothing to sneeze at. Winds can be as high as 110 mph." Her voice was up an octave. "Imagine driving a car at 110 mph and sticking your arm out of the window. Think how that would feel."

Ouch! I'd never thought in those terms. My stomach suddenly knotted. "Maybe we should try to find a hotel."

"Y'all are worrywarts," Penny Sue said, eyeing the clock. "Only a few minutes left of my birthday, and you're whining about something that may never happen." She sashayed to the kitchen and poured herself a Bailey's on the rocks. "Come on, let's party!" She held her drink up.

Ruthie and I shook our heads. One liquor-laced coffee was enough.

"I know what you need." Penny Sue pushed the CD for *Midlife Crisis* into the boom box and turned the volume to high. The musical's spoof of "Heat Wave" bounced from the vaulted ceiling.

Glass held high, Penny Sue twirled to the driving rhythm. Suddenly, she planted her feet. Snapping her fingers like the dance scene in *West Side Story*, she gyrated toward us, stopped within inches of our faces and crooned, "It's a hot flash burning up my spine. ... A hot flash that makes my forehead shine." She snapped her fingers. "Come on," she chided, "don't be sticks in the mud."

The energy was infectious. I glanced at Ruthie, who shrugged and giggled. "What the hell?"

Next thing I knew, Ruthie and I were gulping wine, shaking our booties, and singing three-part harmony.

The heck with Charley! Tomorrow was another day. Now, we were going to party for the last few minutes of Penny Sue's birthday.

Chapter 2

August 13

Rinn-ng, rinn-ng. BAM, BAM, BAM. "Halt, who goes there?" Lu Nee 2's mechanical voice squawked.

I rolled to my side and checked the clock. Eight AM. What dimwit would come calling at eight in the morning? Then I realized it was Friday the thirteenth. Fitting. I hoped this wasn't an omen for the rest of the day. I snatched my robe from the end of the bed and headed down the hall followed by Ruthie. Penny Sue was already at the door, eye pressed against the peephole, hands holding her head. It looked like she'd slightly over-celebrated with the Bailey's Irish Cream.

Penny Sue was a sight, as my mother says, with her hair standing on end and mascara streaking her cheeks. The only saving grace was a spiffy, pink print kimono.

"It's a tall, skinny guy with salt and pepper hair," she whispered.

I nudged her aside and took a look. "That's Guthrie."

Penny Sue regarded me like I'd dropped in from outer space. "Guthrie? Who the heck," she paused to massage her temples, "is Guthrie? What kind of name is that?"

"He's staying in the two-story unit on the far left. His name is Guthrie Fribble."

Her eyes narrowed to slits. "Guthrie Fribble? You've got to be kidding." She turned on her heel. "It's barely light, for godsakes! I'm not in the mood for Fribble's dribble." She stomped past me to the master suite and slammed the door.

BAM, BAM, BAM. Whether Guthrie heard Penny Sue's comment, I don't know, but he was not giving up. "Leigh, it's me, Guthrie. Something's happened! Something bad," he shouted.

Penny Sue must have been listening from her bedroom. The "something bad" apparently got her attention. She barreled from her room and opened the front door.

The three of us must have been an eye full, because Guthrie went mute.

"What happened?" Penny Sue demanded.

Guthrie, barefooted and dressed in baggy jeans with a very faded Arlo Guthrie tee shirt, backed away.

I patted the air soothingly. "Sorry, you woke us up." Guthrie was an old hippie—about 50, I guessed—who might have done a few too many drugs in his youth. Still, he was a neighbor who'd been staying in his aunt and uncle's place for the last few months. My intuition said he was gay, though it really didn't make any difference. He'd always been nice to me and was a good guy as far as I could tell. "What happened?"

"Little Mrs. King's in the hospital. Someone tried to break into her condo, and she had a heart attack."

My hand went to my mouth. I had no idea who he was talking about. "Mrs. King?" I asked sheepishly.

"My next door neighbor."

Oh, that lady. She was a quiet, sweet widow approaching 80, whom I knew as Nana.

"Someone broke into her house?" Penny Sue asked.

"They tried to pry open the window in the garage and set off the burglar alarm. The alarm must have scared Nana and caused the heart attack. She had a weak heart, you know."

"I didn't know about her heart," I confessed, feeling like a dirty dog for not taking more interest in my neighbor.

Guthrie's hand went to his heart. "And now Hurricane Charley …"

"What about Charley?" Ruthie snapped, eyes widening.

I pushed open the screen door, the rusty spring stretching with a loud twang. "Let's talk about this over coffee."

Guthrie took the stool at the corner of the L-shaped bar. Ruthie flicked on the television that was still tuned to the Weather Channel from the night before. While I scooped Columbian grounds into Mr. Coffee, Penny Sue made toast.

"There, see?" Guthrie exclaimed, pointing at the television and a jumble of colored lines fanning out from Charley's location. "Those are computer forecasts of the storm's path. Check out Mr. Yellow."

Ruthie sank onto the sofa, her expression grim. "It goes right through Central Florida and could become a Category 3."

Penny Sue slid a basket of toast, knives, jelly, and stack of napkins on the counter. "A hurricane box is our first priority." She glanced at the clock. "The stores are probably packed already."

"Yeah, sure." I passed Guthrie a mug of coffee. "How is Nana?"

He shrugged. "I don't know. Her alarm woke me. I'm surprised you didn't hear it. Luckily, she wore one of those medical emergency necklaces. Like the ones in the commercial where the lady falls and can't get up. Nana had the strength to push the button, so it couldn't have been a massive heart attack. The police and ambulance arrived at about the same time."

"The burglars didn't get in?"

"No, I guess the alarm scared them away. The police are dusting for fingerprints now. Ten bucks says it was some kids looking for quick cash. Dummies. That window had an alarm sticker on it."

Penny Sue washed down two ibuprofens with her coffee. "Those warnings don't make much difference. So many people put up stickers who don't have alarms, they're not much of a deterrent anymore."

Guthrie nodded. "She doesn't have an outside bell, so the kids probably thought the sticker was a fake. Nana told me the outside bell kept rusting in the salt air, and she was tired of replacing it. She had an extra loud alarm installed inside, figuring that noise would scare away thieves. Seems it worked. Only, it nearly scared her *away*," he glanced at the ceiling, "like, permanently."

Ruthie sat next to Guthrie and snagged a piece of toast. "If Charley comes this way, will you stay?"

"I guess," he said, waving at the radar image on the TV. "Where would I go that's not in the line of fire?"

"What about storm surge?" Ruthie asked.

"That doesn't worry me, unless it's a direct hit. Flooding isn't likely." He dipped his head and grinned devilishly. "Not more than a foot or two, at most."

Ruthie gritted her teeth.

Penny Sue jumped in before Ruthie could say anything. Staring at his Arlo Guthrie shirt, Penny Sue asked coyly, "Is Guthrie a family name?"

Our neighbor finished his coffee and stood. "No. I just have very fond memories of the movie, *Alice's Restaurant.*" He flashed the devilish grin again.

Why the grin? Was that the movie where hippies baked marijuana brownies? I wasn't sure.

"Guthrie's not your real name?" Penny Sue continued.

He swallowed the last bit of his toast. "An old nickname that stuck." He rubbed his arms vigorously. "You ladies keep this place as cold as a refrigerator. Man, I don't have on shoes; my toes are turning blue. I need to go home and thaw out."

Yes, I thought, rubbing my own arms. I'd been freezing ever since Penny Sue arrived. Her hot flashes were out of control, and gods knew what the electric bill would be.

"What's your real name?"

He started for the door. "Fred," he said over his shoulder. The front door clicked shut.

Penny Sue reached under the counter and pulled out the Bailey's. She dumped a large dollop in her coffee and took a swig. "Fred Fribble. His name is Fred Fribble!" She started to giggle and, thankfully, had the good sense to cover her mouth. Otherwise, Bailey's would have sprayed all over the kitchen. "Lord, it sounds like something from a Flintstones cartoon."

Ruthie tittered. "It does, doesn't it?"

Penny Sue choked down a chortle. "Leigh, this place is a hoot. Bodies, burglaries, Guthrie 'Fred' Fribble." She wiped tears from her eyes. "None of this ever happens in Atlanta. It must be you."

I reared back at the suggestion. "Me!? Nothing happens unless *you're* around. You're the one who draws trouble."

She stroked my shoulder soothingly, and then cackled, spraying coffee all over me.

"Gross!" I threw my toast at her. It bounced off her prodigious chest and fell to the floor.

"It is you!" Ruthie agreed, heaving her toast at Penny Sue. It went wide. "There was a hurricane the first time we came after Leigh's divorce, and you started that ruckus with your gun. You draw trouble."

Penny Sue reached into the breadbasket and grabbed the remaining toast with both hands. Laughing hysterically, she pelted us both. "Y'all are old fogeys. If it weren't for me, you'd have no excitement in your life. You need me. Admit it, I spice things up."

Ruthie and I exchanged eye rolls. Geez, now a Spice Girl. Hmmm, which spice? Red pepper? Chinese mustard? Tabasco!

By ten we'd showered, dressed and were ready to whip through our assigned tasks. (Two guesses who did the assigning.) Penny Sue raced to Publix, frantic the store had already sold out of water and toilet paper. Ruthie took my car and headed to Wal-Mart for flashlights, a battery-powered TV, a first aid kit, and molded plastic chairs that would fit in the closet and still accommodate Penny Sue's butt. I was relegated the chore of cleaning out the closet, since most of the stuff was mine.

The iron and ironing board were the first to go, followed by my half-sets of linens, beach chairs, and other assorted household implements and supplies. Sorting the wheat from the chaff was easy until I reached the wire mesh shelves at the back of the storeroom. I decided the lower two shelves would have to go to make room for our chairs. Easy enough—the wire planks merely snapped into plastic brackets on the wall. Finding a place for their contents presented the problem. The utility room was packed with my belongings—I couldn't bring myself to toss the sheets—and the credenza in the great room was already full. If I was lucky, there was nothing on the shelves but outdated canned goods that could be thrown away.

I reached down with both hands and came up with several half-filled bottles of suntan lotion. No dates, they were likely a decade old. I tossed them into the garbage can outside the closet door. Next, corroded, swollen canned goods. Botulism for sure. They hit the wastebasket with a loud thud. I squatted with a grunt and stretched to the back of the shelf. My fingertips skimmed the wall, and then hit something furry. Mouse was all I could think. I fell backward as a tuft of red feathers fell forward and a round furry thing hurled toward me. I scrambled to get out of the way.

"Dum, da da, dum! Dum, da da, dum! Big sleep. Hungry, very hungry," the furry vermin chirped. Lord, it was Ruthie's Furby, May May, and a … a toy bird! I'd forgotten about the Furbies Ruthie and Penny Sue purchased on our first visit. Penny Sue's Furby was named Lu Nee, an incredible twist of fate, considering Penny Sue's personality. Yep, that little guy was a real chip off the old block. Sadly, Lu Nee met an untimely end at the hand of a humorless thug. So, Penny Sue's new remote controlled robot, and purported security guard, was named in honor of her first "child." Lu Nee 2—the perfect sidekick for Penny Sue.

I picked up a red-feathered parrot and the Furby. It sang, "Fun. Party. Dance. Dance."

"That was last night," I told the fuzzy munchkin.

I levered to my feet and placed the toys on the kitchen counter, then pulled out the bottom shelves. Hot and grimy, I'd just poured a diet Coke when the doorbell rang. My stomach clenched at the thought it might be Guthrie, this time with *really* bad news about Mrs. King. I took a deep breath for courage before looking through the peephole. Instead of a grubby tee shirt, I saw a suit-clad, barrel chest, and the lower half of a square jaw. Definitely not Guthrie. I fluffed my hair, smoothed my shirt, and opened the door to reveal a stocky man about six feet tall with thick brown hair and a ruddy complexion.

He flashed a wide smile. "Good morning, I'm with Westside Realty." He held out a business card.

I opened the screen door and took it. Yuri Raykov, Broker/ Agent. I ran my finger over the paper. Embossed print, nice.

"I have a client who wants to buy a condo in this development. Are you the owner?"

"No, this belongs to a friend." I studied him. Was this the guy who'd snatched up the other two condos before I could get the owners on the phone? He certainly was aggressive, going door-to-door. His client must be a big spender. "I know the owner's not interested in selling. I tried to buy the place myself," I added for good measure. Not true, but I was sure the judge would give me first dibs if he ever decided to sell.

"Ah, the owner is your friend. That always helps." He started to leave, then stopped abruptly. "I hear an elderly lady over there," he pointed in the direction of Nana's unit, "is in the hospital. Do you know if she has family?"

Boy, this guy had no scruples. Mrs. King's hospital bed was barely warm, and he'd all but written her off as dead. "She has a minor problem, nothing to worry about."

He gave me smarmy grin. "That's good. Sorry to bother you. Have a nice day."

"Sure."

I watched him walk up the hard-packed sand drive to a shiny, black Jaguar parked on the side of the hill. He gave me a finger wave, swung into the driver's seat, and started to back up. Penny Sue's yellow Mercedes popped the hill at that moment, coming within inches of Yuri's car. She steered hard right, sending a plume of sand over the formerly pristine Jag, and skidded to a stop in a palmetto. Her door flew open and a Steel Magnolia emerged—mad as a hornet, loaded for bear. She stalked to the middle of the driveway and planted her feet. I instinctively checked her hands for weapons. None. Good! I breathed a sigh of relief. Two near misses within twelve hours. What's the probability of that?

"What tha'?" she started.

Yuri was at her side in a millisecond. "I am so sorry, Madame. My fault. It was stupid to park on the side of the hill." He took her arm and nudged her toward the Mercedes. "Are you hurt? Perhaps you should sit down."

She didn't budge, though her shoulders relaxed. She'd shifted out of attack mode.

The real estate agent held his hands up, apologetically. "If there's any damage, I will pay for it. We should check your car." He strode to the Benz, which was idling, and peered at the front end. Futile since it was embedded in palmetto fronds. "May I back it out?" he asked softly.

She smiled demurely. "I'll do it," Penny Sue all but purred.

Oh, boy, I'd heard the tone before. The scent of a man, it got her every time.

She backed the car out and parked in front of the condo. We huddled around the front end, checking for damage. At least, I was checking for damage. Yuri and Penny Sue, eyes locked, were checking out each other.

I got bad vibes from Yuri, making this was one eye-lock I wanted to break. "Wow, a miracle! No damage. Not so much as a scratch." I looked from Penny Sue to Yuri. They were still gazing at each other like dumb goats. "Well, I guess we'd better get the groceries in the house before the ice cream melts," I added.

Yuri took Penny Sue's hand. "Please, let me help with your packages, it's the least I can do."

"That's very kind," she said in her best Georgia peach, Scarlet O'Hara voice.

Sheesh. It was all I could do to keep from sticking a finger down my throat. A gag and vomit was the only appropriate response to his come-on and her syrupy reply. At least he helped bring in the groceries before he stroked her hand one last time and left. Penny Sue had purchased four-twelve packs of toilet paper, six big bags of crushed ice, and enough food to feed a platoon on weekend maneuvers.

"Yuri's a realtor. He stopped by to see if you wanted to sell the condo," I said, hefting ice into the large ice chest that would serve as our coffee table in the closet. Only three bags fit, so I put one in the freezer and the rest in the sink, hoping Ruthie would return soon with a Styrofoam cooler. "I told him your dad's not interested. You don't mind, do you? If the judge decides to sell, I hope he'll give me first dibs."

Penny Sue shoved two bottles of champagne into the refrigerator. "He's not going to sell any time soon. He's started talking about coming down after he retires for surf fishing. Besides, Momma loved this place. He'd keep it for sentimental reasons if nothing else. And," she grinned smugly, "I want it."

She unloaded a brown bag of assorted chips as I stacked the toilet paper on the floor beside the credenza. There was no other place to put it, because I'd already filled most of the condo's free space with the pitiful remnants of my marriage.

Next came a bag of jars and cans. I reached in and came up with a small jar. "Red Salmon Caviar?"

Penny Sue handed me a package of water crackers. "Don't worry, there's some white in there, too."

I shot her the you've-got-to-be-kidding glare. "Champagne? Caviar?"

She squared her shoulders. "Haven't you heard of a hurricane party? Laa, if we're going to be stuck in a closet, we might as well have fun." She dropped a large bag of Hershey Kisses on the counter. "I love chocolate with champagne, don't you?" She plopped a sack of miniature Snickers atop the Kisses, which jostled the counter and Ruthie's Furby. The toy awoke jabbering, "Big sleep. Hungry, very hungry."

Penny Sue snatched the fur ball. "This is Ruthie's Furby. I was so busy unpacking the groceries, I didn't notice it. And, Repeat Parrot," she took the bird with her other hand. "Where did you find them?"

"On the bottom shelf, at the back of the closet."

"I gave the parrot to Daddy for his birthday years ago." Penny Sue cradled the Furby in the crook of her arm and stuck her pinky finger in its mouth. A string of Furby *yum, yum, very good, very hungrys* spewed forth. "The parrot's a stitch. Pete repeats everything you say and is activated by noise. Daddy put him in the guest bathroom and programmed him to say, 'Boy, you have a big behind.'" She chuckled. "He thought it was hysterical. Momma didn't, which is how it ended up in the closet. I'll have to take that home with me. Ten bucks says he puts it in the guest bathroom again."

The Furby's lunch was cut short by Ruthie's arrival. Chairs, cooler, a first aid kit, and a red box.

"Boy, are we lucky," Ruthie said, holding up the red box. "I found a weather radio! A lady was returning it when I walked in the door. I snatched it immediately." Her eyes caught the Furby. "Little May May. Where—?"

"The closet," I said.

Penny Sue surveyed the items Ruthie's stacked on the floor. "No battery-operated television?"

"Too late. They sold out days ago."

"Darn, I told you there'd be a rush on necessities. I guess the boom box radio will have to do. It can pick up local television stations, but no Weather Channel."

"Exactly why I bought this radio. It airs NOAA weather alerts. All we have to do is put in our zip code. When there's a warning for our area, it sounds an alarm and broadcasts the details."

I took the box from Ruthie and read the label. "This is very cool. It works like an alarm clock—only goes off if there's a warning for this county. Great to have in case a storm hits in the middle of the night."

"That's what I thought," Ruthie said. "You should keep this in your bedroom."

It took a little over an hour for us to arrange the closet and program the weather radio. The three chairs fit nicely around the ice chest, while our supplies—chips, crackers, boom box, flashlights, and batteries—were stored within easy reach on the lowest remaining shelf.

Penny Sue surveyed our handiwork with satisfaction. "We're ready for Charley. Bring it on."

"Where is Charley?" Ruthie asked anxiously. She checked the clock over the credenza. "Eleven-forty-eight. It's time for the hurricane update." She dove for the TV remote and punched buttons like a crazy woman. Thankfully, the set was tuned to the station. Dr. Steve, the hurricane expert, had just come on.

The state of Florida appeared on the screen, an ominous yellow cone extending from a red pinwheel in the Gulf of Mexico and fanning out over the central part of the state.

"It's a Category 2," Ruthie murmured, "and we're in the strike zone."

"Don't start panicking," Penny Sue chided. "It's supposed to hit the west coast and move east across the state. Hurricanes always lose strength over land. And, look, we're still close to the bottom of the danger zone—meaning the weak side of the storm. Tropical force winds are probably the worse we'll get."

Ruthie pulled at her lip, not speaking until Dr. Steve finished and a commercial began. "It has the potential to become a Category 3. I think we should evacuate. I'm going to call inland hotels."

"Go ahead, if it will make you feel better. But Charley's going to blow out, and we'll have a fun party," Penny Sue said matter-of-factly.

"What about Frannie May?" Ruthie turned to me.

Frannie May, a.k.a. Fran Annina, was my co-worker at the Marine Conservation Center. A wealthy, Italian widow in her sixties, Frannie had taken me under her wing and become a good friend to us all. She was also feisty, á la Penny Sue. She showed her stuff in our pursuit of renegade bikers by kicking the butt of a man a foot and a half taller. No kidding, she literally kicked his butt. I did a mental chuckle at the memory of Frannie hanging from the guy's neck, her legs flailing for all she was worth.

"Frannie?" Ruthie repeated.

"She's in Boston. Her sister's in the hospital."

"What about Carl?" Ruthie continued.

Carl was Frannie's genius son. He was also a *Star Trek* fan who engaged in role playing games with his MIT-educated buddies. Carl played a Klingon, other friends played Romulans. They kept reenacting something called the Battle of Khitomer. This battle was apparently a big deal in alien circles. I'd intended to get old *Star Trek* tapes and look it up, but never found the time. I had tried to fix my daughter up with Carl, but it didn't work. She wasn't a Trekkie. A shame. A good-looking millionaire, who was kind to his mother, Carl Annina was a catch by almost anyone's standards. Anyone except my Ann, who wasn't drawn to the Trekkie stuff. Oh, well, Ann Annina was a tongue twister. "I know he's working on a project, but he may be in town. Why do you ask?"

Ruthie began to pace. "I'd like to think there's someone around if we need help."

"How about Deputy Ted?" Penny Sue said brightly.

Ted Moore was a very nice guy who worked for the Volusia County Sheriff's office. Recently divorced, like me, we'd struck up a friendship that was beginning to develop. Beginning was as far as it got, however. A front page newspaper photo of Ted and me holding hands at an art fair was enough to get his ex-wife's back up. Suddenly, she needed to confer with him daily on their sons' welfare. The boys were sassing her, hanging out with the wrong crowd, might be doing drugs, and on and on ad nauseum. Her manipulation was crystal clear to me, but not to Ted. When he canceled the third date for a kid catastrophe, I called it quits, telling him to call me when he got his life sorted out. I was having enough trouble sorting out my own life; proof being the huge stack of mismatched sheets piled in the utility room.

I cleared my throat. "We're not seeing each other anymore."

"You're not?" Penny Sue called, fanny up, head buried in the refrigerator. She came out with three cellophane-wrapped sandwiches. "How about a Cuban? I'm starving. All we've had was toast, and we ended up throwing most of it on the floor." She snickered.

Ruthie and I nodded. My stomach was feeling hollow. Besides, eating might divert their attention from Ted. No such luck.

"What became of Ted?" Penny Sue pulled out a skillet and started to grill the sandwiches.

I sat at the counter as Ruthie arranged placemats and napkins. "There's not much to tell. In a nutshell, his life is complicated—young kids and a possessive ex-wife."

"Hmph," Penny Sue grunted as she forcefully mashed the sandwiches with a spatula. "I'll bet his wife wanted the divorce until she found out someone else was interested in Ted. Happens all the time. Once she's sure y'all are finished, she'll dump him again. You watch." She slid a sandwich onto a plate and passed it to Ruthie, who added a handful of chips. "Let's hope he's smart enough to go that route only once. I dated a jerk that did the number three times. Mind you, one time was enough for me. I hear his next girlfriend has already been around that track twice." She scooped out the last two sandwiches and took the stool beside me. "Would you take Ted back?" she asked, biting into the sandwich. "Mm-m, these things are good. They don't do much for the waistline," she patted a newly acquired, perimenopausal paunch, "but do wonders for my mood. If we're going to wrestle a hurricane, we'll need our strength."

I looked sidelong at Ruthie, who'd stopped chewing. Darn, I wish Penny Sue hadn't said wrestle. "Don't worry, Ruthie, Guthrie will be here if we need anything. He's a nice man."

Ruthie stared back at me. She wasn't buying a word of it.

It was after one when we finished lunch. Penny Sue retired to her *boudoir* to *select* an outfit for the hurricane. (Lord knows which personality said that line, probably Scarlett O'Hara. If Penny Sue came out wrapped in curtains, I'd know for sure.) Ruthie—on pins and needles as she waited for the two o'clock storm update—took her cell phone to the deck and started calling hotels. I made my bed, took a quick shower to knock off the closet dust, and called Bert Fish, the local hospital, to check on Mrs. King. She was resting quietly. I tried to wheedle information about her family—like, had they been notified? Had anyone arrived to sit with her?—but the ward nurse was too professional to spill any beans. Next, I called New Smyrna Beach Florist. They were closing early for the hurricane, but I was in luck. The van hadn't left, and they had a nice, cheery arrangement in stock. I put it on my charge card. I guess we had a bad connection, because the storekeeper couldn't seem to get our address right, and made me repeat it twice.

Exactly at one forty-five we all rushed, like trained monkeys, to the living room and the next tropical report. Ruthie watched the broadcast, hands touching her lips prayerfully. I sat on the edge of the loveseat, and I noticed that Penny Sue, normally nonchalant, gripped her diet soda tensely.

A meteorologist I didn't recognize came on and announced that Charley's eye wall showed the storm was gaining strength. If that wasn't enough, the storm was moving faster. Several models predicted it would make landfall around Tampa. New Smyrna was on the lower edge of the strike zone.

Penny Sue took a big gulp of soda. "See, Ruthie? Worse we'll get are tropical force winds. We're home free."

Ruthie shot Penny Sue a cynical look. "If it hits, we'll be on the right—STRONG—side of the storm."

Penny Sue downed the rest of her cola. "For a New Ager, you're awfully fearful. Can't you contact your spirit guides to confirm the storm's path?"

Ruthie folded her arms defensively. "I'm not bothering my guides with earthly matters."

"Enough said." Penny Sue sashayed toward the kitchen, exaggerating the fanny action. "If earthly matters are not worthy of the spirits' time, they're not worth ours. We *are* spiritual beings, right? Ruthie, you need to put your actions where your mouth is."

I glanced at Ruthie whose face was beet red. Penny Sue had lobbed a real zinger!

Thankfully, the doorbell rang at that moment, proof that spirits were looking after Ruthie.

Penny Sue virtually ran to get the door, obviously realizing she'd stepped way over the line. My stomach seized, fearful it was Guthrie with news of Mrs. King. I heard the twang of the screen door, a slight yelp, and the front door clicked shut.

"What?" I called, dreading the answer.

Penny Sue emerged from the hall holding a single pink rose. "Look." She held out the flower with a New Smyrna Beach Florist card attached. The card was addressed to Penny Sue and simply said, "You haven't been out of my mind since I first saw you."

Chapter 3

August 13

"I wonder who sent this?" Penny Sue mused, placing the rose in a bud vase. She turned the card over—no other inscription. "The florist must know." She dialed the number on the card and waited a long time. "Darn, they've closed early for the hurricane."

Ruthie sniffed the rose. "I'll bet it was Rich."

"Rich?" Penny Sue shot back, irritability masking her sorrow. "How could Rich know I was here? He's in the witness protection program, probably sequestered in Timbuktu."

Rich Wheeler was a man Penny Sue fell in love with on our last trip. Unfortunately, Rich got mixed up with some very rough bikers who were engaged in scary activities. They nearly killed Rich, so the Feds shuttled him away for his own safety. How long that would last, no one knew; but Rich vowed he'd return to Penny Sue one day.

"Sorry, Rich was my first thought. Pink roses stand for admiration."

"Admiration? I'll bet it was Yuri," I said.

"Who's Yuri?" Ruthie asked.

"A sleazy realtor who wants to buy up the complex. He's trying to butter you up," I said to Penny Sue.

"Sleazy? I thought he was a nice guy. Not bad looking, either." Penny Sue studied the rose smugly. "He helped us bring in the groceries." She paused again, the wheels in her head whirring. "Admiration. What stands for love?"

"Red roses."

Penny Sue grinned. "I'll bet it *was* Yuri. Rich would have sent a red rose."

"Does that mean Rich is history?" I asked.

"No," she snapped, her brows knitting. "Even though I love Rich, it doesn't mean I have to check into a nunnery. Nothing wrong with an occasional date until he gets home. After all, we're not married."

True, she wasn't married or even officially engaged. Besides, flirting to Penny Sue was akin to breathing, an involuntary biological process. I was certain she'd been faithful to all three of her husbands—even the two who didn't return the favor—still, she'd always been a flirt. The thrill of victory, I supposed, to see how many men she could attract. And lord knows, that was a lot.

A loud horn blared, and Penny Sue's romances were instantly forgotten. Lu Nee 2 whirled in circles, demanding, "Halt! Who goes there?" The Furby woke up too, moaning, "Big sound, scare me!"

Ruthie, Penny Sue, and I stood like slack-jawed fools, trying to figure out where the sound came from. Then, a loud male voice boomed, "At two forty-five, Volusia County issued a mandatory evacuation for all mobile and manufactured homes."

The weather radio! We rushed to the closet.

"Shelters will open at four PM and close to new entrants between eight and nine PM. Tropical force winds are expected by ten PM. Bridges from the beach to the mainland will close when winds reach 38 mph. All Daytona Beach International Airport flights have been cancelled."

Ruthie sank into one of the plastic chairs. "A mandatory evacuation! The airport's closed and there are no hotel rooms to be found. We're stuck."

Ring, ring. BAM, BAM, BAM. The Furby screeched, "Whoa-a-a!" Lu Nee 2 exclaimed, "Where did that come from?"

Penny Sue put her hands over her ears, stomped down the hall, and flung the door open with a thud. There was a long pause then she started to laugh. "Come here, you've got to see this!"

Ruthie and I turned off the weather radio and double-timed it to the door.

I couldn't believe my eyes. Guthrie was on the stoop dressed in his Arlo Guthrie tee shirt, baggy madras shorts (circa 1972) with a chicken tied around his knee. Yep, you heard right, a chicken! A whole, frozen, Purdue roaster.

"Leigh," he began, pitifully, "I've hurt myself, Charley's coming, and I'm all alone. Can I stay with you?"

Penny Sue's eyes were glued to the chicken. "What's with the poultry?" she asked.

"Publix sold out of ice. My freezer's turned to high, but it can't make ice fast enough for drinks and my knee. The chicken is frozen—as good as ice." He put his hand to his forehead. "I'm so upset. My friend isn't going to come—he has to stay with his mother. I can't go to his place, because Mother doesn't approve of our relationship. With Mrs. King in the hospital, I'm all by myself. On top of that, the Russians are coming. Can I stay with you? Or will you come to my place?"

Penny Sue opened the screen door and waved him in. Once again, he took the seat at the corner of the bar, propping his leg up to rearrange the Ace bandage and rotate his chicken.

"Can I get you something?" Penny Sue asked. "Like a stiff drink?"

His eyes shifted from Ruthie to me. "A scotch would be nice. Neat."

Penny Sue poured four fingers of scotch in a glass with a few cubes of ice. "I suppose we'd better conserve our own ice." She handed Guthrie the drink. "How did you hurt your knee?"

"I was upstairs making brownies—"

Marijuana brownies? I wondered. Wasn't that a scene in *Alice's Restaurant*?

"—when I heard a scraping noise coming from the back of our duplex. Low, like maybe the crawl space." He took a good swallow of his scotch. "I listened for a while, and started to think someone was trying to break into Mrs. King's house again. So, I got my Glock—"

"Glock, like a gun?" Penny Sue asked.

He nodded and sucked down more scotch. "I got my Glock, ran to the porch, and tripped over the front door mat. I fell down the first flight of steps and landed hard on this knee. It's horribly bruised and swollen. Want to see?" He started fumbling with the Ace bandage.

I held up both hands. "Not necessary—we believe you."

"Did you figure out what the noise was?" Ruthie asked.

He shook his head. "No, it was all I could do to crawl up the stairs to my condo. Anyway, the noise stopped as soon as I fell. I guess I scared them away." He took another gulp of liquor. "The pain was excruciating. So, I iced my knee down and called Timothy, my friend. I thought he'd rush over to help me." Guthrie wiped his eyes. "No such luck. Timothy's sister couldn't stay with their mother, so he had to bring *Mother*," Guthrie virtually spate the word, "to his house for the storm."

"Why didn't you call me?" I asked. "We'd have helped."

"I couldn't find your number. Leigh Stratton isn't listed."

Right. I was using the judge's phone and had never made the effort to have my name listed. I scribbled our number on a Post-It note. Here, call us next time."

"Thank you." He rotated the chicken and gave us a pitiful look. "The last day has been so trying. I can't face the hurricane alone."

Ruthie, Ms. Sensitive Pisces, stroked his back. "Don't worry, you're welcome here. In times like these, we have to stick together."

Penny Sue closed her eyes and bumped her forehead against the kitchen cabinet. Thankfully, that was all. I could tell she wanted to vault over the counter and strangle Ruthie. I wasn't jumping with joy at the prospect of Guthrie sleeping on the sofa, but he seemed nice enough and definitely needed our help.

"I won't be any trouble," Guthrie said. "I have a sleeping bag. You'll never know I'm here. I'll bring dinner. I'm making a hobo stew out of all of these," he motioned to the chicken, "frozen foods."

Penny Sue gave me the squinty eye. "What else have you used on your knee?"

"Green beans, corn, the usual." Guthrie held his glass up for a refill.

"Peas," she said, her eyes still slits.

"Huh?"

"Frozen peas. That's what they recommend for women after boob jobs." Penny Sue refilled his glass. "They're cold and flexible. I guess corn is about the same."

"Mine was on the cob. Don't worry, I cut off the kernels for the stew. I'm really a good cook. I made brownies before I hurt my knee."

Brownies. Yep, Arlo Guthrie. I still wondered if the brownies contained anything other than the usual chocolate, flour and sugar.

Penny Sue slid his drink across the counter. "What did you mean, the Russians were coming?"

"A Russian realtor showed up right before the scratching started. He came by early this morning, asking if I wanted to sell my condo. I explained I didn't own it. I guess I mentioned that Mrs. King had a heart attack. I was so upset. I babble when I get upset. If I start to babble, stop me. I won't be offended. Really. Anyway, the same Russian stopped by this afternoon asking if I knew Mrs. King's family."

A money-grubber, just as I thought. I smirked at Penny Sue.

"I said no and he left. Within an hour, the scraping started."

"Can you be more specific about the sound?" Penny Sue asked, arms folded across her chest.

"A metal on metal sound."

"Which side of your building did it come from?"

"I couldn't tell."

"I think we should check it out," Penny Sue said in her Jessica Fletcher *Murder She Wrote* tone. "But I'm certain Yuri had nothing to do with it."

Guthrie downed his drink and eased his leg to the floor. "Okay. Can I stay here tonight? I promise not to get in the way."

Ruthie helped him stand up. "Of course, we'd love to have you."

Penny Sue curled her lip.

With a shoulder under each armpit, Ruthie and I helped Guthrie up the hill to his condo. Penny Sue led the way with our new halogen lantern, a crow bar from the utility room, and her .38 stuffed in the pocket of her capris. She thought she'd hidden it from us, but the bulge was unmistakable. Under normal circumstances, I would have been annoyed—her darned gun had gotten us in a lot of trouble. I didn't care this time. I was fairly certain we wouldn't find anything. Why would a burglar come back in broad daylight?

After considerable huffing, puffing, and a few stops, we got Guthrie up the hill to his unit. I noticed he had hurricane shutters, which were already rolled down. Hmmm, maybe we should stay with him. He had shutters and was on higher ground. I'd broach the subject to Penny Sue later. Not now, not with the gun in her pocket. (Penny Sue's hormones weren't completely out of kilter; still, no sense taking chances.)

"Which unit is Mrs. King's?" Penny Sue asked, now sounding like a feminine Perry Mason.

Guthrie pointed straight ahead. Penny Sue did a walk around, while Ruthie and I eased Guthrie to the staircase of his condo. Penny Sue returned with tight lips. Something was wrong.

"Someone's been in the crawl space under Mrs. King's condo. There are scuff marks in the sand, and the crawl space door has been opened."

Penny Sue pointed at Guthrie sternly. He cringed. I didn't blame him, this personality reminded me of The Terminator.

"The door to your crawl space is coated with sand and cobwebs, meaning no one's been in it for a long time. No cobwebs at Mrs. King's."

"Did you look inside?"

Penny Sue handed the lantern to Ruthie. "No, I think Ruthie would be a better fit. The doorway's pretty small."

Ruthie shoved the lantern back at Penny Sue. "Forget it. You know I'm claustrophobic."

They both stared at me, the lantern hanging limply from Penny Sue's fingers. I stifled the urge to smack it away. Why me? Why did I have to do everything? Because I was a big dope. But, I wasn't going to give in this time.

Guthrie broke the impasse. "It was probably the pesticide guy spraying for bugs. I'll bet that's why the door's been opened."

I frowned. "Spraying on a day when everything is closed for a hurricane?"

"Maybe he was already in the neighborhood."

"What about the grinding sound? Was that bug spraying?"

Guthrie studied his chicken. "No," he said quietly. He motioned to his knee. "I'd do it, but—"

I snatched the lantern from Penny Sue and stifled a heavy sigh. "Quit! You big bunch of scaredy cats, I'll look!" I stomped around back, Ruthie and Penny Sue following on my heels. I dropped to my knees and examined the door. It was brown wood to match the building and about two feet wide and three feet tall. I snuck a glance at Penny Sue's rear end. Yep, definitely a tight fit.

She caught my look. "I know what you're thinking. I haven't put on that much weight."

I chuckled and went to work on the slide-bolt lock. After a lot of grunting and a few curses from me, the lock gave. Lantern held high in front of me, I gingerly crawled in as far as my head and shoulders. The bottom of the area was concrete slab, while pipes and plastic conduit crisscrossed above my head.

Penny Sue's chin rested on my shoulder. "What do you see?"

I shrugged, bumping Penny Sue's chin. "Give me some room. I see the underbelly of a house, what do you think?" And something skittering in the distance! I jerked backward, sending Penny Sue sprawling. "Something's moving in there."

Penny Sue scrambled to her feet and pulled out her .38. "A snake?" she shrieked. "There are rattlers around here, you know."

I slammed the door and locked it. "I don't know what it was, and I'm not going to find out. Besides, I didn't see any evidence of tampering. Concrete and pipes, nothing else." I brushed myself off.

"What do you suppose Guthrie heard?" Ruthie asked.

"I don't know, and I don't care. Heck, it was probably someone rolling down a hurricane shutter. That would make a scraping noise. I'll bet most of these shutters haven't been moved in years."

Penny Sue's eyes brightened. "You're right, I'll bet it was a hurricane shutter. That would explain the scraping sound."

"And, maybe he'd been tasting his brownies," I said with a wink.

Penny Sue chuckled, but Ruthie gave me a dumb look.

"Come on, Ruthie, you remember *Alice's Restaurant*. What did Alice put in the brownies?"

Her hand went to her mouth. "Oh-h!"

"Are you sure that was *Alice's Restaurant*?" Penny Sue shoved the revolver back in her pocket.

Now that she mentioned it, I wasn't sure. "Not one hundred percent." I brushed hair out of my face, the wind was picking up.

"We'd better be careful how many we eat tonight."

Ruthie's mouth dropped. "You'd eat them?"

Penny Sue dipped her chin and grinned. "I'll try one. He's a guest, after all. We can't be rude." She started up the hill toward Guthrie's stairs. "You invited him, Ruthie, so you must try one, too."

Ruthie canted her head defiantly. "Not if I'm allergic to chocolate or on a diet."

"Liar, liar, pants on fire," Penny Sue shot back.

"Peace of mind is more important than diarrhea," Ruthie fairly shouted.

That stopped Penny Sue in her tracks. She turned around and gave Ruthie a slow, long look over. "What in the crap—excuse my French—does that mean?"

Ruthie put her hands on her hips. "A quote from Hugh Prather. Surely, you remember Hugh Prather. *Notes to Myself* and *Notes on Courage*. The man is a legend."

Penny Sue put her fist on her hip, thankfully the hip without the gun. "I missed that legend." She started back around the building. "What does diarrhea have to do with peace of mind?" she called over her shoulder.

Ruthie and I huffed after her. I could tell Ruthie was winding up for one of her spiritual lectures. We rounded the corner and found Penny Sue sitting next to Guthrie on the bottom step.

"Hugh Prather's one of my favorite authors," Guthrie gushed. "Hugh was saying that we should be as vigilant with our peace of mind as we are with diarrhea. You know, like, if you have diarrhea—"

"'Nuf said!" Penny Sue raised her face to the heavens. "Two of 'em, heaven help us."

Penny Sue left abruptly, claiming an urgent problem with her peace of mind. Ruthie and I helped Guthrie up the stairs to his condo—no small feat, since the chicken had thawed and kept slithering down his leg. After two attempts to tie it back in place, we gave up and left it around his ankle. It was time for him to move on to pork chops, anyway. We told Guthrie to call for help when he was ready to come over, and then left. The phone was ringing when we arrived. It was Frannie May calling from Boston.

"I'm not sure you should stay there on the beach," she started. "Carl's home, and you're welcome to weather the storm at my house. It's a cinderblock house that's built to hurricane codes. You'll be safe there."

Penny Sue sauntered in from the deck sipping a martini.

"Frannie May," I mouthed.

She shook her head and whispered, "We'll be fine here."

I thanked Fran and promised to call Carl if things got dicey.

I stared at Penny Sue's martini. "You said you were having acute peace of mind problems."

She held up the drink as Ruthie came in from our bedroom. "I was. This is the cure."

"We thought you had diarrhea, and were being polite with the peace of mind stuff," Ruthie said.

Penny Sue squared her shoulders. "If I'd listened to you and Guthrie much longer, I would have had a terrible case of the runs. The way you two went on, I'm convinced there *is* a link between peace of mind and gastric distress." She took a sip. "Want one? It'll cure what ails ya."

Ruthie and I gave each other the she-is-awful look, then nodded.

"Make mine dirty," Ruthie said loudly.

I nearly fell through the floor. Ruthie rarely drank, except in our company, and usually she'd sip a single glass of wine for an entire evening. (Yep, we were a bad influence.) For her to pipe up wanting a dirty martini was on par with the Dalai Lama asking to see an X-rated movie. Okay, maybe not X-rated, but at least PG-13.

"Dirty it is." Penny Sue pulled out gin and a big jar of olives.

As she prepared the drinks, the phone rang again. It was our friend Chris, the former proprietor of a local New Age shop, now owner of a store in St. Augustine. She was worried that I might be staying alone on the beach. We were all welcome at her house—or if things looked bad there, her store. I assured her we were well prepared, and would call if things went downhill.

Penny Sue handed Ruthie a martini with a toothpick skewering at least six olives. Mine only had one.

"Dirty means you add olive juice. The extra olives were my idea," Penny Sue explained.

Shoot, wish I'd known that, I'd have gone for a dirty drink, too.

We took our cocktails into the living room and tuned to the Weather Channel. Charley had taken a turn for the worse; it was now a Category 4 storm. Translation: You'd better write your social security number on your arm in permanent ink, along with the name and phone number of your next of kin. You'd also better have your affairs in order, unless you happen to live in a bomb shelter. Hurricane Andrew was a strong Category 4, and it blew away everything in its path, except the strongest bank vaults. A problem if your bank went for the lowest bid. In that case, your safe deposit box's contents were strewn across Mexico.

Being a Category 4 was bad enough; worse, it was hitting south of Tampa and headed east—our way. At that news, Ruthie stripped all the olives from the toothpick and chugged the rest of her martini. "We have to get out of here," she wailed.

"Out, where?" Penny Sue bellowed. "Look at the strike zone, everything close by is in it."

"Maybe we should tape the windows with big Xs."

"Not necessary. Daddy had all the windows replaced with hurricane-rated jobs."

"Yeah, but what are they rated to? I think we should get out of here and go to Fran's house," Ruthie said.

I had to intervene on that one. Since living in New Smyrna, I'd learned from old-timers that the Inland Waterway was a flood zone. The beach wasn't. Screwy, I admit, but true. It had to do with water building up in inlets versus a straight coastline that allowed the storm surge to spread out horizontally, instead of vertically. "We're probably as safe here as we would be at Fran's."

Ruthie regarded me as if I'd lost my mind.

"Really, I've checked it out. Fran's house is in a worse flood plain than we are. Besides, it's a compact storm and will surely lose steam as it moves over land. If we stay in the closet, I think we'll be safe. This building has been here a long time and weathered a lot of storms." I thought, but didn't say, "I hope those storms didn't weaken the structure."

Ruthie didn't get a chance to argue. Guthrie called. He'd seen the same forecast on the Weather Channel, had given up on the hobo stew, and was ready to come over with his brownies and sleeping bag.

Chapter 4

August 13

It would take all three of us to get Guthrie down to our place. Rain was already falling thanks to Charley's feeder bands, so we donned the yellow slickers that Penny Sue had purchased. When we arrived at his place, Guthrie was waiting by the door wearing an old Pith helmet and a dry cleaning bag in lieu of a raincoat. Once again, Ruthie and I supported him with a shoulder under each armpit. Penny Sue shrugged into his knapsack and carried a large pan of brownies and a tarp-wrapped sleeping bag. She was none too happy about it.

"What do I look like, a pack mule?" she muttered under her breath as we trudged down the slope to our unit.

Don't tempt me, I thought. Her load was a fraction of ours. While Guthrie was fairly slim, he weighed at least one-eighty, not counting the package of frozen sirloin tied to his knee.

"What's in this knapsack anyway?" she groused.

"Frozen food for my knee," he said haltingly as we hopped him down the hill. "And, some protection."

"The Glock?" I asked.

"Looters are always a problem after storms."

The blood drained from Ruthie's face. "Looters?"

"I hadn't thought of that," Penny Sue said, softening toward Guthrie. "Hmph, I need to make sure my gun is loaded."

I gritted my teeth. Not her damned .38, again. Penny Sue and guns spelled trouble.

The light sprinkle turned to a torrential downpour by the time we reached the condo. Ruthie had the forethought to cover the floor with towels so we wouldn't track water. Good thing, too, because we were soaked. We leaned Guthrie against the wall and ripped off his cleaner's bag. Then we shed our slickers in a heap and hopped Guthrie to the living room. The television was already on. Clearly put out, Penny Sue trailed behind, dripping water. She dropped the sleeping bag in the dining room, and plopped the knapsack and brownies on the kitchen counter.

"Are we having fun now?" she asked sarcastically, pulling off her raingear and stuffing it in the sink.

"We will in a minute. Bring in the brownies," Guthrie called, propping his bum leg on the coffee table. "My brownies are guaranteed to brighten your day. Brownies for everyone!"

Ruthie, Penny Sue, and I exchanged wide-eyed glances. We'd never decided if it was Alice, of *Alice's Restaurant* fame, who baked marijuana brownies. Somebody baked them in an old movie—we just couldn't remember which one. In any event, Guthrie's enthusiasm made us leery of his baked goods.

Penny Sue handed Ruthie the pan, a knife, and a napkin. "Thanks, but I'm on a diet," she said.

Ruthie placed the pan on the coffee table and dished up a brownie. Guthrie ate it in two bites. She gave him another. He downed that one just as fast. "Come on, try one," he said, still chewing.

"I had a sandwich a few minutes before you called," Ruthie said.

Spying what looked like lumps of nuts on the top of the brownies, I fibbed, "I'm allergic to nuts."

"Bummer," Guthrie mumbled. "Well, can't let them go to waste." He held out his hand and took a third. "If things get dull, I brought my tape of *Alice's Restaurant*. It's in the knapsack."

"Whoopee," Penny Sue muttered, unzipping the canvas bag.

"You have a VCR, don't you?"

"It's broken," Penny Sue replied languidly, reaching in the satchel. She came out with a well-viewed videotape and a large baggie stuffed with a handgun and ammunition. "Wow, is this a Glock forty-five?"

"Yeah, the compact model. There's a smaller one, but I thought it looked wussy. Man, if you're going to carry a gun, you want something that makes a statement."

Penny Sue smirked at me. "My sentiments, exactly."

Brother, I wish he hadn't said that. Penny Sue's .38 was bad enough, with a little encouragement she'd probably buy an M16.

Penny Sue finished unloading the knapsack of its frozen contents and stowed them in the freezer.

"Flip to Channel 9," Guthrie instructed. "They have a man in Punta Gorda. Charley's coming ashore at Fort Myers."

Ruthie changed the channel. "Hotel rooms in Central Florida are booked with people fleeing Tampa Bay. With the unexpected turn in the storm, there's no place for southern residents to go except shelters," the anchorwoman said. The picture flashed to boats pitching and crashing in a marina. A reporter in Punta Gorda came on by telephone from the hallway of a hotel. He'd barely begun his story when there was a loud ripping sound. "The hotel's roof just peeled away!" the reporter shouted.

"Don't panic, Ruthie. The storm will blow out before it gets here," Penny Sue said.

"Yeah, we're only expected to get Category 1 or tropical force winds," Guthrie added.

"But the eye is supposed to pass over Daytona Beach at eleven tonight. That's only thirty miles north," Ruthie whined.

"Yes, and six hours for the storm to change course." Penny Sue popped the cork on a bottle of champagne and put out a plate of caviar and crackers. "I've never thrown a hurricane party before. Come on, let's get on with it."

We spent the evening eating, channel surfing between the Weather Channel and local stations, and answering the phone. News of the storm's path through Daytona Beach spread fast. Our fathers, my son, Ruthie's daughter, and assorted friends called to check our status. "Don't worry," we told them bravely. "Winds will die down before Charley reaches us."

I hoped our bravery didn't turn out to be stupidity.

By nine o'clock the storm had reached Orlando with high winds, torrential rains, and power outages. We'd finished the champagne, caviar, and a large tray of Stouffer's chicken lasagna. Guthrie had polished off the brownies by eight and taken to teaching Pete, the toy Parrot, to talk. "One," he said. The toy squawked, "On-ne."

"Two." The bird croaked, "Two-o."

"Three." Guthrie kept going to ten.

The three of us sat at the kitchen counter, one eye on the TV, the other on our hippie friend with chopped meat bandaged to his leg.

Penny Sue said, "Hide the Furby."

I covered my mouth and whispered. "He thinks the bird is really learning. I'd say that proves the brownies were spiked with something."

"He ate the whole tray," Ruthie exclaimed.

"He'll probably pass out any minute." Wrong.

"I've taught Pete to count," Guthrie called happily. "Show them, Pete."

"Show them, Pete," the bird aped.

We bit our lips.

"One, two, three-e," Guthrie prompted.

"One, two, three-e."

"And?" Guthrie leaned forward, his face within inches of the bird. "Four, five, six," he whispered.

"Four, five, six," the bird said softly.

Penny Sue sputtered, unable to control herself any longer. Pete cackled like Penny Sue.

"His name is Pete the Repeat Parrot," I said. "He only mimics what you say. He doesn't remember any of it."

Guthrie folded his arms, eyes narrowed. "Man, that was a waste of time." He reached for his knee. "I need to change the bandage. My meat's thawed and started to drip. There should be a bag of succotash in the freezer."

A gust of wind rocked the patio door. Rain pounded the building like shrapnel.

"Man, I'm suddenly really hungry." He spied the candy piled on the kitchen counter. "Those Hershey Kisses look mighty good."

I got the succotash as Ruthie poured the candy into a bowl. He handed me the thawed, bloody sirloin that had leaked and wrapped the vegetables on his knee with the soiled Ace bandage. I put the meat down the garbage disposal. Yuck!

We spent the rest of the evening eating—we even cracked a couple of cans of Vienna sausages—and watched the storm's progress. We had electricity, though there were several ominous brownouts. Fortunately, our stove was natural gas, so we could cook even if the electricity failed.

The wind was howling as eleven o'clock drew near, but except for occasional hits by palm fronds and debris, there didn't seem to be major damage. Still, Ruthie insisted we all go into the closet at ten-thirty. I gave my chair to Guthrie, who propped his leg on the cooler. I sat cross-legged in the floor. We left the TV on in the living room, volume maxed, so we could track the hurricane's progress. At eleven o'clock there was a report of looting in Orange County.

Penny Sue took her .38 from her pocket, slipped it out of the holster and placed it on a shelf in easy reach. "Can't be too careful," was all she said. "Where's your Glock?" she asked Guthrie.

"On the coffee table. It's loaded. If you hear anything, one of you run get it."

About eleven fifteen, the storm passed off the coast of Daytona Beach and we ventured from the closet. Though the wind still raged, blowing rain in horizontal sheets, Charley was kind to us. We seemed no worse for the wear. At least there were no leaks or outward signs of damage.

Penny Sue cracked the second bottle of champagne to toast our good fortune, and we all proceeded to turn in for the night. I helped Guthrie unroll his sleeping bag and blow up the air mattress rolled inside. I rewrapped his knee with a Birds Eye Teriyaki stir-fry and zipped him in the sleeping bag.

"Snug as a bug in a rug," he muttered, either very sleepy or completely stoned. Whichever, he seemed content for the rest of the night.

Wrong again.

"Help! I'm drowning!"

I was in the middle of a dream where I was shopping at Beall's department store. I was standing in a mob at the jewelry counter, eyeing a humongous bottle of Joy perfume. It was hot, and I was sweating. The people around me smelled of perspiration, and I wished I could douse them all in the cologne.

No sooner did I have the thought when the bottle burst. The Joy perfume ran down the counter and filled the store up to my chin. There was a mad rush as customers swam out—

"Help! I'm stuck. I'm drowning!"

This call, louder and more urgent than the first, woke me up. Drenched in sweat, I blinked at the early morning sun shining through the window and tried to separate dream from reality.

A moment later a loud "Damn!" came from the hallway—unmistakably Penny Sue. "The electricity is off and the place is filled with water."

Ruthie and I, in the guest room's twin beds, bolted upright.

Ruthie swung her feet to the floor. "Heavens!" she cried.

I stood up in ankle deep water. "The place *is* flooded." Then I remembered Guthrie on his air mattress, zipped up in a sleeping bag. Lord, he really could be drowning. I slogged to the spot where I'd left him; he wasn't there.

"Over here," he yelled. "Help me."

Lying on the air mattress, he'd floated to the far side of the room, behind the sofa. I splashed through the water, unzipped the sleeping bag, and pulled him to his feet.

"Thanks, man. You saved my life. I was trapped like a big, soggy burrito. I'm indebted to you for life."

"Forget it. You would have done the same for me."

"Yeah, man, but I'm still indebted—your slave for life. If you need anything, just ask." He rubbed his knee. "After this knee heals."

A slave, just what I needed. My own life was tough enough to handle. Managing Guthrie's life was too heavy to contemplate.

By now everyone was in the living room. "Where the hell did all this water come from?" Penny Sue asked, scanning the room with the halogen lantern.

"Storm surge," Ruthie said forcefully. "I warned y'all."

"It couldn't be storm surge. The water would have come in through the glass doors." I pointed to the sliding doors, where dawn was beginning to break. "In that case, Guthrie would have floated down the hall and been jammed against the front door."

Penny Sue dipped her hand in the ankle deep water and tasted it. "It's not salty. This is fresh water."

"Rain," Ruthie said sharply. "It ran down the hill from the other condos."

"Well, open the patio doors," Penny Sue instructed, zinging into her Martha Stewart mode. "If it's coming downhill, we have to let the water drain out. And stuff towels under the front door, so no more gets in."

I opened the sliding glass doors. The water rushed to the deck, leaving us big toe versus ankle deep.

"This doesn't make sense," I said. "There were torrential rains all night—which would have drained down here—and the hall was dry as an old bone when we went to bed."

Penny Sue squinted at me. I could tell she was flipping into Jessica Fletcher or Sherlock Holmes. "You're right. With all the rain, we'd have flooded hours ago if that's the source." She glanced at her watch, six AM. "When the sun comes up, we should go out and investigate. This flood doesn't make sense." Penny Sue poured spring water into a teakettle, and put it on the gas stovetop. "What we need is a cup of strong coffee."

"Coffee? The electricity's off."

Penny Sue smiled smugly, holding up a red box. "There's more than one way to skin a cat. These are coffee bags, like tea bags. Let them steep in hot water, and voilà, fresh brewed coffee."

Guthrie, who'd made his way to the sofa, raised his hand like a first-grader. "Far out. I'll like some. Sugar, if you have it."

"How much?" Penny Sue asked, pulling mugs from the cabinet.

"Three tablespoons."

We all did a double take. "Tablespoons?" Ruthie asked.

"I've already eaten all the brownies."

O-okay, I wasn't sure what that meant. Was he addicted to sugar or something else? One thing I did know, the tile floor was wet and slippery. If we didn't mop it up fast, one of us was going to break her neck—and with my luck it would be me. Or worse, Guthrie. I had a momentary image of the three of us waiting on him for life. Unh uh!

I headed to the utility room for a broom, bucket, and mop. I held up the broom and mop to Ruthie. "Would you rather sweep water out the back door, or mop up afterward?"

She took the broom. The floor wasn't level, and the water pooled in the back corner of the dining area. I pushed the water out of the corner with the sponge mop, and Ruthie swept it out the door. By the time our coffee was ready, we'd made a good dent in the mess. While we rested and sipped our java, Penny Sue took over with the mop.

"Like another cup?" Penny Sue asked, an obvious cue for Ruthie and me to get back to work.

I took back the mop. "How about a bagel with jelly?"

Penny Sue shook her head. "The oven's electric. Momma didn't like cooking with gas, said it made sponge cakes taste like chemicals."

"Do it the old-fashioned way. Use the iron skillet," I said. "Grammy Martin made toast like that on the stovetop. Like Ruth Gordon said in *Harold and Maude*, 'Try something new every day.'"

By now, we'd disposed of most of the water, yet the floor remained slick. I was also tired of squeezing the sponge mop. "Try something new everyday." Old Maude was right. I went to the utility room and returned with a stack of my bottom sheets. I dropped one on the floor and shuffled around.

"What are you doing?" Ruthie asked, in shock.

"Drying the floor." I tossed her a folded sheet.

"These are the linens you're saving."

"Yeah, well, times change."

We finished about the same time as the bagels. Considering the electricity was out, we had a pretty good breakfast. Hot coffee, toasted bagels with jelly, and oatmeal. Sure, it was a tad heavy in the carb department, but after a dinner of caviar and Vienna sausages, what difference did it make? We'd clean up our diet next week, when the dust settled, or rather, the floor dried.

Penny Sue drained her mug, clicked it down on the counter, and stood. "We have to stop the water."

Right. We were running out of sopping material for the front door and I'd already donated my remaining sheets to the cause. The sun was up, so it was time to go into action, even if we had to dig a moat around the front stoop.

Ruthie wrapped her arms around her body as if she had a sudden chill. "I don't have a good feeling about this."

"This what?" I asked.

"The water."

"Not good, how?" Penny Sue waved at Ruthie as if trying to draw out more information.

"Not good, like evil."

Penny Sue, Ruthie, and I went to find the source of the water. Guthrie's knee was still swollen and horribly bruised. It was painful to even look at. I thought we should take him to the hospital, but he refused, saying he hated doctors. Geez. I brought out the battery-powered radio for his amusement and wrapped a bag of Ore-Ida frozen fries around his leg. Before we left, he insisted I give him the Glock and ammo in case there were looters. I wasn't in thc mood to argue, but asked him to call out to us before he pulled the trigger.

Ruthie and Penny Sue, with gun drawn, waited for me at the front door.

"I wish you'd put that thing away," I said, nodding at Penny Sue's gun.

"Heck no. You heard about the looting in Orlando last night."

"Those were stores. Who would loot condos?"

She put her hands on her hips; thankfully the .38's barrel was aimed at the wall and not me. "Crooks know most of these condos were evacuated. TVs, computers, DVDs—that's what they want. Smash and grab. It takes an experienced crook ten seconds to break in. Even with an alarm, they're long gone before the police arrive, especially after a storm. Ted would tell you that."

"Thanks, Penny Sue, that makes me feel real good. I felt secure with the alarm system until now."

"You should get a gun, Leigh, and take some lessons. A lone female on the beach—you're a sitting duck."

Boy, she was on a roll, that made me feel even worse. "For crissakes, Penny Sue, I've got enough stress already. Let's deal with the present situation, and I'll deal with my future another time—like in the future. Maybe I'll go into a convent, ashram, or something. Then, I won't need a gun."

Penny Sue opened the door and stalked out. "That would never work—all they'd give you is gruel and sacramental wine. No ice cream, for sure."

She was hitting below the belt. Mint chocolate chip ice cream was my one—okay, one of several—indulgences. No mint chocolate chip? I'd have to re-think the religious commune angle.

Penny Sue led the way with her gun at ready. I followed close behind, while Ruthie trailed by a good three yards. I hoped Ruthie was lagging because she was getting info from her spirit guides—like we should turn back. Guess not, because she didn't say anything.

"Look!" Penny Sue pointed at the roll-down hurricane shutters on the ocean side of Guthrie's condo. They had been sheered off at the top and were lying on the ground. One of the unprotected windows had blown in. She stopped to examine the closest shutter. "This is really strange. It broke off in a straight line. It's like someone sliced it off."

"Don't look now, but I see where the water's coming from." I pointed to the small door to the crawl space of Mrs. King's condo that we'd inspected the previous day.

"She must have a water main break," Penny Sue said. "We need to find the master switch for the water to her house. Do you think Guthrie knows?"

I gave her a you've-got-to-be-kidding expression. After all, this was the guy who'd spent the previous evening eating brownies laced with who-knew-what and trying to teach a toy parrot to count. "Remember the parrot?"

She got my drift. "I'd better call a plumber. I know one that Daddy helped with a legal crisis. If he's still in business, I'm sure he'll come."

I glanced over my shoulder at Ruthie. She was staring straight ahead with her arms wrapped around her body. "What do you make of this?" I asked.

"Evil. Evil all around us."

Chapter 5

August 14

"I've never seen anything like this." Sonny Mallard was a prince of a guy who had left his own damaged house to help us with Mrs. King's plumbing. He quickly found the main cut-off, solving our water problem, and had moved on to fixing the busted pipe.

Penny Sue knelt in the doorway to the underbelly of Mrs. King's house and watched. I peered over her shoulder.

"This is a new plastic/aluminum composite pipe. I've heard about these, but never seen one before," Sonny said. "Basically, it's three layers. The inner and outer parts are plastic, while the middle is aluminum. Somebody stripped the outside plastic layer. Best I can tell, the aluminum disintegrated. The plastic tube in the middle couldn't take the water pressure and popped like a balloon."

"The aluminum disintegrated?" Penny Sue asked.

He peeled back an inch of the outer plastic and peered inside. "Damnest thing I've ever seen. I guess this was once aluminum, now it looks like rust."

"I didn't think aluminum rusted," I said.

"It doesn't."

"Can you fix it? I'll pay," Penny Sue offered. "Mrs. King's in the hospital with a heart attack—she doesn't need to be bothered with this."

"No time soon. I wouldn't know where to buy this stuff. Best I can do is leave the water main turned off and make a few phone calls. A permit should have been filed with the city and that will give me the contractor's name. I can't find out anything until Monday, at the earliest, though."

Penny Sue turned to me. "Good thing Mrs. King's still at Bert Fish. We should check on her. If we find her contractor, maybe we can have it fixed before she gets home."

Good ole Penny Sue. She didn't even know Mrs. King. 'Course, Penny Sue also had money to burn.

"I'll call you on Monday," Sonny said, gathering his tools. He stood, tugged up his pants, and headed for his truck. "Right now I need to deal with a big, old live oak that smashed my garage."

Penny Sue followed him to the truck and slipped him a couple of hundred dollar bills. "I can't tell you how much I appreciate your coming."

He tried to give the cash back, but she stepped away. "You'll need that for your garage."

He nodded his thanks and left.

Penny Sue was such a generous—and complicated—person, the exchange brought a tear to my eye. Thankfully, Ruthie came from the side of our condo before I *tuned-up*, as Grammy Martin called crying. "I guess we'd better check on the rest of the damage," I said.

"The judge lost some shingles on the roof facing the beach, and the metal chimney blew off," Ruthie reported. "The condo's coated in sand, otherwise in good shape. Your neighbors didn't fare as well. He lost all the outside light fixtures and most of the shingles facing the ocean. The tarpaper even ripped off, exposing a lot of wood. I'll bet the wallboard inside is soaked."

"Did you check on Guthrie?"

"Sound asleep on the sofa."

"We'd better take a look at his place." Penny Sue pointed to the broken window. "Ruthie, would you get his key? I want to know what's what before we drag him up this hill."

I stooped to examine Guthrie's hurricane shutters that had fallen. Roll down shutters, they were constructed of horizontal aluminum slats. Aside from a few chips in the paint, the window covers seemed sturdy, yet both had sheared off in approximately the same place. I studied the sheared edge. It was wavy, but smooth. No jagged edges or creases for that matter. "Penny Sue, take at look at this."

She dropped to her knees beside me.

"Do you notice anything unusual about this shutter?"

She ran her finger along the torn edge. "The side is slick. And look." She held up her finger, covered in a rust-colored powder, just like Mrs. King's wire. "Like you said, aluminum doesn't rust. Something very fishy is going on here." Her forehead creased with thought. "Guthrie heard a scraping sound. Metal on metal, he said."

"Yeah."

"The windows are only about six feet off the ground. Suppose a person took something sharp, like a rake, and scratched off the paint on the shutters."

"Okay ...?"

She cocked her head. "The paint protects the aluminum, and now the metal's exposed to salt air."

I shook my head. "No cigar. It's impossible for aluminum to corrode that fast."

"Maybe the corrosion started, weakening the slat, and then Charley—"

I gave her a thumb-down. "The edge would be ripped, not smooth."

Penny Sue's lips tightened. "Well, maybe someone threw acid on it and that ate through the exposed metal."

"Too dangerous. It might splash on the saboteur."

"He wore a raincoat and hat. And he didn't throw it on, he swabbed the scratch with an acid-soaked sponge."

That might work. Besides, it was obvious she wasn't going to give up. "I'll allow that theory."

She grinned sanctimoniously.

"What acid eats aluminum?"

Penny Sue tilted her chin regally. "I'm not an encyclopedia. You can't expect me to know everything."

I closed my eyes and thought of my dear, departed Grandma Martin. *Grab patience and might,* she used to say in situations like this. "Help me, Grammy," I pleaded silently. "I need a passel of patience for Penny Sue."

Just then, Ruthie returned with the key and we headed up the stairs to Guthrie's condo.

"How's he doing?"

"Happy as a clam. He's stretched out on the sofa listening to the local stations. He's a veritable font of knowledge on all the damage, looting, you name it. Of course, I had to tend to his knee. We were pretty much out of his frozen foods, and I couldn't tell which was ours and which was his. So, I took some ice from the cooler."

Penny Sue frowned. "We have no idea how long the power will be off. We may need that ice for drinks."

"His knee really looks bad. When we finish here, we should insist on taking him to the emergency room. His leg should be X-rayed—he may have broken something."

"I agree. We can check in on Nana while we're there."

The spirits, as Ruthie would say, were obviously looking after Guthrie. The broken window was to his utility room—a washer, dryer, and concrete floor. Granted, the room was filled with water, sand, leaves, and a poor, dead seagull, but nothing that couldn't be cleaned.

Ruthie found a purple towel in the dryer and gently wrapped it around the seagull. We stood in a circle while Ruthie said a prayer. She blessed the gull for all its selfless contributions to our plane (translation: Earth) and commended his spirit to the great gull attractor field in another dimension, where he would never feel pain again.

As a consummate New Ager, Ruthie's service didn't surprise me, except for the attractor field part. That was a new tangent for her. I made a mental note to ask about it later.

Ruthie sat on the porch, lovingly cradling the towel-wrapped gull, while Penny Sue and I finished the inspection. We found no major damage, except for a possible leak in the vent fan in the master bathroom.

"Rain probably blew down the roof vent," Penny Sue said.

I agreed quickly, anxious to leave Guthrie's personal space. Aside from a ten-by-fourteen headshot of a very handsome man, whom I assumed was his friend Timothy, the room was unremarkable except for the incredible clutter. In my experience, gay men's housekeeping put Martha Stewart to shame. Guthrie was clearly the exception. Of course, he might not be gay. Plus, none of it was my business, I told myself wryly.

Guthrie had polished off all the Hershey Kisses and half the Snickers by the time we returned. The electricity was still off, so he was listening to local TV on our boom box. "Man, there's another one out there."

"Another what?" Penny Sue asked sharply, probably peeved he'd helped himself to her candy bars.

"A hurricane. Man, we can't get a break." He noticed the purple towel Ruthie was carrying. "You brought my laundry?"

Ruthie gave him the most hateful look—or as close to hateful as she gets, which is a long shot from most people, like Penny Sue and me—I'd ever seen. "The window in your utility room broke and a poor seagull blew in and died. We need to bury him."

Guthrie bolted upright as if spring-loaded. "Man, that's awful. I'm sorry I was flip." He struggled to his feet. "Absolutely, we need to give him or her a decent burial. I could make a headstone. But, we don't know his name, do we? Guthrie Gull. That fits, don't you think?" He paused. "I'm babbling, aren't I? Sorry, I babble when I get nervous—"

I patted the air, indicating he should sit back down. He complied meekly. I turned to Ruthie. "Where do you think we should bury him?"

"In the sand dune," she said without hesitation. "Ashes to ashes—"

"Sand to sand," Guthrie piped in. "Should we call, like, a priest or something?"

"We said a prayer when we found him," Penny Sue said, still eyeing the half-full bag of Snickers on the coffee table. "Now, we need to lay him to rest respectfully."

"Right. You're absolutely right."

I went to help Guthrie. "Okay, let's go."

Ruthie led the way, Penny Sue followed, and I brought up the rear supporting our hobbling neighbor. Halfway across the deck, Penny Sue relented (apparently deciding to let eaten Snickers lie) and dropped back to help me with Guthrie.

The burial was short and solemn, partly because we'd already commended the gull's soul to the great attractor field, and partly because it started to rain and we didn't have an umbrella. Apparently, Charley wasn't finished with us yet.

We'd only been inside a couple of seconds when someone knocked frantically on the front door. Penny Sue hurried to answer it. "My, my." We heard her exclaim. A moment later, much to Penny Sue's chagrin, it became clear that the visitor was Timothy, the good-looking guy whose picture hung on Guthrie's bedroom wall.

"Is he here?" our visitor demanded, obviously assuming we knew who *he* was.

Penny Sue stepped aside and motioned to the sofa. Timothy rushed past her and knelt on the tile floor beside Guthrie.

"Timmy!"

"Guthrie!"

Geez, it was like a scene from a bad B-movie.

"I came as soon as I got Mother home and settled. She was lucky—her house had no damage and the electricity was on." Timothy gingerly touched Guthrie's bandaged knee, grimacing at the filthy, sirloin-blood-stained Ace bandage.

"It's nice to meet you, Timothy." I held out my hand. Timothy stood to his full six-plus feet of hard-packed muscle. Guthrie's picture didn't do him justice—this guy was truly awesome. "Guthrie's mentioned you several times." I nodded at our friend on the sofa. "We think he should go to the hospital and have his knee X-rayed, but he won't listen to us."

"Don't worry, I'm not giving him a choice." Slipping one arm under Guthrie's shoulders and the other under his legs, Timothy lifted Guthrie like a doll.

"Holy shit," Penny Sue muttered, eyes bulging like Timothy's biceps, triceps, and other 'ceps we'd probably never heard of.

Guthrie tittered, wrapping one arm around Timothy's neck and waving to us with the other. "Like, I guess I'm going to the hospital. Thanks ladies, it's been real."

I ran ahead to get the front door. Timothy raised his chin toward a baby blue BMW. I got the hint and opened the passenger-side door. He placed Guthrie on the seat as gently as a feather.

"I'll stop by later to pick up Guthrie's things. I can't thank you enough for looking after him." With that Timmy peeled off to the hospital.

Penny Sue was standing in the doorway when I returned. "What an Adonis! Laa, he's about the best built man I've ever seen. And he's in love with Guthrie! What a loss for womanhood."

"Opposites attract," I said, heading down the hall, Snickers on my mind.

"C'est la vie." Ruthie turned on her heel and followed me.

"Yeah," Penny Sue said loudly, "but it's a real pisser." She fanned herself, chomping on a candy bar. "It's getting hot in here." She peered out the window. "It's stopped raining. Let's walk around the complex and check the damage." She glanced at Ruthie. "What about the beach?"

"Half of the first dune is gone."

"Could have been worse. One and a half is better than none." Penny Sue snagged ice from the cooler and poured a diet cola.

We went out the sliding glass door to the deck and followed the public boardwalk for the complex. From that angle, we had a better view of the condos' roofs, many of which were missing large swaths of shingles.

Ruthie pointed to the three-story unit on the far side of Guthrie's duplex. A man sat in the corner of the second story balcony. "Someone else braved the storm. Do you know him?"

I squinted in his direction. "That's one of the condos that recently sold. I wonder if he's the new owner."

The man stood, raising his arm. "Seems friendly, he's waving to us." Penny Sue waved back.

Then, we heard a muffled pop. The man lurched against the handrail, the railing collapsed, and he crashed to the ground.

"Magawd," I croaked, my hand fluttering to my heart. Ruthie froze, eyes the size of saucers.

Bless her heart, Penny Sue hailed from heartier stock. Probably the result of all the firearm, Tae Kwon Do, and terrorist avoidance driving courses she'd taken. In any event, this was one time I was happy for Penny Sue to take control. "Ruthie, run get a cell phone. Call 9-1-1. Leigh, you're with me."

Huh? I wasn't good with mangled bodies. She grabbed my arm and yanked, I had no choice.

The man had landed face down in the sand, with one leg folded under his abdomen and one hand bent backward. Penny Sue felt his neck for a pulse and grimaced. "Help me roll him over. I'll try CPR."

One look at his contorted hand and my mouth filled with the taste of Snickers. I gritted my teeth and swallowed hard. "You can do this," I told myself. "You have to do this!"

I placed my hands on his torso, and rolled him to his back. Poised on her knees ready to administer CPR, Penny Sue gagged at the sight of the bullet hole in the middle of his chest and sat down hard. A handgun that looked a lot like Guthrie's Glock was under the body. Blood oozed from the hole in the man's chest. CPR forgotten, Penny Sue and I scrabbled away from the body. At that moment, Ruthie barreled up with her cell phone. She took one look, whirled around, and vomited. Penny Sue and I held our noses and crawled to the side of the building.

"Toss me the cell phone," Penny Sue called to Ruthie. "We'll take care of this. Go back to the condo and clean yourself up."

Ruthie threw the phone and made a half-hearted attempt to kick sand over the vomit while Penny Sue dialed 9-1-1. "You just got a call about an injured man. Yeah, that's the one. Send the police. It's a gunshot wound."

A patrol car and fire truck arrived simultaneously. A female officer bounded from the patrol car, gun drawn. She slowly turned in a circle, searching nearby balconies, while her male partner stooped beside the paramedic. The examination only took a minute. There was no doubt in anybody's mind that this man was dead as a doornail.

Huddled against the side of the building, Penny Sue whispered, "His gun must have gone off when he fell. He might have survived the fall."

"What was he doing with a gun?"

"Looters. After all, someone tried to break into Mrs. King's condo. They would have succeeded if it hadn't been for her burglar alarm. But alarms aren't working now—even the backup batteries have run out of juice."

"I heard a pop, didn't you?" I said.

"The railing giving way. These condos are old, and the wood dries out and rots if it's not properly maintained. That's why so many people are switching to aluminum. A couple of years ago, a balcony down the beach collapsed and a whole family was injured."

The female officer, Heather Brooks, squatted beside us with a notebook and a big roll of yellow crime tape. "We need to rope off this area. Do you live in the complex?"

I nodded. "At the end of the boardwalk, number forty-two."

Heather wrote it down. "Your name?"

"Leigh Stratton. That's L-e-i-g-h."

She tilted her head at Penny Sue. "You're staying together?"

"Yes, it's my father's condo."

"And you are?"

"Penny Sue Parker."

The officer did a double take. "Sorry." She grinned sheepishly. "Could you give me that again?"

"Penny, P-e-n-n-y. Sue—"

The officer held up her hand. "Got it."

"Parker."

Heather consulted the previous page of her notebook. "You made the second call. Ruthie Nichols made the first call. Do you know her?"

"She's staying with us, too. We sent her back to the condo to clean up …" Penny Sue pointed at the pool of puke. "Ruthie isn't good in a crisis."

Heather scrunched her nose. "I see. The three of you witnessed what happened?"

"Yes," I said.

The officer made a notation in her book, stood, and reached down to help us to our feet. I was grateful for her assistance; my knees were still a little wobbly.

"Someone will be down to take your statements as soon as we secure the area. In the meantime, you should keep your doors locked."

Oh, boy. My right knee started to twitch.

Chapter 6

August 14

Ruthie sat at the kitchen counter cradling her head in her hands. She'd changed into a yellow cotton shirt with matching culottes. Un-ironed, since there was no electricity. Normally a fashion plate, ironing was clearly not high on Ruthie's list at the present time.

Penny Sue rubbed Ruthie's shoulder. "You all right?"

Ruthie shook her head no.

"A cola will settle your stomach." Penny Sue pulled three diet colas from the cooler in the closet and poured them into Styrofoam cups with a smidgen of ice. "Not much ice," Penny Sue said, handing the cup to Ruthie. "Who knows how long the power will be out?"

Ruthie spoke without lifting her head. "Electric feeder lines are down. New Smyrna Utilities has no idea when power will be restored. We have to conserve water. Almost all the pumping stations are running on generators. We should limit flushing toilets."

"Toilets aren't a problem, because we can always use ocean water. There are some buckets in the utility room," I said.

"Right," Penny Sue agreed brightly, trying to cheer up Ruthie. "Y'all made fun of me, but we have a ton of food and bottled water. Best of all, we can cook—we have gas!"

Ruthie raised her head and stared at Penny Sue with red-rimmed eyes. "You are bad luck."

Penny Sue tilted her chin haughtily. "I most certainly am not! I had nothing to do with that man," she turned on me, "did I, Leigh?"

She didn't give me a chance to answer, though I was inclined to agree with Ruthie.

Penny Sue went on, "I've never seen him in my life. He was guarding against looters, leaned on a rotten railing, and fell on his gun. You can't blame me for that!"

"You didn't cause it," Ruthie said quietly, "but you're a lightning rod for trouble. Murders don't happen unless you're around."

Penny Sue drew back as if she'd been slapped in the face. "You were there too, for Lord's sake. Maybe you're the lightning rod!"

I held my hands up, trying to calm everyone down. After all, the police would arrive any minute to take our statements. The last thing we needed was a fight among ourselves. Besides, we were all stuck in Florida for who-knew-how long, in case we were required to give statements in the Mafia case. Our initial instructions said we might be called next week. With the hurricane, I had a sneaking feeling the timeline would be extended. I sure as heck didn't want to spend weeks together, at each other's throats.

"We were all present. Don't you see—it's the combination of our energies." I nudged Ruthie's arm. "You always say there are no accidents, right?"

Penny Sue arched a brow in agreement. "Maybe we're destined to fight crime or something like Charlie's Angels." She grinned. "Wouldn't that be fun?"

Ruthie curled her lip.

"Come on, Ruthie," I said. "You're the one who says a person's current situation is the result of all of her past karma. We're not victims of fate—we're here to choose it and to change it, if we made a bad choice in another life." I wasn't sure I believed it all, but if anything would bring Ruthie around, that was it. A smile from Ruthie was all I wanted before the police arrived.

Ruthie regarded me with hooded eyes, then relaxed—her shoulders dropped at least six inches—and, the glimmer of a smile. "You were listening to me all along. I thought it was going in one ear and out the other."

"I listened, too," Penny Sue added hastily. "I kid you about it, but I agree with"—she paused a beat—"most of what you say."

Ruthie leaned across the counter for a group hug. "I'm sorry to be so cross. I don't do well with blood."

The hug made us all a bit misty-eyed. We hadn't had a fight like that since college, and I hoped we wouldn't have another any time soon. They were my best friends, the only people besides my kids I could always count on. To lose that support over a silly disagreement was not what I wanted at this point in my life.

Good ole Penny Sue came to our rescue before we all tuned-up into a blubbering mass. She wiped her forehead, which was perspiring profusely, as they say in the South. Truthfully, she was sweating buckets. The emotion, a dead man, her hot flashes, and the lack of AC all come together in a slimy, stinky (none of us had showered) cascade. "Boy, it's getting hot. Let's open all the windows, so we can get some cross ventilation."

Brilliant. An assignment. Something to take our minds off our disagreement.

Understand, Southern women do not fight: They disagree, have a tiff, or get their nose out of joint, but not from a physical blow, mind you! The distinction between a fight and disagreement may be obscure to non-Southerners—especially when the claws and fangs pop out—yet, there is a big difference. A person from the North might haul off and hit you or spit in your eye. Someone from California will outspend you on clothes, finagle an invitation to an important party, or get a bigger boob job. A Southerner will lob cryptic insults and talk behind your back.

I don't know what people in the Midwest do. They may be the only sane people in the country. They have no accent, which is why television and radio personalities, no matter where they originate, go to schools that teach them to speak Midwestern.

But we're Southerners, and the best thing to end a tiff is an assignment! To dutiful wives, who ministered to everyone during the War of Northern Aggression, there is nothing like a task to get a Southern woman back on track. Without a word Ruthie and Penny Sue went to the bedrooms, while I opened the small window in the guest bath.

As Penny Sue emerged from the master suite, there was a knock on the front door. She peered through the peephole and grumbled loudly as she unlocked the door. Ruthie and I knew that wasn't good. A Southern lady does not grumble vociferously, except in extreme circumstances. I peeked around the corner to see what was wrong. The circumstance *was* extreme. Officer Heather Brooks and Robert "Woody" Woodhead, the local prosecutor and our biggest pain in the derriere, stood on the other side of the screen door.

I won't go into a lot of details, but our college sorority used to spend spring break at Penny Sue's daddy's condo. One summer—I think our sophomore year—Penny Sue met Woody, a local, and they started dating. As usually happened with everything Penny Sue did, things got complicated. Her Atlanta boyfriend, at the time—Zack, my now ex—showed up unexpectedly. There was a big scene between Zack and Woody. In the end, Penny Sue dumped them both, and took up with Andy, the captain of the football team, and her first husband.

No matter what one's opinion was of New Age philosophy, Woody Woodhead was living proof of Ruthie's favorite adage: "There are no accidents." To say the name fit the person was an understatement in his case. As far as I could tell, he was a knot-head in everyone's book.

Penny Sue pushed the screen door, which emitted an ear splitting screech. See, even the door hated Woody, I thought sourly.

"What a surprise," Penny Sue said evenly, motioning them in.

Towering over Woody, Heather dipped her chin when she passed Penny Sue as if to say, "Sorry."

"We don't get many murders in New Smyrna Beach," Woody said, taking his usual seat in the rattan chair by the chimney. "New Smyrna and Volusia police have instructions to call me whenever you're involved in anything." He gave us a crooked grin. "And, here we are again, just like old times."

Heather was a tall, attractive brunette, and I sensed she wasn't particularly fond of Woody. I'm sure he treated her in the same condescending way he had previously dealt with us. To her credit, she was the consummate professional, which Woody was not. Heather stood in the entry to the great room, eyes glued to Guthrie's Glock on the coffee table. Woody the Wuss hadn't even noticed it.

I saw Heather unsnap her holster, ready for action. "That's not ours," I exclaimed, pointing to the Glock. "Our neighbor, Guthrie Fribble, weathered the storm with us last night. He hurt his knee and couldn't walk, so he was stuck on the sofa. When he heard about the looting in Orlando, he wanted his gun within in easy reach, while we checked the neighborhood for damage."

Heather pulled on a latex glove. "Do you mind if I take a look at it?"

"Be my guest," Penny Sue snapped.

The officer picked up the gun and sniffed the barrel. "Doesn't appear to have been fired recently."

Woody steepled his fingers in front of his chest. "Do you still carry a .38, Penny Sue?"

"Yes, perfectly legal."

"Do you mind showing it to Officer Brooks?"

Penny Sue reached in her pocket and pulled out her revolver. Thankfully, she'd put it back in its holster at some point, so she wasn't guilty of carrying a concealed weapon.

Heather slipped the gun out of its leather pouch and smelled the barrel. She shook her head, and gave it back to Penny Sue.

"So the Glock belongs to your neighbor, Guthrie. If he's so concerned about his safety, where's Guthrie now?"

"At Bert Fish, having his leg X-rayed. Call the emergency room, you'll see," I said.

"Wait," Ruthie spoke for the first time. "His real name is Fred Fribble. Guthrie is a nickname."

Woody looked to the ceiling, rolling his eyes. "Fred Fribble. This is a new low for you girls."

All of us, including Heather, cringed at the word *girls*.

"That's his name," I retorted. Woody's condescending attitude reminded me of Zack, which brought up a lot of anger. If Woody wasn't careful, I might forget I was a Southern lady and pop him in the nose. Of course, then I'd go to jail. Not a good idea on second thought. I hated the idea that my kids would have a jailbird for a mother.

Heather called Bert Fish on her cell phone while this exchange took place. "Fred Fribble is in the emergency room," she confirmed flatly.

"You're kidding," Woody replied.

Heather held out her cell phone. "Would you like to speak with the nurse? He's in X-ray right now. Fred fell down some stairs."

At that moment, Woody's beeper went off. He checked the display and stood. "Sorry, something more important has come up."

He nodded to Brooks. "Get their statements and bag the Glock." He turned to us. "You don't mind if we return this to Mr. Fribble ourselves, do you?"

"Of course not. He'll verify everything we said. Woody, there's no reason to treat us like suspects. We were in the wrong place at the wrong time and witnessed a horrible accident," Penny Sue retorted.

"It's amazing how that keeps happening to you girls. Wrong place at the wrong time, that is. Accident? Maybe. So far, preliminary results don't show powder burns on his shirt."

"So?" Penny Sue asked.

"He didn't fall on the gun and shoot himself." Woody started for the door.

"If he didn't shoot himself—" Ruthie started.

"Sniper!?" Penny Sue and I said in unison.

"Wait, Woody, " Penny Sue shouted. "We're in town to give depositions against Al, the Mafia guy."

Woody turned. "The turtle man?"

We nodded.

"I hadn't heard about that." He ground his teeth, obviously annoyed. "I should have been informed." Woody stalked toward the door. "I'll get back to you," he said over his shoulder.

Heather Brooks asked to interview us individually. "One person can influence another's recollection."

"Like the old story about no two people remembering an auto accident the same way," Penny Sue said.

"Exactly. This way I'll get the details from all angles. Who'd like to go first?"

Naturally, Penny Sue volunteered. Ruthie and I found some garbage bags in the utility room and headed outside to pick up debris. We told Heather to holler when she was ready for us.

"We were really lucky," Ruthie said, dropping several shingles into her bag. "The power may be out, but the judge's condo didn't get much damage."

"Tell me about it! I didn't know the windows were hurricane rated. I'm glad he spent the money to maintain the place properly. That's definitely something I need to consider if I buy one of these condos." I picked up a few palm fronds and stacked them in a pile.

"Woody implied that someone shot the neighbor. Do you think it had anything to do with our depositions?"

"No. Why would anyone shoot him? If it had to do with our depositions, they would have shot us." The moment the words were out of my mouth, I wished I could reach out and take them back. Ruthie was skittish, hated confrontation, and was none too keen on the depositions, anyway. For that matter, neither was I. But the judge said that chances were slim we'd be called. The government had a mountain of evidence without our information.

"Don't jump to conclusions," I said quickly. "Let's wait until the police have a chance to fully investigate the death. Woody said preliminary results. Maybe he was wrong."

Ruthie half-heartedly dropped a piece of wood siding into her bag. "You're right. I hope we're called or released by the court soon. I intend to go home on the first flight. I have bad feelings about all of this."

Heather appeared at the front door and called for her next witness. Ruthie handed Penny Sue the trash bag and followed Heather inside.

Instead of continuing the clean-up effort, Penny Sue pulled the Mercedes' remote from her pocket and opened the car. "I need to call Daddy." She sat in the driver's seat and used her car phone. The conversation lasted a long time for the judge. In my experience, he was a no nonsense guy with little patience for chitchat.

Penny Sue emerged from the car with a scrap of paper. "He gave me the name of the insurance agent and a contractor to make repairs. He's also going to make some calls about our depositions. He wants us to come home. He's not at all happy that we've stumbled on another body."

"Neither am I. At least Woody believes us this time. That's something."

"Yeah, and I like Heather Brooks. I told her about the corroded aluminum. She wants to see it as soon as she finishes our interviews."

It took a number of tries, but I finally reached my mother and assured her we were fine and would she please pass the information along, since cellular circuits were jammed. Almost immediately, Heather appeared in the door and waved me in. The interview was short, sweet, and consistent with Penny Sue and Ruthie's stories, judging from Officer Brooks' reaction. I also made a point of the rusted aluminum, stressing the fact that aluminum isn't supposed to rust. Heather's interest was definitely piqued.

"Let's go see this," she said.

The four of us trooped up the hill toward Guthrie's condo and the scene of the crime. Remarkably, Timothy's baby blue BMW pulled in at that very moment. The crime tape, which included Ruthie's puke, extended almost to Guthrie's stairs.

Timothy blasted from his car like a rocket. "What is this? I have an injured man here."

Heather, about Timothy's height, stared him in the eye and introduced herself. "There was an accident, and a man died. The incident is under investigation. Don't cross the crime tape. If you need room to accommodate your injured friend, I'll see about moving the tape." She nodded toward the car. "By the way, is your friend Fred Fribble?"

Timothy flexed his biceps. "Yes, he's been at the hospital."

"I'd like to speak with him."

"He's in too much pain. You'll have to come back another time."

Heather smiled as she reached into the canvas tote slung from her shoulder and pulled out a plastic bag holding Guthrie's Glock. "I wanted him to know that I have his gun. This is his, isn't it?"

Timothy's lips tightened. "Give me a few minutes to get Guthrie settled and then you can speak with him. I warn you, though, he's on painkillers they gave him at the hospital."

"All I need is verification that this is his gun and he had it with him for self-protection."

"Fine." Timothy pulled crutches from the backseat and helped Guthrie out of the car.

Guthrie waved to us with a goofy grin. "Man, the hospital was gnarly. Everyone was in a bad mood, and they wouldn't let me see Mrs. King." He paused as Timothy shoved the crutches under Guthrie's arms. "Nobody believed I'd been a wet burrito and almost drowned." He swayed dizzily. Timothy steadied him and guided him toward the staircase. "I'll catch you later," Guthrie said over his shoulder. "I think I better lie down. A lady doctor gave me some wild pills. She looked really mean, but gave me a lot of them. They're pink—"

"Come on, boy." Timothy grasped Guthrie's waist and guided him up the stairs.

Penny Sue almost swooned over Timothy's bulging arms and thighs. "Such a loss," she mumbled.

Heather chuckled. "Looks like Fred might have had more than one of the pink pills. Okay, let's see this rusted aluminum."

We started with Guthrie's hurricane shutters. I pointed out the smooth edge and the rust residue.

Next, we took her to the crawl space under Mrs. King's house. A big woman, Heather took one look at the tiny door and decided to take our word. "You have a plumber who can verify the strange rust?"

"Sonny Mallard."

"I know him. Good guy. Remodeled my bathroom."

"What about the railing?" I asked.

"What railing?"

"The one that collapsed. Was it aluminum?"

"Let's see." Heather led us under the crime tape to the side of the building where the railing lay. It was wood.

I looked at the bottom of the post. "There's a smooth edge—it didn't break."

Heather and Penny Sue (talk about a pair) nudged me aside. "You're right! The railing support didn't break, so why did it fall?"

I pointed to the balcony that was ringed by short, square boxes—the size that would accommodate the handrail posts. The box on the corner was missing.

"I'll bet a dollar those boxes are aluminum."

Officer Brooks called to her partner who was filling out paperwork. "Have you swept the house? All right if we go in?"

He nodded.

"Come with me."

"I'll wait here," Ruthie said, biting her fingernail.

"We'll be right back." I followed Heather and Penny Sue to the front of the building.

The first floor was empty of furniture and unremarkable, except for the wood interior, which looked like something you'd see in Vail or the mountains. To the left of the door were the stairs to the second floor. We trailed behind Heather, single file. I, for one, was glad she took the lead, since she had her hand on her gun, ready to fire. No goons or nefarious characters appeared. We followed her through the first bedroom that had a door to the balcony. This room was empty except for an Igloo cooler. We trooped to the corner of the porch. Penny Sue and Officer Brooks both stooped to examine the square fittings that lined the porch.

"Looks like aluminum," Heather said quickly. "Both the aluminum and wood were bolted to the deck." She moved to the corner, where the form was missing, and ran her finger over the floor. She held it up for us to see.

"Nothing. No sign of any rust. Looks like the thing just pulled out of the deck. The wood over here is pretty soft."

Penny Sue cocked her head at me. "Heather's right. The rusty aluminum bandit wasn't here."

Damn. I was sure all these weird things were related. Truth be told, I suspected Yuri was somehow involved—trying to scare people out of their houses so he could buy them cheap. So much for that theory. Okay, this accident wasn't related to the aluminum, but the other stuff was very suspicious.

"Something very strange is going on. Do you have a forensics division like the one on TV, you know, *CSI: Crime Scene Investigation*?" I asked as we left the building. "That's what we need. Experts, computers, and scientists. People who can explain how aluminum rusted."

Heather shook her head. "We're a small city. The county doesn't have those kinds of resources. Besides, this railing broke because of rotten wood. Whatever happened to Mrs. King or Guthrie is another matter. There's no evidence of a crime in either case, so there's no reason for us to get involved."

I understood. Guess we'd have to find our own expert if we wanted to pursue it.

Heather thanked us for our cooperation and headed for Guthrie's condo. We found Ruthie and started home.

"I love that show," Penny Sue said.

Huh? Penny Sue had a grasshopper mind, but this transition stumped me. "What are you talking about?"

"*Crime Scene Investigation.* Gil Grissom, the leader of the team, is really sexy. A shame the electricity is off, I think it's on TV tonight."

"If it's a network show, we could listen to it on the radio," Ruthie offered.

"Wouldn't be the same if you can't see the wounds and autopsies. Do you know a forensics expert, Leigh?"

"Not exactly. I was thinking of Carl Annina, Fran's son. With all of his contacts at MIT, if Carl doesn't know the answer, I'll bet he can find someone who does."

"The aluminum rusted, so what?" Ruthie said.

"If we knew how it rusted, we might get a clue about the person who tried to break into Mrs. King's condo."

Ruthie waved off my comment. "I have no intention of playing detective. This is a police matter, they'll handle it."

"Not if Woody's in charge." Penny Sue stopped short and put her hands on her hips. "That weasel called us girls. And, what about him saying he'd instructed the police to call him whenever I'm involved in anything. Harassment, if you ask me. I'm not a criminal." She grinned mischievously. "I'd like to solve this case just to shove it in his face. He is such a jerk. Besides, it gives us something to do while we wait for the depositions. We can't go to any plays or movies without electricity. So many buildings are damaged, it'll be a while before things get back to normal."

Ruthie grimaced. "We could read a book or play cards. Even work on our tan, once the sky clears."

Penny Sue curled her lip. "Bor-ing!"

"You sound like my Furby."

Uh oh, they were getting testy. I turned the corner to our driveway and stopped. A black Jaguar was parked on the side of the lot. "Isn't that Igor's car?" I asked Penny Sue.

"His name is Yuri." She looked around. "I wonder where he is. I'd love to find out if he sent the pink rose."

I tugged her arm. "Come on, you don't want to chase after him like a shameless hussy."

"Maybe he left a note on our door," Ruthie said.

Penny Sue grinned. "Yeah. He probably stopped by to make sure we were okay."

"More likely checking on Mrs. King," I said under my breath.

"What did you say?"

"I need to call the hospital and check on Mrs. King."

"Yes, you really should."

Chapter 7

August 14

There was no note on the front door from Yuri, the hospital was short-staffed and couldn't release patient information except to immediate family, and the condo was as hot as Hades. None of this made for good humor, especially for Penny Sue. Rubbing a coveted piece of ice on her neck and forehead, she moseyed to the front door every few minutes to check on Yuri's car. Disgustingly thin Ruthie, immune to the heat, happily listened to the news on the boom box. As long as our batteries held out, she would be fine. I was somewhere in the middle—hot, borderline cranky, and slightly bored. I snagged one of the few remaining Snickers, which made me feel a lot better momentarily.

"Darn," Penny Sue muttered, stomping down the hall. "Yuri's gone and he didn't even come by to say 'Hello.'" She stopped and watched me. "What are you eating?"

I pointed to the coffee table. She snatched the cellophane bag and held it up to the light. "Three measly bars, that's all that's left? Guthrie ate a whole pan of brownies, all the Hershey Kisses, and most of my Snickers. Some nerve. That, after we were kind enough to let him stay with us."

I swallowed the last bit of candy. "He offered us some brownies."

"Yes, but you freaked us out with that marijuana, *Alice's Restaurant* stuff. The stupid brownies were probably fine. He ate the whole pan and didn't act much different."

"Who can tell? He acts spacey most of the time," I said.

"Well, I wished I'd tried one now. 'Course, then he'd probably eaten all the Snickers." Penny Sue grabbed a candy, ripped the wrapper viciously, and popped the whole thing in her mouth. "Ne-e-ew," she started, then covered her mouth and motioned for me to wait. Finally, she swallowed, ran her tongue over her teeth—behind closed lips, of course—and spoke. "What are we going to do? I'm sure all the stores are closed."

"They are," Ruthie confirmed absently.

"Do about what? Snickers?"

"Candy," Penny Sue snarled with a crazed look in her eye. "We're out, and who knows how long it will be until we can get some more!" She went to the cooler for another piece of ice that she rubbed on her neck.

Geez, this hormone thing had hit her hard. "We have chips and dip," I offered.

She put her hand up her shirt and the ice cube between her boobs. She sighed with relief. "That might work."

Magawd! A menopausal woman with no AC, fans, or anything. What were we going to do tonight? The condo was one floor. Should we leave the windows open for air, or close them for security? Looting was not a joke, and I had no doubt our condos were good targets for crooks who knew that alarm system batteries were dead by now and most of the units were unoccupied to boot.

"How about a glass of Chardonnay with ice?" I suggested. "We can go out on the deck—there's probably a breeze."

She mopped her brow. "Wine. That would be nice." She snatched the bag with the two remaining candy bars and headed outside.

I popped a bottle of Chardonnay and found the Styrofoam cups. "Want some wine, Ruthie?"

Her ear was to the speaker of the boom box. "No, I'm fine for now. I think the batteries are low."

"Extras are in the closet."

I dropped three cubes of ice into each cup, poured the wine, and stashed the bottle in the cooler. I debated whether that was a good idea. Would the wine defrost the ice? Or was it better to chill the wine so we'd use less ice? I sighed. Lordy, these were decisions I'd never faced before.

In Atlanta we had only lost power a few times because of ice storms. Keeping things cool was never an issue. Our house had a fireplace in the den, lots of blankets, and we cooked with propane. I sat on the cooler, still holding the two glasses of wine. When I thought about it, storms in Atlanta were actually kind of fun. We ate off paper plates and snuggled around the fireplace wrapped in sleeping bags and quilts. Zack told ghost stories to pass the time—at least when the kids were young and fell for his outrageous tales. It changed when they grew up. Zack, Jr. was into soccer and girls. Ann was into the dance team and boys. Storms weren't frequent, and we still huddled around the fireplace, yet it wasn't the same.

I wiped a tear from my eye. *They grow up too fast.*

"Anyone home?" a male voice said. In the interest of ventilation, we'd left the front door open with the screen door latched.

Still misty-eyed, I sat for a minute, hoping Ruthie would answer the door. She did. It was Timothy, who'd come to pick up Guthrie's things. Penny Sue shuffled in from the deck to see what was going on. I handed her the cup of wine.

Penny Sue raised her Styrofoam cup. "Can we get you something to drink? Wine, a soda?"

Timothy held up his hands. "No thanks, I don't drink. Gotta stay in shape." He patted his washboard abdomen.

Interesting. Guthrie wasn't shy about alcohol and might even enjoy herbs and other pharmaceuticals, on occasion.

"How is Guthrie?" I asked.

"Nothing's broken, thank God, but he does have a very bad bruise. He'll have to stay off his leg and will be on crutches for at least a couple of weeks."

"Do you think he can manage alone?"

"I'll stay with him for a few days. I have a new house built to hurricane codes, so I didn't get any damage. Others in my neighborhood weren't so lucky. Trees are down, power's out, and lots of roofs are ripped up." He spied Guthrie's knapsack, bedroll, and brownie pan stacked on the loveseat. "I see he brought his famous brownies. I won't touch them myself." He patted his nonexistent stomach again.

"Are you a personal trainer?" Penny Sue asked, sauntering up to him and brazenly giving him the once over.

Honestly, she all but drooled on his biceps. She used to be more discreet. It seemed the demure Georgia peach I used to know had evaporated with her estrogen. Between Penny Sue and Timothy, there was a palpable testosterone overload in the room. He definitely felt it and sidestepped toward the loveseat.

"No, a chemist. I work at the Cape."

"Chemist?" I said too loudly.

He quickly grabbed Guthrie's belongings.

"Sorry, I didn't mean to shout." I smiled sheepishly. "We were just saying how we needed a chemist, weren't we?"

Penny Sue and Ruthie nodded.

Timothy smiled and started backing down the hall, clearly thinking he was about to be rushed by crazed, horny women.

"Something strange is going on," I said, following him.

"Yes, the murder and all," Timothy replied quickly.

"It's more than that. Guthrie's hurricane shutters didn't blow off. We think they were sabotaged."

"Oh, my." He opened the screen door with his rear end and let it slam in my face. Safely on the other side, he seemed to calm down. "I'll be sure to look at that and help Guthrie make arrangements for repairs."

"We'd like your opinion on his shutters. There's rust on the edge where they broke away, and they're made of aluminum."

He flashed a movie star smile—his teeth were blinding white. "I'll look at it and get back to you. I'm sure Guthrie has your phone number, so I'll give you a call. Thanks again for taking care of my buddy." Timothy turned and hotfooted up the hill.

I whirled around, hands on hips, my elbow accidentally brushing Penny Sue's belly. She drew back, squinty-eyed.

"Sorry, I didn't mean to poke you."

She relaxed.

"Penny Sue, you scared the hell out of Timothy. You acted like a sex-starved floozy. I thought you were going to tackle him and lick his arms or something."

Her bottom lip jutted out as her eyes contracted to slits, like a snake. "I am not a sex-starved floozy. If anyone's sex-starved, it's you. I didn't do anything," she said, glaring at Ruthie. "Did I?"

"Don't drag me into this. I'm not taking sides."

Penny Sue put her hands on her hips. "What did I do?"

"You all but drooled on the man."

"Ha ha," she chuckled theatrically. "Who shouted, 'chemist!?' The poor guy nearly jumped out of his skin."

I sighed. She was right. I canted my head apologetically. "Guilty."

Penny Sue shrugged. "Let's forget it. We're all on edge. It's been a helluva few days."

"You can say that again," Ruthie exclaimed. "The vibes in the atmosphere are truly ominous. It makes my skin crawl."

Back in the living room, Penny Sue and I thumped our Styrofoam cups together as a final act of forgiveness.

"There are more hurricanes brewing?" I asked, following up on Ruthie's comment about bad vibes in the atmosphere.

"Two—Danielle and Earl. Danielle's still over by Africa, and Earl's only a tropical storm. They don't worry me. It's more than that." Ruthie glanced around, searching the kitchen. "Where's the wine?"

I went to the closet, retrieved the now chilled Chardonnay, and poured her a glass. We all toasted this time.

Ruthie took a dainty sip. "It's not only the hurricanes, there's bad energy everywhere."

"Can you be more specific?" Penny Sue asked.

I switched off the radio and herded them toward the living area. Penny Sue snatched the bottle of wine as she passed the kitchen counter. Ruthie perched on the loveseat, while Penny Sue and I plopped on the sofa. I held up my hands. "Ruthie, can you tune into the vibes if we're quiet and all concentrate?"

"Probably."

"Wait. Shouldn't we burn some sage or something?" Penny Sue asked.

Burning sage was an American Indian tradition for cleansing spaces of bad energy that we'd used several times before in tense situations. I'm not sure it did any good, though it surely didn't hurt. We were still alive. The only drawback was that the stuff smelled awful, a lot like marijuana, which caused considerable trouble with our prosecutor acquaintance, the spiteful Woody Woodhead.

"Sage?" Ruthie said. "Couldn't hurt."

I found some Spice Island Sage in the kitchen, dumped it in a bowl on the coffee table, and lit it. The fine powder flamed for a moment, then smoldered. I fanned the stuff on all of us, including the living room, saying a silent prayer that Woody wouldn't show up. All the doors and windows were open, since the electricity was still out. The air was hot and heavy with moisture, meaning the smoke hung in the room like stinky clouds.

After a good cleansing with the sage—or as much as I could stand—I placed the bowl on the coffee table and let it burn out. I took my seat next to Penny Sue. Ruthie curled her legs under herself like a pretzel. Penny Sue and I glanced at each other, silently acknowledging that we couldn't get in that position if our lives depended on it. Ruthie placed her hands, palms up, on her knees, thumb and forefinger lightly touching. Penny Sue and I mimicked the movement, though our feet were firmly planted on the floor. (*Where they should be*, as Grammy Martin would say.)

Ruthie closed her eyes and we could tell she was centering. "Om-m-m-m," she intoned.

Penny Sue and I joined in. "Om-m-m-m."

Then silence—a profound silence one rarely experiences. Amazing how quiet things get without electricity. No hum of refrigerators or air conditioners. No televisions or radios playing in the distance. A quiet like people knew in the olden days, I suspected, before electricity and before we were bombarded with electromagnetic waves, continuous noise, and too much information. The quiet was unnerving. I wasn't used to a feeling of such solitude. Finally, Ruthie spoke.

"Chaotic energy. Mother Earth is rebalancing. There will be more storms. There are also hateful energies all around us."

No joke. Drug-crazed punks vandalized Mrs. King's house and a guy just died, probably murdered. That's pretty hateful in my book.

"Can you pinpoint the people responsible?" Penny Sue whispered.

I peeked at Penny Sue and saw her eyes were open and she was sipping wine.

Ruthie thought a moment. "Greed. A rapacious craving for power. That is behind it. There are many greedy factions, all vying for the top spot."

"Can you tell who they are?" Penny Sue asked.

"Only that they're very dangerous."

"What should we do?" I asked.

"There is another storm coming, much bigger than the last. Soon. We should not stay. We should go to the old city, there is protection there."

"The old city? What the heck does that mean?" Penny Sue asked.

Ruthie opened her eyes and shrugged. "I don't know. That's all I got."

"Maybe it means the mainland," I said. "This island was originally named Coronado Beach. The mainland was New Smyrna. The two didn't merge until 1947 and combined the names to New Smyrna Beach."

"Which is older?" Penny Sue asked.

"I don't know. They're probably about the same age."

Penny Sue refilled her cup. "Great, that tells us a lot."

A knock on the screen door ended the discussion. My first thought was Woody. I sniffed the sage. Lord, please, not Woody.

"Come on in," Penny Sue called.

We heard the twang of the spring on the screen door.

"Cool, man, incense. Sage. Are y'all meditating? Can I join in?"

Guthrie. What was he doing here? He sounded like he might have taken another pink pill. He hobbled in on crutches with Timothy walking behind him, supporting his waist. From the look on Guthrie's face, Timothy was the only thing keeping that injured puppy on his feet. Ruthie scooted to the rattan chair and motioned for Guthrie to take the loveseat. He plopped down and put his bum leg on the coffee table.

Timothy had changed into a tank top and running shorts. I had to admit that the man was a fine specimen of humanity. Penny Sue obviously agreed, since she was swigging wine with her eyes fixed on his muscular thighs. Considering the oppressive heat—the heat index had to be 103°—I was afraid she might burst into flames. I once saw a television program about strange phenomena that claimed spontaneous human combustion was a documented fact. Maybe we had the prerequisite combination—heat, humidity, a menopausal woman, and a very well built man.

Guthrie patted the place beside him and Timothy sat down. Penny Sue groaned. Praise be, the spell was broken. I had no desire to be toasted by a flaming Penny Sue.

Guthrie took a deep breath. "Man, I love sage. Terrific for putting you in touch with the Great Beyond. Lavender's good, too. I use that a lot when I meditate. Anyway, I had to thank you for letting me hang out with y'all last night. You saved my life."

"No problem. We enjoyed your company," replied Ruthie, a.k.a. Ms. Manners.

"How did it go with Officer Brooks?" I asked.

"You mean Heather?" Guthrie patted his temple with his forefinger. "That's a sharp lady. Her head is screwed on really tight."

I bit my lip. It was all I could do to keep from saying, "And yours is a little loose."

"Did she give you any trouble about your Glock?" Penny Sue wanted to know.

"Naw. She'd already run the serial number and knew it was registered to me. Besides, Florida has some of the most liberal gun laws, outside of the West. I think everyone carries a gun out West. They shoot each other all the time. Did you ever see that show, *Deadwood*? Man, those cowboys go at it. Do you think George Bush packed a gun? I'll bet he had one in his desk at the Oval Office. Say the wrong thing, and he could pop you, like they do in *Deadwood*. The Secret Service would probably cover it up. Did you see the episode—"

Timothy stroked Guthrie's good leg.

Guthrie eyed Timothy and smiled meekly. "I'm babbling, huh?"

Timothy winked.

Guthrie sat up straight. "I'll be quiet, because Timothy has something to say." Guthrie twisted his fingers in front of his mouth like he was turning a key.

No question in my mind, he'd had another pink pill.

Noticeably embarrassed by Guthrie's antics, Timothy stared at the ceiling. "After the police left, I took a look at Guthrie's hurricane shutters. I agree that they were sabotaged. A highly reactive solvent of some kind. My specialty is fuels, and I've worked for NASA so long, I've forgotten a lot of basic chemistry. I'll have to do a little research, but I promise to look into it. Someone definitely wanted Guthrie's windows to blow out."

"It's not only Guthrie's windows," I added quickly. "The water pipe beneath Mrs. King's condo was sabotaged, too. They both have the telltale rust."

"Whew, that makes me feel better. I thought someone was out to get me. I can understand that someone might want to nail my Aunt Harriet, who owns the condo. She has, like, a personality problem. Crab-b-by doesn't begin to describe her. That's why I moved over here. I couldn't stand her yelling anymore. I lived next door to Harriet in my mother's house. Mom passed a while back—heart attack. Everything was fine for a while, and then Harriet went berserk. I don't know how Uncle Daniel takes it. Anyway, I rented out Mom's house and pay them rent on this place. Works out good. Daniel uses the rent money to hire a nurse, so he can get away to play bingo and cards. I'm telling ya, the man would be crazy, too, if he didn't get away from that old witch."

I waited for Guthrie to take a breath, but he kept going.

"She wasn't always like this, so it's sort of a love-hate thing. Uncle Daniel wants to hold onto this condo until Harriet croaks. He figures these places will be worth a fortune. Then, he can sell and get enough money to go into one of those elderly homes where all the nurses are young and have big tits."

Timothy patted Guthrie's knee.

Guthrie shrugged. "Too much information?"

Timothy nodded.

If I were a writer, this was one pair that would make a terrific novel. Guthrie was like a big, floppy puppy, the kind that gets into everything, rolls in dirt, and likes to give people sloppy, wet kisses. Timothy was flawless—straight out of *GQ* in looks and demeanor. What they saw in each other was beyond me.

Yet who was I to question relationships? I had my own inexplicable marriage to Zack. In retrospect, our relationship was dumb. Back then, young women graduated from college and got married. Besides, a lawyer was a good catch or so everyone said. Seemingly perfect at first, our marriage went downhill fast, which I attributed to the ambitious lawyer syndrome. By then, who cared? Zack worked long hours? Big deal. I had my precious babies to look after.

Yep, Timothy and Guthrie's relationship was none of my business. I hoped they, and everyone on the planet, were blissfully happy—except Zack. (Sorry, Grammy, I know that isn't the right Christian attitude. Forgiving Zack is beyond my ability at the moment, the wound is too fresh. Besides, he's still a jerk!)

"Guthrie," Ruthie spoke for the first time. "You've been around this area for a long time, right?"

"Oh, yeah. I used to come here to surf when I was a kid. Man, we had some great clambakes, better than the stuff in *Gidget*. This was a really cool place. Only problem, there were no bathrooms. See, the place was pretty deserted back—"

Timothy thumped Guthrie's arm. Guthrie smiled.

"—yes, I've been coming here a long time," he finished.

"If someone told you to go to the Old City, what would you think? Does *Old City* mean anything to you?"

Guthrie stroked his chin, in deep thought, or dementia—perhaps Aunt Harriet's condition was hereditary. Actually, I suspected his reaction had something to do with the pink pills for his knee.

"St. Augustine," Timothy said without hesitation. "The old city in this state is St. Augustine. The legend of Ponce de Leon and the Fountain of Youth centers on St. Augustine. Even the first settlers of New Smyrna initially landed in St. Augustine, then followed the St. Johns River down here."

"I never thought of that," Ruthie replied. "I always think of St. Augustine as a great place to shop."

"St. Augustine is full of history," Penny Sue piped in. "I went with Momma when I was a child. Indians, Spanish, and British all fought wars there. Because of that, there are a lot of disjointed spirits."

Ruthie rolled her eyes. "You mean Earth-bound spirits. People who went so fast and unexpectedly, they don't know they're gone. They stay at their old haunts, not realizing they're dead."

Penny Sue waved her arms expansively. "Yes! There are a bunch of ghost tours in St. Augustine."

"And nice hotels," Ruthie added.

"They were all booked for Charley, remember?" Penny Sue chided. "You need to get some dates from your spirits so we can make reservations."

"Reservations for what?" Timothy asked.

I let out a loud sigh. "We did a meditation—y'all smelled the sage—and Ruthie's guides told her a bigger storm was coming and we should not stay. They said we'd be safe in the Old City."

Guthrie's eyes lit up. "Ruthie, you've got guides? Is it the sage? Girl, I'm coming with you."

Timothy put his hand on Guthrie's knee and squeezed. "*If* there's another hurricane, you'll come home with me."

"What about your mother?" Guthrie asked tersely.

Timothy flexed his biceps and set his jaw. "Mother will have to get used to it."

Chapter 8

August 14

As soon as Guthrie and Timothy left, I called Chris, our friend in St. Augustine. A wonderful lady about our age, we met when she owned a New Age shop in New Smyrna Beach. Since then, she'd moved on to bigger and better things, opening The Rising Moon on Spanish Street in St. Augustine. I explained Ruthie's guidance about the old city. Chris said we were welcome to stay in her shop if another hurricane came and the hotels were booked. She'd had no problems there with Charley, except for a brief loss of power. Considering Ruthie's revelation, she'd probably stay at the shop herself.

"Sleeping bags and air mattresses. We want to be prepared if we have to stay in the shop," Penny Sue said after I hung up the phone. Penny Sue fished a sliver of ice from her now empty wine and rubbed it on her forehead. "As soon as the power's back on and the stores re-open, we should lay in our supplies." She scanned the kitchen. "I'm hungry."

"We could warm up some soup," Ruthie suggested.

"You've got to be kidding. Warm is the last thing I need." Penny Sue popped the remainder of the ice into her mouth and swallowed. "What became of the chips and dip?"

Oh, that. I found them in the closet and put them out on the counter, next to Guthrie's *Alice's Restaurant* tape that he'd left behind.

We started with the chips, moved on to Vienna sausages, and finished with Oreo cookies. Not exactly gourmet, but filling nonetheless.

I was still munching a cookie when my cell phone rang. It was Fran, calling from Boston.

"Are you all right? Did you get any damage? I've been trying to call for hours. I finally reached Carl. He said the cell circuits were overloaded."

"We were lucky," I replied, "only lost a few shingles and some other minor damage. How about your house?"

Fran snorted. "That big, expensive behemoth took on water. Carl said rain poured down the kitchen wall and soaked the wallboard. It will all have to be ripped out."

"I'm sorry. Anything I can do? How's your sister?"

"Carl will take care of the house, and my sister's doing well. She should be up and about in a few days. Considering the mess down there, I'm going to stay in Boston until the house is fixed. Allergies. No way I could stand that wallboard dust. Heaven help us if Carl can't get a contractor soon. Mold. He said the power was out, our expensive generator wouldn't work, and the heat index was over a hundred."

Mold. One complication I hadn't thought of.

"I guess I should make this short and free up the circuit. If you need help, call Carl. He'll be around."

No sooner had I pressed the off button than there was another knock on the door, and a quivering woman's voice called, "Leigh? Are you home?"

I recognized the voice. It was Mrs. Holden, a neighbor in the next cluster. "Yes ma'am. Please come in." I rushed to escort her down the hall. A frail, tiny woman who was probably over a hundred and still drove—like a maniac!—she was a definite candidate for slip and fall. I wasn't worried she'd sue me, I worried she'd break something. I took her arm and ushered her to the rattan chair that was higher than the sofa, making it easier for her to get up when the time came.

I introduced Penny Sue and Ruthie, who offered her food, drink— everything but a foot massage. Judging from the way Mattie Holden walked, she might have taken Ruthie up on the foot thing.

"Where's your husband?" I asked.

"Clyde's at home. We stayed in Orlando with my daughter during the storm. She wanted us to stay a few days, but Clyde wouldn't hear of it. He had to get back to check on our house. Did you stay, dear?"

"Yes, ma'am. We were lucky—only minor damage."

"No trouble with crooks?"

"None." I thought of Mrs. King. "Did you have any trouble?"

Mrs. Holden said, "Our front door was unlocked when we got home."

"Were you robbed?" Penny Sue asked breathlessly.

"We don't see that anything's missing, except there's glitter on the floor of our bedroom. Glitter!"

"Glitter?"

"Yes, it's smeared on the carpet. Clyde stepped on it and slid—would have broken his neck if he hadn't fallen onto the bed. Doesn't make sense, does it? Why would someone break into our house and sprinkle glitter on the floor? Clyde's all upset. He's worried someone has a passkey and is playing practical jokes."

The more likely scenario was that they forgot to lock the door, with all the hubbub of the storm and quick evacuation.

The glitter could have spilled from a keepsake they took along. Birthday cards, even wedding invitations, are often covered with glitter. The thing I hate the most is when people stuff the envelop with glitter or tiny hearts and stars that fly all over the room when you open the envelope. Not cute in my book, since it means I'll have to haul out the Hoover. "Maybe the latch didn't catch when you turned the key. I've done that before." Bald-faced lie. "To be safe, maybe you should have your locks changed."

"That's what Clyde thinks."

"Would you like to stay with us tonight?" Ruthie offered.

Penny Sue stared at Ruthie like she's lost her mind.

Mrs. Holden leaned forward to stand. Ruthie rushed to help. "We'll be fine. Clyde has a Colt .38 Super he keeps by the bed. You know, in Florida you can shoot anyone who enters your house and threatens you." She took a few steps with Ruthie cradling her elbow. "Should be like that everywhere, don't you think?"

Penny Sue arched a brow smugly. "Yes, ma'am. I agree completely."

I scribbled our phone number on a Post-It note and gave it to Mrs. Holden. "If you have any trouble, don't hesitate to call."

She patted my cheek. "Thank you, darling. It warms my heart to have nice neighbors like you."

We walked her to the parking lot and her new Cadillac Deville.

"I saw an area roped off by yellow tape when I drove in. Does that mean a sinkhole? Lord, I hope our houses don't slide into a big hole."

"No, ma'am. A man fell from a balcony this morning. The police roped the area off," I said. No need to worry her with the details.

She turned the key to her Caddy and gunned the V-8. "Don't want to compromise the crime scene, huh? I watch that *CSI* show, I know what's what." She shut her door and peeled out of the driveway.

Ruthie went into hysterics. "What a character! I'm not sneaking into her house, that's for sure. Does everyone watch this *CSI*? I guess I'll have to catch it when the power comes back on."

Penny Sue took another ice cube from her drink and rubbed it between her boobs. "I hope it comes on soon, we're getting low on ice. I'd hate to have to put a bag of green beans in my bra."

Ruthie snickered. "Well, you'd definitely be stacked and it would be a lot cheaper than an operation."

"You know, that would be a good invention," Penny Sue said as she went back inside.

"A bean bra?"

"A frozen bra. They could make it out of that gel stuff they use for ice packs."

"Never work, it would soak your shirt as it defrosted."

Penny Sue tossed her hair. "So what? You'd be soaked with perspiration anyway. At least the bra wouldn't leave a salt stain. Better yet, you could wear it like a bathing suit top."

I thought a moment. The idea had possibilities.

Praise be, the electricity came on at about eleven PM so we didn't have to resort to cooling off with soggy vegetables.

"Turn off everything but a few lights, quick! We don't want to overload the circuit," Penny Sue barked.

Ruthie and I scurried to do her bidding. Everything off except lights in the kitchen and living room, Penny Sue and I each stood under an AC vent. Ruthie made for the television and tuned to the local news.

Though Volusia County sustained considerable damage, Orlando fared much worse. Power was out for over a million customers, sewers were backed up, and an untold number of homes and businesses were severely damaged by uprooted trees and flying debris. As bad as that was, electricity could be out for weeks in some places, meaning many buildings would be further damaged by mold.

"Your bra idea may not be so bad," Ruthie said to Penny Sue.

"Yeah, I wonder what it takes to get a patent?"

The next few days were chaotic. We had to deal with the police, insurance company, an endless stream of prospective roofers, and Guthrie.

Although price gouging is illegal in Florida during disasters, many contractors didn't seem to care or were simply willing to take a chance on making a quick buck. A team of contractors went door-to-door offering free inspections and repair estimates. The man who showed up at our door was an attractive, muscular blond named Wayne. Naturally, Penny Sue took him up on the offer. It was amazing how many times she went outside to check his progress and offer refreshments. Ruthie and I shook our heads—we'd seen this drill a thousand times. Penny Sue's acrylic nails had curved into hooks and she was going for the catch. That is, until Wayne walked in with a form that detailed his estimate. The condo needed a whole new roof, there was water in the walls, termite damage, and the old windows really should be replaced. The total price tag was a whopping $80,000, and might go higher if he found more damage when he started work.

I think it was the old window part that got Penny Sue riled. In the blink of an eye, Ms. Sweetness and Light morphed into Cruella DeVil.

"Old windows? What kind of a quack are you?" Penny Sue took the estimate and ripped it in half. "These windows are three years old and hurricane-rated." She stood and pointed stiff-armed at the front door. "Get out of here."

Wayne tried to snatch the torn form, but Cruella was faster. She held the pieces behind her back.

"Get out," I said, "now!"

"If you're not interested, I need the estimate back."

"No way." She glanced at me. "I'm feeling threatened, aren't you Leigh? Get my gun."

Gun got his attention. Wayne high-tailed it out of the house.

Still boiling mad, Cruella shoved the papers at me, unholstered her .38, and ran to the front door.

"You can't shoot him if he isn't in the house," I yelled, chasing after her.

She flung the door open. "I just want him to know I'm serious."

He knew. Not only was his truck peeling out of the parking lot, but so where his buddies.

"I'm going to report him to the Attorney General first thing tomorrow morning. Where's the estimate? What was the name of his company?"

I handed her the top half of the form. Standard office supply stock, no company name or phone number. She waved the paper angrily. "I have nothing to report."

"Maybe the police can lift a fingerprint like they do on *CSI*," I suggested.

"Think so?" Penny Sue carefully placed the estimate pieces in a large baggie. "Worth a try."

We fixed deviled ham sandwiches and sweet tea for lunch and were working up to a nap when the telephone started. The first caller was Guthrie.

"Mrs. King came home today. I thought you'd like to know."

"Did you explain to her about the busted water pipe?" I asked. "Last thing we need is for her to turn on the water and flood us again."

"Yeah, man, I explained all of that to her. She's going to stay with her granddaughter for a while. Also, there are some contractors working the neighborhood, offering to do repairs. Timothy's sure they're unlicensed. If they show up at your place, don't listen to them."

I chuckled. "They've already been here. Penny Sue scared them away with her .38."

"Cool, man. Why didn't I think of that? If Penny Sue's little gun scared them, think what my Glock would have done. Of course, I didn't go to the door because I'm still on crutches, and Timothy doesn't like guns. He got rid of them, anyway."

Yep, I wouldn't argue with Timothy if he took to flexing his biceps.

"By the way, you left your Alice tape here. I'll bring it back if you'd like."

"I don't need it right now. Keep it, man, and watch it. It's a great show."

"Sure, when we get the VCR fixed."

"You can borrow mine. I'll ask Timothy to drop it by this week."

Oh, goody! I thanked him, trying hard to hide my lack of enthusiasm.

The next call was from dainty, little Mattie Holden. "Clyde's beside himself. The estimate to fix our house is over $100,000. We don't have that kind of money—we're on a fixed income."

"You didn't sign anything, did you? We're sure those contractors are fakes."

"Clyde thought the same thing. He wanted to shoot them."

Great, another Penny Sue.

"Now he's not feeling good. I think he has the flu."

"Do you have enough to eat? Do you need anything?"

"No, there's enough food. We have a lot of soup."

"Good. In case you haven't heard, Mrs. King is out of the hospital. Her heart attack was mild."

"Too bad the old bitch didn't die."

My mouth fell open. "Pardon?"

"I said it's too bad the old bitch didn't die."

This was sweet, polite Mattie Holden? "I thought you were friends."

"Nana gets on my nerves. Always bragging about her wonderful kids. She's a pain in the ass."

Better change the subject. "Were you able to get up the glitter?"

"Yeah, Clyde vacuumed."

"If there's anything you need, let us know. Good-bye." She hung up in my ear.

"What's wrong?" Ruthie asked, noticing my expression.

"That was the most bizarre conversation. Mrs. Holden, who's always been prim and proper, called Nana King a bitch. She said it was a shame Nana didn't die."

"You're joking," Penny Sue said.

"No. I've never heard Mrs. Holden talk like that."

"Maybe she had a stroke," Ruthie suggested. "Maybe it's a reaction to all of this stress."

"Or Alzheimer's. At her age the old arteries might have hardened."

I shook my head. "I'm stunned. That's completely out of character for her."

So much for our nap, we were all bummed out after all the phone calls.

"I'm not sleepy anymore. Let's go for a ride," Penny Sue said after a while. "I'm stir crazy. Besides, maybe there's a store open that sells candy."

We piled into her Mercedes and took a right on A1A. Palm fronts and assorted debris, primarily shingles, littered the road, yet it was passable. Utility trucks with bucket lifts were everywhere.

"Utility crews have come from all over the country, some as far away as New York. The news said crews are working twelve hour days." Ruthie opened her backseat window and peered out. "Think how hot they must be, and they probably don't have AC to go home to, either."

"Yes, it's awful. We owe them a huge debt of gratitude, but please put your window up," Penny Sue said over her shoulder. "I'm roasting."

Our first stop was Publix Supermarket. "They must be open, look at all the cars in the lot," Penny Sue exclaimed. She drove to the front and found a spot close to the door. "The spirits are with us, Ruthie. Snickers must be in our future. Maybe some ice cream. Wouldn't that be good?"

Lord, yes. Edy's Mint Chocolate Chip with a little whipped cream—pure heaven. We headed into the store and stopped, dumbfounded. The reason for all the cars was immediately evident. Every aisle that contained frozen or refrigerated food was roped off by yellow tape. Dozens of Publix personnel worked each section—one group stripping the shelves of compromised merchandise, another restocking the shelves.

"Wow!" Penny Sue shook her head. "Sorry, no ice cream, but the candy aisle's open." She literally ran to that section. The stock was low. Almost everything had been sold before the hurricane, and refrigerated food obviously took precedence. Penny Sue dropped to her knees, reached to the back of the shelf, and pulled out a lone bag of Snickers. She cradled it her arms like a baby. "That darned Guthrie. I knew I should have bought more." She gave us a frantic look. "Help me. Who knows when they'll get another shipment?"

Ruthie and I grabbed mints, candy bars, virtually anything containing chocolate. As I was loading my arms, it suddenly hit me that chocolate was an aphrodisiac. Could that explain Penny Sue's attraction to men? Her sweet tooth was to blame? Naw, her sweet tooth had to be a hormonal phase. She'd always been attracted to men and only recently developed an addiction to chocolate.

We paid our bill and dumped the candy in the car. The first thing Penny Sue did was open the bag of Snickers. She chomped one of the snack-sized bars with a sigh of satisfaction. Honestly, her reaction was almost obscene. She took another and had the courtesy to offer one to us. I ate mine in small bites, knowing I'd probably not get another.

Fortified with chocolate, Penny Sue was ready to explore. She took a left out of the parking lot and headed for Peninsula Avenue. The main beachside street paralleling the Intracoastal Waterway, Peninsula was lined with very large houses and stately live oaks. It was also the street that Fran lived on. We hadn't gone far when we realized our mistake. The stately oaks did not get along with Charley. Huge branches blocked the street and had fallen on houses. Road workers wielding chainsaws struggled to carve a path for utility crews. We were definitely in the way and turned around and went home.

"That's why the police asked everyone to stay off the roads. Tree limbs and downed lines—it's very dangerous," Ruthie said sternly.

"Please, no lectures," Penny Sue said as she ripped open another Snickers. "You're right. It also shows how lucky we are—only palm trees on the beach. Those poor people may not get power for weeks."

"Carl," I blurted. "I wonder if he's without electricity?" I took the car phone from its cradle and dialed. He answered on the third ring. There was a lot of commotion in the background, like a party. "Carl, it's Leigh Stratton. Do you have electricity? If not, you're welcome to stay with us. Our power came on last night."

I could almost see him waving frantically at his friends. The background noise suddenly stopped. "I'm fine. We have a natural gas, whole house generator, so I have lights and air conditioning. There was a slight problem at first, but it's fixed now. Mom called. Is there anything you need?"

"We're fine." I thought I detected a sigh of relief on the other end. Ten bucks said there was a big keg party going on around Fran's pool.

"Don't hesitate to call if you need anything."

"You, too." I replaced the receiver. "I think we're missing one heck of a party. I'll bet all the area Trekkies are staying with Carl."

"I feel sorry for the neighbors," Ruthie said. "I hope Carl and his buddies don't start all those Klingon battle cries. They're liable to get arrested."

"I suspect Klingons are low on the list of police priorities today," Penny Sue said. She wheeled into our driveway then hit the brakes hard. Mattie Holden jumped from the scrub under the public boardwalk and waved frantically. Her hair wild, her eyes crazed, she looked like she'd been through hell.

"Help! Help! Scooter and Clyde are dead!"

Chapter 9

August 15

I leapt from the car and grasped Mattie by her shoulders. "Did you call an ambulance?"

Her head bobbled like a toy dog in the back window of a '57 Chevy. "No."

"Where is he?" Penny Sue shouted.

Mattie's eyes were glazed. I shook her, trying to jog a response.

"On the floor of our bedroom, next to Scooter." Mattie started to cry. Scooter was their Pekinese. "I thought Clyde had the flu. I didn't know anything was wrong with Scooter. He curled up under the bed and went to sleep. He does that all the time. But when Scooter didn't come down for his dinner, Clyde went to check. Next thing I know, Clyde threw up and keeled over."

Penny Sue snatched her phone, dialed 9-1-1, and explained the situation. "They're on their way. Come on, I can give him CPR. Hurry!"

I pushed Mattie into the front passenger side of the car and dove in the backseat. Penny Sue was moving before I had my door closed. The front door to Mattie's condo was open when we arrived.

"Where's your bedroom?" Penny Sue cried, jamming the car into park.

Mattie stared blankly.

"Probably on the second floor at the top of the stairs," I answered, already out of the Mercedes and chasing Penny Sue. Ruthie stayed behind with Mrs. Holden.

We found Mr. Holden face down beside his bed in a pool of vomit. Scooter was sprawled beside him, obviously gone to the great dog heaven in the sky. Without missing a beat, Penny Sue slid her left arm under Clyde's chest, raised his face off the floor, and pounded him hard between his shoulder blades. Next, she rolled him on his back, cleared his mouth with her fingers, and began pumping his chest.

I stood beside her, immobilized and awed. Penny Sue could be a hormonal flake, but she was amazing in an emergency.

Penny Sue compressed his chest quickly like a jackhammer. "One, two, three, …" she counted. Twenty, one, two, three … and kept going. She didn't breathe into his mouth, which surprised me. That's what they did on television. I almost said something, but had the good sense to keep my mouth shut. I was a wreck. Penny Sue had the moxie to kneel in puke and attempt to save the life of an old man she'd never met.

"Fifty, one, two, three …"

I heard a siren. Sweat dripped off Penny Sue onto Clyde's face.

"Seventy, one, two, three …"

The sound of people running up the stairs and voices calling to us.

I dashed to the doorway. "In here!"

"Eighty, one, two, three …"

A slender paramedic nudged Penny Sue aside and took over.

Panting from the effort, she crawled over to me. I helped her to her feet and hugged her for all I was worth. "Penny Sue, you're the best in my book," I whispered.

By now the paramedics had produced paddles and given Clyde a couple of electric shocks to his chest. Two were enough. He was gone. The medic who'd taken over for Penny Sue shook his head and sighed. "Probably a massive heart attack," he said.

A policeman and fireman ran through the doorway carrying a stretcher. The paramedic stood, an indication there wasn't any hurry. He motioned us toward the corner of the room. I noticed his nametag—Anthony.

"How was he when you arrived?" Anthony asked.

"Face down in vomit," I answered, since Penny Sue was still panting and not in any condition to talk. "Penny Sue did everything possible to save him. She cleared his mouth and pumped her heart out."

Anthony regarded Penny Sue with admiration. "I heard you say 'eighty' when I arrived. You used that new technique, didn't you?"

She blew out a long breath. "Learned it in an anti-terrorist training course I took in New Mexico."

"Anti-terrorist? Are you Federal?" he asked, looking surprised.

Penny Sue still panted, perspiration streaming down her cheeks. "Her father's a judge, so she's in constant danger from criminals he's locked up," I replied. "She's taken some defense courses as precautions."

Anthony was obviously impressed. "Any idea how long he'd been out?"

"It had to be at least ten minutes," I said. "His wife, Mattie, waved us down in the driveway. By the time we got here, it was that long or longer. Mattie's not acting right. I have no idea how long it took her to seek help."

"They're old. Like I said, he probably had a massive heart attack, and his wife's in shock."

I raised my hands. "Mattie was acting funny before this occurred. She wasn't herself, something's definitely wrong. I, we, thought maybe she'd had a stroke."

Penny Sue locked eyes with Anthony. "Don't write them off because they're elderly. You should do an autopsy. Promise me you'll insist on one."

He winked.

Penny Sue nodded a "thanks," then heaved, "Oh, crap."

I followed her line of sight. Woody and Officer Heather Brooks stood in the doorway. Heather caught our eyes and shrugged.

"Amazing how you turn up whenever there's a dead person in New Smyrna Beach," Woody mouthed off as he strode our way. When he got within a couple of feet, Woody stopped abruptly and squinched his nose.

Penny Sue set her jaw and wagged her finger in Woody's face. "Say one more word, and I'll file a harassment complaint. I'm covered in puke, because I tried to save a man's life."

Anthony gave Woody the up and down, clearly concluding Woody was scum. "She did," the young man said forcefully. "There aren't many people who have her knowledge of CPR and are willing to use it on a stranger."

Woody took a step back, surprised by the vehemence of Anthony's tone. Woody, Mr. Big Stuff, was used to being in charge and having everyone kowtow to him. Paramedics, like Anthony, didn't know or care about local prosecutors. Praise be, someone had perspective, I thought.

"Have you ever given CPR?" Anthony continued close to Woody's face. "For that matter, did you ever sit in vomit to do it?"

Instantly the room went still. Firemen, paramedics, and police stopped whatever they were doing and focused on Woody. Their abhorrence was palpable and Woody felt it.

"I was joking," Woody said to the crowd. "Penny Sue and I are old friends."

I was happy to see that no one thought it was funny. Woody had about as much credibility as Saddam Hussein, judging from the expressions on everyone's faces. Woody started to back toward the door.

"Stop," I said loudly. Woody, and everyone else—even Penny Sue—froze. "This may be a crime scene. Mattie Holden told us her front door was unlocked when they arrived home after the hurricane, and their bedroom floor was covered in glitter. Right after that, she started acting funny, and her husband got the flu. Then, her dog croaked and Clyde died close on Scooter's heels.

"You need to go through this room with a fine-toothed comb to see if you can find this glitter."

"Glitter?" Woody all but spat the word. "Leigh, you can't be serious. You think they were killed by glitter?"

I steepled my hands in front of my chest, a defensive move according to my therapist in Atlanta. She was probably right, but who cared? I found out later she was screwed up herself. "Woody, these are old people whose eyesight was not good. What looked like glitter to them, might not be glitter at all. Check it, that's all I ask."

Woody rolled his eyes. "You're a fan of that stupid forensic show, aren't you? Conspiracies are everywhere. Get a grip, Leigh, the man was old."

"What about the dog?" Penny Sue snapped. "He wasn't old."

Anthony glanced at Penny Sue. "I'll do what I can to get an autopsy on Mr. Holden."

"And, take Mattie, Mrs. Holden, to the hospital for observation. She's not herself," I added.

Woody shook his head. "You girls—" we all cringed, including Heather—"make a mountain out of a molehill."

"Me? Us?" Penny Sue growled. "I've had it with you. I'm filing a sexual harassment suit tomorrow."

Woody scowled. "Sexual? Get serious. I've made no advances, whatsoever."

Penny Sue set her jaw. "Don't worry—Daddy will think of something."

Penny Sue went straight to the shower when we arrived at the condo, then ate four Snickers and drank a big glass of Jack Daniels on the rocks. Another time, I might have criticized her drinking. Today, by golly, she deserved it! I poured myself a small drink, too. Clyde was the second dead body I'd seen in two days time, and that unnerved me. I picked up my glass, the ice in it tingling from my trembling hand.

We were sitting around the kitchen counter, the Weather Channel playing in the background. At that moment hurricanes were the least of my worries, but Ruthie had to be informed. Besides, Jim Cantore was reporting.

"What about Mrs. Holden?" I asked Ruthie. "What did she say while we were upstairs?"

Ruthie took a sip of her sweet tea. "She was barely coherent. She said some mean things. I don't know her, but she surprised the hell out of me."

"She was like that on the telephone earlier—said it was a shame Mrs. King didn't die. Called her a bitch."

Ruthie downed her tea. "Honey, 'bitch' was the least of what she said to me. Seems she hated the dog, too. Scooter was Mr. Holden's pet. Honestly, it was like she was possessed by a demon."

Penny Sue mixed herself a Jack and Coke. Good, she was diluting the liquor. "You're intuitive," she said to Ruthie. "Was she really possessed in your opinion?"

She thought for a moment. "No, I didn't sense another entity. She was under the influence of something, though."

"Like what?" Penny Sue spread her hands wide. "Glitter?"

Ruthie shrugged. "Beats me. Maybe she has senile dementia. The paramedics said they'd get her in the psych ward, so maybe someone there will figure it out."

"Psych ward?" I almost shouted. "She needs to have her blood checked. Some sort of toxin affected them all. Mattie acts like a nut, then Clyde and Scooter bite the dust. Come on, it must have something to do with the glitter. Think about it. Aluminum rusting that shouldn't rust. Glitter on the floor, then a dog and a man die. There has to be a connection!

"We should call Fran's son, Carl," I said. "I know he's throwing a big party, but he has the contacts to solve this. For goshsakes, people are dropping dead all around us. If we don't do something, we may be next!"

"I wish we still had that liquid taser, we could use it now." Penny Sue eyed Ruthie. "Do you think your dad can get us another one? It's better than my shooting people with the .38. I wouldn't try to kill them, if I could avoid it. Still ..."

She picked up the phone. "I'll try."

Ruthie's father was J.T. Edwards, a retired railroad executive who lived in a restored mansion in Buckhead, a very classy suburb of Atlanta. J.T. had inherited money and made a lot on his own, giving him the means to invest in a number of start-up companies. Taser Technologies was one of his investments.

Whereas normal tasers had to touch a person or shoot darts attached to wires in order to deliver an electric shock, Taser Technologies' liquid taser shot an electrified stream of saline solution. That was a huge breakthrough, because it meant one could shoot multiple people with the same weapon. It was still in the development phase, awaiting approvals and licenses, but J.T. had obtained a prototype for Ruthie that proved invaluable in our previous scrapes.

After a short conversation with Mr. Wong, J.T.'s valet who'd been with the family so long he was considered part of the fold, Ruthie spoke with her dad. Sadly, J.T. had lost his mental edge, but not his nerve. He promised to have a new taser to us by Tuesday.

Teary-eyed, Ruthie hung up the phone. "Poppa's fading. I can't bear the thought of losing him."

"It's hard, honey, I know." Penny Sue patted her hand. "I didn't think I'd ever get over losing Mama. Of course, your mother went younger than mine. It's stinking, but I know we're not really losing them; they're going to a better place. I feel Mama's presence a lot. In fact, she was with me when I was pumping Clyde's chest." Penny Sue sighed deeply.

I knew she was holding something back. "Did your mother tell you anything?"

Penny Sue's expression was grim. "Mama said it was hopeless. He'd already passed over. Still, I had to try." Tears started to flow.

Next thing I knew, we were hugging each other and bawling like babies. Death was a rough thing to face, even when you hardly knew the person. We were still moaning and whimpering when there was a knock on the damned door. Honestly, I felt like we lived in Grand Central Station.

"Man, are you all right? We heard the news."

Guthrie—not what we needed. I wiped my eyes and headed for the door.

"Wow, Leigh, you look awful. We heard about the Holdens. Man, that was really brave."

Looking contrite, Timothy stood behind Guthrie. "You're wonderful people. Guthrie's fortunate to have neighbors like you." He stared at Penny Sue. "We heard what you did. May I?" he asked, extending his arms. Penny Sue stepped out on the stoop and fell against his chest. She was in hog heaven and would have wet her pants if she'd seen Timothy's biceps during the clinch.

"Come in." I smiled at Timothy. "We need your help."

Penny Sue poured miniature Snickers into a bowl (I noticed she hid most of them in the pantry) and placed the candy on the coffee table. Big concession on her part! Then drinks—Penny Sue tried to show off Lu Nee 2 for Timothy, but the robot's charge had run down. So, I gave Timothy mineral water while Guthrie took a scotch.

We sat in the living room. Noticing Guthrie was stuffing down Snickers and Timothy only sipped water, Ruthie piped in, "Timothy, can we offer you some vitamins or something?"

He chuckled. "No. How can I help you?" Timothy was a man of action and few words.

I folded my hands in my lap and didn't mince words. "You're a chemist. Something weird is happening in this complex. Two units in our cluster have aluminum rusting, which isn't supposed to happen. Now, a neighbor in the next cluster—and his dog—drop dead after 'glitter' is found on the floor."

"Glitter?" Timothy repeated skeptically.

I filled him in on the details, including Mattie Holden's personality change. I told him I couldn't believe that aluminum would rust and a person would die from glitter in the span of three days. He agreed that mathematical probabilities said the incidents were related, and considering Guthrie's shutters were targeted, Guthrie might be in danger himself. None of us had thought of that—a chill ran up my spine. Timothy had the day off Monday, since NASA, and almost everything else, was closed because of Charley. He promised to look into the problem.

"Man, I'm not afraid," Guthrie bragged, chewing a Snickers. "Anyone throws glitter my way will get a .45 bullet up their gluteus maximus."

Timothy rolled his eyes, and I smiled. It was the look of a parent who'd tried, but had no success with his wayward offspring.

Chapter 10

August 16

The next morning we all rose early. A first. The condo was cool, but despite that, none of us had slept a wink. Penny Sue and I remained haunted by images of Clyde and Scooter. Ruthie was so sensitive, our bad vibes kept her awake. We congregated at the kitchen counter and sipped coffee—as if we needed the caffeine.

"I can't stand staying here another minute," Penny Sue said suddenly. "I'm stir-crazy. Let's go to Orlando."

"Orlando, isn't the place to go," Ruthie said, glancing at the TV. "Damage there is worse than it is here."

Penny Sue waved her arms. "Well, we have to go somewhere. I can't stand this condo anymore."

I crossed my arms on the counter and laid my head down. "I've had it, too. But, we have a dozen things to do today. Sonny's supposed to find out about Mrs. King's contractor. We need to call that federal assistant about the depositions, and I should check on the center."

The Marine Conservation Center was a nonprofit organization dedicated to education and the preservation of the Indian River Lagoon, North America's most diverse estuary. I didn't have a clue what estuary meant when I started work there, but soon learned the term referred to the part of a river where it met the ocean, which in New Smyrna's case, was the inland waterway. I loved my job as part-time bookkeeper and all of my coworkers—a great group who cared as much about each other as they did the environment.

I checked the clock, eight-thirty. Sandra, the center's office manager, would be up. I snatched the portable phone at the end of the counter and dialed her home number.

"No telling when we'll open again," Sandra said wearily. "Our pontoon boat was badly damaged. Bobby"—the boat's captain and a character in his own right—"says it could take as long as a month to get it repaired."

"Is there anything I can do to help?"

"Fortunately, the building didn't get much damage, so there's nothing to do there. Your friends are visiting, aren't they?"

"Yes."

"Then enjoy your time together—as much as you can in this heat. I'll call if I need you."

"You don't have electricity?" I asked, remembering Sandra lived on a picturesque street lined with huge live oaks.

"No. Trees are down everywhere. One squashed my carport. Thank goodness it missed the house."

"Would you like to stay with us? Our power's back on."

"Thanks, dear, I'll be okay. My sister owns a farm in Samsula. She lent me a generator that will power the refrigerator, fan, and a few lights. Electric crews are working the street now, so I hope I'll have electricity by tomorrow."

I hung up thinking that I had a month's vacation. Initially elated, I soon realized it also meant a month of no income. A month with nothing to do. I glanced at Penny Sue whose mouth was screwed up like a prune. Uh oh, I hope it didn't mean a month with my Leo friend. As much as I loved her, a little Penny Sue went a long way. After all, she'd been here less than a week, and there'd been a hurricane and three deaths, counting Scooter.

"We should check on Mrs. Holden. Would you hand me the telephone book?" I asked Penny Sue.

She pulled the directory from the junk drawer. "Here it is, Bert Fish, patient information."

I dialed the number and was connected to her room. Mattie's daughter, Priscilla, answered. We'd never met, but I'd heard Mattie mention her many times. I led off with condolences for her father, and then asked about her mother's condition.

"Sleeping now," Priscilla said tearfully. "They've run blood tests, and I'm waiting for the results. The doctors have ruled out a stroke. They think my parents may have been poisoned."

"Poisoned?!" I knew there was something strange about that 'glitter,' but poison? My friends stared at me, wide eyes demanding details. "Do they know what kind?"

Priscilla sniffled. "Not yet. They're doing an autopsy on Daddy—" She broke down, sobbing. It took her a moment to compose herself. "I heard what you and your friends did, and I'm very grateful." She swallowed hard. "I don't know what I'd do if I'd lost Mom, too."

"The doctors think she'll be all right?" I pressed.

"Yes, they're planning to do some sort of cleansing procedure as soon as they can find the right physician. They suspect the poison was airborne."

"Airborne," I repeated.

Ruthie's face twisted with horror as she mouthed, "Anthrax."

I waved her off. "Priscilla, I don't mean to intrude, but we need to know the cause of your parents' illness. There have been a number of bizarre incidents in the neighborhood, which may be connected to your parents. Would you call me as soon as you find out the cause? It could be very important to a number of other people."

Priscilla choked out, "Certainly, let me find a pen. What's your phone number?"

I gave her my cell number in case we decided to go out. This was one call I did not want to miss. I expressed our condolences again and offered help if she needed anything.

"My brother's coming from Houston," she murmured.

"Take care of yourself," I said softly.

"Airborne? We need to buy some masks." Ruthie started to pace nervously. "Maybe it's anthrax. Do we have any rubber gloves? We should buy gloves, like the ones doctors wear, in case something else happens." Suddenly, Ruthie stiffened as if she'd been struck by a bolt of lightning. "Did you breathe while you were in their condo?"

Penny Sue and I both gave her a you've-got-to-be-kidding glare.

"Breathe?" Penny Sue belted. "I didn't breathe, I heaved my brains out!" She turned to me. "An airborne poison—they don't know what it is?"

I nodded.

"We should all go to the hospital for tests," Ruthie exclaimed.

"Us and everyone else in the room. All the paramedics, firemen, police … and Woody." I added.

Penny Sue lowered her eyes. "Let's not tell Woody."

"You're awful, you know that? Just awful," Ruthie said.

"I was kidding. Ruthie, you've got to loosen up." Penny Sue poured a dollop of the Bailey's in her coffee.

Ruthie pointed at the liquor bottle. "Loosen up like that? Drinking before noon?"

Penny Sue rolled her eyes and took a sip of her spiked coffee. "Sugar, it's this or a tranquilizer. After all, I'm the one who was puffing and blowing in that poisoned bedroom, inches from Clyde's face."

Ruthie's face softened. "You're right. All I did was sit outside with Mattie Holden. You did the real work. I'm sorry—"

Ruthie didn't get to finish; the telephone rang. It was the legal assistant with the Federal Court. Due to the hurricane, our depositions had been put off for at least a week. The assistant would call when the court reopened. I relayed the message, yet before anyone could say a single word—I could tell Ruthie was thinking of flying home—the phone jangled again.

It was Chris from St. Augustine. "How's it going?" she asked cheerily.

Penny Sue shrugged a "Who is that?"

I mouthed, "Chris."

She mouthed back, "Sleeping bags and air mattresses."

I nodded, remembering Penny Sue's idea about what we needed to buy if we went to Chris' store for another hurricane. Penny Sue pointed at the speaker button on the phone.

"We're all here," I said. "You're on speakerphone. As to your question, we're not doing so good."

"What?" Chris asked with concern.

"Two more deaths. A man and a dog," Penny Sue blurted.

"What's going on over there? You need to sage the whole neighborhood," Chris said.

"Heck no, the way our luck's running, we'd be arrested for air pollution," I responded.

"What happened?"

"Too long a story. Don't worry, we didn't kill anyone," Penny Sue shouted.

Chris gave us a big hmph. "I assumed that."

"Let's skip the gruesome details. Are we still invited to your place if there's another hurricane?" Ruthie asked.

"Of course, I'm counting on it. By the way, no one's allergic to cats, are they? I have a store cat, Angel."

"No problem with that. Why are you calling, besides the fact that you think we're wonderful?" Penny Sue asked.

Chris chuckled. "Wonderful? Get a grip!" A New York to Florida transplant, Chris still had the sharp, Northern humor. "Under the circumstances, this may not be the right time to tell you."

"After the last seventy-two hours, nothing would surprise us. Shoot," I said.

"Well," Chris started, "so many people were hurt by the hurricane—many uninsured—a group of us thought it would be fun to have a marathon race to benefit needy victims."

Penny Sue put her hands on her hips. "Race? Are you crazy? I'm not running around a dumb track."

"Not a running race, silly. You think I'd do that? An auto race. Only, not a boring old stock car competition—a marathon race with lots of different events."

"What kind of events?" Penny Sue asked skeptically.

"I spoke with the owner of the New Smyrna Speedway, and he's willing to host it. He suggested a three-part marathon for Labor Day Weekend. Mini-cup cars, school buses, and a bag race. It's all for fun. You know, like the cancer walks where teams get pledges from people for each mile they walk. In this case, teams get pledges for their overall placement. All proceeds go to uninsured and unemployed victims. A few neighborhood associations and a group of NASA retirees have expressed interest so far.

"An-nyway, I thought of a DAFFODILS team, since there are four of us and we're all in that category. What do you think?"

Ruthie's brow furrowed. I thought it would be a hoot. Penny Sue grabbed the bottle of Bailey's and took a gulp. "Hell, yes," she said. "That's exactly what we need, something to take our minds off of all of this trauma."

"But, but—" Ruthie started.

Penny Sue waved off her objection. "Don't worry, Ruthie, you can do the bag race. What you can't see won't hurt you."

"What's a bag race?" she asked.

Chris replied from the speakerphone. "The person driving the car wears a bag over her head and the person in the passenger seat directs 'em. With Ruthie's intuition, she's perfect for the job."

"You mean a bunch of blindfolded people speed around a race track?" Ruthie snapped.

"Well," Chris started, "since they all have bags, no one's going very fast. If you hit something, it won't cause much damage."

Ruthie wasn't comforted. "Much? You're sure about that?"

"Yes, I've been to the track a dozen times. No one gets hurt. For many years, the winner was a real blind man."

Ruthie's expression said she didn't know if that was good or bad. I didn't either.

"Count the DAFFODILS in. We'll kick butt," Penny Sue said.

"Awfully sure of yourself, aren't you? Against NASA retirees?" Ruthie argued.

"You're the one who harps on how our thoughts determine our reality. Hell yeah, we're going to kick their butts; there's no other way to think. Think otherwise and we're doomed."

There was nothing Ruthie could say to that. She was in the bag race, and I had to admit this was a terrific diversion from the rotten stuff going on around us. Besides, we had Carl and his brilliant MIT buddies in the wings. I knew they'd help if we needed them.

"We'll have to practice. You're sure you have the time? You can't do a bag race or drive a school bus cold."

"We'll make the time," Penny Sue said grandly.

We said our goodbyes and I hit the speaker button to end the call. The phone immediately rang, so fast I thought it was a mistake. It wasn't. It was Guthrie.

"Man, have you heard anything about anything?"

"We've heard a lot, more than we want to know. Do you have anything specific in mind?"

"Yeah, like, what about Mrs. Holden or Mrs. King? Any news there? And what about the Holden's little dog, Scooter? That was a cute dog. I kept treats just for him. Is there going to be a memorial service?"

I rubbed my forehead. I liked Guthrie, but felt like I was talking to a three year old most of the time. I wanted to scream, "No service has been scheduled for Scooter! For godsakes, Clyde Holden's funeral hasn't been scheduled yet." Of course, I didn't say it.

"I have no information on Scooter. They're doing an autopsy on Clyde, and Mattie's still being diagnosed. They may have been poisoned. Airborne. Is Timothy there? I think he could help us with this."

Guthrie yelled, "Timothy, an airborne poison killed the Holdens. Leigh needs your help, now!"

I heard some mumbled conversation, and Timothy took the phone. "What's this about poison?"

"Have you had a chance to check your chemistry books?" I asked.

"I did an Internet search this morning and found a *Popular Science* article on aluminum rusting. It's a fairly recent piece and the culprit is mercury. Mercury turns aluminum to rusty mush—and fast. According to the article, a substantial aluminum I-beam turned to dust in a matter of hours. I checked Guthrie's shutters, and they're still deteriorating. I didn't go under Mrs. King's house, but I'll bet her new-fangled water pipe is dissolving, too. No telling how far it's gone. She'll probably have to replace it all."

"Is mercury poisonous?" I asked.

"Are you kidding? It's deadly. Haven't you heard all the press about mercury contaminated fish?"

"Mercury forms little balls, doesn't it? Is it possible to inhale it?"

I could almost see Timothy shake his head. "Mercury vapor is deadly. Anyone working with mercury—stirring it, pouring it, whatever—better take precautions. It'll kill ya. At first you become crazy, then nauseous, and it progresses from there. Not a pretty picture. Don't fool with mercury, whatever you do."

Crazy: Mattie Holden. Nauseous and, maybe, crazy: Clyde Holden. Scooter, who knew? Animals can't tell you what's wrong. Bummer, as Guthrie would say.

"Timothy, that scenario describes the Holdens perfectly. I can call the hospital and tell them we think Mattie may have mercury poisoning, but I think it would carry more weight if it came from you. The docs aren't sure how to treat Mattie—your information could be valuable."

"Who do I call?" Timothy asked. I gave him the number and Priscilla's name.

An hour later Timothy called back. "Positive for mercury on all counts."

"Lord, that's the glitter. Someone must have dropped mercury on the floor and spread it around."

"Every droplet lets off vapor. It would have been a lot better if it had been left in a big lump," Timothy said.

"Clyde vacuumed up the glitter," I said, remembering Mattie's comment.

"Vacuumed?"

I could hear the trepidation in Timothy's voice. "Yes, vacuumed."

"That's how it became airborne. Scooter was so short his nose was in the vapor. The little pooch didn't have a chance. The vacuuming is why Clyde died and Mattie didn't. Mattie was affected, for sure, but the vacuum probably blew the fumes right into Clyde's face. I need to call a HAZMAT team. Don't go over there, whatever you do." Timothy paused. "Leigh, you and Penny Sue should probably go to the hospital to get checked. Is anyone showing symptoms?"

If the first symptom was confusion or acting crazy, who could tell with Penny Sue? When I thought about it, she could have had mercury poisoning her whole life. Considering our bizarre circumstances, I felt fairly normal. "Anyone feel funny?" I asked. "Timothy thinks we should go to the hospital for a blood test."

"Yes! I have a headache, and I didn't sleep a wink all night," Ruthie shot back. "We should go now."

"If it'll make you feel better, we'll go. Give me a few minutes to put on my face," Penny Sue said.

"Slap on some lipstick and wear your big Chanel sunglasses. We don't have time for you to primp. We could be in mortal danger!" The veins on Ruthie's neck were sticking out. That was a first, even though she was skinny. She was wound up tighter than a tick, and I doubted that all the chanting in the world could soothe her.

"Ruthie's right," I said. "With the hurricane, no one's out and about. We won't see anyone we know except other sick people." I winked at Penny Sue. "Let's go now and get it over with."

"You drive, Leigh," Ruthie demanded. "She's been drinking."

Penny Sue folded her arms defiantly. "Aren't we the stickler for detail? I've had about as much alcohol as you'd get from a slice of rum cake. If it will make you happy," she virtually sneered, "Leigh can drive *my* car. Hers isn't big enough for normal people."

My VW bug was so big enough for normal people! It was abnormal humans like Penny Sue—I bit my tongue and picked up my purse. "Fine, let's go." I snatched Penny Sue's keys from the counter and headed for the front door. I started the Mercedes as Ruthie and I waited for Penny Sue. A moment later, a white Taurus with government tags pulled in behind us. Woody got out. I slapped my forehead at the bum luck. If Penny Sue had been a little faster, we'd have avoided his obnoxious presence.

Woody tapped on my window. I opened it reluctantly.

"I heard your depositions were postponed indefinitely," he said.

"Indefinitely? The lady who called this morning said it was only for a week."

"A week, two weeks, no one knows. I spoke with one of the Fed's attorneys. He said it was doubtful you'd be called."

"That's great news," Ruthie said from the backseat. "Can we go home?"

"Not yet, nothing's been finalized."

Woody drove out here to tell us that? He wasn't that nice. Besides, we'd already heard as much from the judge. There was no doubt in my mind that he knew we knew the judge had talked to everyone who was anyone. So why was he here? "Is there anything else?" I asked at the moment Penny Sue dropped into the front passenger seat, her face noticeably turned away from Woody. I knew she was embarrassed that she didn't have on her full face. Woody took it as an insult.

His eyes bore holes into the back of Penny Sue's head. "I wanted to tell you that the man who fell from the balcony was

Antonio Accardo, a known underling for the New Jersey Mafia. You know, the guys you may have to testify against. His wound wasn't an accident. It came from a 9 mm Takarov, a Russian weapon. Old Tony was carrying a Glock."

Penny Sue lowered her head and stared at Woody across the top of her sunglasses. "Get to the point. What does that mean to us?"

Woody shuffled and flashed his smarmy grin. "We're not sure what it means, but I reported it to the Feds. They may take steps."

"Like what?" Penny Sue demanded.

Woody shrugged. "It's up to them."

"You mean, you were told to butt out?" Penny Sue said with a snicker.

"Absolutely not." His body language said otherwise.

"If you have some free time, you may want to go to the hospital," I started.

Penny Sue poked my leg, a shut-up maneuver.

I ignored her. "There's a good chance Clyde Holden died from airborne mercury poisoning. Anyone in that room could have been contaminated."

"Are you sure?" he said, for once sounding sincere.

"Do you think I'd be going somewhere without make-up otherwise?" Penny Sue piped in.

"I guess not." Woody hurried to his car and backed out of our way. Wonder of wonders, he had some manners. Wrong. I glanced in my rearview mirror and saw him on his cell phone. No doubt notifying his troops. Good, it saved us the trouble and the time—we needed to get going now!

Chapter 11

August 16-17

We all had elevated mercury levels, though none of ours were critical. Penny Sue's level was highest, bordering on dangerous—not surprising since she'd been closest to the floor when she tried to revive Clyde. The hospital said they could do a chelation treatment to remove the mercury, but Ruthie was skeptical. "We'll call Chris first," she whispered as the doctor outlined our options.

"Mud. You need magnetized mud. Works much faster than chelation. Not that there's anything wrong with chelation, it's just slower," Chris told us as we huddled around the speakerphone in the kitchen

"Magnetized mud? Where do we get it?" I asked.

"FedEx is running, I'll have some to you by tomorrow," Chris said. "A bath of this will take care of the problem."

"A mud bath?"

"Don't worry, it's really soothing."

The liquid taser and mud arrived the next day on the same FedEx shipment. Ironic. The first was to protect us by shooting/

polluting people with electrified water, the other to remove our own pollutants. Penny Sue immediately plugged in the taser batteries to charge, then headed to her bathroom, the only one with a tub. She was wasting no time. Under the circumstances, I agreed completely.

Chris had shipped eight bottles of magnetized mud that supposedly removed metals and pollutants from your system. Ruthie filled the tub with warm water as Penny Sue stripped. I spooned the mud into the stream of water with my fingertips. It dissolved instantly, turning the water a light tan.

"You don't reckon it will dissolve my fillings, do you?" Penny Sue asked, down to her bra and panties.

Ruthie studied the instructions. "No, says it won't affect fillings—only the toxins in your cells."

"Teeth have cells, don't they?" Penny Sue asked doubtfully.

"Fillings don't," Ruthie replied.

"Right," Penny Sue looked at me, "then put in two jars. I want to get everything out now. Lord, I could become autistic. Surely you've heard about the link between mercury-based preservatives in vaccines and autism in children?"

Sure I'd heard about it, but Penny Sue autistic? Not attached to people, like men? Too late for that, yet I wasn't going to argue.

Ruthie rolled a towel for Penny Sue's neck and she settled into the mush. "Hey, this is nice," she sighed. "Really relaxing. Boy, a glass of champagne—"

"No, you're clearing toxins, remember?" Ruthie said sternly.

"O-okay," Penny Sue said dreamily. "How long?"

"At least a half hour," Ruthie read from the instructions.

"Tell me when it's over." Penny Sue closed her eyes.

We tiptoed out, closing the door to her bathroom and the bedroom. Good thing, we were only halfway down the hall to the great room when the doorbell rang. It was Officer Heather Brooks.

"Sorry to bother you. I thought you should know that we've found another body."

I was momentarily distracted as the weird fisherman passed through the parking lot behind Heather. He tipped his hat.

"Body? Whose? Where?" I asked, opening the screen door and ushering Heather down the hall.

"A man, mid-40s we guess. He was found in the dumpster of the cluster next door."

"The one on the other side of the public boardwalk?"

She nodded. "He was shot once, in the head. No identification except he had Cyrillic letters tattooed on each knuckle of his right hand."

"Cyrillic?" I asked. "What is that?"

"Russian alphabet," Ruthie replied quietly.

Russian? I immediately thought of Yuri. His hands were perfectly manicured and definitely not tattooed. Still, an interesting coincidence. "I don't believe I want to know what you think this means."

"The first victim was Italian. This one Russian, or at least Russian mob related. You ladies are possible witnesses against a New Jersey Italian mob boss. Russians play in that territory, too. All this is off the record, okay? Do I have your word on that?"

"Of course," Ruthie and I said in unison.

"I'm not trying to scare you, just be especially careful. I'm afraid you've landed in the middle of a mob war."

"Mob war?" Ruthie went white. "A mob war? I've never even had a speeding ticket.

"Yesterday was the new moon." Ruthie rubbed the back of her neck, thinking. "And, there was a huge solar flare. Solar flares affect the Earth's geomagnetic field. We are all electrical beings. Our nerves are electrical impulses. A big jolt of electricity from the Sun could send unstable people over the edge. That's it! Someone got a jolt, went berserk, and killed the Russian."

Heather patted Ruthie's shoulder. "I'll take your word for it. I only want y'all to be careful." She scanned the room. "Where is Penny Sue?"

"Don't worry, she's in the bathtub. By the way, have you talked to Woody?"

"Not in the last day."

Jerk. He should have called Heather about the mercury. I filled her in on the details. "If the hospital says your levels are elevated, come back, and we'll give you a magnetic mud bath. It's supposed to clear you of toxins."

"If the mud works on toxic colleagues, I'll be back right after my shift." Heather grinned.

"It probably wouldn't hurt."

As I closed the door on Heather, Penny Sue screamed, "Help, I'm stuck!"

Ruthie and I rushed to the bathroom. Penny Sue wasn't kidding. The magnetized mud had congealed to a Jell-O consistency, and Penny Sue was flopping around like a big jellyfish. Every time she managed to get to her knees, she lost traction and slid back into the slimy mess. I giggled uncontrollably. She wasn't amused.

"Don't laugh, you're next," she said, wagging her finger.

Ruthie and I each took hold of a slick arm and tried to pull her to her feet. She slithered through our fingers and landed back in the tub with a plop.

"Damn, that hurt," she whined.

Ruthie and I bit our lips to keep from laughing. Lord, I wish I had a camera handy. Completely covered in goo, Penny Sue looked like an alien from a low budget space movie. I swallowed hard to keep a straight face. "Did you pull the stopper so it could drain out?"

"The stupid stuff is too thick to go down the drain."

Ruthie nodded. "We probably shouldn't have used two jars."

"I don't think we're going to be able to pick you up." I washed my hands in the sink. "The only solution I see is to drag you over the edge of the tub."

"Drag me? Drag me like a sack of potatoes?"

No, a big side of greasy beef. Of course, I didn't say it. I reached under the sink and pulled out a stack of towels. I took a bath towel, folded it in half, and draped it over the edge of the tub. "This will cushion you." I handed Ruthie a hand towel. "We'll use the hand towels to grip your arms. What do you think?"

Penny Sue folded her slimy arms over her slimy boobs and pouted. "I don't like it one bit."

"If the tub weren't so full, we could try diluting the mud," Ruthie said. "We could scoop some of it into the sink, then try to water it down." She raised a brow hopefully. "Want to try that?"

"Yes, but hurry. I'm getting cold."

I gave her a towel to put around her shoulders. Ruthie fetched a pitcher from the kitchen, and I turned the sink's hot water to a slow stream. Ruthie dipped a container of goo from the bathtub and dumped it in the sink. The hot water washed it down the drain, but very slowly.

"Hell, this will take forever," Penny Sue groused. She tossed her towel on the floor and held up her arms. "Drag me. And, if I hear a single word remotely resembling fatback or slick as a greased pig, I'll shoot you in the foot with the taser."

Ruthie and I wrapped towels around her arms and dragged her out. She landed face down on the floor like a beached whale. "Don't just stand there, help me up," she sputtered, giggling. By now we were all laughing so hard, Ruthie and I didn't have the strength to move. Penny Sue was on her own. She struggled to her knees then pulled herself up by holding onto the sink. Ruthie, literally bent double with hysterics, tossed some towels around her. I dashed ahead to start the shower in our bathroom. A half hour later Penny Sue was stretched out on the sofa sipping green tea, goo-less and good as new.

"Do you feel any better?" Ruthie asked.

"I think so. Relaxed if nothing else. You know, after y'all have your soak, we should go back to the hospital and have our blood tested again. I want to be sure it worked." She gave me a devilish grin. "Your turn."

I studied her, wondering if she had a trick plotted. With Penny Sue out of the tub, the mud level fell considerably, allowing us to turn the shower on low. It worked. By the time I got to the bathroom, the mud had drained out. One thing for sure, I was only using one jar.

I filled the tub, spooned in the mud and settled in. It was surprisingly pleasant. I lay back with my head on a towel. Next thing I knew, Ruthie was shaking me and saying my time was up. Penny Sue and Ruthie both stood in the doorway watching, obviously wondering if I could get up.

I scooped a handful of the muddy water and let it drip through my fingers. "No problem, it was the second jar that did it." Ruthie took my hand and pulled me to my feet. "Piece of cake," I said, smugly. Penny Sue made a disgruntled, feral sound.

I toweled off as Ruthie drained the tub to prepare her own bath. Penny Sue had dressed and put on her full face. I took the hint and ducked into my room. My full face meant a little moisturizer, a swipe or two of mascara, and some lipstick. Penny Sue probably worked on her face the whole time I soaked, while my toilet took about ten minutes. Hey, it's the beach!

Penny Sue was making finger sandwiches of deviled ham and Tabasco olives when I emerged. The combo sounded funny, yet tasted surprisingly good. I downed two, not realizing until that moment how hungry I was. She handed me a glass of iced green tea.

"Ruthie told me about the body in the dumpster. A Russian, she said. It couldn't be Yuri, could it? Ruthie never met him."

I snatched a third sandwich. "I'm sure it wasn't Yuri. Heather said the victim had Cyrillic letters tattooed on his knuckles. I noticed Yuri's hands when he gave me his card—a perfect manicure and no tattoos."

Penny Sue let out a sigh of relief. "I know we don't agree, but I thought he was a nice guy. Not bad looking, either. I'd hate to think he was caught up in a mob war and killed."

"I don't wish him harm, I just think he's buying up all the real estate. You know I'm looking for a place here, and someone—I suspect Yuri—keeps beating me to the punch. His interest in Mrs. King's condition was crass, to say the least. I got the feeling he hoped she'd croak so he could swoop in and buy her place."

"All we know is what Guthrie told us and he goes for dramatics," Penny Sue said.

"You're right, I may be jumping to conclusions. It's partly frustration. I've haven't found a place here, even though I cruise the neighborhood twice a day. Several have been sold, the rug pulled right out from under me."

"Do you have Yuri's card?" Penny Sue asked.

I fetched the card from the top of my dresser. "His office is on the North Causeway." I handed it to Penny Sue.

"Let's drive by there and see what his office looks like. You can tell a lot about a person by their habitat." Penny Sue took a sip of the green tea and stared at the liquid. "I hope this stuff is cleansing my system like Ruthie said. I could sure go for a glass of Chardonnay about now."

"I like green tea. But, if you wait until after the blood test, I'll join you."

"Deal." Penny Sue pursed her lips, thinking. "Have you checked on the units that sold? What did they go for? Was Yuri's company involved? There must be a way to find out."

"We need to talk to a realtor." I checked my watch. Ruthie's time was up.

Most of the people who'd responded to Clyde Holden's death were in Bert Fish's emergency room waiting for blood tests. Our luck—Woody was in line directly ahead of us. We all stopped short, no one wanting to stand behind him. Ruthie finally stepped up to the plate, since our hesitation and frantic whispering were drawing attention. Honestly, Ruthie was so empathetic, she'd probably shake the devil's hand rather than hurt his feelings. Standing next to Woody was close.

Mr. Personality stared at us like we were freaks. "I thought you'd already been tested."

"We have," I answered quickly before Penny Sue could make a smart remark. "We've here for a recheck after our cleansing treatment."

"There's a pill or something that will take care of mercury contamination?" Woody asked.

"Yes, the doctor will explain it to you," I answered. There was no way I was going to mention our mud bath.

Fortunately, the line moved quickly, and Woody struck up a conversation with a fireman in front of him. Heather Brooks also showed up. Heather's presence gave us the perfect excuse to turn our backs on Woody. Penny Sue tried to question her about the dead Russian, but Heather frowned, indicating she couldn't talk. Penny Sue had the sense to drop the subject.

I had to give the hospital staff credit. They'd ramped up for the onslaught of tests, establishing an assembly line. One nurse drew blood; another labeled the vial and passed it off to a lab tech. The results were back in about a half hour—incredible for the average hospital. Most people, including Woody, had very low levels of mercury. A nurse reported their results, advising them to cut back on fish for a while until their systems had a chance to clear.

Woody left, so we were next. A moment later, Penny Sue poked me with her elbow.

"Ouch!" I drew back, rubbing my forearm. "What was that for?"

"Here comes that cute Dr. Samuelson who gave us the first test. Check his hand for a wedding band."

"Wedding band? I'm going to get a bruise from this—" I stopped as the doctor squatted in front of us. He was cute, maybe too cute—meaning too young for us.

"Your test results are amazing. They all show a substantial drop in mercury, especially yours," he said, patting Penny Sue's hand. "When I saw your name on the lab report, I was sure I'd be arranging chelation therapy. Don't get me wrong—your level is elevated, but you're out of the danger zone. What in the world did you do?"

"Well, it wasn't easy—" Penny Sue started.

I held up my hand to silence her. I could feel the story of the mud and being stuck in the bathroom bubbling up. I also had a fleeting fear Penny Sue might ask the doctor to examine her boobs, in case there were injuries from being dragged over the tub. "We used an old home remedy—green tea and a mud bath." Lord knew, I wasn't going to mention the magnetized part of the remedy or give Ruthie a chance to start on the new moon and solar flares.

Dr. Samuelson smiled skeptically and stood. "Whatever you did seems to have worked." He nodded at Penny Sue. "You should have another test next week. Do you have a local doctor?"

"No, I'm visiting," she said in her buttery, Georgia drawl. "I'll have to come here. When are you in?"

Good grief. The emphasis on *you* was embarrassing.

"I work days, but anyone can do the test." He took a step back. "In any event, all of you should go light on fish for a couple of weeks."

"Why fish?" Ruthie piped in.

"You've heard about mercury polluted waters and fish, haven't you? Actually, you're probably safe if your fish is fresh and purchased from a local market like Ocean's Seafood. Most of their stock comes from this area, so there shouldn't be a problem. It's the canned stuff you have to be careful with—no one knows where it came from. It's not a problem for the average person. But, someone like you, who's inhaled mercury, should avoid anything with even a remote chance of contamination."

"I understand." Penny Sue offered her hand. "Thank you, doctor, for all your help. It's so nice to meet a physician who takes time with patients. I know you're under the HMO gun, ruled by a massive bureaucracy of manuals, and accountants, and—"

His beeper sounded. "Sorry, I have to go."

Dr. Samuelson all but ran away, thrilled—I'm sure—for an excuse to ditch Penny Sue.

As soon as the doctor was out of sight, Penny Sue grinned. "No wedding band."

I held my tongue until we got in her car. "I thought you were in love with Rich."

She scowled. "Yes, and as you know, he's tied up indefinitely in the witness protection program. A date or two and a little flirting doesn't hurt. I'm merely passing time until Rich returns." She started the car and headed toward Canal Street.

"Where are you going?" I asked.

"North Causeway, what do you think? I want to check out Yuri's office."

The North Causeway Drawbridge was up and traffic at a standstill, so we turned off onto a feeder road lined by a strip of glass-front stores. Yuri's office was in the middle, closest to an upscale beauty salon. Penny Sue backed up and parked a few doors away so as not to be obvious.

"Not too classy for a realtor," she said.

"The salon down the street is well known. Maybe Yuri hopes to draw in their rich customers."

"Could be," Ruthie observed. "He has a lot of flyers with sold signs taped to the window."

"Go take a peek." Penny Sue glanced at Ruthie through the rearview mirror. "He doesn't know you."

"Me?"

"For goshsakes, it's broad daylight, and his Jaguar isn't in sight. See if any of the sold units are for Sea Dunes."

Ruthie grumbled, but unlatched her seatbelt. In the distance I saw the drawbridge drop into place and a black Jaguar headed our way, leading the line of traffic.

"Here he comes across the bridge," I exclaimed.

Penny Sue made a U-turn and headed the other way before Ruthie got her door open. Doubtless a maneuver Penny Sue had learned in the anti-terrorist driving course, I thought as I hung on to the door handle. I watched for the Jag as she turned left onto the main road.

"Are we out of the woods?" Penny Sue asked.

"Maybe."

"What do you mean, maybe?"

"There's no sign of the Jag, but I think we're being followed by a black Taurus.

Chapter 12

August 17-24

"A black Taurus? What makes you think it's following us?" Penny Sue asked.

"I noticed one behind us at the light when we turned into the hospital. I saw a black Taurus parked on the opposite side of the lot when we left the emergency room. Now, a black Taurus is a few cars behind us."

"We'll see about that." Penny Sue drove straight across Riverside Drive, hung a left on Sams, a right on Canal, then a left on Live Oak. We missed the light at the intersection to Route 44 and pulsed to a stop in the left turn lane.

Ruthie and I scanned the streets behind us. No black car of any make was in sight. "We lost 'em."

"Maybe we weren't being followed after all," I allowed.

"The Taurus is a common rental car," Ruthie said. "With all the tension of the last few days, our nerves are on edge. I'm sure it was merely a coincidence."

The light went green, and we headed over the South Causeway Bridge, back toward the condo. I peeked over my shoulder several times, but didn't find a Taurus. Logic said Ruthie was right, and my imagination was running wild. My gut told me otherwise.

Our development was filled with cars and yellow crime tape when we pulled in the driveway. While one person worked the Italian site in our cluster, most of the interest had shifted to the Russian in the dumpster next door. At least five cars, marked and unmarked, surrounded the green receptacle. A large group of sightseers had congregated on the elevated public boardwalk, giving it an almost festive feel. We drove past the commotion and parked in front of our unit.

"Let's see what's going on," Penny Sue said.

"Give me the key. I'm not interested," Ruthie replied. "Besides, I have to go to the bathroom."

It had been over an hour since she'd checked out a toilet facility. Ruthie was one of those people who simply could not pass a bathroom without going in. We'd counseled her to look into the pee urgency medication. She always blew us off. We finally took the hint and stopped trying to convince her.

Penny Sue handed over the key ring. "You'll come, won't you, Leigh?"

I hated to admit being a gawker, yet I was curious. "Sure."

Since the beach entrance was damaged by the storm, we walked up the driveway to A1A. Guthrie, leaning on his crutches, spotted us coming. "Where have you been? A body was found in the dumpster."

We stepped up on the walkway, an elderly woman close on our heels. Penny Sue and I made our way slowly through the crowd. Many were residents of the development, the rest curious passersby. We wove through the throng, single file, uttering a litany of *excuse me, sorry, excuse me's*. We received a lot of dirty looks, especially from short women who thought we were trying to butt in front of them and block their view. Even as we continued past, I could feel angry eyes boring into my back. The angry looks I could take, it was the amazing number of pistols and revolvers on belts and in hands that made me nervous. I thought Guthrie was being hysterical when he compared Florida to the Wild West, but now I was inclined to agree. Sheesh, I had no idea so many of my neighbors packed weapons. I decided I'd better watch my step in the future.

"Can you believe it?" Guthrie said when we arrived at his side. "Another murder! Rumor has it there's a mob war. A lot of people are talking about selling out. I mean, the hurricane damage was bad enough, this mob war is the last straw."

Selling? My initial reaction was "hurray!" Then, a mental head slap for being selfish. I wanted to buy a place for sure, but I wanted to get it fair and square—not steal it from a frightened retiree. "I'm sure the mob rumor is false," I said loud enough for the people around us to hear. "I'll put my money on a hurricane party, too many beers, and a drunken brawl."

A substantially built woman with shocking white hair nudged me in the back. I did a double take. It was the elderly woman who'd followed us up the walkway.

"Aren't you the lady who drives the little yeller car?" she asked me.

I started to offer my hand and introduce myself, when I noticed she clutched a handgun with a long—real long—ornately, etched barrel. I dropped my arm quickly. "Yes, ma'am. I'm Leigh Stratton. I'm staying at Judge Parker's place down on the beach."

The lady snorted, unimpressed. "You know, things were real quiet around here until you showed up."

Penny Sue whipped around and was about to speak when Guthrie spied the lady's gun. "Man, is that a real 1860 Colt 45? Wow, I never thought I'd see one in person."

The woman eyed him suspiciously. "You the guy staying in Harriet's place, next to Nana King's?"

Guthrie stood up straight on his crutches. "One and the same. Harriet's my aunt."

"Harriet," she grunted.

Penny Sue stepped forward and shoved her right hand at the lady. "I'm Penny Sue Parker, Judge Parker's daughter. With whom do I have the pleasure?" Her lips were stretched in a tight smile.

The lady shifted the pistol to her left hand and took Penny Sue's. "Pearl. Pearl Woodhead."

I gasped so hard, I nearly swallowed my tongue. Was this Woody's mother? Penny Sue didn't flinch.

"You've grown a lot," Pearl continued. "I knew your Momma. I was sorry to hear she'd passed. If she was around, I'm sure we wouldn't be havin' all this trouble."

Where had Pearl been? Penny Sue's mother died over ten years ago.

Penny Sue's smile stayed fixed, but her eyes went slitty and her voice stern. "You're right, Mrs. Woodhead, Momma would have been appalled by this commotion. I assure you that neither Leigh, I, or my friends have anything to do with it. As Daddy says, there's a lawless element that affects even the best people. There's no explaining it."

"Well, my son's been run up the flagpole by the bigwigs a lot since you started coming around. Hard enough to get the respect that's due without having to deal with troublemakers like you."

"Your son is Robert?"

"Yeah, Bobby. Y'all caused him a lot of trouble."

Penny Sue's smile went south. "Mrs. Woodhead, I know you love your son like my father loves me. Your son is paid to do a job, and he's doing it. Let's leave it at that."

Pearl gave Penny Sue a steely-eyed once over. "You're a lot like your mother," Pearl said, dropping her gaze to the pistol.

"Ma'am, is that a real 1860 Colt?" Guthrie asked, oblivious to anything but the gun.

Pearl turned away. "A replica cap pistol. Don't you worry; I have a real arsenal at home. Guns, bows and arrows, knives—I've got it all." Nudging people to the left and right with the barrel of the cap gun, she cleared a path though the crowd.

"Wait," I said on impulse. "What kind of car do you drive?"

"A Ford. A Ford Taurus," she said without looking back.

The gods smiled on us for the next seven days. No one in the neighborhood was murdered or died. We continued our mud baths, sending our mercury levels into the normal range. Our depositions were delayed for another week. Best of all, the weather was terrific. We pulled out our bathing suits and headed to the beach to soak up some rays. It was deserted except for the eccentric fisherman with the fishing machine. Back to the water, he lounged in a chair perusing a newspaper, his fishing pole held by a white tube within reach.

"Don't most fishermen stand and watch the water?" Penny Sue asked, juggling the boom box and a sand chair.

"Maybe the sun was in his eyes," I answered. "I suppose watching the waves gets boring after a while."

"Does he always wear that silly hat?"

The hat in question was covered with hooks and sinkers and other fishing gear. "Yep. Looks like something his kid probably gave him for Christmas a long time ago." I deposited the small cooler next to Penny Sue. "This close enough to the water?"

"Fine with me," Ruthie replied.

The condition of the shore was the only downer to an otherwise idyllic day. Thanks to Charley, the beach was covered with debris and a couple of feet lower than the previous week. Most of the sea turtle nests that had been so carefully roped off by the turtle patrol were gone, swept out to sea.

"This turtle season will be a bust," I said morosely as we shoved trash aside for our chairs. "Cars and night lights are hard on turtles, but there are ordinances to control them. There's no way to legislate Mother Nature."

"All the nests were washed away?" Ruthie asked.

"At least the stakes were. It's possible some nests survived—we just don't know where they are. There were three nests roped off in this area before the storm." I swept my arm in a wide arc. "With all of this rubbish, baby turtles would have a tough time getting to the water if they happened to survive the hurricane."

"Remember that cute little hatchling that got confused and walked in circles on our first visit?" Ruthie mused.

"Yes. The little booger would have died if it hadn't been for me," Penny Sue bragged.

"We helped," Ruthie protested.

"It was my idea. That old lady from the turtle patrol wouldn't let us pick him up and take him to the sea. Hmph, more than one way to skin a cat. If you can't take the turtle to the sea, you bring the sea to the turtle," Penny Sue said, smiling.

I took a diet soda from the cooler and settled into my chair. "Digging that trench from the water to the turtle was a stroke of genius."

Penny Sue grinned. "It was, wasn't it? I ruined my manicure, but it was worth it. Remember how that seagull kept circling, trying to swoop in and eat the little turtle?"

"I remember you shouting and shaking your fist at him," Ruthie said to Penny Sue. "I think you scared the turtle patrol to death. The old lady, what was her name?"

"Gerty," I said.

"Gerty swung wide berth around you, after that." Ruthie giggled.

I cackled. "I was so happy you didn't have your gun with you. If you had, the seagull and Gerty were goners for sure, and maybe a few other members of the turtle patrol."

Penny Sue pointed to the cooler next to my chair. I handed her a bottle of water. She twisted the cap and took a long drink. "You know I wouldn't really shoot anyone."

I shook my head in amazement. "You threatened to shoot us in the foot with the taser the other day."

"The taser's different, because it's not a lethal weapon—though, I guess it might kill a seagull." She lifted her face to the sun and closed her eyes. "Ruthie, I wish your father would get one for me. I'd love to have a taser like yours."

"I'll see," Ruthie murmured, rolling her eyes at me. I tried not to grin.

We sat quietly, enjoying the sun, for all of five minutes.

"Damn," Penny Sue said suddenly.

"What? What?" Ruthie jumped, nearly tipping over her chair.

"I can't rest for worrying about the little turtles. With all of this garbage, they'll never make it to the ocean." Penny Sue pointed at a jagged, brown piece of glass—an obvious remnant of a beer bottle. She struggled up from her low-slung sand chair and angrily snatched the glass. "What kind of heathen would leave a glass bottle on the beach? The turtles could be shredded by this, not to mention children."

"Children?" I said. "What about adults? I walk this beach barefooted all the time."

Hand on her hip, Penny Sue set her jaw.

Uh oh. "What do you want to do?" I asked, afraid of the answer. I'd hoped for an hour or two of peace and quiet.

"Do you remember where those nests are?"

"Generally."

"Do we still have some of those big garbage bags?"

I knew where she was going. So much for relaxation. "Yes, I think we have a few."

"We're going to pick up all of this garbage and clear a path to the sea for the turtles. What do you say?"

Ruthie was already standing and folding her chair. Penny Sue was in the schoolmarm mode. Argument was pointless.

While Penny Sue went to the condo for the garbage bags, I marked off the approximate spots of the turtle nests with a piece of driftwood. Ruthie dragged our chairs to the walkover and watched. I also noticed our friendly fisherman peering over the top of his newspaper.

Penny Sue returned a few minutes later. "We only have two." She handed me the brown, plastic bags. "Y'all get started, and I'll run up to Food Lion for more." She stomped off, not waiting for an answer. Ruthie and I exchanged a puzzled look.

I waved my bag. "What's wrong with this picture? She wants to pick up trash, and here we are doing it."

Ruthie dropped a shard of wood into her bag. "It's Penny Sue—what do you expect?"

In a huff, I plopped on the bottom step of the walkway. "For once, I am not going to do *Her Highness'* bidding. It was her idea, and I'm willing to help, but I'll be darned if I'll break my back while she rides up and down the road. I'll start working when she does."

Ruthie sat beside me. "Good point. I'll wait, too." She started to bite her fingernail. "You know, Penny Sue was born bossy. She's a Leo. It's her natural way."

"I know, you've said all that before. I'm not a Leo, darn it. I get tired of being bossed around. I got my fill of being a doormat when I was married to Zack. I'm not mad at Penny Sue, I'm just not going to jump when she says jump any longer."

"You're right."

A half hour later, Penny Sue flounced down the boardwalk with a big yellow box of lawn bags. We stood when we saw her coming. She punched open the box, pulled out a bag that she snapped open in the wind, and said, "All right, let's get going."

She didn't seem to notice that we hadn't already been working. Hmm, maybe I took her commands too seriously. Or, maybe she forgot the orders as soon as she gave them. Whatever, we worked almost two hours—with several soda breaks—and filled ten large bags with trash. One by one, we lugged the bags to the front of the condo for transport to the dumpster—our dumpster, not the Russian one.

"Whew," Penny Sue sighed when the last bag was deposited next to her car. "Let's take it to the dumpster later. I bought a four pack of those little bottles of Chardonnay when I was at Food Lion. They're in the icebox, chilling. Come on, let's go admire our handiwork."

She breezed through the condo, plucked the carton of mini-bottles from the refrigerator, and led us to the beach. We walked to the edge of the water and surveyed our handiwork. Penny Sue passed out the wine and turned one up. The moment she took a drink, it must have dawned on her that the bottles were glass. "Don't you dare drop those twist caps or bottles," she admonished us.

"Honey, we're not stupid. We picked up enough of this stuff to know better." I gazed at the litter-free sand. "We did good, didn't we?"

Penny Sue sipped her wine quickly. "Do we have a rake in the utility room?"

"You're not proposing that we rake the beach, are you?" My back was already killing me from so much bending. Raking sand was out of the question.

She shot me the old hooded-eye, pitiful look. "Remember how the little turtle kept getting stuck in the holes? I thought we should smooth out the beach."

"Penny Sue, it will be smoothed," I said with a sigh. "It's called high tide. Tomorrow morning this beach will be completely flat. It will also be filled with trash again."

Her hooded eyes widened. "Darn, I never thought of that!"

The idea of cleaning the beach every day proved too much for Penny Sue. She'd downed the last bottle of the four-pack by the time we got back to the condo. Thankfully, the phone was ringing, diverting her attention. It was Chris, calling about the benefit race. Penny Sue answered, and then pushed the speaker button on the phone so we could all hear.

"I spoke with Mr. Hart, the owner of the New Smyrna Speedway. He said he'd make arrangements for us to practice, but we have to make an appointment. The other teams want to practice, as well. So, when are you free?" Chris asked.

We all shrugged. "Tomorrow," Penny Sue said. "Is that too soon?"

"Perfect. I have tomorrow off. How about eleven? I hate to get up early on my day off."

"Eleven it is," Penny Sue replied. "Should we wear something special?"

"Shorts, jeans, clothes you wouldn't mind getting dirty."

"Wait," Ruthie said nervously. "Is there anyone to train us? I don't know a thing about races."

"Mr. Hart said he or his promoters would give us some pointers, but they can't show favoritism. It's a benefit race. We're on our own. By the way," Chris said, "I've heard you speak—none too fondly—of the local prosecutor. Woody? I heard today he's fielding a squad. Seems Woody learned there was a DAFFODILS team and decided to join in the fun."

I saw Penny Sue's jaw muscles flex. "No problem. I welcome the competition," she drawled. "It is for charity, after all."

"Yes, it is. See you tomorrow." Chris clicked off.

Penny Sue turned on us like a wild woman. "Who do we know who knows anything about racing?"

Chapter 13

August 24

Ring, ring. Bam, bam, bam. We heard the front door open. "Hey guys, it's me, Guthrie and Tim. Are you decent?"

"Yes," Ruthie called. "Come on in."

Guthrie hobbled in on his crutches followed by Timothy who carried a VCR and a pan of brownies. "With all the stuff going on around here, we thought we should have a party. We can send out for pizza and watch *Alice's Restaurant*." Our hippie friend cocked his thumb at the brownies. "I made dessert, since you didn't get any last time. What do you say?"

It was only five PM, a little early for dinner, but we knew we'd have to see the dang movie sometime, and now was as good a time as any. Ruthie and I looked to Penny Sue. She sighed. There was no way we could refuse.

"Sure, that will be a lot of fun," she muttered through gritted teeth.

Timothy set up the VCR while we filled them in on the benefit race and our practice session scheduled for the next day.

"Man, I wish I could race." Guthrie slapped his bandaged knee disgustedly. "I'll be the water boy for your pit crew. I should be walking by then. I'll make refreshments. Every pit crew needs refreshments."

"You really don't have to—" Penny Sue started.

He grinned and held up a hand. "No argument, I want to do it. You've done so much for me."

The pizza arrived and we settled down to watch *Alice's Restaurant*. Guthrie sat on the edge of his seat. Timothy rested his head on the back of the loveseat, stoically staring down his nose at the screen. His body language spoke volumes—like, he'd seen the movie a million times and hated every minute of it.

About half an hour into the showing and pizza, we all, except Guthrie, shared Timothy's opinion. The film was one of the slowest, dumbest movies ever made. Guthrie's continuous interruptions and comments—"Listen to this!", "Isn't that wild?", "Alice is such a nice person."—actually added to the show.

In a nutshell, Alice was a good cook, had a restaurant, and invited a bunch of hippies to her house for Thanksgiving dinner. After the big feast, Arlo Guthrie loaded up a VW minivan with trash and set out for the county dump. Being a holiday, the dump was closed. (Yep, this guy was a bubble short of plumb.)

Lo and behold, Arlo happened upon a mound of trash on the side of the road. Figuring a little more garbage won't make any difference; he dumped his trash on top. Predictably, upstanding citizens observed the nefarious deed and reported him to the police. So, Arlo was arrested for littering.

Truly, the story was dull, dull, mundane stuff. The only interesting twist came from the fact that the littering conviction—a criminal record!—kept Arlo from being drafted for the Vietnam war.

Penny Sue's eyes closed after her third piece of pizza. Ruthie and Timothy seemed to be in a meditative (or perhaps catatonic) state. The only thing that kept me awake was Guthrie's exuberance and my determination to see if Alice ever baked marijuana-laced brownies. There was a lot of marijuana smoking in the movie but, not once, did Alice contaminate baked goods. Hmmm, maybe Guthrie's brownies were fine after all.

As the closing credits played, Guthrie shouted, "Brownies for everyone!" which sent our snoozing companions halfway to the ceiling.

I fetched the pan and Guthrie downed a cake immediately. Timothy demurred, patting his stomach. (Pizza was enough pollution for his bodily temple, I suspected.) I took one and nibbled a corner cautiously. Chewing slowly, I searched for any hint of a grassy ingredient. Nope, they tasted like regular old Duncan Hines—probably the double fudge mix I used to bake for the kids.

Penny Sue arched a brow at me, an obvious question if the dessert was safe to eat. I nodded and took a big bite. That's all she needed, Penny Sue dove in like a starving orphan. I swear she ate at least four. Even Ruthie finally relented and had one. She seemed pleasantly surprised.

Guthrie was down to pressing his forefinger on the crumbs and licking it when the doorbell rang. I instinctively checked the clock. Seven-thirty, still light. My spine stiffened. Please, not another emergency.

Penny Sue glanced at us apprehensively as she headed for the door. A moment later she returned with a wide smile. She was holding a yellow rose.

"Another rose," Ruthie exclaimed. "What does the card say?"

Penny Sue sashayed to the kitchen and arranged the yellow rose in the vase with the now withering pink one. Playing the scene for all it was worth—honestly, it was worse than the melodrama of *Alice's Restaurant*—she slowly opened the envelope, read the card, and grinned like the Cheshire cat in another Alice story.

"What does it say?" Ruthie pressed.

Penny Sue tittered. "I'm still thinking about you," she read. "What does yellow mean?" she asked Ruthie.

"Joy and freedom. The roses are obviously related, do you still think it's from Yuri?"

Penny Sue toyed with her emerald necklace, an heirloom from her mother. "I don't know. Joy and freedom sorta sounds like Rich, doesn't it?"

"Yuri?" Guthrie bellowed before Ruthie could respond. "Are you talking about that Russian, criminal realtor who keeps asking me about Nana King?"

Penny Sue shot Guthrie the evil eye. "We don't know he's a criminal." She glared at me. "That's mere speculation."

Timothy was as smart as he was good looking. In a flash he was on his feet and unplugging the VCR. "I have an early meeting tomorrow. We really must be leaving." He slung the recorder under his arm and snatched the brownie pan. Guthrie took the hint and struggled up on his crutches. "We appreciate your hospitality, ..." Timothy said loudly, "and patience," he whispered to Ruthie and me.

"Yeah, man, it's been a blast. Isn't Alice cool? I'm happy you finally tasted my brownies. I'll bake a giant batch for the race." Guthrie glanced at me. "I left out the nuts so you could have some."

My face grew hot, remembering I'd fibbed about being allergic to nuts to avoid the first batch. "That was very thoughtful," I mumbled. "I enjoyed the show." *Liar, liar, pants on fire.* Well, as Grammy Martin used to say, *Let he who is without sin cast the first stone!* Sorry, Grammy, I'm pulling a two stoner this time.

Gushing Southern peace and light, Penny Sue followed the two men to the door. What returned was more akin to Attilla the Hun. "Yuri is not a crook," she stated angrily, arms folded over her chest.

I cackled. "Geez, you sound like Richard Nixon."

"I do not!" She flashed a mean look as she headed for the kitchen to pour a glass of wine. "Guthrie doesn't know anything. That was the dumbest movie I've ever seen."

"Or didn't see," I snickered. "You snored through most of it."

"Snore?!" She chugged her wine indignantly.

I tried to hide my grin. "Okay, breathed heavily; plus every now and then you choked and gurgled."

Penny Sue's eyes turned to saucers. "Choke and gurgle?! I do not!"

Ruthie dipped her chin. "Yes, you do."

"You're kidding," she said, horrified.

I bit the inside of my lip to stop laughing. "You do snore … have for a long time. So what? If you didn't snore, you'd be perfect, and who wants to be perfect? Perfect is boring."

She took the bottle of Chardonnay by the neck and refilled her glass. "I may have a minor flaw or two, but I know I don't snore. Men snore!"

"Women do, too," Ruthie said. "It can be a sign of sleep apnea, especially the choking and gurgling. I was going to say something—"

"What the hell is sleep apnea?" Penny Sue held up the wine bottle. Ruthie and I both gave her a thumbs-up. If ever there was a situation for wine among friends, this was it. Snoring was not a topic Southern women want to discuss.

A Southern woman does not sweat, she glistens, glows—or in extreme cases—perspires. A Southern woman does not wear patent leather shoes after five PM or white (except winter white, which is really cream) after Labor Day. Lord knows, a Southern woman may breathe heavily—after all, it is hot in the South—but she does not snore! No question, not done. Period.

Penny Sue handed us our drinks. "Is sleep apnea a disease, like malaria or something? What makes you such an expert, Ruthie?"

Ruthie sipped her Chardonnay. "It's not a disease; it's a condition. Poppa's housekeeper has it. Her snoring used to shake the walls—kept Poppa and Mr. Wong awake all night. Poppa finally mentioned it to his doctor, who told him she probably had an obstruction of the airway that occurs when people sleep on their backs. Poppa sent her for tests, and she tested positive, big time. Now she sleeps with a mask that keeps her windpipe open, so she doesn't snore."

Penny Sue's face contorted with horror, as if Ruthie had suggested a tracheotomy. "What kind of mask?"

"It covers her nose and blows air down her windpipe."

"Oh gawd!" Penny Sue's hand fluttered to her heart. "You don't really think I have it, do you?"

"Wouldn't hurt to be tested when you get home," Ruthie said. "It can damage your heart."

"Lord have mercy!" Penny Sue started rubbing her chest. "Is there a cure other than the stupid mask? That would kinda screw up your love life. Who wants to sleep with Darth Vader?"

Ruthie dipped her chin apologetically. "The condition seems to come on with age, excess weight, allergies, and alcohol."

Penny Sue's eyes shot darts. "I am not old or fat!"

I noticed she left out alcohol.

"I didn't say that," Ruthie added hastily. "As we age, muscles, like the windpipe, naturally lose tone, and our metabolism slows down."

Penny Sue stalked to the refrigerator and returned with a large jar of olives. She dumped some in a bowl and popped one into her mouth. "Ruthie, you're anorexic. You're hardly one to talk about metabolism."

Ruthie grabbed a handful of olives and downed them all. "I am not anorexic. I'm blessed with a high metabolism. You saw me eat a brownie."

"Half!"

"Whole!"

Yikes, this was going nowhere! And I was not in the mood for bickering. Best to change the subject. "Who do you think sent the rose?" I asked Penny Sue.

She sighed. "I thought it was Yuri. Now I'm not sure. Maybe it was Rich."

"Who made the delivery?" I asked.

"New Smyrna Florist. They apologized for running late."

"We'll call them tomorrow and see if we can get a name."

Another big sigh. "I can't believe Yuri's a crook. He seemed like a nice guy."

Boy, I'd heard that one before. Penny Sue was impetuous and hardly the best judge of male character, especially if the male was good looking, sad, or seemed to have money. "Guthrie and I think he has bad vibes," I said. "Money-grubbing vibes. You have to admit his interest in Mrs. King seemed mercenary."

Penny Sue ate a few olives and started drumming her fingers on the counter. "It's still light. Let's go back to Yuri's office and check out the flyers in his window."

"Are you serious?" Ruthie asked.

"Hell, yes. Grab the halogen flashlight."

Ten minutes later, Penny Sue parked around the corner and once again cajoled Ruthie into checking Yuri's window. "You're the logical choice. He's met Leigh and me."

"You don't think this big yellow Mercedes is a give away?" Ruthie snagged the flashlight and headed down the street angrily. She wasn't gone long. "No units in Sea Dunes listed on the flyers." She slammed her door.

"See, Yuri isn't a crook," Penny Sue said smugly as she put the car in gear, made a U-turn, and headed back across the North Causeway Bridge.

"Maybe," I replied pensively.

Penny Sue stared at me. "What do you mean 'maybe?'"

"If he were involved in a plot to buy up Sea Dunes, he wouldn't post it on his window."

"You're right," Ruthie said. "The listings were all his own. If he was going door-to-door searching for a unit, it would have sold right away and never been listed. A realtor could probably tell us if anything has sold recently, even if it wasn't officially on the market. Don't know a realtor, do you, Leigh?"

"As a matter of fact, I do—a volunteer at the center." I snatched Penny Sue's cell phone from its cradle and dialed. "Betsy, would you do me a favor?" I explained what I needed. She promised to check and call me at the condo.

It didn't take her long. We'd just returned and settled before the TV when Betsy phoned.

"Three units have sold in the last month." I read from my scribbles. "Unit 20C from Wilson Stanton to BB Corp., Unit 14A from Johnson Family Trust to Samuel Adams, and Unit 34B from Naomi King to Magilevich LLC. Naomi King—that's Nana! She's already sold her condo and Magilevich sounds Russian."

Penny Sue snatched the pad from my hand. "Let me see that." She studied the name quietly. "I wonder if there's anyway we can find out who owns this corporation?"

"Sure," Ruthie said, fetching her computer from the bedroom. "It's probably online. Most states have their records posted on the Internet these days." She typed in Florida.gov and had a list of corporations in a matter of minutes. "Here, Magilevich LLC," she pointed at the screen. "Registered agent is a lawyer in Tallahassee. It's a profit company headquartered in Atlantic City, New Jersey."

"What about BB Corp.?" Penny Sue asked.

Ruthie stroked the keyboard. "A profit corporation headquartered in New York."

"I wonder if there's a way to tell what the units sold for," Penny Sue mused.

"I think the county property appraiser posts that information."

In a matter of minutes, Ruthie found the Web site and located the sales. She glanced up at me. "What do you suppose condos in this complex are worth?"

"$400,000 to $600,000, depending on the location."

"All of these units went in the $300,000s."

"Even the beachfront condo? That's impossible!"

Ruthie cocked her eyebrow. "Well, it did."

Something smelled, I told myself, and it wasn't the scent of a rose.

Chapter 14

August 25

Volusia County is sometimes called the home of stock car racing. Old-time North Carolina moonshine-runners may dispute this claim, but Daytona Beach and Volusia County gave the moonshine drivers legitimacy and made it a sport. That's because stock car racing and NASCAR's birth can be traced to the beach/street races held at Daytona Beach in the late 1940s, which eventually evolved into "The World's Greatest Race—The Daytona 500."

While the Daytona races may be the most famous, that track isn't the only speedway in the county. About twenty miles south, at the intersection of county routes 44 and 415, is the site of racing action most weekends. On one corner is the New Smyrna Speedway, the home of FASCAR—NASCAR's Florida cousin. A half-mile stock car track, the speedway also holds eclectic competitions for virtually any motorized contraption that moves—this includes motorcycles, trucks, school buses, go-karts, mini-cup cars, and the wildly popular bag race.

While races at the New Smyrna Speedway are known to get down and dirty, the real dirt is across Rt. 415 at the unpaved track for mud racing. A couple of Saturdays a month, trucks with very big tires bump and slosh through rocks and mud.

"You're sure we're not going to do mud racing, right?" Penny Sue asked as she pulled into a parking space next to a grey Toyota.

"Yes, Chris nixed it—too messy." I cocked my thumb at the Toyota. "That's her new car. It's really cool, an electric and gas hybrid."

"Too small."

"You'd be surprised, it's roomier than it looks. Besides, it gets great gas mileage," I said.

"Well, you won't catch me in one. Besides, I'm not sure I'd fit." Penny Sue swung her huge Louis Vuitton handbag over her shoulder and clicked the Mercedes' locks. She was decked out in a black bodysuit with leopard print capris. If you added a black riding helmet, knee-high boots, and a crop, she could have passed for an overweight jockey or maybe a dominatrix. Ruthie and I wore jeans, tee shirts, and jogging shoes, not exactly sure what was required for racing.

We trooped through the open chain link front gate, past the concession stands and bleachers to the edge of the track. Chris stood in the pit area talking to a man in a white cowboy hat and a woman in a pickup truck with a trailer carrying a miniature racecar.

"Magawd," Penny Sue blurted as we crossed the track, "that car's smaller than your bug. There's no way I can drive it."

"Chris and I already decided she'd drive the mini-car, Ruthie and I will do the bag race, and you'll drive the school bus. You'll fit in the bus, don't you think?" I said over my shoulder.

"Very funny." Penny Sue poked my arm, hard, and then flashed her most winning smile at Chris and the others.

Chris introduced us to Andrew James Clyde Hart, the track owner, and Annie Bronson, owner of the mini-cup car.

"Just call me Andrew," Mr. Hart said with a wink.

Penny Sue winked back, as she gave him the once over. I shook my head. Incorrigible.

"Annie's agreed to let us use her new racer." Chris interrupted Penny Sue's flirtation.

Annie cocked her thumb at the tiny, flat grey car. "Don't worry, that's primer, it hasn't been painted yet."

Penny Sue's eyes lit up. "Annie, if we pay for everything, could we have it painted yellow, with a daffodil on the hood?" Penny Sue faced us, eyes aglow. "And, we could have yellow racing suits made with daffodil patches. The school bus is already yellow. What do you think?"

Chris cut her eyes at Penny Sue. "I think you've watched too much of Paris Hilton. The Daytona Racing Experience has agreed to lend us fireproof suits and helmets. We have to wear them." Andrew nodded. "This is a charity race, not a fashion show. The money would be better spent on hurricane victims than designer outfits."

Penny Sue tilted her chin regally. "It never hurts to stand out in a crowd. Besides, it'll help us get pledges for our team. Why, it may even draw media attention." She wiggled her fanny.

Andrew glanced away, stifling a grin.

"A spiffy group of divorced women would surely get a lot of support. We might even make the *Today Show* or *Good Morning America*. Think what that would do for contributions to the hurricane fund."

The Southern belle and savvy New Yorker stared at each other for a full minute. I held my breath, afraid a fistfight might break out. Chris finally broke the silence. "Good merchandising—you may have something there. What do you think, Annie? It's your car."

Focused on Penny Sue's leopard capris, Annie was obviously skeptical. "It's my new car. I'm planning to paint it pink. The Pink Panther."

Penny Sue gave her the palms up. "We promise to return it to you in exactly the shape it is now." She waved grandly. "In fact, we'll pay for your new paint job and our new suits and helmets. Won't we?"

"Penny Sue, I don't have that kind of money," I objected.

She stared at Ruthie. "We do. Right, Ruthie? Come on, this is for charity. Think of all of those poor people with damaged roofs and huge insurance deductibles, or worse, no insurance at all! This would give us visibility and the chance to draw national contributions. Besides, you and your dad have more money than the Saudis. You'll spring for it, won't you?"

"It is a good cause," Ruthie started hesitantly. "Oh, hell. I'm in. But, it's only because national attention would generate contributions. Those camera-mugging rich people get on my nerves. I'm not looking for personal notoriety."

Penny Sue planned to handle the camera-mugging department, I was sure.

"Good enough?" Penny Sue asked Annie.

Annie glanced at Chris.

"Don't worry, those two have money to burn," Chris assured her.

Annie held out her hand. "Free paint job? A deal."

Andrew headed to the back lot to get a school bus while Chris and Annie pushed the tiny car off the carrier. The car looked smaller on the ground—it didn't even come to our waists!

Annie grabbed the top and flipped it open. "This is the door."

"Thank the Lord," Penny Sue said. "If we had to slide in the window like NASCAR guys, we'd be plumb out of luck." She sized up Ruthie. "You're anorexic, and I don't think you'd fit."

"Hush, I'm not anorexic. Listen to Annie."

"Basically," Annie started, "this is a go-kart with a car body. But it's a fast little booger and can get up to seventy-five miles per hour." She pointed at the front floorboard. "Like a go-kart, there aren't any gears. All you have is a gas pedal and a brake. Be very careful with the brake. Hit that hard when you have some speed, and you'll go into a spin every time."

Annie fetched fireproof coveralls, gloves, and a helmet from her truck and handed them to Chris. "You might as well take it for a spin."

We all studied the paraphernalia as Chris pulled the coveralls over her clothes. Ruthie blanched.

"What's wrong?" I asked.

"The suit's one piece."

"So?"

"We'll have to get undressed to go to the bathroom."

Since Ruthie peed at least a dozen times a day, I understood her concern. She wasn't hot on this race, anyway. The one-piece suit could be a deal buster. Thankfully, Annie came to our rescue.

"If you're going to have them custom-made, you can get two piece suits. I prefer those myself. I know of a good local supplier for custom suits and helmets. I'm sure I have the card in my truck."

"See, no problem," I said blithely.

Ruthie was still worried. "We have to wear a helmet?" she asked.

"Of course," Annie answered. "It's standard equipment."

"I thought I could tolerate the bag, because it would be loose-fitting. A helmet and a bag? I'm claustrophobic—I'm not sure I can handle that," Ruthie said.

Penny Sue slapped her on the back. "Sure you can, just say your mantra. We'll practice wearing our helmets at home, so you get the hang of it. You'll be fine."

Ruthie's scowl said she didn't buy a word of it.

The helmet didn't faze Chris, who put it on, climbed in the car, and strapped in. Annie connected the tethers from the Hutchins device's shoulder straps to Chris' helmet.

"What's that?" Penny Sue asked.

"The thing that might have saved Dale Earnhardt's life," Annie said grimly. "They keep your head from snapping back and forth. Everyone wears them now, even though they limit mobility."

"I'll say," Chris exclaimed. "I can only see straight ahead. Where are the mirrors in this thing? How will I know when it's safe to pass or make a run for it?"

"Your spotter will tell you."

"My what?"

Annie rolled her eyes. "Your spotter. A person who stands on top of the grandstand and tells you want to do." She pointed at a platform over the box seats. "There's a microphone in your helmet. For example, if your spotter says, 'Inside,' it means a car's about to pass you on the left. 'Inside, inside' means two are going to pass on the left. 'Outside' says someone's coming on the right. Your spotter will also tell you about wrecks, spinouts, and how to avoid them—like, 'go low,' 'go high,' whatever. Your spotter is your best friend. Always remember, hold your line unless your spotter tells you otherwise."

"Will you spot for me?" Chris asked Annie.

Annie grinned. "I wouldn't let you drive my car otherwise. There's no traffic, so run a few laps."

Chris turned the key and the tiny car roared to life. Far from timid, Chris floored it and peeled out of the pit area as Andrew entered from the rear in a beat-up school bus.

"Think that's big enough?" I asked Penny Sue.

She curled her lip at me.

As Chris merrily lapped the track—going high and low, slow, fast, and spinning into the infield once (I thought Annie would have a cow)—Andrew acquainted Penny Sue with the school bus. Everything had been stripped out except the driver's high back chair, the first row of seats, and bare necessities. Basically, the bus wasn't a lot different than the go-kart. The driver's seat had been outfitted with an elaborate shoulder harness/seat belt system including clips for the Hutchins device. Fortunately, the bus had an automatic transmission, so there was only a gas pedal and brake to contend with. And unlike the mini-car, it had mirrors—lots of mirrors.

"I don't have a fire suit for you," Andrew said. "It doesn't matter as long as you go slowly to get the feel for driving the bus. When you get your suit and helmet, you can come back and do some real racing."

Annie finally waved Chris in, commenting that the mini-car must be nearly out of gas. Chris removed her helmet, grinning, and climbed out through the roof. "Awesome!"

Meanwhile, with Andrew coaching from the seat behind, Penny Sue inched the bus out of the pit at about five mph. The first few laps were very slow, but by the sixth lap, Penny Sue floored the bus on the straightaway in front of the pits and promptly fishtailed when she braked for turn one. After that, she made a few more leisurely laps and kept her foot off the brake.

"That's tougher than it looks," she said, wiping perspiration from her upper lip when she returned. "The rear end is really loose. Boy, get a few of these on the track together and you've got a traffic jam."

I had to agree. "Do you think it's too much for you to handle?" I asked.

"Of course not. It'll merely take a little practice. If I can evade terrorists and ride a Harley, I can surely master a school bus."

"What about the car for the bag race?" Ruthie asked Andrew.

"That's up to you. Most people buy a cheap junker."

Ruthie went wide-eyed again. "Why? Are there lots of wrecks?"

"Nothing serious. After all, no one is going fast, still you should expect some fender-benders."

"Do you recommend a particular brand of car?"

"Something cheap and sturdy."

Annie gave us the card for the racing shop, promised to call her painter, and headed out. Famished from the morning workout, Team DAFFODILS, as Chris called it, headed to Pub 44 for lunch. We found a table in the windowed corner of the backroom, next to the bar. The place was hopping, primarily with locals on their lunch hour. As we waited for our taco salads and sandwiches, Penny Sue called the race shop and wheedled a fitting for custom suits at three o'clock. Meanwhile, Chris used my cell to phone an old friend who owned a used car lot.

"He has a 1997 Toyota Corolla he'll sell for $3,000, since it's me and for a good cause. A little body damage, the upholstery's stained, but it's mechanically sound, and has relatively new tires. If we have it painted and don't bang it up too bad, he'll buy it back for what we paid. He says the Corolla is rated as one of the safest cars in crash tests." Chris raised a questioning brow at Penny Sue and Ruthie, who would have to finance the purchase.

"I'd feel comfortable in a smaller car like a Corolla," Ruthie said to Penny Sue.

Penny Sue nodded and finished chewing. "Tell him to hold the car. We'll swing by after our fitting."

The rest of the afternoon was a blur. The helmet specialist happened to be at the racing shop when we arrived. So, he assisted with the fitting—business was slow because of the hurricanes—and promised to have the helmets ready by the next afternoon. We picked yellow fabric for the suits and found a commercially available daffodil that Penny Sue licensed for the uniforms, helmets, mini-car, Corolla, and school bus—yep, she was on a Paris Hilton roll!

Although Chris and Ruthie rolled their eyes, I secretly thought it was kind of cool. Especially since I didn't have to pay for it.

The seamstress agreed to rush the order and we left for our final chore—to buy a vehicle for the bag race. We followed Chris to the car lot where Penny Sue bought the Toyota. After that, Chris baled out—I could tell Penny Sue was getting on her nerves—and we headed home.

It was close to six o'clock when we pulled into the parking lot and found the weird fisherman on the bench on our neighbor's stoop. His fishing machine propped against the wall, he sat slumped forward, head in his hands.

"Lord, he can't be dead," Ruthie exclaimed.

Penny Sue slammed the car into park. "I think he'd be sprawled on the ground in that case. He must be sick."

Ruthie was out of the car in a flash. We were close behind.

"I'm borderline diabetic. I think I fished too long," he said without looking up. "Too much sun. Not enough food."

Penny Sue reached in her handbag, pulled out a snack-sized Snickers, and ripped off the wrapper. "Here, take a bite of this."

He popped the whole thing in his mouth. A few minutes later he straightened up. "Thank you, I feel better." He started to stand up, but collapsed back on the bench.

"Come sit with us for a while," Ruthie said. "We'll make you a sandwich."

"I'm okay, really," he said feebly.

"Bullshit," Penny Sue snapped, grabbing his arm. I took the other while Ruthie rolled his fishing gear. "You're coming with us unless you want to deal with me." Penny Sue said, her face an inch from his.

He grinned. "In that case, I think I'll come to your house."

To this point we didn't even know his name. We'd always referred to him as the weird fisherman.

"What's your name?" Penny Sue said as we half-dragged him down the hall.

"Larry. Larry Smith."

We eased him onto the sofa, which gave me a major déjà vu of Guthrie.

"What do you need?" Ruthie asked. "Should we give you sugar, carbs, protein, fat? Heavens, it's all so confusing!"

"The Snickers did the sugar trick. If you have lunch meat or cheese—protein—that will tide me over."

Ruthie stuck her head in the refrigerator. "We have everything. Cheddar? Provolone? Plumrose ham on crackers. Name it."

"Cheddar on crackers."

"Coming up." In a matter of minutes Ruthie had crackers and cheese on a plate before Larry and watched expectantly as he ate one. "Are you feeling better?"

The corner of his mouth turned up. "If I'm not, will you give me CPR?"

Ruthie scowled. "No, Penny Sue does CPR, and all you'll get is chest pounding. No mouth-to-mouth. That's the new technique, you know."

He checked out Penny Sue. "Not necessary, I feel much better. I was being a smartass. I have daughters your age," he said sheepishly. "Truly, I'm a harmless old man who only wants to fish. I'm sorry to have troubled you." He leaned forward to stand, but sank back into the sofa.

"Maybe we should call a doctor," I said.

"I'll be fine as soon as the cheese gets into my system. I knew I stayed out too long, but I was fighting a big one and couldn't give up."

"You sound like my father," Penny Sue said. "He's nearly killed himself trying to land fish. He's thinking of moving down here when he retires. Y'all would be two peas in a pod."

Larry nibbled another saltine. "I'd like to meet him ... always looking for a fishing buddy." He popped the last of the cracker into his mouth and chewed. "You were gone all day. What are you up to?"

"You keep tabs on us?" Penny Sue snapped.

"Let's face it, aside from the murders, you ladies are the most interesting thing around here. You're not the average, dried-up prunes we usually see on the beach. Your absence is noticed by everyone."

Penny Sue's ire dissolved. "Why, thank you, sir," she said in her best Southern drawl. "We've been practicing for a charity race to benefit hurricane victims."

"Race? Like running?" He looked amused.

"No, a motorized marathon out at the speedway. There are three parts: mini-cars, a bag race, and a school bus race." Penny Sue wiggled her brows saucily. "I'm driving the school bus."

"I'm an audio expert. I used to work with stock car headsets. I can improve the range and clarity, plus filter out extraneous noise. Many a race has been lost because the driver didn't hear an instruction. If you'd like, I'd be happy to beef up your equipment."

"That's very nice." Ruthie grinned smugly. "See, there are no accidents. We need help, and he shows up at our front door."

Larry stood, his strength back. "I needed help, and you came along with a Snickers. Let me know when you get your helmets."

I nodded. "Unless something happens, they should be ready tomorrow afternoon."

Chapter 15

August 26-31

Ruthie sipped coffee, eyes glued to the television.

"Good morning." I rounded the counter and poured a mug for myself. She never gave me a glance. Was she mad at me? I couldn't think of anything I'd done to offend her. "What's up?" I asked.

"That tropical wave in the Atlantic has been upgraded to a tropical storm. Frances. Tropical Storm Frances. It's moving west-northwest. If it maintains that course, it'll hit Florida."

"Don't worry, it won't. Danielle stayed over water, and Earl went south and never came close."

Ruthie gave me a moist, doe-eyed look. "Remember my vision of a big storm? The one where we should leave and go to St. Augustine? I think this is it."

Her intensity made me uneasy. "If it is, we'll leave," I promised. "We'll keep an eye on the storm and make hotel reservations. If push comes to shove, we know we can stay in Chris' store."

"I'm getting bad vibes about that, too. Evil and greed surround us."

"Honey, evil and greed are the state of the world." Penny Sue bounced into the room wearing her red, embroidered kimono. "If a storm's coming, we're buying a battery-operated TV today. We can't wait or they'll all be sold. When's Frances supposed to hit?" she asked, pouring a cup of coffee.

"They're not sure ... probably about a week," Ruthie said.

"Next week? Labor Day weekend? That'll mess up our race. We've spent a fortune on this thing—a hurricane cannot hit," Penny Sue declared.

"Anything can happen in a week. It will probably blow out or turn north," I said.

"Right," Penny Sue agreed. "We should still get the TV and put a rush on all our race preparations."

There was no need to rush the helmets. Our helmet specialist called at nine and said they were finished, except for the daffodil decals, which should arrive first of the week. If we were going to be home, he'd drop them by our condo because he had another delivery in our area.

"Sure, come on," Penny Sue said.

Apparently he'd called from the parking lot. Five minutes later we had our newspaper and four sparkly, yellow racing helmets, along with two headsets for the spotter and crew chief.

"This is cool," Penny Sue said, pulling on the helmet marked with a "P". "I'm going to kick butt in that bus race." She flipped the visor down and strutted around the condo barefoot. She was still wearing her red kimono, which really "set off" her ensemble, as Cujo, the TV fashion expert, might say.

Set off? Blast off was more like it, I thought wryly.

"Come on, put yours on," which, with her visor down, came out as a muffled, "Con en, poo youse eh."

Ruthie and I got her drift and complied, but left our visors open.

"Boy, it's heavy," I commented, feeling like a fool in the helmet and my pink chenille robe.

"Youse ge ute ta it. Ah fee ta saa waw ..."

I reached over and opened Penny Sue's visor. "We can't understand a word you're saying."

She screwed her mouth. "I said, 'you'll get used to it. I felt the same way when I first wore my Harley helmet.' Flip your visors down. The yellow tint really brightens the room."

I lowered my visor, careful to leave an opening at the bottom. Although I wasn't as claustrophobic as Ruthie, I wasn't ready to be locked down, either.

Ruthie pushed her visor a couple of inches and tilted her head forward to see through the plastic. "It does make things brighter." She immediately pushed the visor back up.

"Y'all are chickens. Lock down your visors. You can breathe fine. Really."

"I'll do it in my own time," Ruthie said forcefully. "The weight of this thing is bad enough for now."

"We don't have time to waste. It's only a week and a half until the race." Penny Sue took her helmet off. "You should wear yours as much as possible so you get used to it." She wagged her finger at Ruthie.

Ruthie snatched the paper and huffed to the kitchen counter. "Watch it. If you're not careful, you may be short-circuited by a stream of saline, if you get my drift." Jaws locked, Ruthie hunched over the paper and started to read.

Still wearing the helmet with her sea blue, silk pajamas, Ruthie was a veritable sight. If only I'd had a camera handy, her pose was worth a fortune. Of course, the taser belonged to her, too. Best I didn't have a camera, on second thought.

Penny Sue started for her bedroom to get dressed, and I had my coffee midway to my lips when Ruthie squealed.

"Oh, my God! Listen to this: 'Key Witness In Mob Trial Found Dead!'"

Penny Sue and I were peering over her shoulder in a millisecond. "Jack Simpson, a twenty-year-veteran of the FBI and DEA, was found dead in his room at a plush Orlando hotel this morning. The cause of death has not been disclosed. Authorities will only say his death appears suspicious.

"Mr. Simpson was in Orlando for the trial of a New Jersey Mafia boss who faces a long list of charges including drug smuggling, murder, and money-laundering."

Ruthie and I turned toward each other, knocking our helmets together hard. I stumbled backward; her head ricocheted into Penny Sue's boobs.

"Ouch," Penny Sue cried. "Be careful. Y'all have protection, I don't."

"This is where the frozen bra might come in handy." I tapped Ruthie's shoulder. "Good news, I didn't feel anything, did you?"

"No, I didn't. I guess these expensive helmets actually work." Ruthie slapped the newspaper. "What about this article? The agent must have been in town for Al's case, don't you think? And if Al's buddies succeeded in killing a DEA agent, we're sitting ducks."

"I'll bet the guy who fell from the balcony was trying to kill us," I said weakly.

Penny Sue rolled her eyes. "Well, we weren't sitting ducks in that case. He was."

"Probably killed by the Russian mob—the guy found in the dumpster." Ruthie was getting shrill.

"Don't jump to conclusions," Penny Sue said. "There are lots of Federal drug cases heard in Orlando, and New Jersey is the connection for a slew of criminal activity."

"How can we find out if this agent was on Al's case?" Ruthie asked. "Do we have the number of the judicial assistant who keeps postponing our depositions?"

"Calm down. I've got it, and I'll give her a call now. If she won't tell me, I'll telephone Daddy," Penny Sue said, heading for her bedroom to make the calls.

No sooner had her door closed than the doorbell rang. Ruthie and I stared at each other. "I can't go," she said. "My nipples show through these pajamas. You have on a robe."

She had a good point. No proper woman would answer the front door with protruding nipples. "We could ignore it," I suggested.

"What if it's the Feds here to protect us or something?"

"All right." I had the door half open before I realized I was still wearing my helmet. Too late to get the darned thing off. Fortunately, it was Guthrie. Unfortunately, Woody had pulled into the parking lot and was getting out of his car.

"Oh, cool! That's for the race, right? Turn around. You look sharp, girl." He clapped his hands. "I was on the deck having coffee when the man delivered them and couldn't wait to see your outfits."

I pulled the helmet off and cradled it under my arm. Woody now stood behind Guthrie. I nodded hello, very conscious of my faded chenille robe. "We only have the helmets," I told Guthrie. "Our suits won't be ready until Monday. Come back then, and we'll give you a fashion show." I noticed Larry, the fisherman, stop in the background, watching.

Clean underwear and your best nightgown, Grammy always said. Wish I'd listened. This place was like Grand Central Station. Here I was in my rattiest robe—cradling a yellow racing helmet—and all of New Smyrna Beach was at my front door. At least Guthrie didn't notice anything but the helmet.

"I've planned the menu for the pit crew," he said excitedly. "Naturally, brownies—my signature dish. Then, I thought peanut butter cookies. Peanut butter has protein, so the energy lasts. Of course, lots of oxygenated-water—that was Timothy's idea." Guthrie gave me a big smile. "He drinks it all the time. Works wonders. On the peanut butter cookies, I could throw in some chocolate chips if you want a little punch. Timothy suggested I mix in some lecithin and B vitamins. The cookies are kind of heavy, but taste okay."

I glanced at Woody, who was shifting from foot to foot impatiently. "You're the pro; whatever you want is fine with us." I gave Guthrie a thumbs-up.

He winked then peered over his shoulder at Woody. "I thought I smelled garlic. I'll get back to you about the menu, Leigh. I think Mr. Sour Puss is in a hurry."

"Thanks, Guthrie," I called as he walked away and Woody stepped up to the screen door.

"I'd invite you in, but as you can see, we're not dressed."

"No need." He focused on the helmet. "Getting ready for the race, huh?"

Flatter your enemies, then go for the groin, Grandpa Martin used to say. Maybe it would work with Woody. "Yes, we thought we should have helmets that fit properly. We're novices, you know."

"Good move. No sense getting a head injury for charity. The Driving Experience helmets probably *are* too big for you ladies."

What do you know? Grandpa's axiom worked! Of course, Woody's comment assumed we'd have a wreck. "I heard you entered a team. I think it's wonderful that so many people are willing to help the hurricane victims. Let's hope there isn't any more damage, like from Frances."

"It'll probably turn north. Anyway, I'm here to warn you that a witness for Al's case was murdered. Y'all need to be very careful. Penny Sue should carry her gun."

Penny Sue should carry her gun? This from Woody? Things were serious. "What about our liquid taser—can we carry that?"

"I wouldn't take it shopping, but in the car, yes. Be careful. If you see anything suspicious, contact me or the police." He put his nose to the screen door. "This is serious; otherwise I wouldn't be here."

I believed that. I was certain Woody wasn't so cold-hearted he wanted to see us killed, even though a little hassle—from someone other than himself—would make his day. "Thanks for the warning. We just read about the murder in the newspaper and wondered if it was related to Al. Any information about the murders over here? Do you think they're connected?"

He stared at his shoes, a bad sign. "It's under investigation." He backed up and smiled. "I look forward to racing you at the speedway. A good cause."

"Of course, we're only amateurs hoping to get some donations from wealthy friends."

Woody nodded good-bye, a sincere good-bye for once. *Thank you, Grandpa.* Lull them with humility and kindness then kick their behinds. We'd have to do a lot of practicing, though.

Woody left, and Larry stepped up to the screen door. I felt like a woman at the supermarket deli counter. *Next*. Dressed in my worst robe—I resolved to throw it away as soon as everyone left—I now had to face Larry.

"I couldn't help but notice your helmet. May I see it?"

I looked over my shoulder and saw that Ruthie, with her nipple ripples, had scurried away to dress. I pushed open the screen door. "Sure, they just arrived, along with headsets for the spotter and crew chief."

Larry propped his fishing machine against the wall and followed me down the hall. Ruthie appeared in a sweat suit (with bra) and Penny Sue emerged from her bedroom (still in her kimono) as he sat at the counter and examined my helmet.

"Damn!" Penny Sue bellowed. "The murdered agent was working on Al's case, and the judicial assistant—little twerp—

advised us to be careful. A lot of good that does." She saw Larry sitting at the counter with my helmet and smiled sheepishly. "Sorry, Larry, I didn't know you were here. I don't usually use profanity," she drawled.

"No problem," Larry said without looking up. "I've heard that word before and a lot worse. These are good helmets. I'm happy to see you didn't scrimp. This is the most important part of your gear. Nice earpieces." He glanced around. "Where are the headsets?"

I fetched them from the credenza.

We hovered over his shoulder as he examined them. "These are nice," he finally said. "I was afraid you'd go cheap, which is why I offered to help. I can still boost the performance of these babies. Give me the helmets and headsets, and I'll make the modifications today. It's a simple process; I only need to add a piece or two. And, it won't cost you a cent. I think I have the parts in my shop. I can have the helmets back to you this afternoon."

"We'd like to pay you for your trouble," Ruthie said.

Larry waved her off. "The parts cost pennies, and I wasn't in the mood to fish today, anyway. I enjoy doing the old stuff now and then. Makes me feel useful and younger."

"We appreciate it," I said.

"Forget it. What's this stuff about a murdered agent and you should be careful?"

Penny Sue filled him in (with full drama) of our encounter with the Italian Mafia and the possibility we may have to give depositions for the mob boss' trial, which had been postponed repeatedly. She explained that the agent murdered in Orlando had worked on the case.

"Worse than that," I interrupted, "Woody suggested that you carry your gun, and that we keep the liquid taser in the car."

"You're kidding," Penny Sue said. "Woody *wants* me to carry my gun?"

"Yes, and he was actually polite. Although, Woody did mention he had a team in the race," I added.

"He's trying to spook us, so we won't win," Penny Sue said.

"He seemed sincere," I replied.

Larry broke in. "Where's the box for this stuff? I'll take it home and give you the edge you need to kick Woody's skinny rear end."

Penny Sue flashed a big smile. "Right on. There's nothing I'd like better."

Ruthie boiled eggs, toasted bagels, and cut up fruit while Penny Sue and I showered and dressed. Ruthie had already announced that she needed some alone time and was going to spend the morning in meditation. I scarfed down a boiled egg and bagel as Penny Sue made arrangements with the paint shop for the Corolla and the mini-cup car.

Ruthie positioned herself on the sofa in the Lotus position, with the taser within reach.

"Happy meditating," Penny Sue said, waving a swatch of cloth from our suits. She started down the hall, then stopped abruptly. She hustled into the utility room and returned with a brown grocery bag. "If you're going to meditate, you might as well put a bag over your head, so you'll get used to it." She made a move toward Ruthie.

Ruthie grabbed the taser. "Don't you dare!"

Penny Sue tossed the bag on the coffee table. "Fine. I was only trying to help."

"Do you have your gun?" I asked as we settled in her Mercedes.

"Of course."

First, we picked up the Corolla from the car lot and took it to the paint shop. Annie's car was already there. Fortunately, there was a premixed color that matched our suits perfectly, so the cars would be painted by Tuesday or Wednesday at the latest. From there we went to Wal-Mart in search of a battery-powered TV. There was only one model available and it had a tiny black and white screen.

"I was hoping for color," Penny Sue complained. "We'd have to go all the way to Daytona Beach to get one. What do you think?"

I read the box. "This one takes ten C batteries. A color set would probably require twenty. Lets buy this one. We'll only need it for a short period, if at all."

"Good point."

We purchased the TV, two dozen batteries, and a lifetime supply of snack-sized Snickers, which were on special. As I put the package in the backseat, I caught sight of a black Taurus out of the corner of my eye. It was idling at the end of our row. Probably waiting for our space, I told myself. Still, the murder and Woody's warning had rattled me. I slid into the front seat and locked my door.

"What's wrong?" Penny Sue asked.

I told her about the car.

"It's probably not the same car, but keep your eye on it." She backed out and headed for the exit to Route 44. "Did it take our space?"

"No, it's following us. Two cars back."

"Two cars," she mused out loud. "Keeping a safe distance. They don't want us to spot them." Penny Sue hung a right onto the highway, went one block, and made a quick right back into the shopping center. "This will tell us if we're really being followed."

I watched the car in the outside mirror. "It went straight." I stretched to keep the Taurus in view. The car drove another block and doubled back into the shopping center. "Damn, it turned in at the bank."

"Hmph." Penny Sue circled the lot to the Wal-Mart entrance again. She hung a right, floored it, and ran a yellow light. Then she whipped left at the first intersection.

"See 'em?"

"Nope, I think you lost them this time. We'd better call Woody, don't you think?"

"The driver of the car wasn't his crazy old mother, was it? Did you notice any white hair?"

"The windows were tinted, so I couldn't tell who was driving. Besides, why would Pearl Woodhead follow us?"

"Because she's crazy and thinks we've caused trouble for her son. Face it, anyone who'd walk around with a fake gun must be touched in the head."

"No more than the people on the walkway with real guns," I countered.

"You're right. Call Woody."

I did. With nothing to go on except the description of the car—he laughed with I said black Ford Taurus—there wasn't anything he could do. "Next time, get a license number." So much for police protection.

The next few days were an increasingly frantic mix of weather watching and racing practice. By five PM on August 26, Frances became a Category 1 hurricane. At the same time the following day, it had jumped to a Category 3. On August 28, Frances grew even stronger, becoming a Category 4 storm, the same strength as Hurricane Andrew, which had flattened south Florida over a decade before. The only thing that kept Ruthie from hopping an airplane and going home was the fact that the storm was still very far away, and the forecasted track took it south of Florida.

There was also the matter of the race. We all took to wearing our helmets around the condo to get used to them. Penny Sue even donned hers to encourage Ruthie. We wore them watching television (primarily the Weather Channel and *CSI*), cooking, ironing—virtually the whole time we were inside, alone. Day by day, little by little, Ruthie and I lowered our visors until we were finally comfortable wearing the helmets with the visor in place.

At that point, I was finished, but Ruthie still had to contend with the bag. First, we took to leading her around the house with her helmet on, but eyes closed. Then, we taped paper over the visor and led her around. Finally, we put the largest bag we could find—so there'd be a lot of airflow—over the helmet. That was a tough nut to crack, but Ruthie eventually triumphed with a lot of chanting.

When we weren't doing helmet practice, we were racing. Penny Sue visited the track several times to drive the school bus. Chris spent every non-working hour racing the mini-car under Annie's watchful eye. As for the shiny, yellow Corolla with a big daffodil on the hood and the number twenty-two painted on the side (a master number according to Ruthie which insured luck), Ruthie drove the Toyota around *sans* helmet for a couple of days to get used to its feel. Finally, we took her to the middle school parking lot after hours, where she practiced driving with her eyes closed according to my directions. She did amazingly well. Cool, calm, and collected. Of course, the Valium Penny Sue gave Ruthie the first few times might have helped, too.

Finally off crutches, Guthrie accompanied us to several of our practices so he could rehearse refreshments. Basically, that meant a lot of oxygenated-water and brownies. We actually didn't have a pit crew, except Guthrie—and, God help us if he got hold of a microphone during the race—so Timothy agreed to mind the pits and use the second headset if needed. Annie volunteered to spot for all of our races, because she had the most experience.

As if that wasn't enough, there was the matter of sponsors and donations. After all, this was a charity race. Ruthie's dad made a healthy donation, as did the Judge and his law firm. (I know that really burned Zack, my Ex. Ha!) Chris' customers were generous, yet we still needed more money. Considering all the dough Ruthie and Penny Sue had shelled out, we hadn't collected enough to cover our expenses, though we'd always planned to donate that money. It was the principle of the thing—we should at least raise more than we spent!

The realization we were severely in the red pushed Penny Sue into action. She contacted an old friend in Atlanta, Max, who headed a PR firm. In a matter of hours, Max arranged interviews with a local newspaper and television station. He sent over a photographer to take promo pictures of us in our suits, posing beside the cars. The photographer also did a short video, with shots of hurricane damage and interviews with a couple of victims who either were uninsured or could not afford the huge deductibles. Max sent copies of the tape to all the major television stations plus *CNN*, *Oprah, Today Show*, *The View,* and *Good Morning America.* The video was aired in Atlanta, thanks to Max's connections, and brought in pledges of over $10,000 in one day.

Yep, we were in high cotton, so to speak, until mid-day Tuesday, August 31. That's when the shit hit the fan. Frances, a Category 4 hurricane, turned toward Florida.

Chapter 16

August 31-September 3

The phone rang as I started down the hall. Decked out in our race suits, helmets in hand, we were ready to walk out the door for an interview with an Orlando television station.

"Don't answer. We'll be late," Penny Sue said.

I checked caller ID. "It's Chris." I leaned across the counter and snatched the receiver. "Don't worry, we're about to leave."

"That's not why I'm calling. Did you hear about Frances?"

I ducked my head and glanced sidelong at Ruthie. "Uh, no."

"It's headed this way. I received a call from Andrew's assistant a few minutes ago. She said there's talk of school closings and evacuations. If schools close, they're going to postpone the race."

"Fine by me. We could use more practice. We're still meeting the TV crew, right?"

"Yeah, I just wanted to alert you so you can brace Ruthie. I know how skittish she is about storms. I don't want her to hear it from the TV crew and freak out. Not going to be much of an interview if she starts screaming or chanting."

I giggled. "Good point. See you in a few minutes."

Penny Sue guided the DAFFODILS Corolla onto A1A, all the while fiddling with the air conditioning switch. "This AC sucks. I guess you can't expect much for $3,000. What did Chris want?"

"Just checking in, she's en route to the speedway. She also said the race may be cancelled if schools close."

"Frances," Ruthie exclaimed. "The hurricane's headed this way, isn't it? I knew something was wrong. I knew we should have watched the Weather Channel instead of *CSI* last night." She pulled a piece of paper from her pocketbook and furiously punched buttons on her cell phone.

"What are you doing?"

"Making reservations, if we're not too late. I printed out the phone numbers for hotels in St. Augustine. I had a feeling this was going to happen. Damn, this is Labor Day weekend." She let out a loud sigh. "Casa Monica? Do you have anything available for Thursday through Tuesday?" She glanced at Penny Sue and winked. "A deluxe one bedroom suite for $349. Terrific." Ruthie pulled out her American Express card and read the number. "Guarantee that for late arrival. Thank you." She slumped back in her seat. "We were lucky, that was the only vacancy they had."

"I guess so at $349 per night." I said, still in the penny-pinching mode following my divorce. Although my settlement was fair, thanks to Judge Parker, I hadn't fully come to grips with being on my own.

"That's cheap, after all it's peak season and a holiday weekend," Ruthie said.

"I've stayed at the Casa Monica. It's very plush and old. Built like a fortress of coquina stone. That thing won't blow down, for sure." Penny Sue drove through open gates at the speedway to the lane that opened onto the track. The TV news van was already there and a tall, lean reporter talked to Andrew and Chris. One man sat in the bleachers; I supposed the track's public relations manager.

The TV cameraman motioned for Penny Sue to park in front of the low pit area wall emblazoned with "New Smyrna Speedway." A video assistant angled the four of us, dressed in our suits and cradling our helmets, at the rear of the car. Andrew was positioned slightly to the right of the number twenty-two, which gave a good view of the big daffodil on the hood. The cameraman stood on a platform so he could shoot down.

All together, the TV crew shot close to forty-five minutes of tape, though I was sure it would be cut and clipped to a segment of two to three minutes. Andrew led off explaining the charitable purpose of the race, an overview of the participants, total pledges received to date, and the need for more donations. Then the reporter turned his attention to us. Needless to say, no matter what the question, Penny Sue—Southern honey dripping from her mouth—hogged the limelight. That was fine with Ruthie and me, but not Chris. When the reporter asked a question about racing mini-cars, Penny Sue started to answer and Chris cut her off like a slow car on a fast track. Ruthie and I exchanged amused glances. Good for Chris! Penny Sue had finally met her Northern match.

Fortunately, Penny Sue knew when to back off, so ill feelings didn't linger when the TV crew pulled out. "We've made reservations for a suite at the Casa Monica starting Thursday," Penny Sue said to Chris. "That thing is a fortress. You're welcome to join us if the weather gets bad."

"Do they take pets?" Chris asked.

Ruthie shrugged. "I don't know."

"I can't leave Angel, my store cat."

Penny Sue squared her shoulders. "Don't worry; we'll sneak her in. We won't leave her alone."

Chris gave Penny Sue a wide smile, a clear peace offering with a touch of mischief. "I have to warn you—Angel travels with a crowd."

"Other cats besides Angel?" Penny Sue asked.

"Ghosts. My store is haunted, and the ghosts are Angel's friends."

"You're kidding?!" Ruthie and Penny Sue said in unison. Ruthie spoke with admiration, Penny Sue with horror. Not sure if Chris was kidding, I watched with amusement.

Chris wiggled her brows and mimicked holding a cigar like Groucho Marx. "Don't worry, my dear, they're friendly ghosts."

Penny Sue transformed instantly. "Well, if they're friendly, the more the merrier."

For the rest of the day, the hurricane consumed our every waking minute. We made arrangements to garage the Corolla at the paint shop. We went to Publix and purchased a ton of provisions, particularly a lot of wine and chocolate.

The telephone rang off the hook. Guthrie was frantic, although he was going inland to stay with Timothy, regardless of what Timothy's mother thought. The prospect of coming face-to-face with Mother freaked him out. Frannie May—Frances May—called from Boston urging us to evacuate, as she'd done with her son, Carl, the Klingon. My son Zack phoned from Vail to invite us to stay with him. Ruthie's father called. The Judge called. Both my parents called—separately—something they never did. Usually, Mom phoned and Dad got on the line later. Bottom line, everyone wanted us to evacuate as soon as possible. Get out of Dodge. Don't take chances.

Then Sandra, the office manager of the Marine Conservation Center, telephoned and asked if I would cover for her at the center. Her daughter in North Carolina was due to deliver Sandra's first grandchild at any minute. With Frannie May out of town, I was the only one she could count on. Would I stay around to see that the center was buttoned up before the storm? I couldn't say no.

At eight-fifteen AM on Thursday, September 2, the yellow cone for Frances' strike zone officially included New Smyrna Beach. Coastal residents from Flagler to Palm Beach counties were urged to evacuate. The storm's winds exceeded 140 mph, and New Smyrna Beach residents could begin feeling hurricane force gusts by Saturday.

"Y'all go ahead," I told Penny Sue and Ruthie. "Bobby Barnes is going to help me." Bobby was the center's boat captain. "Worst case, I'll be on the road tomorrow. We don't want to lose the reservation at the Casa Monica. Y'all go today, and I'll be there by Friday evening—Saturday morning—at the latest."

"I don't feel good about this—not only the hurricane ... it's the hateful, greedy forces around here. We don't want to leave you alone," Ruthie objected.

"Get a grip," I said lightly, faking courage. "I live here. Nothing can happen. The condo has an alarm system and I have Lu Nee 2 to protect me."

Ruthie shook her head. "I wouldn't count on Lu Nee 2 if I were you."

"I'll be fine. Go! Guthrie's still here—it will be all right."

So Penny Sue and Ruthie went off to St. Augustine.

Not wanting to be alone, I invited Guthrie down for pizza and to watch TV on Thursday night. He jumped at the chance since he was as spooked as I was. For once, Guthrie didn't bring brownies, too upset to cook, he moaned.

We had a large pizza delivered that arrived in less than a half hour—which told me that a lot of people had evacuated. Guthrie and I ate the pie and watched reruns of *CSI,* knowing the Weather Channel would freak us out. At nine-thirty we said goodnight. Guthrie reluctantly headed home—he'd hinted several times about sleeping on the couch, which I nixed—and I prepared for bed, knowing I'd have to be at the center at eight in the morning.

At ten o'clock, just when I was drifting off to sleep, the phone rang. It was Penny Sue. "Did you arm Lu Nee 2?" she asked.

"Yes," I hated to admit it, but I had.

"Do you have the taser close by?" They'd left it with me, since Penny Sue had her gun.

"Yes. It's on Ruthie's bed."

"It's a damned shame you're not with us. The bar is hopping. A contingent from the Hamptons is here, and they're having a high ole time. Flew down on NetJet, but will leave tomorrow if the winds pick up. There are a couple of good-looking single guys."

"You handle 'em. I spent the evening with Guthrie, and men are the last thing on my mind. I'm going to bed. Have to get up early tomorrow."

"Guthrie came down? That's great. We hate to think you're alone. Our suite is spectacular, and this place has walls like a bomb shelter. The concierge told me they were over a foot thick. Drive up tomorrow as soon as you can."

"Will do." I hung up the handset, suddenly feeling very lonely.

I was up at six AM after an uneventful night. Lu Nee 2 didn't sound a peep—praise the Lord, I'd have wet myself if the mechanical monster had started talking. I ate my oatmeal watching the Weather Channel, which nearly gave me indigestion. Frances was still headed our way. Damn. A quick shower, and I dressed in jeans, a tee shirt, and jogging shoes. No sense dolling up to tie down the center. Bobby was there when I arrived. The task we thought would consume half a day took twice as long as anticipated. It didn't help that a clueless man, obviously a tourist, stopped in to ask about our nature cruises. Really, the guy had to be a nut. What sane person cared about nature cruises in the middle of a mandatory evacuation? Thankfully, Bobby informed the man that the boat was out of commission and hustled him away with a stack of brochures. Upshot, I didn't get home until five-thirty. There was no way I had the energy to pack my car and drive to St. Augustine.

I reached Penny Sue on her cell phone to tell her I'd leave the next morning. She answered amid a cacophony of chatter. I surmised she was in the bar.

"Have you filled your gas tank?" she shouted over the din. "They say stations are dry all the way to Georgia. Too many evacuees, not enough gas."

"Yes, I topped it off on the way home. Gas-wise, I'm fine, but I'm tired to the bone. There was a lot more to do at the center than I expected. I'll sleep here tonight and drive up first thing in the morning."

"The traffic will be horrible. I heard I-95 is gridlocked. You should come up Rt. 1 or A1A."

"I'll get up early," I said, "like four AM. Leave your cell phone on and don't be surprised if you get an early morning call."

"These people from the Hamptons are fun, and they love our racing promo shots. They've donated a lot of money—over $20,000—so far. If you and Chris were here, I'm sure we'd get more. I've tried to call Chris, but her cell must be off. Hurry up. The big guys may fly out tomorrow."

After toting bales and lifting—oh, heck, what is the saying?—anyway, I couldn't have cared less about the big guys from the Hamptons. Yes, I wanted donations for the hurricane victims, whose ranks were about to swell. However, fundraising was Penny Sue's niche, not mine. She had the personality for it—brazen.

I warmed a can of Campbell's Clam Chowder with some garlic bread for dinner and started loading my car. Fortunately, Penny Sue's enornmous Mercedes held most of our supplies. I was left with blankets, pillows, a lot of wine, and Snickers in case we ended up staying with Chris at her store. After I loaded the car, I poured a glass of wine and packed my suitcase to the chatter of the Weather Channel. Things didn't look good. The darned storm was barreling straight for us. I was spooked, not only by the storm, but also the black Ford Taurus and Mafia thing. I placed a half glass of wine on the nightstand, set the alarm, as well as Lu Nee 2, and slid between the covers of my bed, giving the liquid taser an appreciative glance. It was only nine-thirty. I'd set the alarm clock for three AM.

I drifted into an uneasy sleep, the kind where your mind is racing, thinking of all the things you should have done. At eleven PM a noise of some sort jarred me awake. I panted, scared to death. Was someone trying to break into the condo? They hadn't succeeded, because the alarm didn't sound. What if it did? What would I do?

I'd jump out of the window and run. Yes, but the window was locked, and there was a credenza in front of it. Best to clear a path, just in case, I thought. I got up in my nightgown, pushed the credenza against the wall and unlocked the window to provide an unobstructed escape route.

I went back to bed and thrashed around, thinking about the Mafia, and the logistics of jumping out the window. If I jumped out the window, where would I go? I threw back the covers and fetched my pocketbook and car keys. I took a sip of wine and slipped back between the sheets.

I lay there fidgeting and thinking. If someone broke in and I had to jump out of the window, it would hurt my feet. After all, the window as surrounded by sea grapes and prickly vegetation. I climbed out of bed, put on my jogging shoes, and got back into the sack with my sneakers sticking out the bottom of the covers.

I couldn't go to sleep because the shoes kept getting tangled in the blanket. I took another drink of wine and recited my mantra. No dice. My mind churned. If someone broke into the condo, I'd jump out the window. My purse and keys were handy, the window was unlocked, and I had shoes to protect my feet. But there was a screen in the window!

I whipped the blanket away, shut off the alarm and Lu Nee 2, opened the window and removed the screen. I brought it inside and propped it up in the hall. Then I shut the window, rearmed the condo, and returned to bed. I rolled over and looked at the clock … a few minutes after midnight.

I grabbed the glass on the nightstand and finished the wine. I snuggled into the pillow, but my mind still raced. Okay, if someone broke in, I would grab my purse and keys, jump out the screen-less window, (which wouldn't hurt my feet because I had on jogging shoes) run to my car and drive to St. Augustine.

But I had on my nightgown. I couldn't walk into a classy hotel like the Casa Monica in my nightgown. I rolled out of bed, got fully dressed, poured a few sips of wine that I gulped down, and sat on the edge of the bed. By now, it was one-thirty.

One more time! I whipped the blanket over me and lay there stiff as a board. A half hour later, I'd had enough. *What the heck?* I locked the window, grabbed the taser, purse, keys, and headed out. The wind had started to howl, and fat drops of rain hit me on the head. Thankfully, no nefarious creatures showed themselves. Good thing, because the taser was charged and my trigger finger was twitching.

I was out of the parking lot and headed for St. Augustine by two-thirty. A few miles down the road I realized my alarm clock would go off at three, sending Lu Nee 2 into a tizzy. Hell with it, I thought, and kept driving north.

Chapter 17

September 3

I decided to take Route 1, even though I-95 would normally be faster. St. Augustine was only about seventy-five miles north, and at seventy mph, one could make it in a little over an hour. But, the local radio station reported heavy traffic because of mandatory evacuations, and the wind and torrential rains meant no one could make good time, regardless of which road they took.

While I-95 was crawling, Route 1's traffic was slow because of the rain, but cars weren't bumper to bumper. I didn't pass anyone going south, and there was a line of evenly spaced cars behind me headed north. I decided I'd call Penny Sue when I reached Palm Coast, which was approximately halfway. There was a straight, deserted stretch of highway, a good place to use the phone. Unlike Penny Sue who could eat, talk on her cell, and drive all at the same time, I'd found multitasking wasn't my strong suit. For that reason, I rarely used my cell phone, except in emergencies, and hadn't bothered to invest in a hands-free headset or one of the newer phones that took pictures and dialed numbers from voice commands.

When I passed the Palm Coast sign, I held the phone at eye level, scrolled down to Penny Sue's number, and hit send. I guess I slowed down, because I noticed a car in my rearview mirror gaining fast. I accelerated and set my speed control to sixty. Penny Sue answered after seven rings.

"You're here?" she asked with a thick tongue. "Lord, it's only three-thirty."

"I'm at Palm Coast, probably forty minutes away. How do I get there from Route 1?" I caught a flash of headlights in the mirror. Two vehicles were close behind me, and the one at the rear—an SUV or, maybe, a pickup truck—had pulled out to pass.

"Best way is to stay on Route 1, then go right on King Street, which takes you straight to the hotel. There's valet—"

"Oh, Lord!" I screamed and threw the cell phone on the passenger's seat. The SUV wasn't trying to pass the car behind me—it was attempting to run the car off the road! I gripped the steering wheel with both hands and floored the gas pedal.

"What's going on?" I heard Penny Sue cry.

"A case of road rage behind me," I screamed. "An SUV is trying to run a car off the road."

"Get out of there!" she shouted.

"I'm trying," I yelled back. My speedometer inched toward 80 as the vehicles behind gained on me, side-by-side, in a sick tug of war. But luck was with me: an exit sign to I-95 appeared. I hung a quick right and slid up the on-ramp, brake pedal pressed to the floor. I skidded toward a long line of cars traveling at a snail's pace. All the while, I heard Penny Sue and Ruthie screaming from the phone in the next seat. *Help me, God,* I prayed silently. He must have heard me. Thanks to a slow-moving eighteen-wheeler, a space opened up in traffic, and I slid in, my speed down to about thirty. I let off the brake, my knee shaking violently.

"LEIGH!"

"I'm okay. Give me a minute to catch my breath." I inhaled deeply, trying to calm myself, trying to steady my trembling hands. The traffic, bumper to bumper, moved at approximately thirty-five mph. I could care less. There was safety in numbers and slow was fine by me. Still panting, I picked up the phone. "Heavens, I don't know who was trying to run over who back there. I thought the SUV was after the other car, then it seemed they were both after me. I'm on I-95 and traffic is creeping. I won't be there in forty minutes."

"Why did you leave so early? To beat the traffic?" Penny Sue asked.

"Yeah." No need to go into my anxiety attack.

"Call when you get to King Street. We'll meet you at the valet stand."

"Evil all around us," I heard Ruthie pronounce in the background.

Great, just what I needed to hear.

"Be careful," Penny Sue said and hung up.

It was after five o'clock when I pulled up to the valet station of the Casa Monica. Penny Sue was waiting, dressed in flowing red silk pajamas, covered by an embroidered, knee-length jacket. She pressed a twenty into the valet's palm and gave me a big hug. "You scared me to death!"

I took my wheeled suitcase from the backseat and handed the car keys to the valet. "The rest of the stuff will stay in the car. You have secure parking, don't you?"

The young man—probably a student at Flagler College across the street—stiffened as if I'd offended him. "You are completely safe at the Casa Monica."

I winked. "I'm glad to hear that. Safe is good." And I wasn't kidding.

Pulling my suitcase, I followed Penny Sue to the fifth floor. My friends had a corner suite in one of the towers. Ruthie waited with a cup of coffee, the TV was tuned to the Weather Channel. (Wonder of wonders!)

The coffee was the best I'd ever tasted (could have been the timing), and the suite truly was spectacular, worth every penny of Ruthie's $349 per night. If it hadn't been for the small bar with a microwave and refrigerator, you'd think you'd stepped back into the nineteenth century. The walls were painted a pale yellow with white crown molding and trim, while brocade drapes with white sheers hung over the expansive windows. The living area furniture had marble-topped tables with a couch and matching high back chairs upholstered in royal blue brocade. An ornately carved cabinet housed the television.

The bedroom had two queen beds with fluffy white comforters and big pillows. Those pillows called my name, yet I had to be minimally sociable before ripping my clothes off and diving into bed. In fact, I was so tired I'd even sleep with Penny Sue.

I sat in one of the chairs and gazed at the green shrimp formation, which was Frances, approaching the Florida coast. "What's the storm doing?"

Ruthie sighed. "Drifting ashore at five mph. Good news—they think it'll hit south of New Smyrna. Bad news—that puts the condo on the strong side of the storm. It's moving so slowly that forecasters predict tremendous flooding."

"Glad I left," I said, noticing the wind speeds at various sites around the Florida map. I held up my cup. "Have any Bailey's Irish Cream for this?"

"Of course, darling," Penny Sue drawled, pulling a bottle from a shelf under the bar. "You're wiped out, aren't you?" She filled my mug and splashed some Bailey's over ice for herself. Ruthie declined, being as it wasn't even six o'clock. "You're pale as a ghost. What happened?"

I gave them an abbreviated—that is, face-saving—version of the noises at the condo and the reason I left early.

"I had a bad feeling about your staying there alone," Ruthie said emphatically.

Next, I filled them in on the bizarre race or road rage incident in Palm Coast. "Honestly, I was doing eighty, and they were gaining on me. I don't know if they were trying to kill each other or trying to kill me." I winked at Ruthie. "I got some divine intervention. At the moment my bug wouldn't go any faster, I saw a sign for the interstate. Needless to say, I took it. I hit the brake and skidded up the ramp. It was short and I had to decelerate from eighty to thirty mph in a matter of yards. The wheels were locked, and I was skidding into bumper to bumper traffic." I glanced at the ceiling. "Someone up *there* helped me. A slow eighteen-wheeler made a space and I slipped into it. If I could find that trucker, I'd kiss him. He saved my life!"

Ruthie smiled. "There are no accidents."

"What happened to the guys following you?" Penny Sue asked.

"They were accelerating when I made my move. *If* they were after me, I lost them."

Ruthie shook her head. "Evil is everywhere; I feel it."

I downed my drink. "I have to go to bed."

I slept until eleven. When I awoke, Ruthie and Penny Sue were gone. From the shape of the bathroom, they'd already showered, dressed, and headed to a late breakfast. Good. I needed some quiet time, and I was famished. The clam chowder I'd eaten for dinner was long gone from my stomach. I called room service for Eggs Benedict and a large pot of coffee.

I found an iron and board in the closet, along with a terry cloth robe that I put on for room service's sake, fished a cotton outfit from my suitcase, and switched on the Weather Channel.

Frances remained just off the coast, moving at a snail's pace. Jim Cantore had been in Daytona Beach earlier in the week, but had gone south, now.

Fed and fully dressed, I located Ruthie and Penny Sue in the gift shop off the lobby.

"We left so you could get some sleep," Ruthie said.

"Thanks, I needed it." I glanced around the shop and the lobby. "This is a beautiful hotel."

"Yeah, too bad most of the fun people left this morning. They were afraid of getting caught by the storm and flew back to the Hamptons."

"Can't say I blame them."

"No big loss," Ruthie said. "I didn't think they were that much fun."

Penny Sue's brows knitted with disbelief. "Yes they were, and they're rich as hell. Our pledges total over $50.000. If we'd found Chris, I know they'd be higher. She's a great salesperson and from New York, to boot."

"Why couldn't you find Chris? Did you call her store?"

Penny Sue gave me a dumb look. "I called her cell phone."

She was clueless. "Penny Sue, Chris works. She probably turns her cell off during business hours. Did you walk down to her shop?"

"Her shop?"

"Yes, the store we're invited to stay in. The store with the friendly ghosts and psychic cat. The Rising Moon! Does that ring a bell? It's only a few blocks away, on Spanish Street."

"That does sound familiar," Penny Sue allowed.

"I hope so, after everything Chris has done for us and the race."

"We'll go visit Chris this afternoon. Come on, I want to introduce you to one of the guys we met." Penny Sue grinned devilishly. "He's single." She charged out of the gift shop and ran smack-dab into a man walking down the hall. There was a quick exchange of apologies, and the man headed out the side door.

"Slow down, Penny Sue. There's no need to rush. Frankie's obviously here for the duration, since he didn't fly home with his friends," Ruthie said.

"Wait," I said, following them into the hallway. "I know that man."

"Frankie?" Penny Sue sounded peeved.

"No, the man you just rammed."

She tossed her hair. "I didn't ram him, it was a minor brush."

"That almost knocked him down." Ruthie snickered.

"Seriously, that guy came in the Marine Conservation Center yesterday. He wanted information on nature cruises. We gave him some brochures and sent him packing. I thought it was strange that someone would be interested in boat tours when the island was being evacuated. Now he shows up here."

"Are you sure it's the same person?" Penny Sue peered out the side door.

"Positive. I recognize the heavy gold necklace he's wearing. It's unusual to say the least—intertwined snakes."

"How tacky," Penny Sue said.

We started toward the lobby. "Forget tacky—what's he doing here?"

"Evil," Ruthie murmured, shaking her head.

Geez, I wished she stop saying that! With murders, wrecks, and hurricanes, even I knew the vibes were awful. I didn't need to be reminded constantly. But, that was Ruthie; she meant no harm.

We took a quick tour of the ornately furnished lobby and ended up in the bar for a cappuccino. Penny Sue insisted, claiming the hotel's cappuccino was the best in the world. I shook my head.

"What's wrong?" she asked.

"Lame. Surely you can come up with a better excuse than that."

"Lame how?" She plopped her purse on a table by the window and sat down. A television over the bar was tuned to the local news.

Ruthie and I took seats with a view of the TV. "Frankie wouldn't have anything to do with your sudden desire for coffee, would he?" I asked.

She waved to the bartender, pointed at the cappuccino machine, and held up three fingers. He got the message. "Maybe. Frankie came here yesterday for lunch."

Chocolate, men, and wine. You could count on at least one being the motive for almost anything Penny Sue wanted to do. She was so predictable, I almost laughed aloud.

Suddenly, Ruthie gasped and pointed to the television.

"Frances?" I asked.

"No, a wreck on Route 1. A black Taurus. They said the driver apparently lost control and ran off the road. He was speeding."

"Where? Did they say where the crash occurred?"

"Just beyond the 298 interchange. That's the ramp you took to I-95!"

"Gracious! I'll bet it was one of the cars following me—one was about the size of a Taurus. I'd better call Woody." I swiveled toward Penny Sue's chair. She was gone. It was a small bar, so she wasn't hard to find. She'd intercepted a lanky, dark-haired man at the entrance. Frankie I presumed. I squinted to get a good look at him. "Crap! I've seen that guy before, too. He was at the racetrack watching us during the TV interview. I know it. Ruthie, there are far too many coincidences for my taste. We have to get Penny Sue away from him, and we need to get out of this hotel!"

"I told you—" Ruthie started.

I held up my hand. "Don't say it—'evil,' I know. The question is, 'What should we do about it?'"

"Pull out your cell phone and pretend you're talking." I did. "Barrett," Ruthie called to the bartender who was making our coffees. She motioned to me. "An emergency. We have to leave, charge it to my room."

"Want me to put them in paper cups?" he offered.

"No time," Ruthie replied, then whispered to me, "Duck your head, and pretend you're crying. Rush past Penny Sue to the elevator. I'll get her and meet you at the suite."

I brushed past Penny Sue and Frankie with my hand over my eyes. Ruthie lingered to speak with them. I found an elevator waiting and took it to the fifth floor. A few minutes later Ruthie and Penny Sue arrived. She rushed to me and gave me a big hug. "Oh, Leigh. Your father?!"

Meanwhile, Ruthie unlocked the door and dragged us in, bear hug and all.

"My father's fine," I said, extricating myself from Penny Sue's grip. "It's Frankie."

She gave Ruthie a hard look. "I thought your father—What do you mean, it's Frankie?"

"I've seen him before. He was at the track when we did the TV interview. He was sitting in the grandstand."

Penny Sue threw her hands up. "You think you've seen everyone. The guy in the hall, now Frankie. Have you had your eyes checked recently? What are the chances that two men you saw in New Smyrna Beach would be in this hotel? The probability is zero!"

"You're right," I shouted, "unless we're being followed!"

"Followed?" Penny Sue slumped into a chair.

"That's not all," Ruthie said forcefully. "While you were sparking with Frankie—"

"Sparking?" Penny Sue threw back her head and laughed. "For goodness sake, where did that come from?"

"It's a nineteenth century hotel, so I'm picking up the vibes. Anyway, there was a wreck on Route 1 last night. A black Taurus ran off the road and the driver, a man, was killed. It was on TV while you were … flirting."

"Really?" The blood drained from Penny Sue's face.

Ruthie was as fired-up as I'd ever seen her. "I told you we were surrounded by bad energy. Now we know who's responsible. Like Leigh said, we have to get out of this hotel."

"How can we do that if we're being watched? They know our cars—they'll follow us anywhere we go."

There was only one way out that I could see. "Chris. Her shop is down the street, and we were thinking of staying there anyway. The men are watching us, not our cars … unless they've been bugged!"

Penny Sue did a head slap. "Damn, I never thought of that. That's the first thing they taught us in the anti-terrorist driving course—check for tracking devices, and it never occurred to me."

"If they're bugged, we can't move them, right?"

"Right, but all our stuff is in them. If we stay with Chris, we'll need our supplies," Penny Sue said.

"I have an idea. We call Chris and have her come pick up the stuff from our cars," Ruthie suggested.

"Chris can't get to them—the cars are in valet parking," Penny Sue objected.

Ruthie smirked. "She can if we tip the bellman and valet enough."

"If we're being watched, won't that look suspicious? I mean, calling a bellman to the room?"

I glanced around. "Don't y'all have something that needs to be pressed right away?"

Penny Sue jumped to her feet, eyes aglow, as Ruthie poured herself a glass of wine. It was all I could do to keep a straight face at the role reversal.

"I see," Penny Sue said excitedly. "We tip the bellman, to tip the valet, to let Chris in and give her the keys to our cars." Penny Sue started to pace. "I know … Chris is a friend that we were helping to move. The stuff in our cars belongs to her and now she's come to get it."

"Good," Ruthie said, handing Penny Sue and me a glass of Chardonnay. "Keep thinking."

Penny Sue took a sip. "Nothing suspicious about having a dress pressed and a friend picking up her belongings." Penny Sue strode to the closet, took Ruthie's black silk chemise off the hanger, balled it up, and sat on it. "Okay, why don't we meet our friend downstairs? That's suspicious. If she's such a good friend, why aren't we there to help her get her stuff?"

"Because we have massages and facials scheduled at the only time Chris can come. We're going out to dinner, which is why we need the dress," Ruthie said.

"That's good, Ruthie," Penny Sue said with true admiration. "You're on a roll."

Ruthie finished her drink and refilled the glass. "I'm getting help. An older woman. Very stately. She used to vacation at this hotel in its heyday. Her name's Millie. She hangs around because she had so much fun here. She particularly liked wine and she could drink when she came here, since no one at home would know."

Lordy be, I thought. 'Evil all around' and now Millie. If I lived through this, I might write a book about it.

"You're possessed?" Penny Sue asked, arching a brow.

"No, only in communication. This lady had a lot of nerve."

"All right, assuming Chris is available and we pull that off, how do we get out of the hotel without being followed?" I asked.

Ruthie screwed her mouth up like we were the dumbest people in the world. "The chambermaid, of course." Ruthie waved her glass grandly. "She'll roll us to the back door in that big laundry cart, where Chris will pick us up."

"You think we'd all fit in it?" Penny Sue asked sincerely.

"Maybe, if you tighten your corset." Ruthie grinned impishly.

Chambermaid? Corset? Ruthie *was* possessed. Whoever thought of it, the plan would work. I held up my hand to Penny Sue, whose face had gone beet red at the corset comment. "Don't take it personally. Ruthie's channeling the other lady, who's trying to help. I think the plan will work."

Penny Sue drained her glass. "I do, too."

Chapter 18

September 4

Chris answered the phone at her shop on the second ring. "I was wondering what happened to you guys. I've called the condo a dozen times. Where are we staying, your place or mine?"

"Yours." I filled her in on the wreck, the guys following us, and our plan. She thought it was a good one. Business was nonexistent because an outer band of Frances had come ashore, and it was raining hard, so she was planning to close early, anyway. Her car was small, but the shopkeeper next door owned a van she could probably borrow. Chris would check.

She called back in five minutes. "I can use the van, but we have to do this right away. He plans to close early, too."

I checked my watch. Almost two o'clock. "Be here at two-thirty—that should give us time to tip everyone."

While Ruthie called for a bellman, Penny Sue rushed to the lobby for cash. She returned before the bellman arrived for the dress, which was seriously wrinkled, considering Penny Sue sat on it for a long time. Ruthie tipped the bellman $20 and gave him $75 for the valet. We would call downstairs with instructions about the person who needed to get into our cars. Penny Sue phoned the valet, told him to expect a $75 tip, and instructed him to give Chris access to our cars so she could retrieve her belongings. Penny Sue read him the number from her valet stub, then put me on the phone to give him mine.

Amazing what money will do! The plan came off without a hitch. The valet escorted Chris to our cars, unlocked them, and even helped her unload the prodigious contents. The only downside was that Chris had to single-handedly lug the stuff into her store in the pouring rain. It was almost four o'clock when she finally called back.

"Phase one accomplished, but you owe me big time. I'm drenched. Ready for phase two? I had to give back the van, so I'm coming in my car."

"We'll phone when we're leaving for the back door," I replied.

Ruthie called housekeeping and requested Carmen, our usual maid. Carmen did a favor for Ruthie, and she'd forgotten to give her a tip. Carmen was at the door in a matter of minutes.

Ruthie gave the performance of her life—honestly, she had to be channeling the spirit of Millie—saying a jealous boyfriend had shown up and threatened us. Ruthie broke-up with him when she learned he'd served time for assault. We were scheduled to have dinner with her new boyfriend and his sister, but were afraid her ex-lover was spying on us and might become violent. Could Carmen take us down to the loading dock in a laundry cart, where the sister would pick us up?" Ruthie waved a hundred dollar bill.

Carmen, a full-figured woman who made Penny Sue look small, smiled and tucked the C-note into her bra. "No problem. My old boyfriend was mean like that. I finally had to swear out a constraining order. I keep a copy in my car's glove department." She shook her finger. "That guy keeps bothering you, call the cops. Men like that are loco."

While Carmen went for the cart, I called Chris and told her to meet us at the delivery entrance in ten minutes.

Carmen was a trooper. Figuring all of us would never fit in one cart, she returned with two plus a bunch of sheets. She wheeled the carts into the room and had us at the back door before Chris arrived. Luckily, there were stairs next to the exit, so we could step up and out of the cart with Carmen's assistance. By the time we'd all climbed out, Chris pulled in. Ruthie hugged Carmen and thanked her, pressing an extra twenty into her palm.

Off we went in the Toyota Hybrid that Penny Sue vowed she'd never ride in. Funny how things turn out. It was almost six, and the historic district, usually full of tourists, was deserted. The only thing missing was tumbleweed blowing down the street. We parked behind The Rising Moon. Angel, the psychic house cat, met us at the door and immediately rubbed against Ruthie's leg.

"She likes you," Chris marveled.

"That's because Millie came with us," Ruthie said.

"Millie?"

"A spirit Ruthie picked up at the Casa Monica," I replied. "Millie helped us come up with the plan."

"Good for Millie," Chris said nonchalantly. "The more the merrier."

Ruthie was transfixed by the shop—it was her kind of place. A colorful display of wind chimes hung in the center of the main room. Stars, moons, fish, and geometric shapes of all sizes tinkled to the air conditioner. There was a large selection of New Age merchandise mixed with handcrafted wares from around the world. The far wall displayed an array of African masks and wooden bowls as well as a poster about Fair Trade.

"New Age and Fair Trade in the same store. How perfect," Ruthie enthused.

Chris grinned playfully and patted herself on the back. "A natural fit, if I do say so myself, because they both raise human consciousness."

Ruthie spread her arms wide, Angel still rubbing her leg. "That's why we're supposed to be here. These are good vibes."

Penny Sue covered her mouth and whispered to me, "What the heck is free trade?"

Chris—still dripping wet, and how should we say, a little out of sorts?—overheard Penny Sue's comment. "It's fair trade, not free trade. It means the craftsmen and artisans are paid a fair, living wage for their work. The middlemen are eliminated and the workers are paid directly—no sweatshops or child labor.

"Did you know that of the $5 you pay for a cup of designer cappuccino, less than fifteen cents goes to the farmers? Fair Trade attempts to level the playing field so the producers get a square deal."

The mention of child labor got to us all. I thought Ruthie and Penny Sue might whip out their American Express cards and buy the entire inventory as they oohed and awed up one aisle and down another. The thought of children being exploited bothered me, too, but I couldn't afford to buy out the store. I'd wait to see what was left over. Hopefully, stuff that wasn't too expensive.

Angel, the cat, started to growl—a low, guttural sound only a cat can make that has the same effect as fingernails scratched across a blackboard. Was the cat annoyed that I wasn't going to spend enough? Was she reading my mind and thinking in terms of Fancy Feast gourmet food? "What's with Angel?" I asked.

Ruthie put her hand to her throat and thought. "There is a lot of energy here. Millie says old spirits, much older than she is."

"I hope they're positive, like Casper the Friendly Ghost," Penny Sue quipped.

"They are, for the most part," Ruthie replied. "Millie's talking to Angel. Millie said you," Ruthie pointed at me, "must call the authorities immediately."

Authorities? The cat must mean Woody who'd told me to contact him if we had any trouble. I glanced at my watch. "It's after five."

"Call him," Ruthie said forcefully as Angel yowled. Boy, talk about being hounded, or was that catted?

Wonder of wonders, Woody answered his cell phone. I related the story of the cars following me, the black Taurus' wreck, and the two men at the Casa Monica whom I'd seen before. For once, Woody listened without making a smart aleck remark.

"Where are you?" he asked.

"St. Augustine. The Rising Moon on Spanish Street."

"I'll make some calls." He clicked off.

I stared at the phone. Even when Woody tried to be nice, he was still offensive. Abrupt, some would say. Rude by Southern standards.

Penny Sue, Ruthie, and Chris stared at me. I threw up my hands. "Woody said he'd phone some people, then hung up."

"Common," Penny Sue said. "That man is plain common. No good-bye, or fare-thee-well?"

"Nothing." He was common!

"Hell with him," Chris said. "We can take care of ourselves." She went to a cabinet in the backroom and pulled out large black squares of material outlined with grommets. Chris nodded at Penny Sue. "You're the tallest, help me."

"With what?"

"Cover the windows, so the bad guys can't see us. Then, we can hang out and party. I couldn't help but notice how much candy and wine you brought."

Penny Sue grinned ear-to-ear. "Well, there's no telling how long this hurricane will last. It's a slow mover."

"Yes, and we should check its status," Ruthie said as she rummaged through a box of our supplies. She pulled out the tiny TV we'd purchased at Wal-Mart, unwrapped the cord, and plugged the set in. "Thank God, the electricity's on."

"And the AC," Penny Sue remarked as she helped Chris cover the windows.

"Even so, we should light a couple of candles," Chris said. "It's going to be real dark in here when we cover the big window. If the lights go out, we won't be able to see our hands in front of our faces."

I lit a half-burned candle by the cash register and put our flashlights beside it. If the power failed, we'd be ready. Meanwhile, Ruthie found a local television station broadcasting hurricane news. She stood back from the tiny screen and watched.

"Gracious, Frances is drifting westward at five mph. It's not expected to make landfall until late tonight or early tomorrow morning. Look! Tony Perkins from *Good Morning America* is in New Smyrna Beach."

"Jim Cantore was in Daytona Beach earlier in the week," I piped in.

"I missed Jim Cantore?" For a moment I thought Ruthie might cry. "Did you tape him for me?"

Tape him? It was a weather report. "It never occurred to me."

She sat on the edge of a display dejectedly. Angel jumped in her lap and started licking her arm. "My big chance, and I missed it for some snotty people from the Hamptons."

"Snotty, but fun," Penny Sue said, wiggling her hips as she fastened the last grommet. "Now it's time to party!"

We all gave her a sour look. "Doing what?" I finally asked.

Penny Sue pulled a deck of cards out of her purse. "Poker!"

The wicker chairs and table from the front porch had been brought inside earlier and Chris quickly found another chair and stool in the backroom. Weather forecast blaring in the background, we settled down to an evening of poker, popcorn, candy, and wine. By ten thirty that night, torrential downpours pelted St. Augustine, and Tony Perkins of *Good Morning America* could hardly stand up in New Smyrna Beach. He reported that the bridges had closed, meaning if anyone beachside hadn't evacuated, they were stuck.

"Aren't you glad you're not there?" Ruthie said to me, laying down four kings. She was beating us like a drum.

"Is that cat helping you?" Penny Sue demanded as Ruthie raked the penny pot toward her substantial pile.

Ruthie grinned. "Millie is."

Penny Sue raised her face to the ceiling. "No fair, Millie. Can't you help me for a while?"

Chris stretched. "I think I've had enough fun for one evening. Between lugging in your stuff and everything on the front porch, I'm beat. Besides, the Vienna sausage sandwich gave me heartburn. Remind me never to eat another one of those vile things."

Penny Sue took a bottle of Tums from her pocketbook. "They did taste nasty, didn't they? It's probably because we bought the chicken kind and not real Viennas." She popped a Tums and handed the bottle to Chris.

Chris downed three. "Might not have been so bad if we'd had some kraut. Let's try to get some sleep."

We all staked out an area on the floor, then laid out our comforters and pillows. No sleeping bags and air mattresses like we'd planned—the stores sold out as soon as a new shipment came in.

Ruthie spread her blanket by the front door and cuddled up with Angel. We turned off the lights except for a battery-operated lantern, in case of a power outage, which Penny Sue asserted was akin to carrying an umbrella to ensure it didn't rain. I, for one, hoped she was right. The air conditioning felt deliciously cool, and it didn't take long for us to drift into an uneasy sleep.

All was well until about three o'clock, the witching hour according to Ruthie. All of a sudden, the wind chimes clanged violently, and Angel catapulted from Ruthie's arms to the center of the room, her back arched and tail standing straight up.

Chris propped up on her elbow. "It's just a blast from the AC. Nothing to worry about." She plopped back down.

"No, it's not," Ruthie whispered as she sat up. "Someone just tried the door handle, and there's a shuffling noise on the porch."

Penny Sue crawled across the floor to her purse and found her .38. I scooted to the box by the front wall and snatched the liquid taser. There was a tap on the window, and Angel let out a loud screech.

Chris snatched the keys to her car and turned off the lantern. "Let's get out of here!"

"Millie agrees!" Crouched low, Ruthie scrambled to the back door.

"What about Angel?" I asked.

"She'll be fine. She has hiding places inside of hiding places," Chris assured me.

As Chris fumbled with the deadbolt, we heard the unmistakable sound of a gunshot on the front porch. Adrenaline surged. We nearly ripped the door off its hinges, ran across the back porch, and piled into Chris' car. The hybrid started like a normal vehicle, but quickly switched to the virtually silent electric mode. Lights off, Chris crept down the driveway to Spanish Street. To our horror, a man lay sprawled across the sidewalk a few feet away from us. Chris made a right on Spanish Street and floored it, causing the gas engine to kick in. The sound of the engine got the attention of two men on the porch, who hopped the railing and raced to a big sedan parked across the street. Before they had a chance to start their car, a black Cadillac sped by and more shots rang out.

"There are two groups, and they don't seem to like each other," Chris shrieked.

"Like the wreck on Route 1," I mumbled.

"Well, they're not getting me. This baby can outmaneuver those lardass boats any day." Chris took a right at the first intersection, a left on Cordova to King, and onward to Route 1. "Do you seem them?"

"Yes, but they're far back."

"Good, I know where we can lose them." She hung a left on Route 1, drove a ways, switched off her lights, and turned into the San Lorenzo Cemetery. We bumped down a dirt road and parked behind the caretakers' building with a clear view of the entrance. We stared at the gateway, praying headlights would not appear. No such luck.

"Damn! They probably bugged your car," Penny Sue cursed. "We're sitting ducks—we've got to get out of here."

We exploded from the Toyota and made a beeline for a chapel in the middle of the cemetery. I lugged the taser, Penny Sue had her .38. We left our pocketbooks behind, which showed how scared we were. No Southern woman would be caught dead without her pocketbook. It was the dead part I didn't like. Hell with tradition, the purses were on their own!

"Millie says we should find a guy with a skull, then run to the right, toward the woods," Ruthie panted.

"Guy with a skull?" Penny Sue called over her shoulder. "Are you sure Millie's a friendly ghost?"

"Look, I just call it as I get it," Ruthie snapped.

We reached the chapel and scanned the area for a man with a skull. All we saw was row after row of small crosses.

"Millie says nuns," Ruthie nodded at the crosses, "and we should go around to the front."

We picked our way slowly, hugging the side of the building. The car that turned into the cemetery had parked behind ours.

"Hurry," I started to say, but stopped as another car entered the graveyard and cut its lights. "Geez, more company." We rushed around the corner and came face-to-face with a giant marble statute of a man holding a skull.

"Crissakes," Penny Sue exclaimed, backing up. The skull glowed in moonlight streaming through a break in the clouds. "Who's that, the saint of death?"

"I don't know, and I don't care," Ruthie replied in a controlled shriek. "To the woods. Here they come!" We bent down as low as we could and ran like hell toward the trees.

By this time, the men who'd parked behind the Toyota realized we weren't at home and had started searching for us with halogen flashlights. Their view obstructed by the caretaker's building, they obviously didn't realize they had company. Three lights fanned out from the first car, heading in our general direction. A moment later, our worst fear materialized. One of the beams caught Ruthie, who was in the lead. "Millie says jump." And Ruthie disappeared.

We stopped in our tracks. "What tha—?" Penny Sue started.

"Down here. Jump!"

Lordy, Ruthie had jumped into a pit—no, a freshly dug grave!

"A grave? I'm not hopping in a grave," Penny Sue declared.

A shot rang out, and one of the flashlights fell to the ground. That was all the encouragement needed, we jumped and landed in a thick layer of mud. Thankfully, I'd held the taser over my head, so it wasn't damaged.

We sat on our haunches in a good foot of mud, too scared to move. A flurry of gunfire reverberated around us. We heard a man scream, then a loud curse in a foreign language. Silence. Another shot, and a curse in a different foreign language. Then the weirdest thing happened, the sky above lit up with a pulsating blue. The light bounced off the thunderheads and filled the pit, giving us the first look we'd had of each other since we left the store. Faces full of terror, covered in mud, we were a pitiful sight, to say the least.

"Remember that Speilberg mini-series about the little blonde girl who was really an alien?" Penny Sue said, her voice trembling, face raised to the heavens. "I think we're about to be beamed up like she was at the end of the show."

"You think you're an alien?" I quipped.

"Not me ... Ruthie! This is exactly the way it looked when the aliens came for the little girl."

As Penny Sue searched the sky for a spaceship, Chris inched upward to peer over the edge of the grave. "Aliens, hell. It's the cops!"

Chapter 19

September 6-8

The next day at eleven-fifteen AM, the East Coast alerts for Frances were officially lifted. Chris, Ruthie, Penny Sue, and I raised our Mimosas and toasted the hurricane's departure as we sat in the bar area of the Casa Monica Hotel with a good view of the TV.

"And, to Woody, who helped us for a change," I added. Chris and Ruthie tipped their glasses. Penny Sue scowled. "Come on, Penny Sue, Woody deserves some credit, you have to admit that."

"He was doing his job."

"True, but he saved our hides."

She squinched her nose, yet begrudgingly lifted her drink. "To Woody. About time he did something constructive."

The information I gave Woody about the wrecked Taurus and our being followed made its way to the St. Augustine Police Department and the area office of the FBI. While we played poker at Chris' store, the FBI checked our cars in the Casa

Monica garage. They found tracking devices, deciphered the frequency, and gambled that the gang would use it again. They were a little late staking out The Rising Moon, so missed the action there, but located Chris' car in the cemetery and arrived in the middle of the shootout.

"Quite a catch," John, the lead agent for the FBI task force, gloated when we picked the two men out of the lineup who'd followed us from New Smyrna Beach. Frankie, Penny Sue's heartthrob, turned out to be an underboss in the Italian Mafia. The guy with the snake necklace was a notorious character from the Russian mob. Who was chasing whom, and for what reason, was unclear, since no one would talk. In any event, the FBI thought both gangs would lay low for a while, putting us in the clear.

So we were celebrating and biding our time until we could go back to New Smyrna Beach. According to Woody, damage was extensive—a combination of wind and thirty-six hours of rain—and the power on the island remained off. He advised us to stay in St. Augustine for a while (probably hoping we'd stay forever), since many roads were impassible from downed trees, not to mention the massive traffic jams and gas shortages caused by returning evacuees.

Another time we would have headed for St. Augustine's Old Town shopping district or the outlet malls. On this Labor Day, most stores were closed, so we had to settle for massages at the hotel. Too bad, oh, twist my arm! I, for one, intended to plop in the hot tub as soon as we finished lunch.

Our sandwiches arrived. "Wait," Chris said, catching Penny Sue with a wedge of club sandwich halfway to her mouth. "One more toast." Penny Sue put her sandwich down reluctantly and reached for her Mimosa. Chris stood and we followed suit. "To us!"

"To us."

"And Millie," Ruthie added.

"To Millie."

"And victory in the race!"

"Victory!" We clicked our glasses and did a sloppy high five.

I was about to chomp down on the biggest, juiciest hamburger on the planet when my cell phone rang. I checked the display—it was Guthric. I longingly eyed my burger and debated whether to answer. Guess I should—he might be calling about the condo. "Hello?"

"Man, are you all right?" he asked.

"Fine. I'm in St. Augustine with Penny Sue and Ruthie. How about you?"

"Peachy, considering there's no electricity and," I could hear him cup his hand around the mouthpiece of the phone, "Timothy's mother is driving me batty. She calls me Guppy and is crazy as a loon. Like, when are you coming home?"

"The electricity is out all over the island. We're planning to stay here for another couple of days." I glanced at Penny Sue who'd already eaten half of her sandwich. "Can I call you back? We're in the middle of lunch."

"No prob. I'll be here playing Scrabble with Mother." His hand went around the mouthpiece again. "She cheats!"

Suffering from news deficit with all the commotion of the past few days, Ruthie carried the tiny battery-operated TV to the spa. How anyone could relax with a massage as she watched the news was beyond me. I suppose being informed was a security blanket for Ruthie, insuring she wouldn't be surprised like she had been by her ex-husband, Harold. Trusting soul that she was, Ruthie had no inkling Harold had run around on her all through med school.

While Ruthie and Penny Sue were kneaded and rubbed, I lounged in the hot tub and called Guthrie.

"Devastated. Just devastated at the beach. Roofs gone, dunes eroded, still no power. I fear what we'll find when we get home. I hope you're coming home soon," he whispered. "I, like, can't stand it here much longer. Mother makes Aunt Harriet look good."

"Hold on." I called to Ruthie and Penny Sue, "Think we'll head back tomorrow?"

"If the power's on," Penny Sue answered. "I need to check the condo. I hope we didn't get any damage."

"As soon as the power's back on," I relayed to Guthrie.

"Fab, man. I'll check every hour and let you know the minute the juice is back. Like, I really can't stand much more Scrabble and rummy."

Ruthie suddenly moaned. Not good. It wasn't an I'm-so-relaxed moan, it was of the oh-shit variety.

"What now?" Penny Sue asked peevishly.

"Tropical Storm Ivan has been upgraded to a hurricane."

"No!" I held a towel over my face. "I don't want to know."

The electricity in our complex didn't come back on until late Tuesday evening, so we headed home Wednesday morning. By then, most of the traffic had cleared, although there was still precious little gasoline. Fortunately, we both had half a tank and knew we could make it. Penny Sue led the way with me following. The further south we drove, the worse the destruction became. By the time we reached Port Orange, we saw that most of the blue tarps covering roof damage from Charley were flapping in the breeze. There were also large portions of roofs, tarps still in place, piled on the side of the road.

I got a sick feeling as we approached the South Causeway Bridge and saw police stopping traffic and checking IDs. A precaution to prevent looting. No one without an official ID that showed they belonged on the island would be allowed to pass. Thankfully, Bobby Barnes had clued me in and vouched for my employment at the center, so I was able to get a business and resident pass. Without his help and the passes, I wouldn't have been allowed on the island, since I'd never taken the time to get a Florida driver's license. I quickly called Penny Sue and told her to pull over.

"If we get out of line, we'll never—" she started.

"Hush. Without a pass, you won't get home at all. I have one for you."

They worked like a charm. We flashed the passes, and the police waved us on. We drove slowly, single file, overwhelmed by the downed signs and debris. About the time we reached Ocean's Seafood, my phone rang. It was Guthrie.

"They won't let me on the beach because my driver's license has my old address," he wailed.

"Park in the hospital lot, I'll come back for you." I hung up, hit redial for Penny Sue, and told her to pull into Publix's parking lot. "Guthrie's stuck, I need your pass."

The lot was full of Publix eighteen-wheelers and a bunch of cars. The cavalry had arrived to restock the frozen food. Penny Sue would be happy about that—it probably meant they had ice.

She handed me the decal. I nodded at the grocery store. "Might be a good time to pick up some ice." I started for my car.

"Wait," she called. "You're not going to invite Guthrie to stay with us, again, are you?"

"Geez, we don't know what we'll find when we get home. We may need to stay with him."

Her brow furrowed. "You're right. I was being pissy. We'll do what we have to do."

Leaving the island wasn't a problem, and I quickly located Guthrie and handed him the pass. We were both in shock when we finally got home. With rubble piled on both sides of A1A, the area looked like a war zone. He went to his condo, I went to mine … er, the judge's. I found the front door ajar and the tile floor covered with damp sand. Ruthie and Penny Sue were in the great room, inspecting the windows and furniture.

"Water must have run down the hill and under the front door," Penny Sue said.

"It rained for thirty-six hours," Ruthie said quietly.

Lu Nee 2, our robot security guard/maid, stood in the far corner of the room, perfectly still. Penny Sue patted her head. "Little Lu Nee is dead!"

"Probably out of power, a recharge should fix her up," I said, remembering I'd forgotten to turn off my alarm clock, which had undoubtedly sent Lu Nee into a tizzy. For hours the robot probably demanded, "Halt, who goes there?" until her life was spent.

"You're right." Penny Sue stepped under an AC vent. "Cool air. Hallelujah!" She hurried to her room and returned with Lu Nee 2's charger.

I gazed out the salt-coated windows. The image of the beach was fuzzy, still the water seemed a lot closer than it used to be. "We should check outside," I said. "The ocean looks awfully close to the deck. We should go down the cluster walkway."

Ruthie pressed her nose against the window. "You're right, I think we've lost the last dune."

We trooped out the front door and ran into Guthrie. "It's a disaster," he wailed. "The windows without the shutters blew out. The condo is soaked. The wallboard has swollen up like a sponge. Frances even blew the pictures off the walls. What am I going to do?"

Ruthie put her arm around him. "You'll stay on our sofa until we get this straightened out."

I could tell Penny Sue wanted to strangle Ruthie, but like a true Southern lady, she smiled instead. "Of course, you're welcome to stay with us," she murmured, all the while giving Ruthie the evil eye. Ruthie returned the hard look and gave Penny Sue a stealthy hand gesture, something I'd never seen her do before. That's when I first suspected that Millie had followed us home!

The four of us trooped down the cluster walkway and stopped abruptly a few feet beyond our condo. The rest of the walkway was gone, ending in a steep five-foot drop to the beach. Thank goodness, we didn't step out on the deck—the side closest to us was hanging in midair.

Penny Sue's hand went to her chest. "Gawd, it's worse than I imagined." She inspected our roof. "At least the roof held—probably because it was replaced when we did the windows."

Debris—huge planks, poles, concrete slabs—the remnants of decks and walkways from who knew where covered our beautiful beach. "Larry won't being fishing any time soon," I said, pointing down the now non-existent dune line. "All the stairs to the beach washed away."

"The turtle nests were lost, that's for sure," Ruthie said ruefully.

Guthrie motioned to the other half of the judge's duplex where the blue tarp covering Charley roof damage flapped. "Man, a shame they didn't get a new roof when you did. I'll bet there's water inside. Do you know the people who live there?"

"Pat and Gary Wilson still own it, I assume. Like Daddy, they hardly ever come down, rent it out instead. I think they're holding it for their kids." She turned to me. "This could be your chance. They may be willing to sell now."

I gulped. "I might not be interested when I see the mess."

"They're not making any more beachfront property. The dunes will come back, they always do. Besides, it's worth a call," Penny Sue said. "If you want a condo here, you can't dillydally."

"You're right. Do you have their phone number?"

"I think it's in the kitchen junk drawer, and a local realtor has the key. We'll call and offer to check on their damage."

Guthrie, still limping, hobbled home to nail plastic over the broken window, tell Timothy where he'd be, and gather his stuff. Meanwhile, Penny Sue called the Wilsons, who were thrilled to hear from 'little Penny Sue' and grateful for her offer to check on their place. Their realtor handled over a dozen rental properties and wasn't sure when she could get to it. The Wilsons debated whether one of them should fly down from Wisconsin, but were worried about the other storm that was on the way. Mr. Wilson promised to call the realtor and have her bring Penny Sue a key.

"As soon as we see the damage, you can decide if you want to make an offer," Penny Sue said. "Ruthie, maybe you should check on Ivan. It's worrying the Wilsons."

She didn't have to ask Ruthie twice. The Weather Channel was on in a split second. As Ruthie waited for the storm update, I pulled out a bottle of ammonia and a large trash bag. "I'll clean the icebox. It's been off for five days; the food is all spoiled."

"Good idea, we want to get that icemaker going ASAP. Publix had already sold out and said the first shipment of ice went in less than an hour." Penny Sue peered over my shoulder as I opened the freezer. The ice cream and everything else had melted, then refroze when the power came back on. The bottom of the compartment was covered in a disgusting mishmash of drippings. "That is nasty! Hand me the ice bins," Penny Sue said, holding her nose. "I'll wash them in the sink."

I unplugged the fridge as Penny Sue filled the sink with warm water. "The goop in the bottom needs to thaw," I explained as I tossed containers in the trash bag.

"Good news," Ruthie called. "It looks like Ivan's going to miss us. It's supposed to brush the coast of South America and head into the Gulf of Mexico. The Florida Panhandle will probably be hit again."

"That's what they said about Charley," Penny Sue said sourly. She brushed her foot on the gritty tile. "If you're finished there, Ruthie, how about vacuuming?"

"Sure, no problem." As Ruthie started for the utility room, we heard a loud knock on the front door.

It was Anastasia Clements, the Wilsons' realtor. Dressed in jeans, a tank top, and running shoes, Anastasia didn't look like your typical realtor. She plunked a digital camera on the counter and started working a key off a large ring. "I was across the street when the Wilsons called. I'm glad you're going to check on their place—that's one less thing I have to worry about." She put the key and her card on the counter. "All of my clients are calling, each one in a state of panic. I'm losing my—" Her cell phone started to play the theme from *Rocky*. "See. Sorry, I need to take this."

She turned toward the hall. "Hello? … Pearl, I'm up to my ears in alligators right now, and besides, you know I can't divulge that information. We've been through this before … Yes, I know who your son is … I'm sorry, I have to go. I'm with a client now. Goodbye."

Anastasia let out a long sigh. "That lady will be the death of me. As if I don't have enough trouble, I have that old biddy breathing down my neck."

"That was Pearl Woodhead, wasn't it?" Penny Sue asked.

"Is she your friend?" Anastasia asked tentatively.

Penny Sue grunted. "Hardly. One of the rudest people I've ever met."

"Rude and delusional," Anastasia said. "Pearl thinks she's some sort of princess and this is her kingdom. Claims she's going to buy up this complex and wants a list of all my clients." The realtor snorted. "Mad as a hatter, if you ask me. Pearl barely has a pot to pee in. I know for a fact her condo is mortgaged to the hilt, and her son makes the payments for her."

Penny Sue arched a brow. "Which condo is hers?"

"A B-unit in the first cluster. Pearl and her husband were among the initial residents. He passed away a long time ago. I never knew him, but people say he was very nice. A woodworker, if you can believe it. Woodhead, woodworker." Anastasia chuckled. "Sometimes truth is stranger than fiction, huh?"

Penny Sue snickered. "Lord's truth."

Anastasia checked her watch. "If you have a digital camera and a computer, would you take pictures of the Wilsons' place and email them? That's what I'm doing. When you speak to them, ask if they'd like me to arrange repairs." She picked up the camera. "Honestly, Charley repairs haven't been completed and now this. There's a shortage of shingles, and roofers are booked for months." She scanned the room. "Did you get much damage?"

"No," Penny Sue replied. "We replaced the roof and all the windows a few years ago. Our only problem is erosion. Frances washed away the sand underneath the deck, and our stairway's gone."

"Count yourself lucky. Call me when you're ready for me to pick up the key."

"We will," Penny Sue dried her hands and walked Anastasia to the door. "Thanks. Don't work too hard."

"I wish."

Penny Sue handed me a bowl and a spatula to scoop out the slush on the bottom of the freezer. I filled the bowl; she dumped it into the sink and doused it with hot water. By the time the slush went down, I'd filled the bowl again. As we continued our assault on the freezer, Ruthie vacuumed the master bedroom.

"What does this remind you of?" I snickered, handing her another bowl of grossness.

"Magnetized mud. And you're tacky to bring it up. My boobs still hurt from being dragged out of the tub." She shoved the bowl back at me.

"It was your idea to use two jars. We were only following instructions."

"Well, it wasn't so funny on my side of the tub rim." Putrid steam rose from the slushy drippings as she sprayed them with hot water. She leaned back, holding her nose. "This is truly disgusting."

"Only one or two more bowls before I'm ready to wipe it down with ammonia." I handed her another load. "Speaking of disgusting, what do you make of that stuff about Pearl?"

"You mean Princess Pearl?" Penny Sue cackled. "Princess of Darkness, Princess of Doom and Gloom. Hey, if she's a Princess, what does that make Woody? Is he a prince? Woody, Prince of Doom and Gloom—that fits."

"Do you think she's the person buying up all the real estate?"

"Of course not. We know the last three units were sold to different groups. Besides, Anastasia said Pearl is mortgaged to the hilt. And, Woody is a government employee. He probably does pretty well, being a lawyer and everything, but I'm sure he's not getting rich."

"He's married; maybe his wife has money. He's a lawyer, so he'd know how to set up dummy corporations. In fact, maybe that's why Pearl's place is mortgaged—they're using the equity for down payments on the condos they buy." I handed her the bowl. "This is the last of it."

"Praise the Lord, I can't tolerate much more of this stinky steam." She dumped the bowl and doused it with water. "Down payments are one thing, making the mortgage payments are another."

"Interest rates are at an all time low right now, meaning payments are low, too. Besides, they'll rent the units to cover the payments."

Penny Sue rinsed the bowl and filled it with warm water and ammonia. "Here," she handed me the bowl with a sponge.

"Gee, thanks. Wouldn't you like to take over now?"

She waved flippantly. "You're doing fine. Besides, I need to call Daddy and tell him we're all right. He may know something about the Woodheads. Pearl apparently knew Mama."

My eyes rolled up to the ceiling. "Why me, Lord? Why did I always end up with the dirty work?"

Before I could protest, Penny Sue took the portable phone into the guest bedroom to call her dad. A few minutes later, Ruthie showed up with the small cooler from the Mercedes. I'd forgotten all about the cooler we'd packed with ice and soft drinks for the trip.

"I need a break," Ruthie said, hopping on a stool. She popped the top of a cola. "What's your pleasure? Tea, cola, water?"

"Green tea. I think my system's polluted by all of this ammonia." I made a final swipe of the freezer wall, closed the door, and plugged in the refrigerator. We still had the lower compartment to clean, but this would get the icemaker started.

I sat at the counter beside Ruthie. "Penny Sue's calling her father to see what he knows about Pearl Woodhead." I took a sip of tea. "You know, Pearl said she knew Guthrie's Aunt Harriet." I took my cell phone from my pocket. "Maybe I can get him to do a little detective work, too."

After all the calls I'd received from Guthrie, I only had to hit "send" to reach him. It took several minutes, but he finally answered. "How are you doing?" I asked.

"Man, the place is worse than a disaster. It's, like, a catastrophe. You're lucky I'm alive. I forgot the power had been off and opened the refrigerator for a cola. Whoa, I almost passed out. Gnarly. The worst smell of all time, like, there's no word to describe it."

"Nasty?"

"Man, that's it—nasty. Yeah, it was totally nasty."

"How's your knee?"

"I'm getting tired, and it's starting to throb."

"Don't hurt your knee again by overdoing it. We'll come up tomorrow and help you clean out the fridge."

"Wow, that's really nice of you, Leigh, because this thing is so disgusting I think we should, like, load it up and take it to the dump. You know, the way Arlo did in *Alice's Restaurant*."

I chuckled. As Grammy would say, he was *eat up* with that movie. "Don't worry, there's nothing wrong with the icebox we can't fix with ammonia."

"Gee, you're wonderful. Because, I think I'd, like, throw-up if I had to clean it. I'm doubly, triply, quadrupl—"

"Hey, no problem. Have you talked to your aunt and uncle about the condo yet?" I asked.

"No."

"Would you do a favor for me?"

"Anything, man, I owe you my life, my—"

"You don't owe me anything. I do need a favor. Remember the old lady, Pearl Woodhead, we met on the public walk when everyone was checking out the Russian in the dumpster?"

"Sure, she had an 1860 Colt 45 cap pistol. That thing really looked real, didn't it?"

"Right. Remember, she claimed to know your Aunt Harriet, which means your folks might recall her. Do you mind asking your uncle what he knows about Pearl?"

"You want me to play detective? That's cool. What are we looking for, commander?"

Gawd, now I'm his commander. I stared at the phone, not sure info about Pearl was worth it. Still, I'd gone this far. "We heard she thinks she's some sort of princess and this development is her kingdom."

"That's really twisted. I'd say Pearl's Colt is a cap shy of a full strip."

I rolled my eyes at Ruthie and Penny Sue who were listening to my end of the conversation. "It is twisted, but she apparently believes it. We're trying to figure out how she came up with such a wild idea."

"A-okay, commander, I'm on the case. Ten four." He hung up.

I smiled grimly. "I'm now Guthrie's commander. He's going to call his folks."

"Lord, I hope he doesn't start saluting you," Penny Sue said.

Me too. Brownies were one thing, salutes—over the line!

Chapter 20

September 8-10

Since I scraped and scrubbed the freezer, I insisted Penny Sue clean out the lower compartment. She reluctantly agreed. Like always, Ruthie and I would end up doing most of the work. Ruthie offered to wipe the compartment down with ammonia after it was emptied, while I agreed to assist with recyclables. Ruthie and I should have inspected the fridge before making our magnanimous offers. Most of its contents were glass and plastic, meaning Penny Sue's task was merely to hand me the jars and bottles to be dumped down the disposal and rinsed. Ruthie would do the hard work, later, with the ammonia. Once again, Penny Sue came out on top but, it also gave her time to talk.

"Daddy said the Woodheads were a nice, private couple. He doesn't remember much about Pearl, except that she always seemed out of sorts. Everyone called her husband Gerry, an Anglicized version of his American Indian name. He was apparently three-quarters Indian and his family had lived in these parts for generations, the last of a long-forgotten tribe. Gerry told Daddy this area was originally his tribe's land."

"Pearl thinks she's an Indian princess?" I said as I dumped salad dressing into the sink and rinsed the container.

"I guess so. If he were the last of a tribe, I suppose that would make him chief. Is the chief's wife a princess or a queen?"

"Darned if I know." I took a jar of mayonnaise and scooped it into the sink. Ruthie sat in the other room watching the weather forecast for the umpteenth time. "Anything new on Ivan?" I called.

"No, still far south and expected to move into the Gulf."

"How would you like to take a stroll while you're waiting your turn at the icebox?" I asked.

Ruthie leaned against the counter. "Why? What do you need?"

"You haven't met Pearl, so she probably doesn't know who you are. How about taking a stroll over to her condo?"

"Good idea. It's one of the B-units in the first cluster," Penny Sue said. "Pretend you're checking out damage. Just walk around and see if you notice anything unusual."

"What does she look like?"

"About Penny Sue's size," I said, "with shocking white hair. The hair's the giveaway. You can't miss her."

"I doubt it'll do any good, but I could use some exercise," Ruthie said. "Let me change shoes."

Guthrie telephoned right after Ruthie left. "Commander, mission accomplished. It took some doing—I had to go through Harriet to get to Uncle Daniel. Anyway, the Woodheads had one child, Robert. Pearl's husband was named Gerry, and he was a Native American. Uncle Dan said he was a super guy. Gerry was a woodworker who made beautiful tables and things out of stumps and driftwood. Uncle said they were, like, works of art. But, get this—Gerry's true specialty was totem poles. Man, isn't that awesome? Woodhead, totem poles!"

"That is wild," I agreed. "His family must have Anglicized their last name based on his craft."

"Yeah, man, like the old English did. Millers, Smiths, Weavers—they all took names from their trades."

Penny Sue was getting ahead of me and had placed a long line of jars and bottles on the counter. I figured I'd better get to the point. "Does your uncle know anything about Pearl?"

"He didn't like her. Uncle Dan said she was conceited and put on airs. She ragged Gerry a lot about not getting the proper respect. Gerry always blew her off, which made her madder. Seems she thought somebody owed him something. Uncle Dan tried to steer clear of her, because she reminded him of you-know-who."

"Harriet?"

"Yeah, only worse. Hey, I'm almost finished here. Want to go out to dinner?"

"Go out to dinner? What's open?"

"I saw Larry, the fisherman, in the parking lot. He told me the Pub brought in refrigerated trucks for its food and is grilling stuff out back."

"Want to go to the Pub for dinner?" I asked Penny Sue. "They're grilling food out back."

"Yes, if they have ice and cold beer."

I glanced at the clock. "We're still cleaning the icebox. How about six?" I arched a brow at Penny Sue. She nodded.

"That's cool."

"We'll pick you up and bring your stuff down after dinner."

"That's a plan, man."

Penny Sue finished emptying the bottles, and I started wiping the icebox with ammonia. I was almost finished when Ruthie returned.

She sat at the counter and fished a bottle of cold water from the cooler. "It's a long way up there, and the heat index must be over a hundred. There's considerable damage, mainly roofs and decks. It's a disaster." She took a long drink and grinned. "I found Pearl's place, and you'll never guess what's next to the stairway."

I smiled back. This was too easy! "A totem pole?"

Ruthie's jaw dropped. "How did you know?"

I filled Ruthie and Penny Sue in on my conversation with Guthrie.

"Respect?" Penny Sue mused. "The other day, on the walkway, Pearl said something about Woody not getting respect."

"That's right." I closed the icebox and washed my hands—they reeked of ammonia. I made a mental note to buy the lemon-scented variety in the future. "I think the name thing is a hoot—Woodhead, totem poles."

"Parker. I guess my ancestors parked buggies." Penny Sue elbowed me, giggling. "Your ancestors, Martin, must have been birds." Penny Sue pawed to the bottom of the cooler and found a beer. "What about Guthrie? Fribble. What's a fribble?"

Ruthie hopped down from her stool and pulled a dictionary from a drawer in the credenza. She thumbed the pages and went into hysterics. "It's here! Fribble means a frivolous person."

"Truth is stranger than fiction!"

"Wait," Ruthie said. "There's something else I forgot to tell you."

She had our attention.

"Pearl drives a black Taurus."

The next few days were a blur of activity. Phone calls from concerned family and friends, phone calls to insurance agents who never answered or showed up when promised, busy lines and answering machines at any establishment remotely related to roofing or construction.

Guthrie spent nights with us on the sofa and worked to clean up his condo during the day. Mold, he said. Even though we had electricity—which many people still didn't have—he was afraid the wallboard had been infected during the five steamy days without power. Although there were no outward signs of mold, it was a definite possibility.

We trooped next door to the Wilsons' the morning after we spoke with him and found extensive damage. Like in Guthrie's condo, moisture swelled the wallboard, and the saturated carpet would have to be replaced. We took a bunch of digital pictures, cranked the AC down to seventy-two—mold!—and emailed the pictures to Gary in Wisconsin. One look and Gary Wilson decided he'd better fly down. Besides, Ivan seemed certain to pass us by.

We hadn't been home long from Gary's when Chris called wanting to know if we needed any help. She also informed us that the New Smyrna Speedway was covered with debris—all the billboards had blown apart—and was closed until the first of October. That news was truly a bummer, as Guthrie would say. Our court depositions had been delayed indefinitely, and we were counting on racing practice to give us a break from cleaning and construction.

"You're welcome to come stay with me and do some shopping," Chris offered.

"Thanks, but we wouldn't feel right running off and leaving Guthrie and Gary Wilson to fend for themselves," I said.

Penny Sue, sipping a Bloody Mary, gave me the evil eye. I blew her off by curling my lip like Elvis.

"The offer stands," Chris said. "Call if you change your mind. Meanwhile, I'll check around St. Augustine to see if there's another place we can practice."

The moment I clicked off, the phone rang again— Frannie May from Boston. How were we? Did we get much damage?

Her sister was doing great, but Fran was going to stay up North until the repairs to her house were completed. Carl guessed it would take another week or two. Was there anything we needed? If so, call Carl. He'd be happy to help.

I assured her we were fine and told her about the charity race, which would probably be in early October. I said we hoped she'd be back in time.

"Wouldn't miss it for the world," she replied. "I'll put two thousand on your team. Be sure to call Carl if you want help with your cars."

I thanked Fran and said goodbye, then pointed to Penny Sue's Bloody Mary and winked. She got my drift and started making one for me.

"Weak," I exclaimed, as she took the vodka, poised to pour without a jigger. "How much money do we have pledged so far?"

"If the Hamptons' people come through, which I think they will—except maybe Frankie, who's in jail ..." Her face scrunched with concentration. Math was never Penny Sue's best subject. "... about $45,000."

"Make that $47,000, thanks to Frannie May." I took a taste of the drink she slid across the counter. "Hmmm, that's good."

Ruthie appeared from the bedroom. Penny Sue raised her glass, "Want one?" she asked.

Ruthie held up a can of green tea. "I'm fine."

"You know, I think we should use our free time to raise contributions," I said. "After all, there are more hurricane victims now than before."

"Yes," Ruthie said emphatically. "I heard on TV that because the two hurricanes are separate disasters, homeowners may have to pay the deductible twice—which for most is two percent of the insured value. That's thousands of dollars working people can't afford."

"It's that much?" Penny Sue asked. "We're lucky Daddy replaced the roof and windows, otherwise we'd be in the same boat. This is a vacation home. If the whole thing went," she waved her arm, "we wouldn't be hurt."

My eyes widened. "Who wouldn't be hurt? I wouldn't have a place to live!"

"Sure, but you wouldn't lose money."

Ruthie slammed down her green tea—totally uncharacteristic—and motioned to Penny Sue for a Bloody Mary. "You're right. There are people out there who have lost everything. Think about it. So many businesses have been damaged—especially on the beach—families not only have lost their homes, but their jobs. At the very time people need money for repairs they have no income! We have to help. Penny Sue, call your PR friend. We need TV spots. We need *Good Morning America* and the *Today Show*. We need national contributions." Ruthie chugged her Bloody Mary.

I was astounded. I'd never heard Ruthie speak with such passion, which was my second clue that Millie had followed her to New Smyrna Beach.

Pumped up with righteous indignation, Penny Sue threw back her shoulders. "Damn straight, it's the least we can do. Leigh, please hand me the telephone."

Penny Sue reached her friend at the Atlanta PR firm and laid it on thick. Her description of the hurricane damage sounded like a nuclear holocaust, and Max quickly agreed to run the news circuit again.

"Tony Perkins from *Good Morning America* was in New Smyrna Beach. That should buy credibility," Max said. "I'll contact them. The Weather Channel was in the area, too. I'll give them a call, since they're here in Atlanta. Jim Cantore may be willing to do a short spot."

"Jim Cantore," Penny Sue mouthed to Ruthie who all but swooned. Penny Sue hung up the phone, smirking. "We're on our way."

Sonny Mallard, the wonderful contractor who had fixed Nana King's water leak, agreed to help Penny Sue with the deck. What we needed were a few truckloads of sand to anchor the exposed supports. Sand, what's the big deal? Seems anything involving the beach was a very big deal, we soon found out. First, you needed a permit and permission to drive equipment on the beach. Secondly, you needed native sand—that is, matching sand. Any old sand wouldn't do. Whether through luck or connections, Sonny obtained the permits in a few days. The sand was another matter. He put in an order for several truckloads, but unfortunately there was a waiting list. If we were lucky, they'd get to us in a couple of weeks. Under normal circumstances, a reasonable scenario; in our case, not so hot. Every high tide eroded the sand under the deck a little more. At the rate it was going, the deck could collapse before the sand arrived.

"Sandbags are the only solution I can thing of," Sonny advised. "I know a place in Sanford that stockpiled them for Frances and may have some left. If you can borrow a truck, you could get a load and place them around the deck supports. That should give you a little protection until the sand arrives. I'd do it for you, but I'm booked solid. Ten-hour days for the foreseeable future."

Gary Wilson, the other half of our duplex, had flown in the previous day. He had the same problem with his deck, so quickly offered to help with the sandbags. It took several phone calls, but we finally found a dealership willing to rent us a used pick-up truck. Since the cab only held three people, one of us had to stay behind.

"Ruthie, why don't you stay here and peek in on Pearl Woodhead?"

"Pearl Woodhead?" Gary loaded a shovel and wheelbarrow into the back of the truck. "She called last night, wanting to buy my condo."

Whoa, Pearl was worse than Yuri, I thought. "If you're thinking of selling, I hope you'll give me a chance to bid on your condo. I'm looking to buy something in this development, and your unit would be perfect."

"Pat and I haven't decided what to do yet. I'm waiting for all the estimates. If we decide to sell, I'll be sure to let you know."

"Thanks, units around here are snatched up before the listing even hits the newspaper."

We were very grateful to have Gary with us, because the sandbag place was a load-your-own affair. After ten minutes Penny Sue and I were worn out and drenched with sweat. Yeah, it was stinky, dirty sweat—none of that sugarcoated, Southern perspiration stuff. Gary, in his early sixties, was in better shape still, the chances of our filling the back of the truck without help were slim to none.

That's when Penny Sue spied two young men hanging out at the bus stop. She reached in her purse, pulled out two fifties, and headed in their direction, her fanny swaying in full gear. They followed her back.

"Meet Darin and Lee. They can help us for an hour," she said.

Fifty bucks an hour was terrific wages for manual labor in Florida, and those young men earned every bit of it. Darin waved us aside, picked up a sandbag and *tossed* it to Lee, who stood in the back of the truck. They swapped positions several times, but had the truck loaded in fifty minutes. We'd have been in cardiac arrest and on our way to the local hospital. They were happy for the money and hotfooted it to the convenience store across the street.

"Youth," Gary said, starting the truck. "You can take vitamins, Viagra, anything you want, but there's no substitute for youth."

"Gospel truth," Penny Sue said with a devilish grin.

Uh oh, I knew her all too well ... there was a story behind that grin, but I wasn't going to probe in front of Gary. A young Atlanta Brave, perhaps, back home in Roswell? Anything was possible with Penny Sue.

We found Ruthie waiting with a big pitcher of lemonade when we arrived home. "I thought you could use some good old Southern vitamin C after your ordeal." She gave us the once over. "You look like you've hardly broken a sweat."

Penny Sue flexed her bicep. "Piece of cake! We're in good shape."

"I'd love some lemonade," Gary said, taking a seat at the kitchen counter.

"Coming up." Ruthie filled large glasses packed with ice.

"Umm-m, this is good. Just what the doctor ordered. And, to set the record straight, it was Penny Sue's wallet that was in good shape. She found two strapping young men who had some time to spare," Gary said.

"I found out some interesting poop while you were gone." Ruthie took a long drink of her lemonade.

"Don't keep us in suspense," Penny Sue snapped. "Speak up!"

"Well, in case Pearl saw me yesterday, I figured I needed a disguise. So I took an old pair of jeans and cut the legs off to make shorts."

"Not the Moschinos?" Penny Sue blurted.

"Yeah, they were getting shiny in the seat."

I shook my head. Two hundred dollar jeans and she cut off the legs for a disguise! *More money than sense*, Grammy Martin would say.

"Next, I sheared off the sleeves of one of my tee-shirts."

"Don't tell me which one," I said.

"Anyway, I tucked my hair up in a baseball cap, wore your flip flops," she pointed at me, "and Penny Sue's big sunglasses."

"Those are expensive Porsches. They've come back in style. Didn't you notice that some of the guys from the Hamptons wore them?"

"They look fake with the gold frame and all," Ruthie said.

"Fake?" Penny Sue nearly shouted. "The frame's eighteen-karat!"

Ruthie snorted. "Do you want to hear my story or not? Besides, I was confident Pearl wouldn't recognize Porsche sunglasses and would think they were fakes. I couldn't go back today dressed like I was the last time."

Penny Sue sighed. "Go on."

"When I got there, Pearl was coming out of her garage with a bag of garbage. I hid behind the building to watch. You won't believe this."

"What?"

"Pearl stopped at her neighbor's stairway, reached in the garbage bag, pulled out a milk carton and a chicken bone, and put them on the bottom step."

"That's sick," Penny Sue muttered.

"That's not all. Next she took a rotten head of lettuce and put it on top of the mailboxes. By then, she was at the dumpster, tied the bag and slung it in."

Gary held his glass out for a refill. "Sounds like the old lady's lost a few marbles."

"Was that it?" I was disappointed. Pearl's strange behavior merely confirmed what I already thought—that she was seriously nuts.

"There's more. As Pearl was walking back to her condo, a big black limo pulled in. It stopped, picked her up, and drove to her house. I ran around the back of the building to spy on them. Three men got out with Pearl. Two men had dark brown hair, well-tailored suits, and were very tan. They'd either just come from the tanning salon or were Mediterranean, you know Greek, Italian, Spanish, or something. The third man was unmistakably American Indian. His hair was shoulder length and pulled back in a braid. He wore slacks and a print shirt with one of those string ties that guys out West wear. He also had on a lot of turquoise and silver jewelry."

"Did you go to Pearl's door and listen?" Penny Sue asked.

"Heck, no. The driver in the limo would have seen me. I strolled around pretending to inspect hurricane damage. After about a half hour, Larry came by with his fishing machine, and I figured I'd better skedaddle. Even with the big sunglasses, he might recognize me and get suspicious."

Thinking, Penny Sue stroked her chin. "Larry was probably trying to find a way to get to the beach. All the walkways are gone, and there's a five-foot drop in most places." Penny Sue folded her arms across her chest and chewed a fingernail. "What does all of this mean? Pearl thinks she's an Indian princess, is trying to buy up the complex, and an Indian and two apparently well-heeled men come to visit. What's the connection? She's obviously crazy, so why would they fool with her?"

Gary drained his lemonade. "Ladies, it's getting late, and the truck has to be back by tomorrow afternoon. I think we should get started on the sandbags. It's going to take us a lot longer than it took Darin and Lee."

"A shame we couldn't have brought them back with us," Penny Sue said.

Gary stood. "Not a chance, this is Friday night. I'm sure those young men have plans."

Chapter 21

September 11-22

Timothy was spending the weekend with Guthrie (Yeah, we got our sofa back!) and offered to help us with the sandbags. We mapped out a plan of attack the night before. Gary determined that our sidewalk was secure all the way to the end where it had been sheered off by the storm. Our job was to load the sandbags into the wheelbarrow, roll it to the end of the sidewalk, tip it forward, and dump the load. Meanwhile, Gary used a ladder to climb down the sheer sand cliff to the beach. Once we dumped the sandbags, he'd place them around the deck supports. Simple, right? Simple in theory, hard to execute. The sandbags weighed at least a million pounds when loaded in the wheelbarrow.

If it hadn't been for Timothy with all of his bulging 'ceps, we'd never have finished. Guthrie couldn't help because of his bum knee, but lent another wheelbarrow to the cause and played oxygenated-water boy. Timothy loaded the wheelbarrows; we pushed them down the sidewalk and tipped them over. Either we were completely out of shape or the darned handcarts actually weighted a ton, because it took two of us—one on each handle—to push and dump. Being there were three of us, we devised a rotation plan so that one could rest after two trips.

With two carts and Atlas unloading the truck, we finished before poor Gary. A huge pile of sandbags had stacked up on the beach. With the heat index hoveringly around a hundred, the three of us were sprawled against the truck, every pore spouting oxygenated-water. Timothy, aka Atlas, merely glistened and went to Gary's aid. If Penny Sue hadn't been so tired, she'd probably have licked Timothy's ankle as he passed by. The fact she didn't give him a second glance showed her utter exhaustion.

Guthrie offered to drive the pickup truck back to the dealership, while I followed in my car. Penny Sue proposed to call in orders for pizzas and antipasto salads that we'd pick up on the way home. I ran to the bedroom for a quick shower when I returned and emerged as Timothy and Gary arrived. Exhausted, famished, but clean, we all twisted the cap off a beer—even Timothy!—and quickly found places at the table. Conversation was scarce until everyone had consumed several slices of pizza and hefty helpings of salad. As Gary and Guthrie continued to munch, the rest of us settled back and twisted the cap off a second beer.

"Man, I'm sorry I don't have any brownies for dessert. I've been so busy cleaning the condo, I couldn't get in the mood to bake, ya know what I mean?" Guthrie pointed his beer at me. "I meant to tell you, Pearl called Uncle Dan wanting to buy his condo. She told him there was a six-month wait for repairs and other storms were coming. If he was smart, he'd sell the unit while it was still worth something."

Other storms? We all gazed at Ruthie.

"Ivan's out there, but it seems headed for the Gulf," our resident weatherwoman replied.

"Did Pearl make an offer?" I asked.

"Yeah, she offered $299,000. With all the repairs the place would need, that was generous, she said."

"Your uncle didn't take it, did he?" Penny Sue asked.

"Heck no. First of all, he doesn't like Pearl. Second, he's holding the place as his nest egg for when Harriet dies. Uncle Dan hopes he'll get enough money for one of those retirement homes where all the nurses are young with big tits."

Gary, who'd just taken a bite of pizza, almost choked. Ruthie pounded his back. He took a sip of beer. "Sorry," he sputtered.

"What is Pearl up to?" Penny Sue asked no one in particular.

Ruthie clunked her beer on the table. "She's trying to scare people into selling cheap, then she'll turn around and sell them for a big profit."

"Anastasia said she's not rich. How could Pearl afford to do that?" I asked.

"The men in the limo are backing her," Penny Sue said emphatically. "I'll bet they're trying to buy the place to put in big, high-rise condos. Pearl is the front man. She's probably earning a commission." Penny Sue's eyes lit up. "A commission Pearl needs because she's a compulsive spender, which is why her condo's mortgaged to the hilt." Penny Sue leaned back and wagged her finger. "And Woody's told her she has to change her ways, because he's not making her mortgage payments anymore. What do you think?" Penny Sue took a satisfied sip of water.

"You've lost me," Gary said. "But this is prime real estate, and I'd hate to see a high rise go in here." He swiveled toward me. "Don't worry—if we decide to sell, you'll get the first call." He folded his napkin and placed it on the table. "Sorry to eat and run, but I have to fly home tomorrow. My realtor will send someone to rip out the carpet and will coordinate with the insurance company, if they ever send an inspector." Disgusted, he shook his head. “Pat and I appreciate your help. It’s hard to live so far away and nice to know you have friends.” Gary stood and patted Timothy on the shoulder. “Thanks, big guy. I wouldn’t be standing without your help.” They shook hands, and we said our goodbyes.

While Penny Sue walked Gary to the door, Ruthie told Guthrie and Timothy about Pearl, her strange behavior, and the limo.

“Chicken bones?” Guthrie said. “Like, maybe, that’s some kind of Indian hex. Whoa, I find chicken bones on my steps, and I’m gonna sage the place.”

Penny Sue returned and plopped an ice bucket of beer in the center of the table. “Ya know, I’ll bet Pearl’s in on the mercury sabotage.”

“Pearl couldn’t have done that,” I said. “She’s old. Pearl wouldn’t have the strength to hold up the tool that scratched Guthrie’s storm shutters. Besides, she’s stiff as a board—no way could she have crawled under Nana King’s house.”

“The guys in the limo have lackeys who did it.” Penny Sue stood. “Would anyone like a scotch?”

Guthrie raised his hand like a child. “I would.”

Penny Sue departed for the kitchen. “We need more information,” she said. “Someone’s trying to frighten people away from this complex.” Penny Sue handed a glass to Guthrie. “Ruthie, can you use your computer to get a list of all the owners in this development?”

“Probably—the Volusia Appraiser’s database is online.”

Penny Sue pointed at me. Good grief, she’d flipped into the schoolteacher mode. “Leigh, you want to buy a condo in this complex, right?”

My brows furrowed, wondering where she was headed. “Of course.”

“Does anyone have a printer?” Penny Sue asked.

Ruthie and I gave her a dumb look. "Not here," we said in unison.

"I have a portable in the trunk of my car. It's inkjet, but you're welcome to use it," Timothy said, clearly intrigued.

"Thank you, Timothy." Penny Sue started to pace. "There's something sneaky going on, and we're going to find out what it is. Ruthie, your mission is to get the names and addresses of all the owners in this development. Leigh, you're going to send them letters saying you want to buy a condo, and would they please contact you if they decide to sell."

"What about Yuri, who's going door-to-door?" I asked.

"Screw Yuri," Penny Sue said.

Geez! The heat, work, beer, and scotch had gotten to her. Never in my life had I heard Penny Sue use that term. Could the spirit of Millie move around, I wondered? I thought Millie was attached to Ruthie, because of her psychic abilities. Maybe not. "Do you think Yuri's involved?"

"No way. Otherwise, he wouldn't be going door-to-door. Pearl and her guys are undercutting him, which is why he had to resort to personal contact," Penny Sue said.

Made sense. For once, she might be right.

"Okay, let's do it." We all did a clumsy high five.

Hurricanes are the pits, but that's the cost of living in Florida. It could be worse; you could live in California where the earth moves. That has to be the scariest experience of all, I think. In a hurricane, at least the ground's solid and you're blown around. In an earthquake, nothing's solid.

The next week and a half passed in a blur of tedium. Ruthie obtained the addresses for the development, and I sent out the letters. Gary's carpet was ripped up and dumped in our driveway. Guthrie got his insurance appraisal, which nearly sent Uncle Dan into cardiac arrest. Timothy was his hunky self—always good looking, eager to help, but never revealing much.

Ruthie kept doing reconnaissance on Pearl's place. So Ruthie wouldn't continue cutting up her expensive, designer clothes, I took her to Gone Bonkers for local attire. She purchased several cotton outfits that she really liked. "I can't believe I bought this much stuff for this amount of money," Ruthie said, thumping the receipt with her finger.

"Welcome to the beach," I said. "This isn't Atlanta where you're judged by how much your outfit cost. Here, nobody cares what you wear, which is what I like about the place."

A big hat, sunglasses, and regular clothes provided the perfect disguise for Ruthie. Unfortunately, she didn't learn much from her daily treks except that Pearl was truly a brick shy of a full load. Pearl snuck around the development hiding her garbage in neighbors' plants, stairwells, mailboxes, cars, and anything else she could get into. The old girl also had sticky fingers. She stole the welcome mat from one condo and a man's swimsuit that had been draped over a railing to dry.

"Whoa, that's seriously kinky," Guthrie said, when Ruthie recounted her story. "You think Pearl's doing, like, an Indian counting coup thing?"

"What's that?" Penny Sue asked.

"It was a way Indians gained honor by getting through the enemies' defenses. All they had to do was touch the enemy, or take something, to prove they were superior."

"Pearl's proving she's superior by dumping garbage everywhere and stealing things?"

Guthrie held up his hands. "Stranger things have happened."

The other thing Ruthie learned from her daily walks was that fisherman Larry was doing a lot of walking, too. "Likely because he can't get to the beach to fish," she surmised.

"Or the fishing's lousy with all the debris in the water," I suggested.

"That's probably it," Penny Sue agreed. "That depression off the coast was just upgraded to a hurricane, and some weather forecasters think Ivan will go out to sea in New England, then turn around and come back here as a nor'easter."

"You're kidding!" Ruthie raced to the television. With all the activity of the last few days, she'd slacked off on her weather watching. Besides, Penny Sue had become hooked on *CSI* reruns that we'd watched most evenings. A few minutes into the tropical update, Ruthie moaned.

"What, what?" Penny Sue rushed to the living room.

"Ivan made landfall in the Panhandle this morning. It's been downgraded to a tropical storm and is supposed to bring lots of rain all the way to New England. But the worst is Tropical Storm Jeanne that was initially predicted to bypass Florida. It's now a hurricane and expected to take a northwest turn, following in Frances' footsteps."

"English, Ruthie, English. What does that mean to us?" Penny Sue asked.

"We'd better restock the hurricane supplies."

Penny Sue and I both groaned.

The next week was Pearl and weather hell. What probably got Pearl's back up were the responses we started receiving from the condo owners we'd written. Almost to a person, each owner said they'd been contacted by Pearl Woodhead, but would let us know if they decided to sell. I suppose someone told Pearl about my offer. On Saturday morning we found a typed note stuck to our door with chewing gum: "MIND YOUR OWN BUSINESS."

"Put on gloves," Penny Sue shrieked as I started to pull the gum off the door. "The crime lab can probably check it for DNA."

I shook my head. "Penny Sue, get serious. The police are not going to check this note for DNA."

"It's a threat, and we know Pearl did it."

I let out a long sigh. "You may be right, but there's no overt threat."

Ruthie appeared with a baggie. *CSI* had obviously made an impression on her, too. "Doesn't hurt to preserve the evidence. Don't you guess we should call the police?"

"Not for this," I said. "But if it escalates ..."

And, it did.

That evening Gary Wilson phoned to tell us he and Pat had decided to sell. If I wanted the condo, it was mine. They'd been leaning in that direction, but Pearl Woodhead pushed them all the way. The night before, Pearl called the Wilsons and tried to pressure them into selling. When Gary told her he had promised me first choice, Pearl went berserk, claiming it was rightfully her land, and she'd put a hex on him, his children, and his children's children. Gary told her he'd heard enough and hung up in her face. Pearl phoned several more times—they could tell from caller ID—but the Wilsons didn't answer. Pearl finally stopped about midnight their time.

I told Gary I thought the beachfront condos previously sold in the $550,000-$600,000 range, but considering the repairs, would he consider taking less? "Absolutely, wouldn't dream of charging you full price," he assured me. He'd give me with a figure when he received all the repair estimates.

I was ecstatic for about ten minutes. "Gary will sell," I exclaimed. "I'm not homeless anymore!" I did a little victory dance as Penny Sue passed around wine to toast my good fortune.

"Best yet, you'll be right next to me. Won't that be fun-n?" Penny Sue drawled.

I swallowed hard. Hmmm. I had to think for a minute. Oh, well, Penny Sue wouldn't be there much, so it would be fun. We toasted again, just as the phone rang.

"Leigh," Guthrie whispered. "Turn on your front porch light. Someone's messing with your car."

I flew down the hall to the light switch. Penny Sue followed, pulling her gun from its holster as Ruthie slapped the battery pack into the taser. My heart pounded. "Okay, on three. One, two, three-e." I flipped the switch and flung open the door. At that moment, a halogen spotlight from Guthrie's upper deck switched on, illuminating the culprit and Timothy creeping toward the parking lot.

Pearl stood beside my car. She was holding an egg carton and a jar. As I approached her from the front, Timothy snuck in from the rear. Pearl's lips curled back with a crazed look of contempt when she saw me.

"You stole my condo," she said. Before I could stop her, she took an egg and broke it on the hood of my VW. "This is my land." She threw an egg at me, which missed, and prepared to heave the jar. Luckily, Timothy had reached her by then and snatched the jar before she could release it. Pearl whirled around, eyes wide, and smashed the egg carton in Timothy's face. He staggered back, blinded.

Penny Sue shoved her gun into my hands and raced to Pearl. With one swift move, Penny Sue swept her leg in a low arc and knocked the old woman flat on her behind. Then, Penny Sue grabbed Pearl's wrists and held them tightly. "Call Woody. She's lost her mind. Ruthie, bring me a scarf or something I can use to tie her hands. Nothing rough, her skin's like tissue paper."

A two hundred dollar Chanel silk scarf is what Ruthie brought back. What a waste. I sucked air as I watched Penny Sue tie Pearl's hands behind her with the expensive silk and lead her into the house to wait for Woody.

Guthrie appeared with a washcloth and wiped the egg off Timothy's face, all the while Timothy studied the jar. He let out a low whistle. "Be glad Pearl didn't throw this," he exclaimed. "It's mercury!"

My jaw dropped. Was Pearl responsible for Clyde's death?

"Got a hose?" Guthrie brought me back to the present. "The egg will ruin your paint job."

I absently pointed to the side of the house and followed the others inside.

Woody arrived in a half hour. The moment Pearl saw him she started screaming. We'd stolen from her, assaulted her, none of it was her fault. She spit at Penny Sue.

"Mom, if you don't shut up, I'm locking you in the bathroom," he said sternly.

She gave him the most hateful look I've ever seen. "You wouldn't dare."

"Don't tempt me." He stared her in the eye. "What happened, here?"

Timothy started the story, telling Woody how he and Guthrie were sitting on their deck and saw Pearl sneak up and start messing with my car. Penny Sue finished the story as Timothy held up the jar of mercury.

Woody took the jar and examined it. The veins in this neck bulged as he rotated the jar and watched the large silver globule side around in one piece. Finally, he thrust it in his mother's face. "Where did you get this?"

"A friend gave it to me."

"What friend?"

"A relative friend."

"What relative?"

"One of us," she said defiantly.

"Us? Us, what?"

"Our brother. An Indian."

Woody shook his head and put the jar on the coffee table. "Mom, you're not an Indian, Dad was. Can't you get that through your head? You're not an Indian princess."

"Your father was the chief."

"Chief of what? The tribe is long gone." He asked us, "Have any of you heard of the Surruque?"

We shook our heads.

"No one has. Dad was the last of the line."

Pearl sat up straight. "No, son, you are. This is your rightful land. I'm making arrangements to get it back for you, so you'll get the respect and riches you deserve."

He gave us an expression of total defeat. "I'll pay for any damage. Do you want to press charges?"

"No," I said. "Not if you get her some help. Woody, at her age, she may have Alzheimer's. Ruthie's seen her do some very strange things."

"Yeah, man, like kinky," Guthrie added.

"Thanks." Woody helped his mother up. Ruthie untied the scarf.

"I'll call you tomorrow," Woody said as he walked his mother down the hall.

So, the Pearl part of our hellish week came to a fairly satisfactory conclusion. The paint on my car was ruined, but Woody had Pearl committed to a mental hospital for observation. I'm sure that was because of the mercury she had and a secret fear that Pearl might have been involved in Clyde Holden's death. In any event, she was out of our hair.

It was the weather that proved to be the hell of hells. For most of the week Hurricane/Tropical Storm Jeanne did a loop-de-loop in the Atlantic, north of Haiti. It posed no immediate threat, but the way it kept getting upgraded and downgraded over and over, moving north, east, south, and west was enough to make you crazy. I honestly feared for Ruthie's sanity, she'd become so obsessed with Jeanne.

If Jeanne wasn't enough, Ivan the Terrible did what a few forecasters predicted. It dumped tons of rain on the East Coast, went out to sea in New England, and then circled back to Florida as a nor'easter. So, as Jeanne did loop-de-loops, Ivan slid to Jeanne's inland side and pounded us with wind gusts and torrential rains. In fact, the evil booger wasn't satisfied he had already hit the Panhandle of Florida—it crossed the state, reformed as a tropical storm, and hit the upper Gulf Coast a second time.

Though we were in St. Augustine for Frances, locals who stayed for that wicked witch told us Ivan was nearly as bad. For three straight days gale force winds, rain, and high tides clobbered the coast. It was the wind and high tides that did us in. The first day we watched a few sandbags float out to sea. By the second day, several dozen were missing. On the third day, the rest of the bags went, and one side of our deck collapsed.

And that was from a nor'easter and mere gale force winds. Little did we know that two days later Jeanne, tired of running in circles, would head for Florida as a Category 3 hurricane.

Chapter 22

September 23-25

Penny Sue and Ruthie left for Publix at eight AM to buy more hurricane provisions. I stayed home to arrange to have my car painted. The Volkswagen dealership would take it that afternoon. Good, I figured the car would be in a garage if Hurricane Jeanne actually came our way.

Remembering the ice shortage during Hurricane Charley, I had the brainstorm that blocks of ice would melt slower than ice cubes or the bags you could purchase. So, I pulled out every mixing bowl in the condo, filled it with water, and put it in the freezer. If I filled a couple of coolers with the blocks of ice, they would last a long time. I hoped. Halfway through my project, the doorbell rang. Of course, my first thought was Guthrie. I figured he'd seen the weather forecast and had come to beg for a place to stay.

I opened the door, not bothering to check the peephole, and came face-to-face with a stout American Indian and a greasy, but well dressed, New York-type. They were standing inside the screen door. I noticed a gun tucked in the waistband of Greasy's trousers. A big black limo sat next to my car.

Greasy reached in his coat pocket and took out a piece of paper that he carefully unfolded. It was a copy of the letter I'd sent to the owners. "Are you Leigh Stratton?" he asked, looking none too happy.

A vision of the *Sopranos* flashed through my mind, a particular episode where Tony beat a man to death, then chopped him up into little pieces. I smiled, stupidly, wiping my hands against my shorts. Think, girl, think! You were married to a lawyer for over twenty years; you must have learned something about bullshitting people.

Dumb! Play dumb. Stall for time. Maybe someone would walk by. Where were all those nosy neighbors when you needed them? "Oh, are you a homeowner interested in selling? I'd really like to buy a unit in this development. It's so pretty with the sand roads and native vegetation."

Greasy ripped the letter into tiny pieces and threw them in my face. "No, I'm not a homeowner." He stepped forward and shook his finger in my face. "You are a really dumb bitch. What did you think my note meant?"

"No-ote? What note?"

"The one that told you to mind your own business."

I gave him a silly grin. "Oh, that note." Yuk, that was his gum I touched! "I thought Pearl wrote the note. She's old and has been acting funny lately. I didn't take it seriously."

"You should have. Where's Pearl? What did you do with her?" he sneered.

"I didn't do anything with Pearl, her son did. She came over and threw eggs on my car." I pointed at my yellow VW bug with bubbled paint on the hood. "We figured Pearl must be having a spell, so we called her son. He put her in the hospital for observation. You know, at her age, Pearl could have

Alzheimer's or dementia or hardening of the arteries. Maybe a stroke."

Greasy reached in his waistband and pulled out the gun. I didn't know what kind it was, but it looked like a cannon to me. He waved it in my face and nodded at the Indian. "You've screwed up our plans, and we don't like it one bit. Your meddling has cost me millions."

"Gee, I'm sorry. I only wanted to buy a condo."

"I warned you, and you wouldn't listen." He glanced at the Indian and shook his head. "Only one thing I can think of doing with a meddlesome bitch." He raised the gun.

POW!

Greasy's gun hand went limp, and he fell into my arms. A moment later, I felt something wet and warm. BLOOD! I stumbled backward, and Greasy fell flat on his face. Blood spurted from a hole in his back. The limo driver floored the car, clipped my VW trying to turn around, and spun away. The Indian was no warrior. One look at the hole in his partner's back, and the Indian took off down the hall. I raced after him. He reached the glass door in the great room and gave me the look of a caged animal. He fumbled to open it.

"Noo-oo," I shouted.

The Indian didn't listen. He slid the door aside and started across the deck, which promptly collapsed.

By this time, Guthrie had hobbled down from his condo. Glock in hand, he had on nothing but boxer shorts covered in red hearts, an obvious Valentine's present from years gone by. He hopped to the corner where the deck collapsed, flung open the glass door, and pointed the Glock at the man tangled in a mass of sand and wood.

"Make my day, and my friend, Mr. Glock's. One move and you'll get it between the eyes."

As Guthrie held the Indian at bay, I called the police. For once, a patrol car was nearby. Two uniforms arrived. One checked the body in the front door, while the other—Heather Brooks—raced into the great room. Her lips tensed at the sight of Guthrie's shorts and boney legs, but she went into action fast. "Call for medical," Heather barked, as she headed back out the front door and around the building to the deck. She carefully picked her way down the sand slope to the Indian. Once she had him, Guthrie flopped down the sofa, spread eagle. "I need a scotch," he whimpered.

After all he'd done, a scotch was the least I could do. I was handing him the drink—his legs still spread eagle in his heart-covered boxers—when Penny Sue and Ruthie rushed in.

"Wha—" Having negotiated a bunch of police and stepped over a dead body, Penny Sue saw us. Her eyes were the size of saucers. "What's going on here?" she demanded.

"It's not what you think. Call Woody. Tell him to get here quick. It has to do with his mother."

For once, Penny Sue followed my directions, then went to the kitchen and poured herself a scotch. "Geez, we leave you for a minute and all hell breaks loose."

"It wasn't my fault," I said, getting a glass of wine. "I was making ice blocks when all of this happened." My hand shook so badly, more wine went on the floor than in the glass. Ruthie finally took the bottle from me and poured some for both of us.

"Ice. Lot's of ice," I said faintly.

By this time Woody had arrived. He frowned at the sight of us drinking.

"Hey," I said loudly. "We started drinking after the commotion. Everyone was stone-cold sober when this came down." I considered giving Woody a hand gesture, but didn't, since I *was* a Southern woman. Yet, the urge was there, and strong. "These are the guys who were using your mother," I said sternly.

Woody's expression changed instantly. "What? Who?"

"That's your mother's Indian they're fishing out of the collapsed deck. You know, her relative and friend? The 'brother' who gave her the mercury."

Woody stomped out the front door and down the sidewalk.

We sat drinking as paramedics scraped Greasy from our doorway and extricated the Indian. Guthrie and I agreed we were even. I had saved his life, and he had saved mine. Still, he asked if he could stay with us if Hurricane Jeanne hit.

"If Timothy takes his mother, I have to come here. I can't stand that woman. She calls me Guppy and cheats at Scrabble. Forget dictionaries, she's right, the dictionary is wrong. Yeah, like, she could write a dictionary."

"Sure, you can stay with us," I said smiling. It wouldn't seem like a hurricane without Guthrie.

It's a real bummer when your home is a crime scene. They rope it off, the neighbors stand around and gawk, and it's basically the pits. The police did allow me to take my car to the shop (on Woody's orders) with Penny Sue following.

Ruthie stayed at the condo with Guthrie, who was close to falling down drunk, so Penny Sue and I had a chance to talk.

"Do you suppose there's any chance Guthrie shot the Greaser in the back?" Penny Sue asked. "If Guthrie did it, he was protecting you. I wonder if I should call Daddy."

I ran my hand through my hair, which must have been frightening, since I'd done it a lot in the last few hours. "You know Guthrie. I don't think he'd shoot anyone in the back to kill them. Of course, it could have been an accident. Maybe Guthrie was aiming for the guy's thigh, and his bum knee gave way."

"I think he'd do that," Penny Sue said. "Not kill someone, but try to protect us." She glanced at me across her sunglasses. "Guthrie can be a pain in the butt, but he does like us. He'd try to protect you." Penny Sue picked up the car phone, hit speed dial for Judge Daddy, and told him the story. The Judge said he'd see what he could do, especially since the altercation took place in *his* condo.

When we arrived home, only Ruthie and Guthrie were there, and believe it or not, even Ruthie was half-tanked. Timothy was on his way, since Guthrie had called him at work and laid on scotch-laden dramatics. Penny Sue and I immediately suggested that we warm some soup and make sandwiches. There was also the matter of the hurricane provisions they'd purchased. Needless to say, the ice in Penny Sue's trunk had melted by this time. Water droplets had probably followed us around town like breadcrumbs.

While I prepared lunch for our traumatized, drunken friends, Penny Sue brought in the groceries. I noticed an incredible amount of toilet paper, water, chocolate, and wine.

Judge Daddy had contacts everywhere and could quickly cut to the heart of a matter, since all of his friends were high-level types with no time to waste. A few hours later the judge called with the story.

Mob-types of the gambling persuasion were trying to entice American Indians into casino projects with promises of vast riches. Since certified Indian tribes came under Federal law, not state authority, if the Federal government recognized a tribe, it could engage in gambling. Which is what Pearl's 'friends' had planned. They set out to buy up the development with the idea of building a hotel and casino. According to the Indian, Pearl's so-called friend, he and his casino cohorts did the research and knew Sea Dunes was the original territory of the

Surruques, an obscure tribe, of which Woody was the sole survivor.

The casino group easily sucked Pearl into the plan since she was half crazy and already thought she was a princess. Once they purchased the development, the group figured Woody would fall in line through greed or fear for his mother's safety.

That was the plan, the judge reported. A bullet in the back of the Greaser convinced the Indian to sing like a bird and disrupted the scheme. The slug came from a Russian 9 mm Takarov, the same type of weapon that killed the man on the balcony. That proved Guthrie didn't kill Mr. Greasy. It also meant the gang war was in high gear.

By one o'clock the Indian and Greaser were long gone and Timothy had escorted Guthrie home for some clothes. Ruthie had recovered from her morning libations and was glued to the television. Penny Sue and I lounged on the sofa and tried to catch our breath.

"This has been a heck of a few weeks," Penny Sue said. "What else could possibly happen?"

The words were hardly out of her mouth when a loud rumble sounded on the beach, followed by a foghorn. We exchanged deer-in-the-headlights glances. The horn blared again, and Penny Sue bolted to the glass doors.

"Glory be. The cavalry has arrived!"

Ruthie and I raced to the window. Three truckloads of sand and a bobcat sat idling in front of our condo. Sonny Mallard and two men with shovels stood on the beach inspecting the deck and shaking their heads.

"What happened here?" Sonny shouted, pointing at the part of the porch that the Indian fell through.

"A long story," Penny Sue yelled. "Think you can shore it up?"

"That part needs a good carpenter. Best I can do is push sand in front of it. That should give you some protection from the tides." Sonny waved to the trucks. One by one they dumped their loads into huge piles and rumbled off.

"If there's enough sand, push some under my neighbor's deck," Penny Sue shouted.

"I was planning on it. Sand won't do you any good if the dune next door is scoured. Another couple of truckloads are on the way." Sonny swung onto the bobcat and started pushing sand toward the deck. The men with shovels heaved the earth against the condo's foundation and spread it around the deck's supports.

"See," Penny Sue said, beaming. "Just when it seems things couldn't get any worse, something good happens. I think this means our luck's changed." She glanced at Ruthie, who'd shifted her focus back to the television.

"I believe you're right," Ruthie said with a smile—the first smile I'd seen in several hours. "It looks like Jeanne's going to land to our south, close to where Frances hit. That means we'll probably get Category 1 winds at the most."

"So, you don't think we need to evacuate?" I asked, puzzled Ruthie hadn't mentioned it earlier.

Ruthie cocked her head as if listening to an unseen person. "No, we'll be fine here."

Our luck had changed, or so we thought. Chris called to say the race had been rescheduled for Saturday, October 2, under the lights. She'd also located the owner of an abandoned racetrack in St. Augustine who agreed to let us use it for practice, as long as we signed a liability release. Timothy's mother decided to weather the storm with his sister, so he and Guthrie could stay together in Orlando. With sand piled under and around our deck, we had our own private dune. And we had the key to the Wilsons' condo with its empty garage—a place for Penny Sue to park her car.

Yep, life was good until eleven PM. Dressed in our pajamas, we huddled around the TV for the tropical update. In retrospect, that was a mistake. We would have slept a lot better if we'd simply gone to bed. We didn't like what we heard. Hurricane Jeanne was gaining strength, had taken a northward jog, and its eye was expected to hit thirty miles north of us in Daytona Beach on Sunday evening.

The telephone rang at eight AM. It was Max, Penny Sue's PR friend in Atlanta. "All the news outlets are descending on Daytona Beach. I've lined up a spot for you with an ABC affiliate. It's a background piece. Can you meet them at eleven o'clock?"

Penny Sue gave us the thumbs-up. "Sure, we'll be there."

"Wear your racing suits," Max said. "I hear Jim Cantore's headed that way, too. I'll see what I can do." She wrote down the address for our interview and gave him her cell phone number in case Max could arrange something with the Weather Channel. She hung up the phone, jumping up and down. "We're on our way."

"Chris," I exclaimed. "She has to be there."

Chris was as excited as we were, vowing to close her store if she couldn't find someone to fill in.

Three hours notice isn't much time, especially for Penny Sue. We wolfed down Raisin Bran, took showers, and put on our gear. Two hours later—a record for Penny Sue—we were in her Mercedes, headed for Daytona Beach. We arrived at the same time Chris did and were met by Melanie, the production assistant. The backdrop for the interview was a boarded-up store on the waterfront with a blue tarp covering its roof.

"We're starting with an interview of the storeowners," the perky young woman explained. "That will lay the groundwork for your segment, because they're going to talk about the high deductibles—one for each storm—and how they haven't been able to get the old damage fixed. They're also going to say that their ten employees are out of work, and as much as they hate the situation, they can't afford to pay them. They're afraid Jeanne will wipe out what's left of their store and thirty years of hard work." She consulted her clipboard. "You're holding a charity race to benefit people like this, right?"

"Yes," Chris jumped in before Penny Sue had a thought formed. "Donations from the race will help needy people with their deductibles, as well as the many who are uninsured and unemployed. We've put together a panel of respected community leaders to review claims. All monies are being held and disbursed by a major local bank. Every penny donated goes to the fund. New Smyrna Speedway, which is hosting the event, has donated one hundred percent of their time and expenses."

Melanie nodded. "Good, be sure to mention that."

I noticed that Penny Sue's eyes narrowed slightly at Melanie's direction to Chris.

"People are leery of these fundraisers," the young woman continued, "because so many charities use most of the donations for their own expenses."

"Yes," Penny Sue jumped in, looking sidelong at Chris. "We're paying for these uniforms and all of our expenses. Not one penny will come from the fund."

"We think this spot may be picked up for the national news. Do you have a toll free number people can call to make donations?"

Chris recited the number before Penny Sue's lips moved, while Melanie made a note on her clipboard.

"And they take credit cards," Penny Sue added quickly.

Melanie studied our outfits with the big daffodil on the chest. "Daffodils ... that's an interesting insignia. Does it stand for anything?"

Unh uh, we're not going to go there! I answered quickly, "It stands for spring and new beginnings."

Melanie nodded. "That's nice. I hope you win."

The interview went surprisingly well, thanks to Melanie's background work. The storeowners—plain, hardworking people enduring terrible times with gumption and grace—gave the perfect lead-in to the charity race. My fear that Chris and Penny Sue might come to blows proved unfounded. They did amazingly well—sort of a Northern and Southern tag team of information. At least Melanie and Sean, the reporter, thought the segment was terrific and sure to make the national evening news.

Chris had to run back to her store, which she'd closed, and Ruthie had to locate a bathroom. But we left feeling up and sure we would win the race, Hurricane Jeanne willing.

We made a quick stop at a McDonalds for hamburgers, milkshakes, and a bathroom. We went through the drive-thru while Ruthie checked out the women's room. Ruthie said her outfit got a lot of stares. Thankfully, we'd spent the extra money for two-piece suits, otherwise Ruthie's milkshake would have melted before she undressed, tinkled, redressed, and returned to the car. Air conditioner cranked up to max—the suits were hot!—we headed home, planning on a nap. The last two days had taken their toll.

So much for a peaceful nap. We discovered that while we were doing our interview, Jeanne had been upgraded to a Category 3 storm. It was still zeroed in on our area. Jim Cantore was en route to Daytona Beach.

Ruthie kicked the leg of a chair. "Darn, I'll miss him again." She stared into the distance. I realized it one of those looks that said she was communicating with someone. “It wasn’t meant to be. He won’t be here long.”

“What do you mean?” I was spooked by a Category 3 storm. “Do you think we should go inland? Timothy said we were welcome at his house.”

Ruthie cocked her head. “We’ll be fine here.”

Penny Sue and I rolled our eyes, both hoping Ruthie’s spirits knew what they were talking about. Apparently, they did.

We took fitful naps, alarms set to wake us for the five o’clock update. We hovered around the tube like men watching a play-off game. Praise be, Ruthie was right. Jeanne was now predicted to hit Saturday morning in Vero Beach. Though expected to parallel the east coast of Florida, inland, its winds should die down by the time it reached New Smyrna Beach on Sunday.

Category 1? No big deal. We had sand under the deck, we had food, and our interview made the ABC national news.

Hurricane Jeanne gave us a break, which is not to say we got off scot-free. It could have been a whole lot worse. The storm blew ashore as a Category 3 a mere five miles from the place Frances made landfall. Moving up the middle of the state, Jeanne steadily lost strength. The strongest winds, Cat 1, hit New Smyrna Beach at about three AM. We sat in the closet, lights on, listening to the local weather forecast that blared in the great room. We’d cranked the AC down as low as it would go to get the place as cold as possible in case there was a power failure. All of our coolers, and a few new ones, were filled with blocks of ice.

Rain pounded the windows, and the racket of waves crashing against our deck could be heard over the television. About three-thirty Penny Sue ventured into the great room and flipped on the spotlights that shone on the deck. She quickly flipped them off.

"What's wrong?" I asked, peering into the darkness.

"You don't want to know. But we might want to move our stuff into my bedroom at the front of the condo."

"Why?"

"Remember all the sand Sonny brought in? The sand and the deck are gone."

"Oh, boy." We dragged the supplies into Penny Sue's bedroom, which had its own TV, and lounged on the bed listening to the local broadcast. The patio of the Breaker's Restaurant, a New Smyrna Beach icon, had washed away, as well as the Flagler Street seawall and boardwalk. On site reports showed sea foam piled up like snow and debris strewn a block up the street from the ocean.

At some point we all dozed off and awakened to the awful sensation of complete silence. The electricity had gone out, but the sun was up, the floors were dry, and we were safe. We trooped into the great room and gingerly peeked out the glass door. Where the deck and sand had once been, there was now a six-foot cliff!

"Easy come, easy go." Penny Sue drew the blinds to shut out the warm morning sun. "We should keep the doors and windows closed so it'll stay cool as long as possible."

"Want me to make some coffee?" I asked.

"No way we're going to turn on that hot gas stove. We'll get our caffeine from colas."

Ruthie hauled out the battery-operated television and tuned it to the local ABC station. "A major feeder line's down," she reported as I dumped cereal into bowls and Penny Sue poured colas. "Electric crews are already working on it."

"I hope they work fast," Penny Sue said. "Either I'm having a hot flash or this place is already starting to warm up."

The crews did work quickly, because the outage only lasted about eight hours. The time flew with our phones ringing off the hook. Virtually everyone had seen our TV spot and called to congratulate us on a fine performance. Max was particularly pleased because the story was still running in most major markets. “If that doesn’t generate contributions, nothing will.”

And it did. Total contributions were over $400,000 by noon.

“I wonder how the speedway fared?” Penny Sue mused after taking nearly a dozen calls. “We announced the race was this coming Saturday, so it must go on.”

I phoned Chris who, as usual, was one step ahead of us. She’d spoken to Andrew Hart. The track received minor damage this time, because Frances had already destroyed most of the billboards, so there wasn’t much to clean up. The race could go on, it just didn’t come off exactly as planned.

Chapter 23

October 2

The race was scheduled to begin at seven-thirty, but teams were required to meet in the infield at five o'clock to set-up and receive instructions. There were seven teams in all: The DAFFODILS, Woody's team, NASA retirees, a local realtor, and three teams named Racing Thunder, Hell on Wheels, and Speed Demons. Our team was a standout, what with our custom suits, newly painted mini-car and Corolla, and our spotter, Annie, who wore an obviously expensive headset. Timothy had the spare headset with strict instructions to keep it away from Guthrie. We were also the only team with a pit crew. Timothy, dressed in black bike shorts and a spandex tank top, carried a large washtub of ice and oxygenated-water. Guthrie was, well, Guthrie. He had on his Arlo Guthrie tee shirt, baggy khaki shorts, and lugged an old-style metal TV tray and five large pans of brownies.

The Demons had chosen the right name. They were big, scruffy, and scary looking. Racing Thunder all looked alike in their Diving Experience fire suits and helmets. They were medium height, clean-shaven, with dark, slicked-back hair. Hell on Wheels was a bunch of teenagers ("They could be dangerous," Annie whispered.), while the other crews appeared to be nice, normal folk.

We drew numbers from Andrew's cowboy hat for pit assignments, then went to move our cars and store our gear. Guthrie set up the TV tray with a pan of his 'signature' dish. "These are for you," he said, indicating the team. "No nuts. Have one—you need the strength."

I chomped down on a brownie, and had to admit this was a good batch. I waved at the other pans. "You don't expect us to eat all of those, do you?"

"They're for the other crews. It's not polite to eat in front of people."

Huh? Since when did pit crews pass out brownies to their competitors? I was about to say something when a familiar voice wafted from the track.

"Back off, buddy, I'm with them." It was Frannie May, shooing away a speedway employee who blocked her from crossing to the infield.

"Frannie May," I waved and nodded to the employee who let her pass. "Our good luck charm has arrived. I was afraid you wouldn't make it." I gave her a big hug.

"Almost didn't, my plane was late. Carl, Jr. and his friends are in the grandstands. See them? The center, toward the top."

I followed her arm and was pleased to see Carl and his buddies, *sans* their *Star Trek* Klingon and Romulan battle gear. I waved; they stood and whistled.

"Have a brownie?" Ruthie offered. "No nuts." She nodded at Guthrie. "Our friend made them."

Frannie eyed the pans Guthrie held. "I like nuts." She pulled up the corner of the foil covering the top pan. "Do these have nuts?"

Guthrie whirled around putting his back between Frannie May and the brownies. "You can't have these—they're for the other teams."

Frannie gave us a what's-with-him frown. Timothy shrugged. I gave her a palms-up and whispered, "He's a little high strung."

"I see that. What did you do, put Metamucil or something in those brownies?" Frannie May teased.

Guthrie's brows furrowed. "Of course not." He stalked off toward the other teams.

"Wouldn't be a bad idea, would it? Use a little Exlax instead of cocoa," Frannie joked.

My eyes went wide. Certainly Guthrie wouldn't do that. Would he? I didn't have time to ponder the question. Andrew called the crews to the infield to go over the rules. I noticed almost everyone was eating brownies and all of the teenagers had one in each hand.

"Remember, this is a charity marathon, and it's all for fun. We don't want anyone to get hurt. We want a nice, clean race because there's a lot of news media here." He searched our faces. Everyone nodded.

"Okay, we'll start with the mini-cup cars. Ten laps. Spotters are only allowed for this and the school bus race. Spotters, you can go up to the top of the grandstand now."

Annie winked at us and headed across the track with six men.

"The second race is the bag race." Andrew's assistant handed him a heavy brown paper bag. The sack had several strips of silver duct tape across the center. "As you know, the driver in this race must wear a bag over his or her head. The passenger directs the driver. I don't expect a problem with this group, but people have tried to cheat in the past by putting pinpricks in the bag over the eye area. That's why we've added duct tape, and my assistant will distribute the bags just before the race begins. Also, to insure the passenger doesn't 'accidentally' steer the car, both of the passenger's hands must be on the top, outside of his window throughout the race.

"The final leg is the bus race. It's the most fun for fans, but the most dangerous for drivers. This is a short track, and the buses are light in the rear. I know you've all practiced. Be careful out there, I don't want any buses going over the wall."

Everyone nodded again.

"I hear donations total over a half million dollars and some teams have matching offers. This is a good cause, so be safe." Andrew clapped his hands. "Okay, let's do it!"

We all jogged to our pit areas. Our team was number four, putting us on the outside of the second row. That was a definite disadvantage for the school bus race, mainly because they were cumbersome, but shouldn't make much of a difference for the other two cars. I was so excited my skin tingled. Chris looked like she was about to jump out of her shoes. Ruthie was serene, doing her mantra, I supposed. Penny Sue was Penny Sue, swishing her butt and waving to the crowd. Timothy handed us all a bottle of water. I looked around. Where was Guthrie? Water was his job. I spotted him dishing up brownies to the Demons.

Chris took a swig of water, gave us a thumbs-up, and vaulted through the roof of the mini-car. Timothy attached the Hutchins device to her helmet, and Chris did several microphone tests with Annie on the spotters' platform that overlooked the track.

"Ladies and gentlemen, proceed to the starting line," the announcer said over the speaker system.

The mini-cars sprang to life with a loud roar. One by one they left the pit area, lapped the track, and stopped, two-by-two, at the finish line in front of the grandstand. A hush fell over the crowd, all eyes glued to the starter who stood on an elevated platform. I held my breath.

The starter, a wiry guy with a gift for dramatics, gave the green flag a vigorous swirl. The mini-cars peeled out. Chris was trapped behind the two starters, Hell on Wheels in the number two spot and Racing Thunder with the inside, pole position. The Demon car was on the inside of the second row on Chris' left. As the cars approached the first turn, Racing Thunder lagged behind and started to drift toward Chris. The Demon car, either annoyed or not paying attention, bumped Racing Thunder from the rear, sending it through the infield. The bump created a temporary opening that Chris zipped through. She floored it and pulled in front of Hell on Wheels, taking the lead.

Meanwhile, Racing Thunder ran through the infield and spun onto the far side of the track just as the pack of cars came around. Drawing a bead on the Demon car, Thunder rammed it from the side, sending it into Hell on Wheels. Hell hit the wall, bounced back into Demon, which then rammed Thunder. Thunder skidded into the infield followed by Demon and Hell on Wheels. Thankfully, Chris was far enough ahead to miss the melee. However, the realtor car caught a piece of Hell and went into a three-sixty degree spin that landed it in a puddle of mud and out of the race.

The starter waved the caution flag with one hand and angrily thrust black and red flags at Demon, Thunder, and Hell who were now pursuing each other around the infield. Obviously intent on getting even and not the race, the mini-cars ignored the starter and chased each other in circles until they all eventually were bogged down in muck, the final remnants of Hurricane Jeanne.

The race finished under the caution flag with Chris in the lead followed by Woody and Team NASA.

Chris lapped the track one time, then pulled in at the finish line. Timothy was waiting to unhitch her helmet. A moment later, the top of her car popped open and Chris stood, arms held high and bowed to the crowd. Carl and his *Star Trek* friends went into a frenzy of extraterrestrial victory cries. The people sitting around them probably wished an alien ship would appear and beam them up.

The announcer called a brief intermission as Mr. Hart, the starter, and several speedway security personnel stomped across the track for a conference with Hell, Thunder, and the Demons. A lot of finger pointing, hand waving, and nodding later, the track crew stalked back to the grandstands and the bag race was announced.

Considering the bizarre shenanigans that had just transpired, I was absolutely stunned by Ruthie's serenity. We took our places in the Corolla and put on our helmets. Ruthie snapped her visor shut without hesitation. A clue I missed at the time. Once again, Timothy hooked the Hutchins tethers to our helmets.

"Ladies and gentlemen," the loudspeaker blared, "proceed to the starting line."

Good thinking, no bags until we were out of the pits. We lined up in front of the grandstand, outside second row. A moment later, Andrew's assistant reached in the window and placed a bag over Ruthie's helmet. I didn't detect a wince or whimper. Something was very strange. Had Penny Sue given Ruthie a couple of tranquilizers? Lord, I hoped not.

"Are you okay?" I asked.

Ruthie flicked her wrist. "Better than ever," she said loudly.

Uh oh, I knew that tone. It was Millie! Gawd, should I be happy or sad? Millie had lived a long time ago. Could she drive? Did they even have cars in her day? The starter shook his finger at me, and I put my hands on the outside of the car. "Now, let's start off slowly, going straight. Like we practiced," I started. "When I say—"

"Thanks, Leigh, but we'll be fine," Ruthie replied.

Oh, crap was my last thought before the green flag came down.

Ruthie eased on the accelerator, and we were off. The Demon car to our left was moving erratically and suddenly went through the infield where it promptly mired.

"The guy on our inside just ran off the track," I told Ruthie. "If you ease to the left, you can pass the lead cars on the inside."

Ruthie waved off my comment. "We're fine, Leigh, don't worry."

Ruthie turned the wheel and expertly guided the Corolla to the inside, passing the cars in the lead.

"Millie's directing you, isn't she?"

"Yes, she thinks it's fun. She wasn't allowed to drive in her day." Ruthie giggled.

Good Lord, what was I in for? "Don't drive too fast," I cautioned. "Go just fast enough to stay ahead. If you zip around the track, the judges will know something's up."

Ruthie nodded. "Millie wants you to know that she was always honorable and wouldn't commit this dastardly deed if the race weren't for charity."

As it turned out, my worries about being conspicuous were unfounded. The cars behind us provided such a show, no one noticed the DAFFODILS car. Out of the clear blue, Racing Thunder simply crashed into the wall. Luckily they weren't going fast. Then Hell on Wheels moved into second spot, only to be bumped by the NASA team. The two cars spun into the infield. That left Woody and the realtors—driving cautiously. To them, five laps must have seemed like an eternity, but to us—thanks to Millie—it was a piece of cake. I had a slight tinge of guilt about our otherworldly help, but shed it fast when I remembered the storeowners from the interview.

Once again the DAFFODILS crossed the finish line first. As we did the victory lap to the finish line—Ruthie was allowed to take off her bag to insure we made it—I told Millie, "You have to leave now. We like you, and we appreciate all the help you've given us, but it's time for you to go home. Millie, do you hear me?"

On the back straightaway, Ruthie twitched and immediately opened her visor. "Millie's gone back to the Casa Monica. She says there's a good party going on there. If we get a chance, Millie said we should come up. She had fun with us."

Ruthie was back to her shy self by the time we reached the finish line. She waved self-consciously to the crowd and took off for the pits. Once again our alien friends—the Klingons and Romulans—went into full victory whoops.

The third, final, and toughest contest was the bus race. It was fitting that Penny Sue was the driver, considering all the terrorist avoidance classes she'd taken. True to form, Penny Sue took a swig of oxygenated-water, slapped on her helmet, and strapped into her seat. She and Annie did several sound checks, then Penny Sue raised her thumb, ready to go.

There was some confusion at the starting line with buses getting out of the proper order. Too difficult to fix, the judges decided to leave it alone, meaning Hell on Wheels (the teenagers) were on Penny Sue's inside instead of the Demons.

"Annie, we've won the last two races, I'm going to win this one, too," Penny Sue said.

"You will if you listen to me," a male voice replied.

Penny Sue glanced at the spotters' booth where Annie was pointing to her headset and shaking her head.

"Who the hell are you? Get off this channel, I can't hear my spotter."

"Who worked on your helmets and headsets?"

"Larry?"

"I go by that name sometimes. Listen carefully.

There are some very mean people who plan to kill you in this race. I'm here to see that they don't succeed."

"Where are you?"

"I'm in what remains of the billboard next to the digital time clock. Penny Sue, you have to do exactly what I say. Your life depends on it."

"Okay, but who's after me?"

"Racing Thunder, which is part of Al's mob. They don't want you to give a deposition. They figure if they kill you, Leigh and Ruthie will be too scared to talk. The Speed Demons are Russian and trying to protect you because they want you to testify. Their mob wants Al put away so they can horn in on his drug operation. It was the Russians who nailed your assassins."

"Our assassins? The guy on the balcony and the casino guy?"

"Them and a couple of others. Now listen, whatever you do, stay to the inside. Racing Thunder is going to try to push you over the wall."

"Inside? I've got Hell on Wheels next to me."

"They won't be for long. Stay exactly beside them. Don't try to pass or make a move. I'll take care if it. Are you with me?"

"How do I know you're who you say you are and not one of Al's goons?"

"You haven't been out of my mind since I first saw you."

"You sent the roses?"

"An old friend of yours from Roswell asked me to send them, Honey Bunny."

"Rich!"

The starter waved the green flag and the buses took off. Penny Sue stayed against the wall, matching the speed of her second row opponent.

"Take your foot off the gas, now."

Hell on Wheels moved ahead and there was a sudden ping. Hell's front tire started to go flat and the bus dropped back, finally pulling into the infield.

"Pull into that inside spot!"

Penny Sue did it, with Woody slipping into her position. As this was going on, Racing Thunder was running next to the Speed Demons and nudging them at every opportunity.

"Drop back, Thunder's trying to flip Demons over the wall and Thunder may succeed at the next turn."

Penny Sue did as instructed and Woody pulled ahead, right on the tail of the Demons. As they came down the backstretch, another ping sounded. What do you know? Thunder's front left tire started to lose air.

"Drop back, drop back, give him room."

Penny Sue let off the gas and was rammed from behind by Team NASA. The rear of her bus skidded to the right, dusting the wall. She hung a hard right and corrected the skid.

"Good move," Larry said in her ear. "Watch Woody, he's starting to weave."

For that matter, everyone except Penny Sue was driving like they were drunk.

"These people are crazy," Larry called. "Drop low and floor it."

"Don't worry, I know what to do."

Penny Sue set her jaw, hung a left, and put the pedal to the metal. She passed the other buses as if they were standing still. The starter was berserk, stabbing the black flag at the other buses. Penny Sue ignored it all and kept a hefty lead for the rest of the race.

Once again, the DAFFODILS came in first—a clean sweep. Of course, we had some help, but hey, it was a charity race! All the money went to hurricane victims. Our clean sweep also meant the Hamptons crowd had to pony up an extra $100,000. Oh well, they could afford it!

We were in our pit area, ogling the trophy and doing press interviews, when a small caravan of grey Crown Vics with dark windows sped down the track and surrounded the Speed Demons and Racing Thunder. Men with guns piled out of the cars and circled the teams. Surprisingly, the mobsters put up little resistance. In fact, some of them seemed to be laughing.

"I wonder what that's about?" Ruthie said.

"I'll tell you later," Penny Sue replied nonchalantly. Then suddenly panic crossed her face. "Where's Guthrie?"

"Here I be," he answered, staggering up.

Timothy's eyes narrowed. "Guthrie, have you been into the booze?"

Guthrie stumbled backward. "No man, like, I was helping win the race."

Timothy was not amused. "Win the race? I did everything you were supposed to do."

"I made the brownies." Guthrie gave us a goofy grin.

"Big deal," Timothy said. "They were good, but nothing special."

Guthrie swayed like a wet sock in the wind. "Yours weren't, but theirs were."

"Exlax," Frannie May exclaimed. "I knew it!"

Timothy gave Guthrie the squinty eye. "It wasn't Exlax, it was grass, wasn't it? You promised you'd given up all that hippie stuff."

"Well, I had a few bags left from the olden days." Guthrie was still wobbling. "I knew this thing was for the hurricane victims, and the Hamptons people had promised a lot of money if the DAFFODILS won every race." Guthrie put his face within an inch of Timothy's. "You know, I us-sed to be an accountant. I got a list of pledges and figured the victims would get the most money if the DAFFODILS made a clean sweep. So, like, I decided to make sure they won." Guthrie shook his head. "I wasn't being crooked or anything, I only wanted those poor people to get the most money they could get."

"If that grass was from the olden days, it had to be moldy. You may have poisoned people," Timothy said sternly.

"It was vacuum packed in those boiling bags you see on TV and I've kept it frozen."

"Frozen? How could you keep it frozen for twenty years, through all of these hurricanes?"

Guthrie swayed. "I was careful. What do you think I needed the ice for when I put the chicken on my knee?"

Timothy put his hands on his hips and stared. I held my breath. Was he going to deck Guthrie? Suddenly, Timothy threw back his head and laughed. "All these years you had me bringing you ice and dry ice, it was to store your old grass? Man, you are one piece of work." Timothy reached out and pulled his staggering buddy to his chest. "You are the biggest pain I've ever known, but your heart is in the right place." Timothy sat Guthrie on the ground with a bottle of water. "Tell me the truth, is that the last of it?"

Guthrie looked sad. "Yeah, that's it. My youth is over. I guess I'll have to be responsible now."

Fat chance, I thought, trying not to smile.

As this drama unfolded, Annie was busy loading her mini-cup car on its trailer with Chris' help. Finished, she returned to the group at about the time Timothy sat Guthrie on the ground.

"Penny Sue, I don't know what happened in the bus race," Annie started to apologize. "My headphone went dead. I have no idea what happened. Our sound checks were fine. I'm sorry I let you down, but it looks like you didn't need me after all."

Penny Sue put her arm around Annie's shoulder. "It wasn't your fault." Penny Sue pointed at a man coming our way. "He's the culprit."

Frannie May took one look at the man and went into hysterics. "Enrico! I thought you were dead!"

Our Larry, the fisherman, was Fran's Uncle Enrico? Enrico, the man of mystery that no one in Fran's family knew how he made his living and was afraid to ask? Uncle Enrico, who'd vanished one day without a trace, leaving behind a large trunk stocked with sniper rifles, knives, and other weapons that Fran kept stored in her attic?

Fran ran toward Larry/Enrico. He picked her up and twirled her around with kisses and mutterings about Little Francy.

Back on her feet, Frannie May gave him the once over. "You look good. But, you worried me to death!" She smacked his face lightly. "How could you do that to your family?"

Penny Sue interrupted, "Fran, we thought he was a fisherman, but he was watching our behinds the whole time you were away. Larry saved my life in the bus race. And he is in contact with Rich!"

All of us nodded, knowing that meant Enrico was FBI, DEA, Secret Service or some other clandestine government something.

"What the heck?" Fran said, slapping Enrico's shoulder. "Everyone has to do something. Come back to the house, I'll cook you a real Italian dinner. I have a big tray of my lasagna in the freezer, and you can meet Carlo, your great nephew, who's a—"

I interrupted. "—a Klingon."

Larry/Enrico chuckled. "*Star Trek* is one of my favorite shows." His lips tensed, then slowly stretched into a grin.

“I *would* like to get my trunk. If I come to your house, it can be only you, Carlo, and me. I can’t stay long, and you’re sworn to secrecy.”

Fran patted his cheek. “Anything you want is fine with me. Secrecy? No problem, we’re family.”

Epilogue

October 3

It was noon, and we'd already done more than most people do in a whole day. Ruthie's father had taken a fall—a broken wrist and luckily not a hip. In any event, she needed to go home as soon as possible. She was driving back with Penny Sue—seven hours, close to what it took by plane when you considered airport security and the commutes to and from the airport. We'd packed the Mercedes with their essentials and I promised to send the rest by UPS the next day.

We sat at the kitchen counter ruminating over the events of the last eight weeks. Three hurricanes, a nor'easter, six deaths counting Scooter, a grand slam at the races, close to a million dollars in contributions for hurricane victims, and I had purchased the condo next door.

All of that was weird, but the strangest event was the phone call we received that morning from the Federal judicial assistant who had kept postponing our depositions. Al passed away during the night from a heart attack, so our services wouldn't be needed, after all.

We should be happy, yet the news was so unexpected it left us numb. Al and his mob had been hanging over our heads for close to a year. The Russian component—and Enrico!—was completely unexpected. Who would have guessed the Russians were trying to protect us? Who would have guessed Larry/Enrico was with the government? Who would have guessed that Pearl and her casino chiselers were a separate issue all together and not connected to the mob war?

The doorbell rang as we were about to click our cans of green tea and say goodbye.

Penny Sue huffed down the hall. "You know it's Guthrie." She flung open the door. Wrong. It was Woody with a giant bouquet of flowers.

"Can we call a truce?" he asked. Penny Sue unlatched the screen door and waved him in.

"Flowers, how nice," I said. I found a vase under the sink and filled it with water. "This is unexpected."

Woody looked as uncomfortable as any person could be. "My mother's been diagnosed with Alzheimer's, pretty advanced. You did me a big favor when you didn't press charges against her. With her mental state, she might have gotten off if she'd been charged, but it would have caused my family a lot of heartache. It's hard to believe Mom went downhill so fast and I never noticed."

I took the flowers, put them in the vase, and fluffed them. I thought of my marriage with Zack. "Yeah, sometimes we're too close to a situation to notice what's really going on. Anyway, I've purchased the condo next door," I said brightly, hoping to lighten the mood.

"Then we'll be neighbors. I'm moving my family into Mom's condo, our native land. Our tribe was absorbed into the

Seminoles, but this area has special meaning to me." He ducked his head, seeming very sincere for a lawyer. "I hope we can put the past behind us and be friends."

In unison, Ruthie and I parroted one of her favorite adages, "The past is gone, it can touch me not."

A tear streaked down Woody's cheek. Now Penny Sue was uncomfortable—dumbfounded to be more accurate. Typical Penny Sue, not knowing what to do, she offered Woody a scotch.

Read an excerpt from Book One
of the DAFFODILS Series

The Turtle Mound Murder

Chapter 1

Roswell, Georgia

"Damn, girl, you look like hell!"

I slid into the booth next to the window at the Admiral's Dinghy, a locals' hangout in the restored district of Roswell. Penelope Sue Parker, my long-time friend and sorority sister, was already finishing a glass of wine. From the gleam in Penny Sue's eye, it might have been her second.

"Thanks, that makes me feel real good," I said sarcastically.

Penny Sue studied me, sipping wine, sunlight bouncing off the two-carat diamond on her right hand. "You look like you haven't slept in a year. Heavens, you have dark circles under your eyes." She raised her glass, signaling the waiter. "What's wrong, honey? You still depressed?"

"I'm going to change my name," I said in a rush.

"I don't blame you. I'd get rid of that skunk Zack's name as soon as possible. I'm surprised you haven't done it sooner. As far as I'm concerned, you'll always be Becky Martin."

"Leigh," I corrected. The waiter arrived with two glasses of wine. I stared at the glass the waiter put in front of me. "What's this, Penny Sue? You know I shouldn't drink; I've been taking antidepressants off and on for months."

"Pooh, one little glass of wine won't kill you. It'll help you relax." Penny Sue pouted, fingering the substantial emerald hanging from her neck. "What's this stuff about Leigh?"

"My middle name. I'm sick of being Becky. Good old Becky; sweet, cute Becky; dumb shit, blind Becky."

"You were just too trusting," my friend assured me.

Stupid, trusting, the label made no difference; Zachary Stratton had played me for a fool. As soon as the kids were off to college, my loving husband took up woodworking. Each night when I went to bed, he'd retire to his shop in the garage for a couple of hours. A partner in Atlanta's most prestigious law firm, Zack claimed rubbing and sanding wood relieved the stress of his hectic day.

Wood, hell—it was silicon breasts!

While I snored blissfully, Zack sneaked out to meet a strip club dancer he'd set up in a house a few blocks away. The scam worked for over a year until Ann, our younger, was picked up for DUI late one night. I rushed to the garage to tell Zack. The tools were cold, and his car was gone.

A staunch believer in a person's right to privacy, I'd never intruded on Zack's domain. I made an exception that night. In a matter of minutes, I found a carton of wooden figurines identical to the ones he claimed to have made. In a sickening flash I realized the find's implications and gagged, recalling the times I'd ooed and awed over the silly statues. Rage suppressed the tears and gave me the strength to carry the box to the center of the garage. When Zack returned home, I was waiting, feet propped up on Exhibit A.

"I'm forty-six; Becky is a child's name." I took a drink of wine and glared. "Leigh, now there's a woman's name. Momma got it from *Gone With the Wind*. You know, Scarlett, Vivien Leigh. I deserve that name, don't you think?"

"Absolutely," Penny Sue said, raising her glass in salute, "Leigh it is. What in the world brought this on?"

"My therapist said it would help me release the past."

"Are you still seeing that squirrelly guy downtown?"

"No, I gave him up months ago. He was too strange."

Penny Sue threw back her head and laughed. "Of course, dear, he's a therapist. They're all weird. You teach what you need to learn." The New Age explanation for the purpose of life, the phrase was Penny Sue's pat answer to everything. "Why did you drop Dr. Nerd?"

I scanned the room to see who might be listening. "The jerk crossed the line when he suggested I attend a Sufi ceremony, saying a novel experience would help my depression. It was novel, all right. By the time I arrived, everyone was naked, lying in a pile. My therapist was on the bottom."

Penny Sue snorted with amusement. "Figures. I would have guessed as much. What about that other one? The attitude healer in Vinings? Did you ever try her?"

"Yes, lord, another dead end."

"What happened? Ruthie said she was good."

I sat back and folded my arms. "That's not saying much—Ruthie hasn't been right since she drove off the bridge and cracked her head. I signed up for the *Heal Your Mind, Heal Your Life* workshop, figuring it would give me a chance to see the therapist in action, before going for a private session. Am I glad I did; that lady's in dire need of analysis herself.

"Waltzes in the first meeting and announces she's a reincarnated priestess from ancient Egypt. Then, she starts in on visualizing the future we want." I waved expansively. "Nothing wrong with that; except we can't just imagine it, we've got to visualize her way. We have to cut out pictures from magazines and make paper dolls. She did it, too. All her pictures came from bridal magazines. Paper dolls? Bridal magazines? Does that tell you something? And I'm supposed to follow her advice? Yeah, right."

Penny Sue chuckled. "That explains why Ruthie liked her. Ruthie's always had a fetish for wedding gowns. Remember how she wore one to the Old South Ball at Kappa Alpha each year?"

"I'd forgotten about that. The gown wasn't so bad, it was the veil—"

"With sunglasses! Wasn't she a sight?"

"How's Ruthie doing anyway?" I asked.

"The same. Lives with her father; works on charities and an occasional political campaign. She's still into New Age stuff; you know, meditation and crystals. You should give her a call. She's always going to meetings and seances. I've been a few times, it's fun. Nothing else, it would get you out of the house."

I leaned forward. I could already feel the effects of the wine. "Maybe I will." Getting out with people was what I needed; I knew I'd become almost reclusive, dreading the thought of running into old friends and having to re-tell the story of The Big Split. Yet, the loneliness fed the depression, which made me more reclusive, and on and on until there was nothing except a dark emptiness. A great, gaping void in the center of my chest; a black hole which could not be filled by therapy or pills. "Does Ruthie ever date?"

Penny Sue said, "Heavens no, she'll never remarry, at least as long as her father's alive."

Ruthie's father was J.T. Edwards, a retired railroad executive who lived in a restored mansion in Buckhead. I blinked back tears. "Probably just as well."

"What's got you so down?"

I blotted my eyes with the back of my hand. "Zack moved out last week while I was visiting my folks."

"That's terrific news! Y'all living under the same roof while you fought over the property settlement was sick. I told Daddy so." Penny Sue's daddy was Judge Warren Parker, founder of Zachary's firm. "Daddy likes you and feels bad about the situation, but Zack's a valuable asset to the firm, because of his connections with the telephone people. They love him."

"Naturally," I said. "He takes them to strip joints whenever they come to town. That's how Zack met Ms. Thong."

"Who?"

"His little lap dancer. I found a picture of her in a silver thong bikini at the bottom of Zack's sock drawer."

Penny Sue shrugged. "Daddy promised to have a word with Zack, advise him to give you a fair shake. You know, fifty-fifty."

My cheeks flamed. "It worked," I said, trying hard to control my anger. "Mr. Fairness took half of everything in the house. Half of the pictures on the walls, half of each set of china, and half of the furniture, right down to one of Jack, Jr.'s twin beds."

"Half the Wedgwood?" Penny Sue asked. I nodded. "No wonder you're depressed."

"The Wedgwood's the least of my worries, he could have had it all. It was the spite that gets me. We're supposed to sign off on the property settlement tomorrow. I can't imagine what else he's got up his sleeve. A person who'd take half the sheets—I mean all the top sheets, no bottoms—is capable of anything."

"No doubt." Penny Sue drained her glass and clicked it down. "Girl, you need a vacation."

"Vacation? After tomorrow I may not be able to afford lunch. Besides, I have to sell the house."

"Hire a realtor; you need a change of scenery. New Smyrna Beach is beautiful in the fall, and Daddy hardly ever uses his condo anymore. Remember what a good time we had there in college? Come on, Beck—er, Leigh—it'll be relaxing, do you a world of good."

"I'll see how the settlement goes," I replied.

Thankfully, the waiter arrived to take our order, shutting Penny Sue down. I chose the Caesar salad, while she ordered quiche with a Dinghy Dong for dessert.

"A Dinghy Dong? Isn't that the extra large chocolate eclair?"

Penny Sue cut me a look. "So?"

"Comfort food? What's wrong, did you breakup with the Atlanta Falcon?"

Penny Sue raked a hand through her meticulously streaked hair. "Honey, I'm dating a Falcon *and* a Brave, now. But, a Dinghy Dong's something else; I always have room for one of them."

From Parker, Hanson, and Swindal's twenty-third floor conference room in downtown Atlanta, the people on the street looked like ants foraging for crumbs. I could sympathize, I had a bad feeling that's what I'd be doing at the end of the day.

I should never have quit my job, I thought ruefully. Until the fateful night when I found out about Zack, I'd been a part-time bookkeeper for a local car dealership. Money wasn't the issue, though I enjoyed having funds of my own. The job gave me a sense of purpose, something to think about other than bridge and local gossip. But I couldn't concentrate and started making mistakes after I discovered Zack's other life. Afraid I might do serious damage, like fouling up an IRS report, I decided to quit.

Although most of my sorority sisters were pampered Southern belles, my family was a hundred percent middle class. I was one of only two sorority pledges who had not "come out" at a debutante ball. That never bothered me, or them, for that matter. By my senior year I was president of the sorority and a regular at all the posh, hotsy-totsy balls.

Which was how I got hooked up with Zachary. A six-foot-one handsome blond from a poor, farming family, Zack was in his last year of law school when we met. He'd dated Penny Sue initially, but was dumped for her first husband, Andy Walters, the amiable, if dumb, captain of the football team.

I see now what a shameless social climber Zack was. I suppose he figured that if he couldn't have Penny Sue, I was an acceptable second, since I traveled in all the same circles. Second indeed. Considering Zack's lackluster grades and dirt farming roots, Parker, Hanson, and Swindal would never have given him a glance if it hadn't been for my friendship with Penny Sue.

Which was an ironic twist—I set Zack up in the firm that was about to squash me like an ant. I turned my back to the window angrily. Well, this was one bug that wasn't going to roll over and die.

I sat at the end of the conference table and fished a thick file of documents from my briefcase. Where was my attorney? Max Bennett promised to come early. He knew I didn't want to face Zack alone, especially on his own turf. How could Max be so insensitive? *Easy, he's male and a lawyer*, I answered my own question.

I had really wanted a female attorney, but decided a woman would be powerless against Zack's firm and the Atlanta good-ol'-boy network. Bradford Davis was handling Zack's case, a PH&S senior partner whose great-great-grandfather was a Confederate General who defended Atlanta in the War of Northern Aggression. I figured I needed a legal heavyweight of my own. I chose Max because his ancestors on his mother's side went back to Colonial times, and he'd handled several high profile divorces with good results. In any event, he'd seemed nice enough the few times we'd chatted at charity events and cocktail parties.

Appearances can sure be deceiving. However the day turned out, I would be happy to be rid of Max Bennett. I'd had a bellyful of his red, sweaty face; off-color jokes and patronizing remarks—not to mention the fact that he hadn't done one thing right.

The process had dragged on for nearly two years because Max couldn't or wouldn't stand up to Bradford Davis. The present meeting had been postponed four times at Bradford's request, once to accommodate a state bar golf tournament. In fact, Max was so openly solicitous of Bradford, I'd wondered if the two had something going on the side. I voiced the theory to Penny Sue, figuring she might have some insight since her second husband had turned out to be bisexual.

"Who can tell?" Penny Sue said. "Even straight men act like a pack of dogs, sniffing each other and posturing. All that butt slapping and carrying on, it's in their genes, goes back to ancient Greece where they played sports in the nude."

The idea of Max and Bradford romping around buck-naked was too much. I laughed out loud at the very moment Max, Bradford and Zack arrived. Clearly thinking I was snickering at them, each instinctively checked his fly. Even they noticed that synchronicity, which made me laugh even harder.

Scowling, Bradford and Zack took seats at the head of the table in front of an ornately framed painting of Judge Parker. Max sat next to me at the opposite end. He nodded coldly as way of greeting.

"I believe we can dispose of this matter quickly," Max said, passing a three page document to me. "Mr. Stratton provided a list of your joint assets and their market value. He wants to be fair and proposes to divide your belongings right down the middle. Since a quick sale could depress the value of your property, Mr. Stratton has offered to buy-out your share by making monthly installments over a five year period. In that way, he can dispose of the property in an orderly fashion."

I flipped to the last page of the document. The total was $1.1 million, including $550,000 for the house. "This can't be everything."

Max cleared his throat. "Uh, no, it does not include household furnishings, which have already been divided, or personal items such as your cars."

The total was far too low. My rough calculation put our assets at well over two million. I scanned the list. All the values were ridiculously low, and a number of investments were missing altogether. Zack was trying to cheat me, just as I'd feared. "These estimates are wrong," I said loudly, staring defiantly at Zack.

Bradford smirked. "You must remember, Becky dear, that the markets have been off the last few years."

"Leigh," I corrected.

"As you wish, *Leigh,*" Bradford replied, putting particular emphasis on my name as if it had a bad taste. Zack snorted with amusement. "Names aside," Bradford continued pompously, "the property was evaluated by Walker & Hill, the most reputable *independent* appraiser in Atlanta. Surely, you cannot find fault with that."

Independent, hell! Zack played golf with Taylor Hill at least twice a month. I gave Max a pleading look. He patted my hand and flashed a thin, sleazy smile. I wanted to backhand him in the mouth. Luckily, Judge Parker entered the room at that moment and stood by the door, listening. I was too angry to meet his eyes.

"In our experience, it is difficult to get full value from the disposal of community property," Bradford continued. "Buyers expect bargain basement prices in the case of a divorce. It's very difficult to overcome that mind set."

"I've found the same thing in my practice," Max chimed in.

I glared at him. *Who's side are you on?* I wanted to scream. Of course, I knew the answer: he was a good-ol'-boy, a member of the *club*, and they were all going to stick together. "What about the stocks and bonds?" I demanded through tight lips.

Bradford consulted another list. "The securities were liquidated last November to take care of family debts."

November? Zack went to the Caribbean on business in November. Could he have sold the stocks and deposited the money in an off-shore bank? "What debts?" I demanded hotly. "I want to see proof."

"General household expenses." Bradford looked to Max. "We provided all of this to your attorney. There were several credit cards—"

Credit cards? "I haven't seen any proof!" Could Zack have spent that much money on his stripper? Then, it dawned on me. Zack had opened a bunch of accounts, taken-out cash advances and deposited the money in tropical banks. What a sneaky jerk ... all our savings gone and I didn't have a prayer of finding it.

Bradford continued, "Your attorney has reviewed these documents. We've also filed a copy with Judge Nugent. Of course, the judge would like a property settlement before he grants the final decree."

I pushed the paper away. "This is not fair; Zack has hidden our assets. I won't sign it." I caught Judge Parker from the corner of my eye; he winked and canted his head. I wasn't sure what that meant, and Bradford gave me no time to think about it.

He slammed his folder shut. "That is your prerogative, Mrs. Stratton," Bradford intoned snobbishly. "However, I caution you that a court battle could be *very* long and expensive."

The emphasis on *very* was crystal clear. While Bradford was probably handling Zack's case for free, I had to pay my own legal fees. Max's tab already topped $30,000. Holding out for a trial might double or triple the bill. And, what did I stand to gain? Nothing. The good-ol'-boys would protect each other to the end. I glanced at the Judge who nodded slightly. Damn, I hated giving in! But, the deck was stacked against me, it was time to throw-in my hand. My eyes stung with tears, from frustration more than anything. I blinked them back and raised my chin resolutely; I would not give those men the satisfaction of seeing me cry.

I jabbed Max with my elbow, hard. "Give me a pen," I spat the words. He rolled his chair back and handed me a Cross ballpoint. I signed the document with an angry flourish, pocketed the pen, and strode stiffly past Judge Parker and out of Zack's life.

* * *

I called my therapist as soon as I got home.

"How do you feel?"

"Angry, betrayed, hurt. Those men made me so mad." I tugged my scarf off and wrapped it around my fist, wishing it was Zack's throat.

"No one can make you feel anything. You choose your feelings. If you're mad, you've chosen to feel that way."

Chosen to feel that way? Those scuzz balls ganged up on me. "It's the injustice that angers me. No one—not even my own lawyer—did a thing to help me. Bradford, Max, and Zack walked in *together*. Don't you see, it was a done deal before anything was said. I was set up!"

"So, you feel like a victim?"

"Yes, I'd like to cut off their private parts and hang them from their ears." I unraveled the scarf and pulled it tight, like a rope.

"Violence doesn't solve anything, does it?"

"For godssakes, I wouldn't really do it. It's a fantasy; a delicious fantasy at this moment." I balled the scarf up into a tight ball.

"Lashing out is a common reaction to situations like this. Let's talk about it. I can work you in tomorrow morning at eleven."

"I'll get back to you." I slammed down the receiver. *Lashing out is a common reaction.* I hurled the scarf against the wall.

Damn! Then, I drew the blinds and went to bed feeling more depressed than I'd ever felt in my life.

But, sleep did not save me. My head had hardly hit the pillow when I was awakened by the sound of a siren ... no, the doorbell. And shouting.

"LEIGH. BECK-KKY LEEE-EIGH. We know you're in there."

It was Penny Sue. I had on my slip and didn't bother to find a robe. I looked through the peephole at the optically-widened images of Penny Sue and Ruthie, who was holding a gigantic bouquet of flowers. I cracked the door; Penny Sue barged through.

"Get dressed, girl. We're going to celebrate."

"Celebrate what?"

"The divorce, of course. Free at last, free at last. Praise the Lord, free at last! Besides, you're now qualified to be in the DAFFODILS."

Ruthie thrust a vase of daffodils into my face as Penny Sue fastened a silver and gold brooch to my slip strap. Both women were wearing the same pin, a circular swirl of graceful leaves, stems and daffodils in full bloom. Penny Sue's brooch served as the clasp for a wispy Chanel scarf; Ruthie's accented the square neckline of her black silk chemise.

"The what?" I asked testily, eyeing the daffodils and brooch that hung limply from my slip strap.

Penny Sue replied, "DAFF-O-DILS: Divorced And Finally Free Of Deceitful, Insensitive, Licentious Scum."

Deceitful, Insensitive, Licentious Scum. A smile tugged at my lips. I was definitely qualified, and so were Penny Sue and Ruthie.

I figured Penny Sue had probably founded the club. Her second husband, Sydney, was a television producer who'd had an affair with his male assistant. As painful as Zack's infidelity was, at least I hadn't been thrown over for a man. The huge settlement the Judge got for Penny Sue (Daddy took Sydney's escapades very personally) undoubtedly helped. Her third husband, Winston, wasn't much better; he had an eye for young secretaries.

Ruthie had also endured her share of heartache. Harold, her ex, was a cardiologist in Raleigh, North Carolina. A heartless cardiologist at that. (Maybe Penny Sue was right about teaching what you need to learn.) Ruthie worked as a librarian to put him through medical school, only to be ditched for a nurse the week after Harold finished his residency. Not one to mope, Ruthie Jo had packed up Jo Ruth, their only child, and taken a train back to Atlanta, where she'd lived with her father ever since.

I studied the bouquet of flowers. The symbol of Spring and new beginnings, there was something intrinsically happy about a daffodil. "Where in the world did you find daffodils at this time of year?"

Penny Sue responded, "My florist in Buckhead stocks them for me."

"A lot of members in the club, huh?"

"No, I just like daffodils." Penny Sue quick-stepped a jig. "Perk up, girl, it's party time."

I ignored her antics and headed for the kitchen with the flowers, my friends following close behind. "I appreciate the offer, but it's been a terrible day. I don't feel like celebrating." I put the vase on the sideboard and filled a glass from the kitchen tap. "Want something to drink?" I asked, holding up the glass of water.

"You didn't take any pills, did ya?" Penny Sue asked, eyeing me like a mother hen.

I sat down and buried my head in my hands, the brooch clanking heavily on the tabletop. "No, nothing like that."

"Good, 'cuz we've got champagne!" Penny Sue pulled a bottle of Dom Perignon from her oversized Louis Vuitton bag as Ruthie searched the cabinets for stemmed glasses.

"What are you doing here?" I asked, accepting a glass of the fizzing liquid.

"Daddy called me," Penny Sue replied.

My spine straightened reflexively. "*Daddy?* Why didn't Daddy help me today?" I said through gritted teeth. "I was rolled, raped ... swindled. Swindled! Lord, I can't believe it took me so long to make the connection—Parker, Hanson, & SWINDAL. I never stood a chance!"

I was shouting now and it felt good. Hell with my therapist. At that moment, I chose to be mad—foot-stomping, dish-throwing mad. Mad, furious, LIVID. I gulped the sparkling wine.

"Daddy wanted to help, but he couldn't interfere overtly. He called Judge Nugent after the meeting—they go back a long way, you know. Anyhow, he asked Albert to go ahead and grant the divorce, but to take a close look at the property settlement."

"What does that mean?" I asked wearily.

"Monday: the marriage is history. Tuesday: Zack will have some explainin' to do."

"Glory, there is a God." I stood and raised my glass. "To the DAFF-O-DILS."

"DAFFODILS." We clinked our glasses.

"Now, get some clothes on. We're going to have a fancy dinner and plan our trip to the beach."

More Fun From The DAFFODILS

THE TURTLE MOUND MURDER

ISBN 0-9710429-5-0
EAN 978-0-9710429-5-7

Rebecca Leigh Stratton is divorced, depressed, and thoroughly disgusted. Thanks to her two-timing, asset-hiding, lawyer husband, Leigh faces the prospect of starting over at forty-six. Fortunately, her sassy, Southern sorority sisters, Penny Sue Parker and Ruthie Nichols, are old hands at divorce. The three single-again ladies take off for New Smyrna Beach, their college-days haunt. What they don't bargain for are old flames, fist fights, and gunfire. And, that's just the first day!

"What planet are you from?" Rick asked, snickering derisively.

Penny Sue set her jaw, pointed the gun at the ground and squeezed the trigger. "Georgia."

BIKE WEEK BLUES

ISBN 0-9710429-7-7
EAN 978-0-9710429-7-1

LOVE IS IN THE AIR FOR THESE SASSY, SOUTHERN DIVORCEES,

Yet Secrets From The Past Threaten Not Only Their Happiness, But The Security Of The United States Itself!

Leigh is building a new, single life at the beach. Ruthie's in town for a spiritual seminar. Flamboyant Penny Sue, hot on the trail of her latest soul mate, buys a Harley and follows him to Bike Week. In true DAFFODILS fashion, no sooner do the sorority sisters reunite, then all hell breaks loose. Bullets are flying, a body is found, and all clues point to Rich, Penny Sue's new love. Unfortunately, Rich has disappeared into the hubbub of a half million bikers, beer bashes, and cole slaw wrestling.

With the help of Frannie May, a savvy, Italian widow from the South (South Shore of Boston, Massachusetts, that is), and a motley crew of bikers, Trekkies, and Navy Seals, the DAFFODILS must find Rich and unravel the mystery to protect themselves and the entire East Coast.

Also From Inspirational Fiction ...

FIRST RUNNER-UP, 2001 COVR AWARD FOR FICTION
FINALIST, 2002 IPPY PRIZE FOR VISIONARY FICTION

Is today's freak weather caused by ocean currents and global warming? Are electricity blackouts really the result of inadequate supplies? Or is something momentous about to occur ...

Starpeople

Mankind Gets A Second Chance

The Sirian Redemption

a novel by

Linda Tuck-Jenkins

The X-Files meets *The Celestine Prophecy* in this fast-paced thriller centering on ordinary people who must come to grips with alien encounters and their destiny of helping humanity make a leap in consciousness.

ISBN 0971042993
EAN 978-0-9710429-9-5
Read an excerpt: www.starpeoplebooks.com